BURY
YOUR
SECRETS

BURY YOUR SECRETS

KERRY WATTS

embla
books

First published in Great Britain in 2024 by

embla books

Bonnier Books UK Limited
4th Floor, Victoria House, Bloomsbury Square, London, WC1B 4DA
Owned by Bonnier Books
Sveavägen 56, Stockholm, Sweden

A CIP catalogue record for this book is available from the British Library.

ISBN: 9781471416910

This book is typeset using Atomik ePublisher.

Printed and bound in Great Britain by Clays Ltd, Elcograf S.p.A.

Embla Books is an imprint of Bonnier Books UK.
www.bonnierbooks.co.uk

MIX
Paper | Supporting
responsible forestry
FSC® C018072

For anyone struggling right now.
The world is a better place with you in it.

Prologue

3rd May, 9 a.m.

The knife moved back just enough for him to gasp out a single breath. But it didn't slow his racing heart, which – judging from the pain bursting from his shoulder to his neck – he thought might explode at any second. Simon had never felt pain like it. Having barely finished his coffee and gotten ready to leave the house, he couldn't compute what was happening. Half an hour ago all he'd had on his mind was the hope that the doctor would be able to help him. Now, this . . .

'Please . . . Why are you doing this?'

'Don't tell me that you haven't feared this day was coming. You must have known. If it had been me, I would have thought about it every single day, been unable to shake the guilt. But then we're very different, you and me.'

Simon panted to control the pain. 'What day . . . Argh, no, please.'

'*What day,*' the man sneered.

'Really, I don't know, just tell me,' Simon begged, wishing he could see through his swollen, bloodied eyes. The attacker had come at him from behind, slamming him into the wall head first. The voice was familiar, but too hard to make out through the ringing in his ears. It had all happened so fast.

'Whatever it is . . . Argh . . . I'm sure we can sort it out.'

'Oh, we're long past sorting it out.' The man gave a sinister laugh, the sound barely audible through the whistling that had overtaken Simon's hearing.

It made no sense.

1

'There's plenty of cash in my wallet. It's on the sideboard in the hall. Take it. My debit card too. My pin number is . . .'

The man laughed again. 'Money won't fix this. You should know that!'

'But if this isn't about money then, please, just tell me what you want. You can have anything. Just . . . just . . .'

'You really don't have a clue, do you.'

Simon didn't get a chance to reply before the knife was forced deep into his chest, twisting slowly, cruelly, cutting through flesh like a butcher's blade. Slicing and tearing with ease. A taste of copper hit Simon's tongue. He tried to cry out, but the excruciating pain stole what little breath he had left.

'No . . .' His words became choked by the blood gurgling in his throat. 'No . . .'

The knife pulled back; the pressure was gone. It was blissful respite until a single blow smashed into his ribs. A stomach-curdling crack. One punch right in the centre of his chest, making him drop like a stone, panting. On his hands and knees he made a futile attempt to save himself, blood dripping from his mouth. He crawled slowly towards the backdoor, his body screaming with pain, his arms and legs weak beneath him – but he had to try. He had to warn Molly. He had to stop her coming home. If only he could reach his phone.

Heartless, mocking laughter rang in his ears until the room fell eerily silent. The pulsing of his own blood rushed through Simon's ears. As he paused, desperately listening for his attacker, a heavy boot slammed down, forcing his battered body flat to the cold wood floor. The force on his back pinned him in place as his face was lifted violently and the knife gleamed at his throat.

Simon could smell his attacker's breath – sweet, tinged with cheap wine. He opened his bloodied mouth to beg for his life until a clump of what little hair he had was snatched up, his attacker's lips next to Simon's ear.

'People like you think you can get away with anything. That you can say anything. Do anything. With no regard for the consequences and – for what? A bit of fun. A bit of attention.' The man sneered.

A jumble of thoughts tumbled through Simon's head, but none that could explain this.

'You just got on with your lives, didn't you. Some of you have done pretty well for yourselves. Shame it will all be wasted.' The words gnawed at Simon's mind. 'In a way you almost did get away with it. Were you hoping that it would all be forgotten about? I'm sorry to disappoint you, but something like that never goes away. Don't worry, though, I'll be catching up with every last one of you. After all, you weren't in it alone. It would be unfair of me to make you the scapegoat.'

It was then that the horrifying realisation hit, but it was too late to say sorry. Simon couldn't go back. None of them could. If only he'd listened to that little voice inside him back then telling him it was wrong. Simon hadn't wanted to do it. It was him, all *him*.

He tried to say the words, but there was too much blood in his mouth. 'I . . . I . . .'

And then it became impossible to speak as the sharp blade sliced across his throat. Blood spurted in gulps onto the immaculate wooden floor, quickly picking up the crumbs from breakfast as it trailed away from his body. The man was just standing there, watching, smiling, as Simon's life poured out. The smile grew wider, then wider still, until his grin stretched ear to ear. He was coming back. If he could, Simon would have begged, pleaded with him to stop. There were no words for the depravity of this final barbaric twist. The knife was coming closer again, still closer, until Simon could smell the metal of the blade. Mercifully, his body went into shock.

The slam of the backdoor and the sound of footsteps on the gravel driveway were the last things he heard as his life ebbed away.

He wouldn't be able to warn them.

1

3rd May, 11 a.m.
'How are you doing?'

Detective Inspector Fraser Brodie shook his brother's outstretched hand when he sat down opposite him in the prison visiting area. It was drab and grey, much like the prisoner's matching T-shirt and joggers. He shivered, the cold of HMP Barlinnie a stark contrast to the warm early May sunshine outside. As always the smell of stale sweat and coffee wafted uninvited into his nostrils. He often wondered how Adam had stuck it for so long – although, granted, he'd had little choice in the matter. It was easier for Fraser to travel to Barlinnie than the years that his brother had spent in maximum security HMP Perth.

Adam Brodie shrugged and scratched his fingers over the improvised tattoo of a skull which poked out from under his shirtsleeve.

'Meh – you see it all.'

'You look well,' Fraser said, as he slid the authorised snacks across the table: one bar of Dairy Milk chocolate and a packet of salt-and-vinegar Hula Hoops.

'Wish I could say the same aboot you. You look like shit.'

'Cheers for that.' Fraser yawned.

'Have you lost weight?'

'Honest as ever, thanks, but I'm fine. Don't you worry aboot me. I'm all right.'

Adam wasn't wrong. Fraser did look like crap. Being six-foot-four meant even losing a couple of pounds made him look thin. His peely-wally Western Isles complexion didn't help. He hadn't slept well for weeks. The recent deterioration in their father's health had triggered a return of the nightmares that had plagued Fraser many years ago. Getting to sleep was a piece of piss. It was staying asleep that eluded the fifty-five-year-old Detective Inspector.

'I got a letter aboot Dad,' Adam mentioned, without looking at Fraser, instead focusing his gaze intently on the floor as he nibbled his short, ragged thumbnail.

'Aye, the care home rang me as well.' Fraser shrugged. 'It is what it is. We always knew it would end like this.'

'They said they think he's entering the final stages.'

'I know.'

'Are you goin' to see him?' Adam asked.

'I havnae decided yet.' Which wasn't a lie and was probably the reason for Fraser's sleepless nights.

'At least I dinnae have to make that choice.' Adam half-smiled when he said it.

Part of Fraser envied his twin brother for that. He could absolve himself of all responsibility for the monster who had brutalised his sons during their childhood. Instead it would be Fraser alone who would have to deal with the arrangements once it was all over. He supposed he could leave it to the state; that option was definitely not yet off the table. Johnny Brodie probably deserved that.

'Aye, that's true.'

'Do you think he's suffered?' Adam asked. 'Because I hope he has.'

Fraser didn't blame him for thinking like that. Johnny Brodie was a bully. There was no other word for him, although it was an understatement if ever there was one. Dementia, caused by years of heavy drinking, was a fitting punishment. Fraser had also never blamed their mother for leaving when they were just young boys, although on that he and Adam had always differed. Fraser just wished that she'd taken them with her to wherever it was she fled.

In Adam's mind she had abandoned them to their fate, but to Fraser she had done the only thing she could to survive. Johnny Brodie would have killed her if she had stayed – or if she had taken them with her.

'It cannae have been easy for him, I don't suppose. No knowing where you are, or if it's new year or New York,' said Fraser.

'Aye, well, he brought it on himself, didn't he.' Anger still poured out of Adam. Even after all these years. Although thirty-five years inside had given him plenty of time to dwell on it.

'I cannae argue with you on that,' Fraser replied, glancing across his brother's shoulder to be met with a cold glare from a face he recognised. The name escaped him; it wasn't the first time he'd had death stares from men he had put in here. If looks could really kill, Fraser would have been dead multiple times over.

Fraser noticed that Adam seemed tense. More stressed than he'd seen him for a long time.

'Never mind Dad. Are you all right? You look—'

'Look like what?' Adam interrupted, a flash of irritation in his words.

'Like you've got somethin' on your mind.'

Adam avoided Fraser's eye for the second time. 'I'm fine.'

Fraser scanned the room. In the past other prisoners had taken a dislike to his brother once they'd discovered what he'd done; their disgust had radiated off them. But today all he saw were men who showed little interest in Adam. It couldn't be that then. It wasn't worth pressing, he decided. Adam would tell Fraser if and when he needed to. That's how it had always been.

'OK,' Fraser said and left it at that.

Adam screwed the chocolate wrapper into a tight ball and slid it back across the table at Fraser before splitting open the bag of crisps. He offered the bag to his brother.

'No, thanks. You can keep them.'

'Suit yourself,' Adam replied through a mouthful of food, spitting crumbs onto the table.

'You still eat like a pig.'

'You'd be the same if you only got treats as little as I did.'

Fraser shook his head. 'Whatever you say.'

'How's it all goin' with you anyway?' Adam asked. 'You busy?'

Fraser didn't dare say that things on the island had been quiet. That was always the kiss of death for his peace and quiet. 'Och, no bad. Cannae complain,' he said instead.

On Lewis, the most populated island in the Outer Hebrides, crime was steady but not anything the force couldn't handle.

'Bit of cattle-rustling and sheep-shagging, eh,' Adam laughed.

Fraser always found Adam's throwaway comments like that strange given what he had done thirty-five years ago. His crimes were far worse than a bit of theft, and had left a lasting legacy in some strands of the community. Even Fraser's return to Lewis after retiring from the army had been met with distaste, given how he had supported his twin unconditionally. But what choice did he have? All they had was each other.

'Aye, summin' like that. Got to keep my eyes peeled for stray shaggers right enough.'

Fraser's phone buzzed in his pocket, and he lifted a hand to apologise to the prison officer. It must have slipped his mind to switch it off. He frowned when he saw it was his DS, Carla McIntosh, because she knew not to disturb him when he flew to the mainland for his monthly visit to see Adam in Barlinnie jail.

'I'm sorry,' he whispered to Adam, who indicated that it was no bother.

Fraser balked as he listened to Carla's update. A shiver shot through him at her description of the crime scene. It sounded like something out of a horror film, and he hadn't dealt with the like for a very long time. A forty-five-year-old mechanic had been found murdered in his home. Adam's brow was crumpled as he stared at Fraser. It was like he knew.

'OK,' Fraser said, exhaling deeply. 'I'll be back as soon as I can get a flight.'

'Bad news?' asked Adam.

'Aye, I'll need to get back.'

'A bit more than cattle-rustling this time then.'

'You could say that, aye.'

Fraser said goodbye and quickly left the prison, hoping there would be a seat on the next flight back to Stornoway.

2

DS Carla McIntosh hung up and stuffed her phone back into her trouser pocket. She replaced her face mask and tidied her long blonde hair into a neat ponytail with a scrunchie, relieved the call was over. Though he was a man of few words, she knew DI Brodie's time with Adam was precious, to both men, and she hadn't enjoyed telling him he should come back.

She re-joined her colleague DC Owen Kelly inside the crime scene. It was one of the worst she'd ever experienced and had almost caused her to puke her breakfast onto the immaculate flower-bed out front.

'How did he take it?' Owen asked.

'Better than I thought.'

'Aye, but you'll be losing brownie points for that, phoning him when he's at Bar-L.' Owen's wry smile made his dark, chocolate-brown eyes crinkle at the edges above the mask.

'I didnae have any choice, did I,' she muttered. 'That in there, that's . . .' She pointed to the kitchen, shaking her head. 'That's horrific.'

Carla was surprised by the younger man's wisecrack. Having become a detective through the Met's direct-entry training programme Owen was a book copper, not a beat copper. Perhaps his ill-judged attempt at humour was a coping mechanism.

'You're not wrong,' Owen replied, then frowned at her and asked, unexpectedly, 'Are you OK?'

'Aye, I'm fine. I'm fine. It's just . . .' She heaved a huge breath. 'I didnae realise it would be that bad.' They were silent a moment before she started to feel embarrassed that he'd seen her so shaken up and added, 'Go and search the couple's bedroom, will you? See if there's anything up there that can tell us who'd do something as barbaric as this.' She nodded towards the kitchen door where there was a hive of activity round their victim. 'This was no burglary gone wrong, that's for sure.'

'Sure,' Owen replied, and he quickly headed off, taking the stairs two at a time in his protective overshoes, acknowledging a young uniformed officer he passed.

Forensics had arrived quickly and were examining Simon Carver's house. Carla steeled herself to go back into the kitchen where she spotted pathologist Julia Carnegie – a woman in her forties whose personality more than made up for her diminutive size.

'Dr Carnegie,' Carla said.

Julia looked up from examining Simon Carver's body. 'DS McIntosh. Don't be shy.' She flicked a gloved hand at her. 'Come through. He won't bite.'

Carla was used to the pathologist's dark sense of humour – also, no doubt, a coping mechanism for her work. They all had them. Carla supposed hers might be Terry's Chocolate Oranges and Pringles. Less healthy but so satisfying.

'I suppose it's a stupid question, but can you give us a cause of death yet?'

'It could be any one of these.' Julia stopped what she was doing and counted aloud. 'Six, seven, eight, nine, ten stab wounds, although cutting the man's throat would have delivered the killer blow.'

'Do you think he was still alive when his tongue was removed?' Carla balked at the thought.

'Judging by the amount of blood, yes.'

Her answer sent chills through Carla's whole body. 'Have you got any idea what kind of murder weapon we're looking for? Kitchen knife?'

'I'll know for certain once I've been able to examine the cut marks fully. If I had to make a guess right now, I'd say probably a blade approximately eight inches. Might even be a chef's knife, something keen cooks would have in their arsenal at home. I actually have one myself. They are sharp and very efficient.'

'So like a kitchen knife then,' Carla said again.

'Possibly. I won't know until I've done a more thorough examination.'

Carla made a note, shocked that it could be a simple item that some people had in their kitchen that had done such horrific damage to the man on the floor in front of them. 'OK. Thank you.'

'I'll send DI Brodie my full report when I'm done with the post-mortem.'

Carla nodded, fearing images of Simon Carver's body would plague her dreams for days to come. She scanned the counter-top for a knife block to check for missing items. The one she saw had no missing knives but that didn't mean one of them wasn't their murder weapon. Before talking to their victim's wife she approached one of the CSIs, a man, shorter than average, in his fifties.

'Bag that knife block. I want to check them for traces of blood and DNA.'

The man looked across to where she was pointing then indicated for one of his colleagues to do it.

'Thanks,' Carla continued. 'What have you got by way of fingerprints?'

'I've found a couple of strong prints on the backdoor handle, kitchen table and on the cold tap. A couple of lighter thumbprints on the kitchen door-frame; hopefully they'll be useful to you. A partial palm print, but I don't think it's enough for a positive ID unfortunately.'

'Hopefully one of them belongs to our killer,' she muttered. 'Although it does seem a bit sloppy to leave such good evidence behind.'

'Makes your job easier though, eh,' the CSI pointed out.

'If only it was that simple.' She gave a brief smile.

Carla thanked him as she took in the flurry of activity around her. This killer wasn't going to get away with this. There were too many people on the case for him to hide for long. He'd left evidence behind somewhere and they'd find him. They had to.

A female uniformed officer was sitting with the victim's wife in the couple's pristine living room. She was still trembling, the shock of finding her husband sliced up like a slab of meat on their kitchen floor etched on her pale face. Carla couldn't fail to notice the contrast between the two rooms.

Carla edged past one of the crime-scene photographers and joined Molly Carver.

'Mrs Carver, I'm DS McIntosh. Carla. I know you've had a terrible shock, but do you mind if I sit down and ask you some questions? It's better while everything is fresh in your mind.'

When she got no response Carla sat on the armchair opposite, noticing how clean and tidy the room was. On the fireplace next to her, which was spotless, sat a row of anniversary cards. Carla counted ten, all laid out neatly either side of a big bunch of red roses. Reaching across the space between them she patted the distraught woman's leg softly.

'Mrs Carver, Molly . . . Is it all right if I call you Molly?'

The dazed woman looked up, her eyes red and sore from crying.

'I'm so sorry for your loss,' Carla pressed on.

'Fresh in my mind.' Molly spoke quietly, her voice hoarse. 'This can never be anything but fresh. Ever.'

'It must have been a terrible shock. I'm so sorry you had to see that.'

Molly started to cry. 'I can't believe this is happening.' She shook her head. 'This isn't happening. This is just a nightmare. Isn't it? It can't be real. It can't.'

Carla pinched a handful of tissues from a box on the spotless glass-topped coffee table that sat between them and held them out to her. 'I need to ask you some questions, Molly. Is that OK?'

Ignoring the proffered tissues, the woman swallowed hard. 'All right.'

'You told the officers that you came in from shopping at about ten o'clock, is that right?'

'Yes,' Molly replied, her words barely a whisper.

'And you said Simon was lying on the kitchen floor?' Carla allowed time for the question to be processed.

'Yes.'

'Were you aware of anyone else either in the house or outside?'

Molly's eyes momentarily held Carla's. 'No. No one.'

'Did you pass a vehicle on your drive home that you didn't recognise?'

'No. I don't think so.' Molly's brow crumpled; she was seemingly searching for information. 'I can't remember, my mind is all over the place.'

'It's OK, don't worry,' Carla replied.

Molly Carver turned and stared at the kitchen door. 'I was only gone for an hour, ninety minutes at most. What if they'd still been here when I got back?'

Carla noticed the woman's face turn white at the thought and didn't blame her. If Molly had returned earlier they might have been examining two bodies.

'Is it normal for Simon to be home on Friday mornings?'

'No. He normally leaves for work at eight, but he had an appointment at half nine so he had arranged to go in late.'

'An appointment where?'

'It was a doctor's appointment. Why does that matter?'

'We just need to gather all the information we can about Simon.'

Molly stared at Carla for a beat. 'He hasn't been sleeping very well recently and he wanted to ask the doctor for something to help.'

'I see,' Carla replied, noting it down. 'Did anyone else know that Simon would be home at that time this morning?'

'I don't know,' Molly said.

'And what time did you leave the house?'

'Nine o'clock . . . no, half eight. It must have been nearer half eight. I had to pop into my sister's before going to Tesco.'

'Where does your sister live?'

Molly's brow crumpled. 'What?'

'Does she live close by?'

'They live near the harbour. Why does that matter?'

'They?'

'Wendy and her husband David. With my niece, Eva. What's this got to do with . . . with . . .'

'I'm sorry. I know some of these questions seem strange but it's procedure. I'm going to need your sister's details.'

Molly opened a drawer in the console table, took out a notebook and wrote down her sister's name and address. After tearing the page out she folded it slowly and neatly and handed it to Carla.

Tears fell again. This time Molly snatched a handful of tissues for herself.

'Thank you. I'm sorry. I know this is difficult,' Carla acknowledged.

'You're only doing your job.' Molly sniffed then blew her nose. 'What else do you need to know?'

'OK then. Molly, is there anybody you can think of that would want to hurt your husband? Someone he's had an argument with recently?'

Molly shook her head forcefully. The suggestion appeared impossible.

'No, nobody. Simon is a popular man. He has lots of friends. Maybe too many,' she attempted to smile. 'He was never at home, always out playing football, watching football, coaching boys' football.' She sunk back in the large black leather sofa. 'I can't think of anyone who would want to do that to him.' Then she paused. 'There was . . . No, never mind. He's not capable of . . .'

'Who's not capable of what, Molly?' Carla's interest was immediately piqued.

'Oh, nothing, never mind.' She took a breath, shook her head. 'My brother-in-law.' Molly stopped abruptly, seemingly deciding that was enough information.

'Your brother-in-law?'

'Och, it was nothing, and David wouldn't do that. My God, he wouldn't do that.'

'Did the two men argue?'

Molly nodded. 'David asked for money and Simon said no.'

'Was David upset by this, do you think?'

'I know he was. Came round here shouting one night when he was pissed, but they've sorted it out now.'

'So there's no longer any bad blood between the two men, that you know of?'

'It was never bad blood. It was just . . . Just family stuff. Simon and David go back further than that. They were friends at school too. David's got a drink problem, sometimes lashes out when he's had a bit too much.'

'What does lash out mean exactly?' Carla pressed. 'Has your brother-in-law ever been violent towards anyone?'

'No, David's anger is more verbal, shouting, swearing,' Molly told her. 'He wouldn't . . . wouldn't . . .' Tears filled her eyes. 'I mean, he's punched a few doors and walls but he's never, *would* never, lay a hand on someone. I'm sure of it.'

'So your sister has never said he's been violent to her during their marriage,' Carla suggested as she wrote down everything Molly had just told her.

'No.' Molly shook her head, then stopped. 'Well, there was that one time . . . I don't know, David pushed her and she fell against the kitchen table, bruising her arm. My sister was so embarrassed when she realised I'd seen the marks on her. Simon was all for going over there and lamping him but . . .' She stopped to wipe her face.

'Do you remember when this happened?'

'Last year I think, but David was so apologetic afterwards. He couldn't do enough for my sister for months after that. He was sober for at least three months after it too.'

Molly might be adamant that her brother-in-law wasn't capable of committing such a brutal crime but Carla wasn't so sure of his innocence. Alcohol could remove inhibitions in even the mildest of people.

'What did David need the loan for?'

'He told Simon that they were behind with their credit-card payments. Swore he would pay him back as soon as he could but we knew David wouldn't, couldn't, because he was suspended from work. He used to work with Simon at the garage.'

'Why was he suspended?'

'The drinking. Someone made a complaint about him, said he wasn't safe to be around heavy equipment. When I asked my sister about it, she said they didn't know who'd made the complaint.'

Molly's expression suggested that she knew.

'Was it Simon?' Carla asked.

Molly nodded. 'He asked me not to tell my sister. He said he didn't want to hurt her, but he had to act because David almost caused a serious accident with a heavy piece of equipment in the garage, you see.' Tears fell again. 'I'm sorry.'

Carla reached across, lightly brushing her fingers on Molly's arm. 'You're doing great,' she said softly.

Molly took a breath to compose herself, a thin smile coming and going quickly from her lips.

'You mentioned that you popped in to your sister's this morning,' Carla continued.

Molly frowned. 'Did I? I'm sorry, my mind is so muddled up. Yes, that's right, I did. I got to theirs at about quarter to nine.'

Carla noted the time down. 'Was David at home when you were there?'

Molly stared anxiously. 'No, he wasn't.'

'Have you got any idea where he was?'

Molly shook her head. 'I didn't think to ask.'

'Was everything all right with your sister when you were there?'

'What do you mean?' Molly asked.

'Did she seem upset about anything, worried perhaps?'

Molly shook her head. 'No, she was fine.'

'OK,' Carla said, before looking sympathetically at Molly. 'I'm sorry, but this next question is something I have to ask,' she continued, hating this part of the questioning. 'Was everything all right between you and Simon? Were you happy together?'

Molly's shocked expression wasn't a surprise. Carla would feel the same in her position if anything ever happened to Dean. Even if he *was* to blame for their recent financial problems . . . He called them 'problems'. She called it a nightmare.

'Everything was fine between us, Detective.' Molly's answer was short but to the point. Then she added. 'Simon was the sweetest, kindest man I've ever met. He didn't deserve . . .' She took a breath. 'He didn't deserve that.'

'I'm sorry. Like I said, I have to ask.'

'I understand. It's just, I mean . . . If you met him, you would know. It's a cliché perhaps, but everyone loved Simon. He treated me like a princess, my sister always said. It was our wedding anniversary last week. We don't have children. I can't have kids so . . .' She paused, a trembling breath leaving her lips. 'We've not long had that beautiful kitchen refitted so that I could . . .' Her eyes filled again. 'It was an anniversary present to ourselves,' she sobbed. 'More for me because he knew how much I love cooking.'

Before she could continue DC Kelly's voice called out, 'DS McIntosh?'

'Excuse me a wee minute,' Carla said and started up the stairs. 'What have you found?' she asked when she reached him.

DC Owen Kelly held up a letter inside a clear evidence bag with his gloved hand. 'Addressed to Simon Carver.'

Carla pulled on a pair of plastic gloves and lifted the letter from the bag.

I know what you did. I'll be seeing you.

'I know what you did?' Carla repeated. 'I'll be seeing you . . .'

'Did the wife mention this?'

Carla shook her head. 'Where was it?'

'Back of the drawer in the bedside cabinet.'

'The husband's side?'

'Must be,' Owen nodded. 'There's a load of man stuff in it – a watch, condoms . . .'

'Condoms?'

Owen nodded again. 'Yep, and a box of matches on top of a half-empty packet of fags as well.'

'Mmm, that's interesting. She says she can't have kids. OK. Thanks, Owen. Keep looking, and when you're done could you go next door and talk to the immediate neighbours? I'll go and ask her about this.'

Carla headed back downstairs with the letter in her hand. 'Hello again.'

'What's that?' Molly asked, wiping tears from her face.

'I was hoping you'd be able to tell me.'

Molly frowned and took the bagged letter out of Carla's hand.

'I've . . . I've never seen this before.' She was about to open the bag until Carla stopped her.

'I'm sorry, I can't let you take it out. It's evidence.'

'Evidence?' Molly repeated Carla's word, looking dazed. 'Does this have something to do with Simon's murder?'

'Did your husband ever mention to you that someone had been threatening him?'

'Never. He would tell me if that happened. We don't keep secrets from each other. I don't understand . . .'

'You're absolutely sure?' Carla insisted. 'You're not aware of Simon having had a problem with anyone other than your brother-in-law?'

'I've already told you . . . Simon gets on with everyone. I just . . . I can't . . .' She stumbled over her words. 'I can't believe this is happening.' Tears started falling again, this time harder and faster. 'Why didn't he tell me about that letter? We could have faced it together. Gone to the police. Instead he . . . he hid it and . . .'

Carla knew her next question would be awkward but it had to be asked.

'While searching in your bedroom we found some condoms. Is it possible that Simon was having an affair?'

'No. Simon wouldn't do that.' Molly looked away. 'Those are . . . we use them and it's none of your business.'

It was obvious how uncomfortable Molly was now. Carla didn't want to make things worse. She pulled a card from her pocket and placed it on the coffee table. There was no use pushing Molly further now. She would talk to her again later. The information she'd already given about her brother-in-law was a good lead.

'I think we should leave it for now. Do you want me to help you pack up some things? I'll get someone to take you to your sister's,' Carla suggested. 'You won't be able to stay here.'

'No, no. I don't want to leave here. I'll stay with Catherine next door. I don't want to go far.'

'All right. My colleague is going to talk to your neighbour soon. He can make the arrangements for you, but if you think of anything else before I see you again please call me. It doesn't matter how small you think it is, any detail could be significant.'

Molly lifted the card Carla gave her and pressed it tightly between her fingers. 'I will, but remember what I said about David – he couldn't do that. He's a drunk, not a murderer.'

Carla couldn't give Molly the reassurance she was angling for. 'I'll come and see you again later,' she said instead. As Carla went to stand Molly grabbed her arm.

'What's going to happen to Simon?'

Both women could see the private ambulance pulling up outside the couple's home.

'Simon will be taken to the mortuary, where our pathologist will carry out a post-mortem.'

'No,' Molly gasped, seemingly appalled. 'Do you really need to cut him up more than he already has been?'

'I'm sorry, it's procedure. And it could help us find who did this.' She indicated for the female officer who had been sat with Molly earlier to rejoin them. 'This officer is going to stay with you for a while, but if you need anything else please just call.'

Carla could tell Molly had said something in response, but her reply was muffled by sobs. She walked away and met Owen at the bottom of the stairs.

'Arrange with the neighbour for Molly to stay with them, will you,' Carla asked. 'Catherine someone. She doesn't want to go to her sister's.'

'Sure thing. Anything useful?'

'There was a falling-out between Simon and his brother-in-law.'

'Bad enough to do that to him, do you think?'

'She doesn't think so,' Carla said. 'But the guy has a drink problem and a volatile temper. He definitely needs looking at.'

'What's his name?' Owen asked.

'David Sutherland. Do you know him?'

'Sutherland . . . Sutherland. I can't say I do, but I'll check the address for domestic-abuse reports if he's a drinker with a temper.'

Carla held up the paper that Molly had given her with the address on it, and Owen took a photo of it.

'Good idea, Owen. Brodie's right, you're not just a pretty face.'

'Ha bloody ha.' Owen winked. 'You're just jealous.'

'Aye, right. Seriously, though, good call.'

'What did she say about the letter?' Owen asked.

'She'd never seen it before.'

18

'And you believe her?' Owen suggested.

'Her response seemed genuine. So unless she's a good actor, she was shocked by it.' Carla's phone buzzed in her trouser pocket. She wasn't surprised by the caller ID but wished it was anybody but them. She answered it as she walked away but turned to Owen before she took the call. 'You go and speak to the neighbours.'

'Sure thing.'

She watched his playful salute and wished she could be as carefree as he appeared. The man was thirty but some days it seemed like he was half that age. No wonder Brodie called him The Boy.

Carla cringed when the woman's voice on the phone said her name. 'Yep, that's me.'

Already knowing what the woman was going to say, Carla fought hard to stop a tear from trickling down her cheek.

3

3rd May, 11.45 a.m.

Owen had seen Carla looking like that when she'd answered her phone a few times now. Something was up and it had nothing to do with work. She thought he didn't notice, but she was wrong. She thought a lot of things about him that weren't true. But he'd prove himself to her eventually. And the gaffer.

Owen knocked on the door of the detached bungalow a few feet from the Carvers' home. Such a nice quiet location, but not far from Stornoway. He could see the appeal of the two newbuild properties. Until recently he'd not been sure whether Lewis was where he wanted to be, but after meeting Sandy his mind was made up. All Owen had to do now was find a place within their budget to buy so he could get out of the rented flat that was costing him way more than it deserved to. There were several derelict cottages he passed on his way to the station every morning. He could see himself renovating one of them.

Slow deliberate footsteps shuffled along the hallway and he held his ID up in front of him while he waited for the door to open. A small, elderly woman leaning heavily on a stick greeted him with a sombre smile.

'Hello, Officer. I've been expecting you.'

'Catherine Price? I'm Detective Constable Kelly. Is it all right if I come in and ask you some questions?'

'Of course, yes. Come away in. Come away in. Excuse the mess. I've not been able to keep on top of things since I broke my hip a few weeks ago.'

The reason for the stick, Owen thought. But she had no need

to make excuses. Her house was clean and reasonably tidy, and smelled of citrus, orange perhaps. He spotted a bowl of pot-pourri on the hall table: the source of the scent. Maybe that comment was just something people say. He wiped his boots on the doormat and followed the old woman inside.

'Thank you.' Owen closed the door after himself and followed her into a large kitchen, fitted out almost completely in pine: cupboards, table, chairs. It reminded him of his parents' home in Inverness. His mother was a huge fan of pine and his father was a huge fan of keeping his wife happy.

'What on earth has happened next door?' Catherine asked. 'One minute I was drinking tea in bed with Ziggy and next all hell broke loose: sirens blaring, lights flashing.' She shook her head. 'It must be something bad. It is, isn't it?'

A large ginger cat leaped onto one of the kitchen chairs, and Owen figured it must be Ziggy.

'I'm afraid so, Mrs Price.'

'It's Ms, not Mrs,' she corrected him. 'But call me Cathy.'

'All right then. How well do you know your neighbours, Cathy? The Carvers.'

'As well as any neighbours can know each other, I suppose. We're not friends per se, but we're friendly. Simon has been dragging my wheelie bin out for me since my operation and we take in parcels for each other, that kind of thing.' She rubbed her hip and winced. 'Pull out a chair for me, will you.'

'Sure, of course.'

'Thank you. But what's happened next door? Should I be worried about my own safety? I do live alone, after all.'

Owen wished he could reassure her, but until they found whoever was responsible he couldn't lie to her.

'I'm afraid Simon Carver was found dead earlier this morning.'

'Dead!' All the colour drained out of the woman's face as she gasped and crossed herself. 'Dear Lord, rest his soul.'

Owen nodded. 'I'm afraid so. Did you see or hear anything out of the ordinary this morning? Particularly between the hours of eight and ten.'

'Is that when he was killed!?'

'We think so, yes.'

'I was...'. She was flustered. 'I was still in bed.' Her eyes were flicking left and right. 'Dead? Simon? Oh how awful. Is Molly all right?'

'She's fine; she wasn't home at the time. Very shaken, as you can imagine, but unharmed.'

'Thank the Lord for that.' She made the sign of the cross on her chest again.

'So you didn't hear anything around that time, or see anyone apart from the Carvers coming or going from the house?' Qwen feared the shock wasn't good for the old woman because her already white face grew paler and her hands trembled.

'I didn't see anyone this morning, no. I don't think so.' She frowned. 'Oh, my mind is in such a fizz now.'

'Can I get you a glass of water?' Owen asked. Telling her the nature of Simon's injuries was completely out of the question.

'No, no, you're very kind but there's no need. I'll be all right in a minute.' She took a deep breath. 'Dead? I can't believe it. I was only talking to him last night.'

'How did he seem when you spoke to him?'

'Happy. Mind you, I think he'd had a fair bit to drink.' She smiled gently. 'Simon likes a nip or two or three.' Then a sombre expression crossed her face. 'Liked, I mean.'

'Did he often come home drunk?'

'Simon was never drunk. He was happy. Not like Molly. She's got a wicked tongue on her when she's been on the vodka. Poor Simon bore the brunt of it, of course. Between you and me, I think she was very jealous.'

'Jealous? Why do you think that was?' Owen asked.

'Because Simon was bubbly and friendly. A bit too friendly sometimes, if you know what I mean.'

'So there was tension between the couple?' Owen asked.

'Maybe. A little. Sometimes. Nothing major, it's not like I ever heard them shouting or anything.'

He made a note of that, then thought about what Carla had said about the brother-in-law.

'Mrs Carver told us about an argument that Simon had with his brother-in-law?'

'Oh, yes. The two men came to blows over something. I've no idea what, but I think they sorted it out because I've seen them together since and everything seemed fine.'

'Do you recall seeing a vehicle parked outside the Carvers' house this morning?'

'No.'

'Did you happen to see what time Molly Carver's car left this morning?'

Catherine shook her head. 'Like I said, I was in bed and my room is at the back.'

Owen jotted that down and took a card from his blazer pocket. 'You've been really helpful Ms . . . Cathy. If you remember anything else then please give me call on this number.'

'I will.' She went to stand up until pain made her stop. Her brow crumpled and she gently tapped Owen's arm. 'This will be DI Fraser Brodie's case, I'm guessing.'

Owen noted that she avoided his eyes. 'Yes, that's right. DI Brodie will be in charge of this investigation.'

Catherine Price sighed deeply, her lip trembling slightly. 'I see.'

Owen frowned. 'Are you all right, Ms Price?'

'Helen Price was my niece,' she said, without explanation, her voice barely a whisper.

'Forgive me, I don't follow,' Owen said.

She was looking right at him now. 'I asked about DI Brodie because Adam Brodie murdered my niece.'

Immediately berating himself for his idiocy, Owen stammered, 'Ah, erm, OK, I'm really sorry. I-I . . .' What the hell should he say to her? Thankfully she eased the tension for him.

'It's not your fault, lad,' she said kindly. 'I shouldn't have mentioned it.'

'Don't apologise. I understand why you did.'

'Thank you,' Catherine Price replied.

'No problem. Listen, we'll be in touch if we need to talk to you again. I'll see myself out. Unless there's anything I can do for you before I go?'

'Oh, no, dear, I'll be fine. You'd be better seeing yourself out.' A thin smile came and went quickly. 'You'll be waiting all day for me.'

'Oh, I almost forgot,' Owen blurted. 'Would it be OK if Molly stayed here with you for a bit? Until her home is . . .' He paused, trying to decide the best way to describe it. He needn't have worried.

'Yes. Of course she can stay. The woman needs all the support she can get right now.'

4

Reverend Denzil Martin tossed aside the weeds with a wry smile on his face.

'Aye, you thought I hadn't noticed you encroaching on my tulips, ya wee bugger,' he muttered, and returned to digging.

Footsteps on the stone churchyard made him turn. He was immediately horrified by the expression on the face of the dishevelled man who approached. Was that blood on his T-shirt? Denzil rose quickly, wiping dirt off his hands onto his trousers.

'Mark. Is everything all right?'

The distressed man now rocked back and forth, back and forth, mumbling something inaudible under his breath.

'What's wrong?'

Startled by Denzil's approach, the man held up a bloodstained hand and called out, 'Dinnae come near me! I've the devil in me. I've the devil in me.' He clutched his hands over his ears. 'Stop. Stop. I've the devil in me.'

Denzil had never seen Mark as bad as this before.

'Come on,' he spoke softly, edging forward slowly. 'Let's get you washed up and then you can tell me what's happened.'

He was almost within touching distance when Mark suddenly jerked back.

'I said stay back! I've the devil in me.'

'All right. All right.' Denzil held up his hands. 'I'll stay here. I promise.'

Mark's eyes flitted quickly left and right. He snatched a glance over his shoulder then asked, 'Are you on your own?'

25

'I am. I was just aboot to have lunch. Are you wantin' to come in and have a sandwich?'

'No, no . . . I . . .' Another flick left and right. 'I'm no hungry.'

'Come away in and wash up though, eh.' Denzil pointed. 'You've got yerself in a bit of a mess there.'

Eyes wide, Mark looked down at his hands as if seeing them for the first time.

'Aye, all right, but I'm no eatin' anythin'.'

Denzil stepped forward to pass him but Mark stepped aside.

'Don't get too close. I don't want to hurt you too because of him . . . the devil in me.'

'OK. OK. I won't. But come on. Let's get you inside, eh.'

'Will you be able to help me?' Mark cried. 'They said you'll help me.'

'I'll try.'

'Do you promise?' Mark implored.

'I promise, Mark. Now, come on, let's go inside and talk.'

Jerking back from Denzil's outstretched arm, Mark pleaded, 'Please, help me, Reverend. I've got nobody else and I've done something terrible.'

'Whatever it is, I'm sure we can sort it out.'

Mark stared straight ahead. 'Not this time.'

5

3rd May, 2.45 p.m.

It was always the taking-off that bothered Fraser. Once he was in the air he was fine, but after reading somewhere that a plane is more likely to crash in the first couple of minutes than at any other time during a flight he began to whisper a little prayer to a higher power each time he headed down the runway. Unlike large swathes of the island community, Fraser was not religious at all. The things he'd seen in his life would make anyone question the existence of God. He was lucky to get a seat on this flight, though, so maybe there was a higher power at work.

The landing didn't worry him as much, despite the familiar shooting pain in his ears and the accompanying temporary deafness as the plane descended onto Stornoway's small runway. A plane was still a better option than the ferry from Ullapool – compared to seasickness his fear of flying was easily the lesser of the two evils. Besides, the ferry took too long and the port was miles away from Barlinnie and Adam.

Fraser was frustrated to have had to abandon his monthly visit to Adam. The visits meant a lot to both of them – especially this month, given the development in their father's condition. And it was obvious that there had been something else on his brother's mind that morning. Fraser could feel it. He knew Adam better than he knew himself – and vice versa he supposed. At least he'd always thought he did until Adam had done what he did . . . But despite his frustration he was impatient to get back to his team. This was a serious case; Carla would never have called otherwise.

Fraser sifted through the facts again. The victim had been brutally murdered in his own home, possibly by a burglar – Fraser could only speculate at this stage, until he had more information. Although going by Carla's description of the injuries it was unlikely they were caused by someone looking for iPads and expensive jewellery. The Boy must have struggled with seeing that bloody mess . . . Fraser liked Owen Kelly but wasn't yet ready to share that with the young constable. Better that The Boy keep trying to impress him. As for his detective sergeant, he knew the case was in very capable hands until he got back, even if he did not tell her that often enough. Carla would keep Owen Kelly right, of that he was sure.

Carla McIntosh had a gentler way about her than Fraser, but that was not to say she could not be tough when it was needed. Some years ago he'd observed her tearing strips off a drug dealer who had been messing them around; he'd never been prouder than in that moment. Carla had been an islander all her life, apart from the short time she'd spent at the University of Liverpool, where she'd met Dean McIntosh. The young couple had had their problems, not least the culture shock for Dean when they'd moved to Stornoway after Carla had joined Fraser's small team. Everything being closed on Sundays, for example, even Tesco. There were other issues, too, that Carla kept to herself most of the time. But yes, she could be strong if she wanted to be, and she had a way of connecting with people that Fraser didn't possess and never had.

The discipline and routine Fraser had found upon joining the army at sixteen had made him more clinical. Analytical, even. The routine there had made him feel safe, probably for the first time in his life. Leaving Adam behind was his single biggest regret. Maybe that was why he felt so responsible for him, for what his twin brother had ultimately done, the abhorrence of which still weighed heavily on him. Fraser had occasionally allowed himself to ponder whether their father ever felt regret for his own actions, but the outcome of those brief musings was always the same: Johnny Brodie didn't care about anyone except Johnny Brodie.

Was he happy that their father was dying? The question left Fraser feeling uneasy. Not because he was definitely unhappy about it, but because he just could not put his finger on how he felt. Adam was delighted to think that their dad didn't have long left to live and had admitted to Fraser that he was counting down the hours and days. But the man was still their father. That had to mean something, didn't it?

'The sun is shining, at least,' the elderly woman in the seat next to him said. Her gentle island lilt broke into Fraser's train of thought, and it took him a minute to process what she had said.

'Good to leave the Glasgow drizzle behind isn't it?'

'Aye, it is that,' Fraser replied and got up from his seat, trying not to bang his head as he uncurled himself to his full six-foot-four.

The rosy-cheeked elderly woman leaned heavily on a stick and seemed to be struggling to get her bag down from the overhead compartment. Fraser reached across and lifted it down for her.

'Must be great to be that tall.' She grinned at him.

'Aye, it's come in handy a fair few times, right enough.' Fraser smiled back and followed the other passengers outside into the bright island sunshine.

It was a welcome that was hard to beat. Sunshine didn't have to be scorching hot to be appreciated. All he needed was enough heat to warm his face and to be able to leave his coat at home. That, and the white-sand beaches in the Scottish islands, something people flocked here for in their thousands every year. Uig Sands was Fraser's favourite happy place. It was like the fresh sea air made it the only place on the planet that he could really breathe, and so he'd bought a place within walking distance for himself and his loyal companion, Napoleon.

Outside of the tourist season the island was a quiet place: a place where you could think. Fraser liked thinking – analytically rather than wistfully. He left that to philosophers and those who attended the various spiritual retreats that kept popping up on Lewis. Each to their own. If people wanted their chakras rearranged that was their business. But with the busier season fast approaching it was vital that Fraser and his team got to the bottom of this man's murder and fast. Although Fraser didn't know him, Simon had been a man who by all accounts was everyone's friend.

Fraser unlocked his Range Rover and tossed his rucksack onto the back seat, yawning deeply as he slid into the front. Barely sleeping, on top of a seven a.m. flight to Glasgow, had caught up with him. And now he'd missed out on an early night in the Travelodge on Paisley Road after a meal in his favourite restaurant in Sauchiehall Street. Just thinking about Steak and Cherry made his mouth water. God, he could do with an S&C Legend Burger right about now. Mushrooms, caramelised onions, bacon, cheese and onion rings. His monthly treat when he went to the mainland to visit Adam would have to wait.

Traffic on the island's roads already looked busy despite it only being early May, a good few weeks before the holiday season really got under way: a time when dawdling island-hoppers often got right on Fraser's nerves. Hikers tackling the Hebridean Way challenge didn't help either. The island's single-track roads were not designed for walkers paying attention to the scenery rather than his car. Not that he could blame them for coming . . . The Western Isles were a magical place where the ability to escape other people was easy. The option to be alone was simple there, just the way he liked it. Even major tourist attractions like the Calanais Standing Stones or the acclaimed Gearrannan Blackhouse Village were never crowded. Luskentyre Beach on Harris resembled the Caribbean, yet a person could absorb themselves in the absolute solitude of the place. Though if it was the hot weather they were searching for, they would be disappointed.

Something Fraser never admitted to, though, was that he hadn't always loved his island life. Growing up in a house of horrors had made Fraser run away as soon as he could. Joining the army took him as far away as he could possibly go at sixteen.

Violent crime was almost unheard of on the island but, as Fraser and Adam knew well, sometimes the worst crimes were kept behind closed doors. And thirty-five years ago, Adam Brodie himself had done something unspeakable. Something he'd been locked up for ever since.

Despite being in need of a hot shower and a shave Fraser headed straight to the station. The sooner he got there the better. He smiled at two uniformed officers as he locked up his vehicle and headed in.

'DI Brodie,' the desk sergeant greeted him. 'Welcome back, although not what you had planned for this weekend, is it?'

The fact that Fraser's trips to the mainland were to visit a serial killer would be shocking to most people, but it was just how it was for his colleagues now. The norm.

'That it is not. Carla and The Boy back yet?' Fraser asked, heading deeper into the station as the sergeant nodded.

'Boss, you're back.' Carla got up from her chair. 'Cup of tea?'

'Aye, that would be braw, lass. I'm gasping.' Fraser hung his jacket on the coat-rack in the corner of his office and slid his rucksack under the desk. 'Owen.' He nodded.

The young detective hung up the call he'd just finished and looked up at Fraser. 'Hey boss, how was your flight?'

'Same as ever. Uncomfortable and nippit, but I'm here in one piece.' Fraser lifted a pair of reading glasses from his desk drawer and started to read the letter the officers had picked up from Simon Carver's house.

'Here you go.' Carla laid a mug of strong tea on the desk in front of him and Fraser picked it up immediately, gulping back as much as he could as quickly as he could.

'You make a damn good cup of tea, lass. Have I ever told you that?'

Carla smiled. 'Aye, you've mentioned it once or twice.'

'So, we've got a victim. Please tell me we also have a murder weapon.'

It was disappointing to see his detectives shaking their heads.

'Dr Carnegie will let us know as soon as she can what type of weapon we should be looking for,' Carla said. 'She suggested it was a chef's knife but will confirm that once she's done some more tests,' she added. 'I've arranged for the couple's own knives to be examined. She likes to cook apparently.'

'Good thinking,' Fraser acknowledged. 'OK. Well, let's start at the beginning.' He stood in front of them, pacing slowly back and forth before pointing at Carla. 'Simon Carver. Tell me about him. Who is he? Who wanted him dead?'

Carla sipped from her mug of tea and opened her notebook.

'Simon Carver. Forty-five. Married to Molly for twenty-three years. Worked as a mechanic for Haddon Haulage since leaving school. Very popular man. Lots of friends. Ran various football clubs. Adult and kids.'

'Great, thanks, Carla.' Fraser pointed at Owen. 'What does cutting out someone's tongue suggest to you?'

'That our killer is a real sicko,' Owen replied.

'That much is obvious, lad. What else? Why is the tongue significant?'

'If you've no got a tongue, you can't speak,' Owen suggested. 'Can't tell us something?'

Fraser turned to look at Simon's photo. 'Did you have something to tell, I wonder,' he muttered to himself, his lips pursed. Then he flicked back around and continued.

'All right, what do you two make of this letter then? *I know what you did.* Do we know of anything Carver might been mixed up in? You said he ran a football team. Everything there's above board is it?'

'I'll take a closer look at the club,' Carla said. 'But it's just a wee amateur outfit.'

'Thanks, Carla. His name has been put through all the usual searches I assume?'

Carla nodded. 'Aye, nothing unusual was flagged. I've searched his name and address but there's nothing. Apart from a social-work record about the couple of years he spent in a kids' home.' She stopped, looking at him curiously.

The memory of his and his twin brother Adam's time in care must have been instantly visible on Fraser's face. It was like a punch in the gut. He took a minute to compose himself, pulling his reading glasses off and chewing the end of one of the arms. 'On the island?'

'Yes, he was in the Lodge from '89 to '92.'

The island's kids' home, closed since the late nineties. The same place he and Adam had been. Carla flicked over to the next page in her notebook.

'What about his financial records? Have we got them yet?'

'Not yet, but they should be through soon,' Owen piped up.

'Good, good. Forensics on scene. What do we have so far?'

'The prints found at the scene. There were three in total other than our victim and his wife. Two of them have matches,' said Owen.

'When did you find that out?' Carla asked, frowning.

'I got a phone call about two minutes before DI Brodie walked in.'

'Oh, I didn't realise.'

'And? The prints.'

'Sorry, boss. Yes, so two of them are on file. What's the chances of that, eh?' His comment fell on deaf ears. 'David Sutherland, the brother-in-law who worked with him at Haddon Haulage. Prints are on file for a drink-driving arrest last year.'

'Who we already know has a drink problem, a volatile temper and previously had a confrontation with our victim,' Carla added.

'Correct, but I'm no sure he'd cut a man up like that for a few quid though, would he?' Owen countered.

'Did you find out if there was a history of domestic-abuse complaints at Sutherland's address?' Carla asked.

'There was nothing, but then folk don't always report it, do they. We know that.'

'Molly, our victim's wife, said that she was at Sutherland's home around the time her husband was murdered and her brother-in-law wasn't there,' Carla mentioned.

'Does she know where he was?' Fraser asked.

'She didn't ask, but he couldn't have been at work because he's currently suspended.'

Fraser's interest piqued at that. 'What was he suspended for?'

'Someone made a complaint about him being drunk at work. It's a busy garage with lots of heavy equipment.' Carla flicked through the pages. 'And it was Simon Carver who made the complaint. He didn't want someone to get hurt.'

'Oh,' Fraser said. 'His own brother-in-law. Was that the reason for the confrontation then?'

Carla shook her head. 'No, Molly doesn't think he knew it was Simon who made the complaint. The two men fell out because Simon wouldn't give him the loan he asked for.'

'How do we know about the volatile temper?' Fraser asked.

'Molly said he snaps, shouts, punches walls when he's drunk. There was an incident last year. Wendy Sutherland, Molly's sister, told her that he pushed her and she fell, leaving her with some bruising.'

Fraser approached the whiteboard where a photo of a smiling Simon Carver hung next to a photo of his dead body lying chopped and slashed on his kitchen floor. He drew a line from it in black marker pen and wrote David Sutherland's name at the end, circling it three times. A habit.

'You said there were two sets of prints on file,' Fraser said. 'Who do the others belong to?'

'The other set belong to a Ryan Melrose,' Owen told him.

Fraser frowned. 'Melrose. Melrose. Why do I know that name?'

'Andy Melrose,' Carla said. 'He's serving time in Barlinnie for drug trafficking. Heroin.'

That's when Fraser remembered. A nasty piece of work. 'Aye, I remember him now. So who's Ryan, then? His brother? What's he got to do with Simon Carver?'

Owen flicked through his notes. 'Ryan is his sixteen-year-old son.'

'Sixteen.' Fraser balked. Just then Adam's face flashed, uninvited, into his mind. Age is no barrier to committing violent crime; his brother's first offence was at just fifteen. The thought that history might repeat itself was horrifying. The idea made Fraser's heart rate quicken unexpectedly. All kinds of terrifying scenarios raced through his head. If Ryan's father was Andy Melrose then that lad had not had a great start in life either. 'Did Molly Carver mention Ryan? We need to establish if the lad is a regular visitor to the house, has a plausible reason for his prints to be there.'

Carla shook her head. 'No, Ryan's name never came up.'

Caught off guard by his gut instinct about the teenager, it took Fraser a minute to refocus.

'So, the third prints. They're not on record then?' He paused. 'Actually, why do we hae that laddie's prints, as a matter of interest?'

'Him and his dad were caught burgling someone's house,' Owen said.

'Ah, right. OK, nothing violent then. OK. OK.' Was that OK? Burglary didn't mean Ryan couldn't be violent.

'*I know what you did . . .*' Fraser muttered while he stared between the two photos. '*I'll be seeing you.*' He turned quickly to face Owen. 'We should get that letter over to Forensics. Go and get that arranged, lad. The sooner it's examined the better.'

'Will do, boss.'

'Are we sure that Sutherland doesn't know that it was Simon that made the complaint?' Fraser asked. '*I know what you did* suggests our killer discovered something significant. What about the wife? What does she say about the letter?'

'Says she's never seen it before,' Carla told him.

'Did you believe her?'

'Yes, I think so. She seemed genuinely surprised when she looked at it.'

'What's she like?'

'Distraught, as you might expect.'

'And their marriage was good, was it? No skeletons there that we should know about?'

'Not yet, but maybe the financial check will give us something. Forensics have found Carver's phone so they're going through that too.'

'The neighbour next door confirmed about the argument with the brother-in-law, and said Simon liked a drink too,' Owen told him. 'She also mentioned that she thought the wife could be a bit jealous at times.'

This piqued Fraser's interest. 'Is that so? Hmm, a jealous wife and a dead husband.'

'No way,' Carla interjected. 'When you meet Carver's wife you'll scrap that idea.'

'You think?' Fraser asked.

'Aye, no, it's no the wife. It's too brutal.'

He looked at Owen. 'What's your gut saying?'

The two younger detectives looked at each other before Owen replied, 'My gut says follow the evidence, boss.'

Fraser pointed at him. 'Correct answer.'

Then he wrote the word 'Fingerprints' and underlined it. In a single column he wrote the names. Ryan Melrose. David Sutherland. Unknown. After hesitating for a second he added Molly Carver. He gave Carla a brief glance before circling Molly's name. She raised her eyebrows.

'All right,' Carla said.

'Humour me. Nothing and nobody gets ruled out at this point.'

'Understood.'

Before they could continue, Carla's phone buzzed on the table. Fraser was confused to see her immediately press decline, the look on her face sombre. Seconds later it buzzed again.

'They seem persistent. I don't mind if you need to answer it.'

'No. It's fine,' Carla said, tapping the decline option again, a light flush of pink on her cheeks. 'I'll call them back later.'

'Are you good?' Fraser pressed, noting that her mood had changed.

'Aye, I'm good,' she replied.

If the case wasn't so urgent he might have pushed her further, but they had work to do.

'Right then, Owen, you get over to the haulage place. What's it called again?'

'Haddon Haulage,' Carla reminded him.

'Aye, that's it, get over to the Haddon place, will you. Talk to them about Simon Carver and David Sutherland, their relationship, work or otherwise. See if they'll let you search their lockers, workspaces, that kind of thing. If not we'll have to get a warrant and I really cannot be arsed with that today.'

'Will do, boss,' Owen replied.

'But organise the letter first. The sooner we find any DNA on that the better.'

Owen nodded and gave Carla a small smile before heading out the door.

'Where do you want me?' Carla asked.

'Could you go to Sutherland's home? Find out where he was and check out any alibi ASAP. Talk to his wife, ask her about it.' Fraser stopped, seemingly rethinking his phrasing. 'Press her about Sutherland's drinking, possible physical abuse. Obviously tread as lightly as you can, she might be vulnerable, but we need to know.'

'I can handle that,' Carla assured him.

'I know you can, lass. That's why I'm sending you and not The Boy.' He said it without looking up from staring at the whiteboard.

Then, grabbing his coat and keys, he added, 'I'm going to the Melrose place to talk to Ryan.'

'Do you think a sixteen-year-old could do that?' Carla nodded towards the photo of Simon Carver's body.

Fraser wished he could say no, but his own brother's past meant that would be a lie.

Ryan Melrose rounded the corner to his house as the ringtone from his phone played loudly in the pocket of his grey joggers. He sniffed and tucked the fat, brown envelope he was carrying into the front pocket of his black hoodie. An old woman walking a small black terrier nearby tutted in his direction, seemingly not impressed by Ryan's choice of music for a ringtone. Eminem. He ran his fingers through his brown hair, long overdue a cut.

'What are you looking at?' He scowled, and spat chewing gum onto the pavement.

Another tut later, the woman gave the lead a tug and walked away, shaking her head.

'Hello?' He answered the call and listened while the caller spoke. Ryan looked around him as he reached his front door. 'Aye, it's done,' he told them, wishing that he could be left to get on with things in his own time. 'Trust me. I know what I'm doing.'

6

Phil Harrison dropped the post onto the desk and sighed. Last night had been a late one and he had the hangover from hell, although it had been worth every throb of his pounding headache. Being his own boss meant he could come to the office when he pleased, which today was after three o'clock. The work still got done, even if today it would mean staying until after nine. He quickly sank his third cup of coffee of the day while he looked out of the second-floor window of his island law firm's office near the ferry terminal. The dark clouds developing over the frothing open sea beyond looked ominous. Starting the practice had been a risk, but Phil had always been a risk taker. He thrived off it. It was probably the only time he felt alive. The business had gone from strength to strength, mainly in property law, with a little family law from time to time – he'd never go hungry, that was for sure.

He never got tired of the view, and didn't miss the noise and smell of the cities on the mainland. Phil waved across the road to the pretty young jogger who always looked up as she passed. Getting to know her better was high on his list of things to do. He was single now, free to pursue whomever he chose. Not that he had been happy to see the end of his ten-year marriage, but he had to admit the opportunities for a single man in his forties – even on a small island such as this – were very good.

Phil laid his coffee mug down, the caffeine finally kicking in, and sat down behind his desk. The envelope on the top of the pile of his post was handwritten and looked personal, so he opened that first, his curiosity getting the better of him.

I know what you did. I'll be seeing you.

'What the fuck is this?' he muttered under his breath, taking another gulp of coffee. Phil frowned and turned the paper over. That was it. That was all it said. Probably some prank that someone thought was funny. The alternative explanation – that he had upset one of his wealthier, more exclusive mainland clients – came and went momentarily. Sending hand-scribbled notes wasn't their style. His mobile rang before he could finish figuring out what it was about.

'Hello, Molly, how's it—' He was silenced by the sound of his friend's wife crying, her words difficult to understand through the sobs. 'Wait a minute, slow down, I don't know what you're trying to say.'

When he could finally decipher her choked words his blood ran cold.

'What do you mean *dead*? I only saw him last night. I don't . . . erm . . .' He paced back and forth, scratching his head, trying to compute what he was being told. Was this really possible? No, it couldn't be. 'Hang on, Molly . . . Wait there, I'm on my way.'

Phil hung up, stuffed his phone in his trouser pocket, grabbed his car keys and dashed out of his office.

She said he'd been murdered. *Murdered.* He couldn't get the word out of his head. Simon had been murdered. His head spun, pounding from more than the single malt he and Simon had knocked back last night, as he sped through the lanes and single-track roads towards his friend's home on the outskirts of the town. How could he be dead? Phil had only spoken to him last night after football practice. They'd had a couple of beers with their usual Glenlivet chasers at McNeill's. Simon had looked fine. He'd been looking forward to the summer, and a holiday to Turkey he and Molly had planned. This couldn't be happening. The two men went back a long way. Long before Phil had come back to set up his law firm.

The tyres of his black Mercedes screeched as he came to a stop on the road outside the Carvers' gravel driveway. Molly appeared from the front door of the house next door. Crime-scene tape stuck to Simon's home made him feel physically sick.

'Molly!' Phil rushed forward without even bothering to lock his car.

She fell into his arms in the neighbour's doorway. 'Phil, I can't believe this is happening. Please tell me it's just a horrible, horrible dream.'

'What the hell happened? I mean, how did he . . .'

Phil didn't know where to start, and Molly didn't look like she was capable of answering any of his questions.

'He was just . . . just . . .' The words seemed stuck in her throat. 'He was just lying there, all cut up.' She succumbed to tears before getting any further.

'Shh, it's OK, you don't have to tell me now.' He squeezed her close and kissed the top of her head. His best friend's wife. Simon's widow. 'Come on, let's get you back inside.'

He took another look at Simon's home before closing the door behind them. From the neighbour's kitchen window he could see suited and masked forensics officers coming and going. The scene was surreal, like something out of a movie, and it was happening to someone he knew. Someone he'd cared about since the two were boys. Someone he'd loved like a brother. Simon couldn't be dead. No way.

Molly pulled back from him and wiped her face. 'I'm so glad you're here.'

'Are you all right, sweetheart?'

Molly fell back into Phil's arms, sobbing again, her words difficult to understand.

'Shh, hey, come on.' He wiped his fingers across her cheeks. 'What have the police said to you?'

'Nothing really, a detective just asked me some questions about Simon, and our marriage.'

'They asked about your marriage?'

'Yes. She kept apologising, saying the questions are procedure. I know she's right. Isn't she? You're a lawyer. You tell me.'

'Yes, they have to ask uncomfortable questions, but I don't want you talking to them again without me.'

Molly's eyes stretched wide. 'What? Why?'

'Just because you're vulnerable. You need someone with you when you speak to the police. They can take even the slightest comment out of context and it's easy for a misunderstanding to turn into a nightmare of accusations and, God forbid, an arrest.'

'But she seemed really nice,' Molly said. 'Like she really cared.'

'I know. I'm not working as your lawyer but still I'd prefer it if you had me there.'

'All right. If you think that's best.'

'Trust me. It is.' Phil wanted to tell her not to worry, but this could go in any direction at the moment. The spouse is always looked at in a murder investigation. Even though it would probably never come to anything, he didn't want her implicating herself accidentally.

Molly nodded. 'Oh, that detective gave me a card with her number on it.' She rummaged in the pocket of her cardigan and handed it to him. 'Here.'

'Good. Can I keep this?'

'Sure, but what if I remember something I think she needs to know?'

'Tell me and we'll talk to them together.'

Molly closed her eyes and nodded, then turned to fill the kettle. Phil stared back out the kitchen window again, relieved that she had accepted his offer of help. He owed it to Simon.

7

3rd May, 4.35 p.m.

Carla noticed the difference in the two sisters' homes immediately. Where Molly lived in a flashy semi-detached newbuild, Wendy and her family had bought a nineteen-twenties former council property. From the outside it seemed well kept with the lawn neatly cut and flower-beds filled with roses and stunning scarlet tulips. She knocked on the front door and readied her ID. While she waited she recalled the look on Fraser's face when she'd declined those calls. Carla wished she could tell him, she really did, but it was too humiliating. That thought drifted to the back of her mind when footsteps tapped along the hallway before the door opened. A thin teenage girl with shiny, short black hair greeted Carla with a stare.

'Hello,' Carla began, holding her ID in front of her. 'I'm DS McIntosh. Is your mum or dad home?' The words had barely left her lips when a woman drying her hands on a red-and-white checked tea-towel joined them. It was immediately obvious that she was Molly's sister. The two women had the same eyes and nose.

'This woman is looking for you,' the teenager announced and walked away.

Wendy Sutherland glanced at Carla's ID. 'What is it? What's happened? Is David all right?'

'Hello, Mrs Sutherland. Would it be all right if I came in and asked you a few questions?' Carla said. Clearly the woman hadn't heard about her brother-in-law yet. Strange. Why hadn't Molly called her sister? She'd only seen Wendy a short time before finding Simon's body. Usually such a traumatic shock made people reach out to family.

'Yes, yes, of course.' Wendy opened the door wide and indicated for Carla to come in. 'We can talk in the kitchen. First door on the right.'

'Thanks.' Carla wiped her feet on the frayed doormat and stepped inside, the smell of fried bacon wafting into her nose.

'David didn't come home last night,' Wendy said, a look of concern on her face. 'Have you found him?' She chewed her lip, flicked her gaze to the floor. 'Has he done something?'

Interesting; she went straight to questioning whether he'd done something.

'When did you last see David?'

Wendy Sutherland took a slow, sombre breath, pulling out one of the pine dining chairs that sat round the matching circular dining table in the middle of the small room.

'I suppose you may as well know he and I argued last night and he stormed out. He's not answering his phone. I must have tried it about a hundred times. So have you found him or not?' she asked impatiently. 'That's why you're here, isn't it?'

The couple's daughter caught Carla's eye, a sullen expression on her face, as she walked past the open doorway before slinking upstairs, her footsteps stopping at the top.

'Have you reported David missing?'

'No, not yet.'

'So it's safe to assume that you don't have any idea where your husband was between eight thirty and ten o'clock this morning?' Carla asked.

'Did you not just hear what I said?' Wendy exclaimed. 'I haven't seen him since last night!'

'And how did he seem when you last spoke to him?'

'Oh, I don't know. Angry. Sad. I don't know.'

'Had something happened?' Carla asked. 'What was the argument about?'

Wendy reached into the drawer behind her and pulled out a pile of letters. The top one had the letters CCJ on it in bold, red writing. She retrieved another envelope and took out the letter. After taking a huge breath she handed it to Carla.

'*Had something happened*,' Wendy repeated, tapping her finger on the pile. 'Take your pick from that lot.'

Carla read the letter she'd been given. It was from the Sutherlands' bank.

'This says that there's a possibility that your house will be repossessed,' she pointed out.

'Yep. We've exhausted all possible ways to keep it.'

Carla handed the letter back. 'I'm sorry,' she said, and she meant it. The woman looked beaten down by it all.

'So, have you found him?'

Carla shook her head. 'No, we haven't. I'm here because something has happened to your brother-in-law, Simon.'

Wendy's face flushed red on hearing that name. 'What's happened?'

'I'm sorry to inform you that Simon has been murdered.'

'Oh my God!' Wendy clasped her hands to her mouth. 'Is Molly, is she,' she stuttered. 'Is Molly all right?'

'Your sister is fine; don't worry.'

'When did he, I mean … When did it happen? I mean, how did he …'

'Simon was killed sometime between eight thirty and ten o'clock this morning,' Carla told her. 'He was stabbed.'

Wendy's brow crumpled, then she gasped. 'That's why you asked where David was this morning!' She burst into floods of tears, her hands trembling.

'Can I get you a glass of water, Mrs Sutherland?' Carla stood without waiting for an answer.

She ran the tap and filled a mug she found on the draining board. 'Here you go,' she said.

'Thanks.' Wendy sipped, her hands still shaking. 'He wouldn't. David has a temper but … No … He couldn't. We kissed. That was all and we had both been drinking and … No, David wouldn't hurt anyone.'

'When you said *we kissed*, what do you mean exactly?'

'Me and Simon. *I* kissed *him* to be precise. It was just a stupid mistake and it happened so long ago. I only told David last night because I was so angry that he'd got us into this mess. But David was very hurt, especially because he thinks it's Simon's fault that all of this is happening to us.' She pointed to the letters.

'Does Molly know?'

'God, no, I mean, I don't think so. Simon promised he wouldn't tell her. I begged him not to. It was a stupid, embarrassing mistake.'

Jealousy is a powerful motive, Carla considered. Jealousy and money. This case had both in play.

Remembering what Molly had mentioned about David pushing Wendy she asked, 'Has David ever been violent?'

The woman avoided Carla's eye. 'No, never.'

'Are you absolutely sure about that?'

'Yes, I'm sure.'

'Your sister mentioned that . . .'

'Molly doesn't know what she's talking about,' Wendy snapped before Carla could finish. 'Besides, what's that got to do with Simon's death anyway?'

'We're trying to establish who might have had a reason to hurt your brother-in-law. We know that David asked Simon for money and he said no. I imagine that was upsetting given your financial problems. If your husband has a history of violence then . . .'

'He doesn't.' She was adamant, yet still didn't look at Carla. 'Anyway they sorted that out. Simon said he couldn't afford to lend us that amount of money. David was all right with it. Besides, the two men were more than just brothers-in-law. Simon and David went to school together.' She wiped her face with the tea-towel. 'They go way back.'

The noise of a text arriving chimed out, and Wendy grabbed her phone from her jeans pocket. A look of relief filled her face.

'It's him.'

'What does the message say?' Carla asked.

Wendy held her phone out for Carla to see. It simply read –

I'm sorry

'Call him,' Carla insisted. 'Tell him to come home, but don't tell him I'm here.'

Wendy frowned. 'Why not?'

'Please, Mrs Sutherland. Just call him.'

Wendy hit the call button and listened to it go straight to voicemail. Shaking her head, she looked at Carla. 'I think he's switched his phone off.'

David vomited on the ground as soon as he'd hit send on the text. He sighed to see that there were twelve missed calls on his phone. His mind felt like it was stuffed full of cotton wool. Again. He'd got drunk as quickly as possible last night after their argument. How could she do that to him? Images in his mind of his wife with *him* filled David with rage. How could *he* do that to David. He'd passed out before midnight behind the wee paper shop, and woken with the shakes at five a.m., nausea clawing in his guts. Thank God for Ravi, the shop's owner, who had a relaxed approach to alcohol sales. David had downed half a litre of Smirnoff before his phone read five forty-five a.m. He must have blacked out again soon after because the can of cheap lager had still been half full on the ground beside him a short time ago.

David got up and wiped dirt from his trousers. He rummaged in his jeans pocket for his wallet and keys.

'Shit,' he mumbled when he found neither.

Then he noticed the cuts on his palms. They stung to the touch, but it was the bruises on his knuckles that shocked him the most. As hard as he tried, no memory of how they'd happened would come. He and Wendy had argued, he remembered that well, but had he . . . No, he couldn't have. No, he'd never hit Wendy. Maybe he'd punched the wall, but that didn't explain the cuts. The drinking had to stop.

A young woman pushing a toddler in a buggy threw him an anxious stare before quickening her step. David tried to smile at her but knew he must look a fright. He would run away from himself if he could.

Then he spotted the drops of blood on his white T-shirt.

8

Fraser took a detour to Simon Carver's home on the way to Ryan Melrose's. He wanted to see the crime scene for himself and the Forensics team wouldn't mind his presence. They knew Fraser well enough to know he liked to do things his own way. Simon Carver's body was gone but Fraser wanted to see the place. He stared at the large, drying blood pattern on the couple's wooden floor. Poor bastard. What a horrible way to die. Stabbed, sliced and hacked to death on your own kitchen floor. Fraser hoped that Carver had at least been unconscious when his tongue was cut out. The irony of his name would be funny if the crime hadn't been so abhorrent.

'That's a lot of blood,' Fraser muttered to himself, tracing the trail with his eyes. 'You were crawling to the door, but you became too weak. The attacker was able to easily overpower you. You'd lost too much blood already.'

He caught sight of a chair pulled away from the kitchen table, a single fingerprint in blood on the back of it. 'They sat and watched you fight for your life from that chair.' He pursed his lips. 'How long did they wait before hacking out your tongue? Five minutes, ten?'

Fraser checked out the sink to see tiny blood drops on the taps. 'The attacker's blood?' He glanced at his own hands, imagining the scene. 'They cut themselves, knife slid through their fingers, slippery from the blood. They washed it off in this sink.' He needed to know as soon as possible if any DNA could be recovered.

Fraser's eye was attracted to a smudged mark on the wall with a numbered label next to it, then he looked back at the stained floor. The killer had torn the man's tongue out and nailed it to the wall. Fraser had seen some barbaric things in his life but this defied humanity.

'Displaying the tongue suggests what – pride at what they'd done? They were showing off', Fraser continued. 'Or is it a warning? A punishment? That's more of a gangland thing.'

A warning to who though? Us? Fraser mulled over the idea. He thought of all the reasons Ryan Melrose might have had to carry out this repugnant crime. How did the two men know each other? If indeed they did. The women Adam had killed weren't known to him. It was just their tragic luck that his brother had chosen them on that particular day. Wrong place, wrong time. If Ryan was the killer, had he chosen Simon at random? Or was he a planner? Adam had told psychiatrists that the thrill of killing was a high like none he'd ever felt before. He'd started to crave it and knew he wouldn't have stopped. He explained that he couldn't. Murder had become an addiction.

Fraser pushed thoughts of Adam back into the box at the back of his mind as he crossed the kitchen, stopping at the backdoor. 'So is this our entry and exit point then?'

He stared, scanning the door top to bottom, left to right, taking in every scratch, every spot. 'No sign of forced entry, so you either knew your attacker or trusted them.'

Fraser turned to look around the kitchen, trying to visualise what had happened there just a few hours earlier. While he'd been on his way to see Adam, a man was being brutally murdered in his own home. A place where he should feel safe.

'Your killer comes in here. Did you know them? Did you invite them in?' He tightened his lips. 'Or were they waiting, hiding round the back. You went out to investigate when you heard a noise.'

Then Fraser considered David Sutherland as a suspect. He knew Simon well, had done for many years. Simon trusted him. Simon would have had no trouble inviting him in despite their arguments. By all accounts Simon was a decent enough guy. He would welcome the chance to sort out any problems they had. Was that when David had taken his chance to kill him? Sutherland's life sounded chaotic, disordered, with a serious drink problem. If he was drunk when he attacked his brother-in-law then that would surely have impaired his abilities? The rage was there for sure, but the coordination, the skill, the accuracy . . . They needed to know exactly where Sutherland was at the time of the murder as soon as possible. Taking out a tongue would have required a steady hand – then there was nailing it to the wall. That meant something. Was this the killer's calling card? Was the letter part of the elaborate build-up? But then why send a letter at all? Did the killer need Simon to think he was being watched? It didn't sound to Fraser like Sutherland was capable of orchestrating a plan like that.

And there was a third set of prints. Maybe he was focusing too much on Sutherland and Melrose. Fraser shuddered to think that this third person might be even more sinister than them.

Reverend Denzil Martin thought about his conversation with Mark. He should check on him. The poor man's mind was in chaos, ranting about the devil being in him. Mark had seemed desperate to tell him something earlier but said *they* wouldn't let him. *They* being the voices in his head. *They* warned him it had to be a secret. Denzil couldn't help but notice the spots of blood on his shirt but Mark was too distraught to be questioned about them. Instead Denzil gave him a clean shirt from the bag of donations recently handed in to the church. Whatever had happened it had scared the living daylights out of the man. Denzil had never seen Mark so terrified. Schizophrenia was such a cruel illness.

He dialled Mark's number and waited. When it went straight to voicemail, he sighed and hung up. Tapping the iPhone gently on his chin, he considered his next move, and dialled again. Still no answer. This time he left a brief message.

'Mark, it's Reverend Martin. I'm just calling to see if you're all right. Give me a ring back when you get this.' He sighed. 'If not then I'll pop over to the caravan and see you in the morning.'

9

Owen indicated left as the sign for Haddon Haulage came into view. After he'd parked up he opened the text Carla had sent him about her conversation with Wendy Sutherland. It seemed that there were even more reasons for David Sutherland to hate his brother-in-law. Notably, an intimate moment between Wendy and Simon. And the man was a heavy drinker, they already knew that. Owen didn't want to assume he was an alcoholic yet. That term was bandied about too much in his opinion. 'Problem drinker' Owen would say. It sounded like his behaviour became problematic for those around him for sure. And then there was the fact that Simon wouldn't give the man the money he needed, and it seemed the couple's financial state was dire. The possibility of losing his home may have pushed Sutherland over the edge, or finding out his wife had kissed the very man who had refused to help might have driven him to kill – and Sutherland hadn't been seen since last night.

The nature of Simon Carver's injuries suggested frenzy to Owen, right up until the tongue. More precisely, going to the trouble of displaying it on the wall. The two just didn't match up in Owen's mind. Then there was Sutherland's motive. Jealousy didn't extend to that final horror, in everything Owen had learned. The stabbing suggested passion, yes, but the tongue was another thing altogether. He would even go as far as to say psychopathic. His theories were all very well until it came to telling DI Brodie though; he wanted to be sure before he told his boss, to have some chance of impressing him enough to lose his unwanted nickname. Talking to Carver and

Sutherland's work colleagues would help him get a fuller picture of both their lives.

Owen locked up the car and headed for the site office, where he was greeted by a large woman with tight, greying curls locking the door after her as she made her way out.

'I'm sorry but the office is closed. You don't have an appointment, do you?' On seeing Owen's ID held aloft, she fumbled with the key. 'Oh, right. Erm, come in.'

Owen noticed a flush of pink on her cheeks.

'Thanks,' Owen replied and followed the woman inside the cabin that was used as the company's office.

'Is everything all right?' she asked. 'I'm sorry, what a daft thing to say. Of course it's not, otherwise you wouldn't be here,' she babbled, fidgeting with the cuffs of her white blouse.

'Firstly, can I have your name please?'

'Maggie Munro. I'm the office manager.'

Owen made a note then said, 'Hello, Maggie. I'm Detective Constable Kelly. I was hoping you could answer a few questions about two of your employees. Simon Carver and David Sutherland.'

The woman's face immediately flushed an even hotter pink.

'If I can, yes, absolutely. Is this about the complaint Simon made?'

'It may be a factor, yes,' Owen agreed, then cleared his throat before telling her. Giving bad news wasn't something he had much practical experience of yet. 'I'm afraid that Simon Carver has been murdered.'

'What!' The woman dropped into a chair, clasping a hand to her face. 'When? I mean, how? I only spoke to him this morning. Oh, that's horrible. What happened?'

All the colour had drained from the woman's face. So the news hadn't reached her yet. This woman's relationship with Carver was obviously not a very close one.

'He was found dead in his home earlier this morning.'

'I can't believe it. That's horrible.'

'What time did you speak to Simon this morning?' This was a development that could narrow down his time of death further.

The woman frowned. 'It must have been around quarter past

eight, maybe twenty past. What time did he . . .' She paused to take a breath. 'I'm sorry. This is so messed up.' She shook her head.

'How did he seem when you spoke to him?'

'Fine. Simon was fine. He said he had a doctor's appointment so would be in late. I know he's had some trouble sleeping recently. He said he was going to see if he could get something for it.'

'Were the two of you close?' Owen asked.

Her thin smile came and went quickly. 'We're a small firm. More like family actually. Sometimes we talk about stuff that's going on our lives.'

'Do you ever talk to David Sutherland about his life?' Owen moved the conversation along, spotting that her reaction immediately changed.

'The less said about David the better at the moment.'

'Why is that?' Owen noted her body language stiffen.

'Jekyll and Hyde is the best way to describe David. When he's sober he's fine – I mean he's never been particularly friendly – but when he's had a drink . . .' She tutted loudly. 'That man is a monster.'

Monster. That was a strong description. Neither Molly nor Wendy had gone that far. 'Volatile' was what Molly had said.

'Tell me more about him. How long have you known him?'

'Myself and Simon started working here on apprenticeships at around the same time. David came a couple of years later after studying mechanics at college on the mainland. Inverness I think it was. Simon and David had been friends at school but I think they had lost touch a bit until David started working here.' Her gaze briefly flicked sideways. 'Me and David went out for a little bit. Before he met Wendy of course.'

'What was he like with you?'

'He was all right back then,' she said. 'But he didn't drink so much then.'

'Was he ever violent towards you when you were with him?'

'Gosh, no, never. But like I said, he didn't drink so much back then.'

'Were you aware of any animosity between Simon and David?' Owen ploughed on. He didn't want to direct her response by using the words 'argument' or 'fight'.

'I knew they had argued about money although neither of them told me that directly. I overheard someone talking about it in the post office. Stornoway is a small town.'

'Did David know that it was Simon who had made the complaint that got him suspended?' Owen continued.

'If he did he never told me,' Maggie replied, fidgeting with her cuff again. 'I'm sorry, I'm probably not being much help, am I.'

'On the contrary, you're a great help. Did Simon and David have lockers? I'd really appreciate it if I could take a look in them.' He knew he was chancing it without a warrant and had purposely avoided using the word 'search'.

'Erm, yes, through here.'

Owen followed her out of the cabin and into a workshop, past a white lorry cab missing a wheel and into a small room that he assumed was the staff break room. Four tall, grey lockers stood at the furthest end of the room, next to a table with four mismatched chairs around it.

'You have four mechanics?' Owen pointed at the table and chairs.

'Not anymore. It has just been Simon and David since our two other mechanics retired. Until David's suspension.' Tears filled her eyes. 'Now it's . . .' Her words tailed off then. 'Anyway, here you are. They're not locked.'

'Thank you, Maggie,' Owen said, as he pulled on a pair of gloves. The sombre expression on her face as she watched him betrayed her grief.

'No problem. I'll leave you to it. I'll be in the office if you need anything.'

Owen waited until Maggie had gone then opened Simon's locker first. The smell of sweat invaded his nostrils immediately, causing him to instinctively lift a hand to his nose. It wasn't just sweat, it was mixed with something else. Oil, perhaps. He rummaged through a pile of dirty rags and receipts. Picking one up he read that it was from Tesco, dated two days before Simon was murdered. He had purchased a packet of chocolate digestives and toilet roll. Another was from Halfords for a tyre and a bottle of screenwash. Mundane, boring items that Simon hadn't lived long enough to use. Owen placed the receipts back into the locker.

On the floor of the locker was a pair of steel-toecapped boots with a sock sticking out of each, as if their victim had just stepped out of them. It was a haunting sight. Something leaning against the back of the locker caught Owen's eye. He bent down and picked up an iPad that had a sticker on a black cover. Property of Haddon Haulage. Owen switched it on, grateful that it didn't require a password. He examined the search history, most of which were work-related websites for engine parts. Batteries, tyres, wiper fluid. Although one search was for hotels in Paris which he assumed was for a surprise for Molly. The homepage had a link to Paddy Power, a gambling site, and another to a racing results website. Why were they on his work device? Owen made a note just in case it was relevant. Perhaps Simon put on his bets and checked his results during his tea breaks. Owen placed the iPad into an evidence bag and put it on the table. There was a forensic examination already being carried out on a laptop and phone that had been taken from his home. Owen closed Simon's locker then turned his attention to David Sutherland's.

The whiff of vodka hit him before the door was completely open.

'Bloody hell,' Owen muttered on seeing the state of Sutherland's locker. It seemed the difference between the two men extended into their workplace.

Simon Carver's wasn't exactly perfect, but what he was seeing here was nothing short of shambolic. Dirty, too. Sticky coffee stains covered the small shelf next to a Celtic football team mug that had a ring round the inside of it halfway up, where a thin layer of mould was starting to develop. His work boots were laid on their side facing in opposite directions. A set of overalls sat scrunched up in the corner. Owen moved them aside and found an empty half bottle of Smirnoff vodka, its lid off next to it. The source of the smell. Owen hated the stink of the stuff and wondered how anyone could enjoy something as rank as that. He turned his attention to the shelf and reached into the back of it. That was where he located Sutherland's iPad.

'Let's hope you aren't password-protected either,' he muttered, as he switched it on. When the battery indicated it was low, Owen typed quickly, scanning the search history as he'd done with Simon Carver's. Porn, poker sites and the same type of work-related stuff Owen had seen on Simon's – until a recent search caught his attention.

'Well, well, well, Mr Sutherland. Your defence lawyer is going to have their work cut out explaining this away.' This discovery just added to the evidence against Sutherland. DI Brodie should know this as soon as possible.

Just then the device switched off automatically.

'What is it?' Maggie Munro's voice startled Owen; he hadn't heard her return.

As he placed the second iPad into an evidence bag he noticed the mug of tea in her hand.

'I thought you might like a cup of tea. I wasn't sure what you took in it so I just put in a splash of milk. There's a bowl of sugar on the work top. You might even find a clean spoon there too.'

Owen noticed that the mug in her hand was a Rangers football club one. The rivalry between the two teams, Celtic and Rangers, was legendary the world over. It was probably unimportant but he noted it nonetheless.

'Thanks, Maggie,' Owen said as he took it from her.

'You're welcome. Have you got any idea how much longer you're going to be?' she asked, glancing at her watch.

Owen took a sip of tea, savouring it. Working with DI Brodie had caused the man's tea habit to rub off on him. Owen had never seen anyone who loved tea as much as the boss.

'I'd like to take these iPads. Is that all right? They are property of Haddon Haulage, aren't they?' He put the mug down onto the table.

'That's right, they are. Of course, take whatever you need,' Maggie said.

'Thank you. Well, I won't take up any more of your time,' Owen said, on seeing her glance at her watch again.

As he walked to his car, a text arrived. The forensic examination of Simon Carver's financial records had been completed.

'That's interesting,' Owen muttered, knowing the boss would also want to know about this development right away.

* * *

'Dad,' Eva called out. 'Where have you been?'

'Where's your mum, darlin'?' David Sutherland said, instead of answering her question. Their daughter didn't need to hear it. What the hell could he say? *Don't worry, your old da' has been blackout pished behind some manky bins.*

The door at the end of the hall opened and a stoney-faced Wendy appeared.

'Go up to your room, Eva. Me and your Dad need to talk.'

'Yes, right,' the teenager huffed. 'You want me to fuck off so you can scream at him again.'

'Eva!' Wendy snapped. 'Don't you dare talk to me like that. Get your arse up them stairs now!'

Eva stepped between her parents. 'I'm no leaving Dad with you.'

David gently brushed his hand across her back. 'Do as your mum says, darlin.'

After giving Wendy a filthy scowl, the teenager slunk upstairs, banging her bedroom door shut after herself.

'Wendy,' David walked towards his wife until she stepped back.

'I don't want to hear it,' she spoke through gritted teeth. 'Pack your bags and get out.'

'You don't mean that. I'm sorry, I fucked up, but I'm going to go to the meetings again, I swear. I'll phone the rev once we've talked.' He reached out to take her hand, but her body stiffened to his touch.

'The police were here looking for you.'

David frowned. 'Why?'

Tears filled Wendy's eyes but the words failed her.

'Wendy, what is it? Why were the police here?' David's heart pounded. The bruises, the cuts. Shit, what had he done?

'Did you do it?' Wendy's voice cracked.

'Do what? Wendy! Just tell me, why were the police here?'

'Uncle Simon has been murdered.'

Neither of them had heard Eva's bedroom door open so didn't know the teenager was listening at the top of the stairs.

'What!' David gasped, looking at Wendy in confusion. 'Wendy! What the hell's going on? Is that true?'

'Yes, it's true. Molly found his body this morning.' Wendy succumbed to a tide of tears. 'Pack your bags,' she sobbed. 'I don't want a murderer in my house.'

'What?' David exclaimed. 'You can't possibly believe I had anything to do with it.'

'Dad didn't do it!' Eva shouted. 'He didn't, he didn't.'

'I'm going out,' Wendy cried, looking up at her daughter. 'Come on, love, you're coming with me.' Then she stared at David. 'I want you gone when I get back.'

'I'm not going anywhere,' Eva huffed.

'It's all right, Eva. Do as your mum says, darlin'.'

David couldn't compute what was going on. Simon couldn't be dead. He tried to remember when he'd last spoken to his brother-in-law. Things were fine, weren't they? He'd been angry on hearing that Wendy had kissed him but David hadn't gone to Simon's. He had just got blackout drunk instead in a bid to forget, hadn't he? But the bruises, the cuts. And there was blood on his shirt . . .

'How did he . . . I mean.' This made no sense. 'How did he die?'

'He was stabbed to death,' Eva announced.

'Stabbed! Oh my God.'

As soon as his wife's car left, David grabbed his phone, irritated that the battery was dead. He had to call her. Where the hell was his charger? Why the hell did Wendy keep moving his stuff? The throbbing headache was getting worse, the sick, sour taste growing viler by the second. The ringing in his ears became almost deafening. This was a nightmare. Once the charger had been located he plugged it in and with trembling hands he scrolled his contacts for Molly's number but he couldn't do it. He couldn't bear to hear her voice.

David's legs weakened under him until he was on the floor, sobbing harder then he thought possible.

'Oh God!' he screamed. 'No . . . What have I done?'

A moment of lucidity flashed through him. Grabbing a black binbag from the cupboard under the sink, he stripped off his blood-spotted T-shirt and jeans. Then his boxers and socks were thrown in. David tied a tight knot in the bag and dropped it on the floor before rummaging in a basket of clean laundry on the kitchen table. His navy jogging bottoms and black T-shirt would do. After gulping a huge glass of water he washed his face and hands.

Snatching hold of the bag of clothes, he fled out the backdoor.

10

3rd May, 6 p.m.

'I ken you're in there so I'm no going away.' Fraser let the letterbox fall back down for a third time then muttered under his breath, 'Three, two, one.' Seconds later the key turned in the lock, before Ryan Melrose's door opened to reveal a pasty-faced, bleary-eyed Suzanne Melrose, her blonde hair tied loosely in a messy bun.

'What do you want?'

'I'm looking for Ryan,' Fraser said, glancing over her shoulder into the hallway, noticing how untidy it was. That wasn't a surprise. The place had been a cowp the day they had taken Andy Melrose in. It seemed nothing had changed since then except, he hoped, there were fewer drugs in the property.

'He's no in.'

'You and I both know that's no true,' Fraser replied. 'So dinnae waste my time pretending it is.'

'Aye, it is true,' Suzanne Melrose insisted, the pitch in her voice lifting as she spoke, as if for emphasis. 'He's no here. I dinnae ken where he is.'

'Dinnae annoy me, Suzanne. Gie your son a shout.' Fraser was losing patience. 'Tell him I need to speak to him.' He paused, seemingly for effect. 'Now.'

It was irritating to Fraser that shoving her aside and taking her son out by the scruff of his neck was frowned upon. That would be far simpler and more efficient than pussyfooting around with protocol nonsense.

'You've got some brass neck, Fraser Brodie,' she seethed. 'Rocking up here, treating folk like this.'

Choosing to ignore the comment, Fraser continued. 'Go and get Ryan, please.'

Suzanne stared, then her lip curled into a scowl. 'You might think folk have forgotten what your brother did, but I havnae.'

'Suzanne,' Fraser said as coolly as he could. It wasn't like this hadn't happened before. 'Where's Ryan?'

'I bet you think that becoming a cop makes up for everything, don't you,' she snarled. 'That's a bit like shutting the stable door after the horse's bolted, though, eh.'

The horrible fact was, she might be right. 'Suzanne, where—'

'Why do you want to speak to him anyway?' she snapped. 'What's he supposed to have done?' She tutted. 'Ryan isnae like his dad.'

'Where was Ryan this mornin'?'

'I dunno.'

'So where is he now?'

'I already told you I dunno,' Suzanne repeated, much to Fraser's annoyance.

'You dinnae mind if I come and have a look for myself, do you,' Fraser took a single step forward until Suzanne came outside, pulling the door shut behind her.

'Aye, I do mind. My bairns are asleep and I'm no wanting you coming in and waking them. Anyway, you need a warrant because I'm no letting you lot in without one. Last time I did that you carted Andy off.'

Fraser wanted to throttle the damn woman, but she was right. 'We've found Ryan's fingerprints at a crime scene and I need to ask him about it. It would be easier for everyone if he talks to me willingly.'

'Easier for you to pin it on him, more like. You never said what's he supposed to have done, anyway?'

Before he could answer, his phone vibrated in his pocket. The caller ID said it was Owen and as he moved away from the house to answer it, Suzanne slammed the door on him.

'I hope you've got good news for me.'

'I think so. Carver's financials have just come in, boss. They show regular monthly payments from his account for five hundred pounds to an account under the reference M.'

'Interesting. Are we tracing the account?'

'Forensics are on that now, they thought we'd like that information as soon as. What's Ryan Melrose saying?'

'Absolutely nothing, because the wee cherub isn't here according to his mum. Good work, Owen.'

'But that's not all I found out,' Owen continued. 'A search of David Sutherland's work iPad showed that he had searched websites that sold knives, boss.'

'Any particular type of knife?'

'Not exactly. The search history was random but definitely worth investigating, I thought,' Owen said.

The boy was right. That did need chasing up, as did Sutherland's whereabouts that morning.

'Good work,' Fraser said. 'You get on that. I'll see you back at the station.'

As soon as Fraser hung up the phone rang again. It was the prison payphone number: Adam. Seconds later Adam spoke.

'How's it goin'?'

'I'm all right, I'm right in the middle of something actually.' Fraser felt guilty saying it, but the clock was ticking.

'Oh, all right, I'll no keep you then. See you later.'

'No, no, it's all right. I can take five minutes,' Fraser sighed. 'I could do with it actually. I'm knackered.'

'You need a holiday.'

'Aye, maybe.'

'Or retirement,' Adam added.

'Fuck off,' Fraser replied. 'What the hell would I do if I gave up working?'

'Find a hobby,' Adam laughed. 'You could start crocheting blankets or something.'

'Aye, right. Ha bloody ha.'

A silence fell between them. Fraser waited, his instinct saying Adam wanted to tell him something. Just like it had that morning . . . Adam broke the silence first.

'So you're busy then. That call you took must have been about something serious.'

'You could say that.' How else could Fraser put it?

'What's happened?' Adam asked plainly.

'A man was murdered and it wasn't pretty.'

'How bad?'

'Really bad.'

'Shit, Fraser, I'm sorry.'

The thought that ran through Fraser's mind surprised him but it shouldn't have. Adam had been the same age as Ryan when he started killing. His spree lasted four years. If this murder was the work of the teenager then there was no way in hell Ryan could be allowed to continue. If there was anyone else in the world who could relate to the lad then, as abhorrent as Fraser found it, that person was Adam, but there wouldn't be time now to put that suggestion to his brother. Quickening footsteps slapped the pavement behind him. Fraser turned to see Ryan bolting from the back of the house and away in the direction of the Tesco car park.

'Shit, I have to go!' he yelled, pocketing his phone and racing off after him.

11

Chasing a teenage boy had made Fraser think about what Adam had said about retirement. Maybe his brother was right. The exertion had been futile.

'Wee bugger gave me the slip,' Fraser told Owen when he returned to the station. 'I've got uniforms out looking for him as well as Sutherland.'

'We'll find him,' Carla cut in.

'If that's no a sign of a guilty conscience I don't know what is.' Fraser pulled out a chair next to Owen. 'Show me those bank statements you told me about. Have we got any idea who or what M is?'

'Not yet, boss,' Owen replied, stifling a yawn. If he thought Fraser hadn't noticed, he was wrong.

'I'm sorry, lad, are we keeping you up?'

Carla shook her head and smiled.

'I'm sorry,' Owen said.

'What about the website searches? Have you gone through them yet?'

'Not all of them but I'm working on it.'

'Good lad. When Dr Carnegie tells us what type of blade was used it will be useful to see if Sutherland has searched for that particular one. We still haven't found him yet, I assume.'

'Not yet,' Carla confirmed.

'All right. In the meantime I've also made finding Ryan Melrose a priority. Slippery wee shite won't be able to hide for long.'

'Have you considered that he might have run for another reason?'

Carla chimed in. 'He's a teenager and Andy Melrose is his father, remember. He probably doesn't like the police.'

Fraser looked at her. 'You could be right, so the sooner we find him the better.' Then he returned his attention to Owen.

'The bank statements,' he said.

'Right, yes, so Simon Carver's account has been depositing the money to this account here.' He tapped his finger on an entry. 'Reference M.'

'Five hundred is a lot of money,' Carla said. 'Is it a loan – car maybe? Do you think it's the reason he didn't give Sutherland the money he asked for?'

'No, I checked. It doesn't match any lenders,' Owen said. 'It's going into a personal account. I'm hoping the bank will give us the account holder's details without a warrant.'

Bloody red tape, Fraser thought to himself. A man was dead. Why couldn't they just march in and search whatever they damn well wanted?

'OK, good work,' Fraser said as he began to walk away. Then he stopped, turned. 'Any chance of a cup of tea? I'm gasping.'

Then he spotted that Carla had *that* look. She was a great detective with sharp instincts and it was clear her and Fraser's opinions on this case differed already. Owen must have noticed too.

'Aye, I'll go and put the kettle on,' Owen said and walked away.

'Go on then,' Fraser invited Carla. 'Say what you're thinking.'

'All the evidence points towards Sutherland,' she said plainly.

'Not all of it,' Fraser replied while looking at the board. 'Melrose's prints are at the house and he ran when I wanted to talk to him. Innocent people don't do that.'

'I heard that drug squad are looking into whether Andy might be reviving the business. Perhaps Ryan is helping with that and that's why he ran, boss.'

'So what are you saying, Ryan Melrose is acting CEO or something?'

'I'm just pointing out that Sutherland is a better fit,' Carla said.

'Do we have any idea where the brother-in-law was yet?' Fraser bristled.

'Not yet.'

'Do we know where Ryan Melrose was yet?'

Carla shook her head. 'No.'

'Well, then, both names stay in play, DS McIntosh.'

Mark Tait paced back and forth before sitting at the table in his caravan. He picked up a pencil and tried to finish his latest sketch. If he could just get her eyes right, capture her spirit, her beauty, she would be so happy with it. But it was no use, the voices were too loud. He couldn't concentrate; they were shouting at him.

'Leave me alone!' He stood abruptly, knocking his pencils and paper onto the floor. 'Please!'

You've got the devil in you! You've got the devil in you!

Over and over and over, growing louder and louder and louder.

'Stop!' Mark pressed his hands tightly over his ears. 'Please stop! I'm sorry. I did what you asked! Please leave me alone,' he sobbed.

They're going to find out. The voice inside his head had changed, and they were laughing. Usually it was a woman. His cruel mother. Mark looked up. This new voice was a man's, one that Mark didn't recognise. *They're coming for you,* the words hissed inside his head. *They're coming.*

Footsteps outside of his caravan drew his attention. He panicked. The voice was right, they were coming for him and they were here. He rushed into the bathroom and tried to lock the door but it had broken months ago. His heart racing, he heard the caravan door squeal open. They had found him. Mark screamed with fright.

'I did what you asked!' he shouted. 'Please leave me alone.'

Footsteps grew closer before someone knocked on the door. There was no point in fighting it. What he'd done couldn't go unpunished. Mark uncurled his fingers from the handle and let it swing open slowly.

12

'Is that you?'

Jenny Baird still called out to Fraser every time she heard the door open. The octogenarian had been his housekeeper for nearly twenty years and had known both him and Adam since they were boys.

He'd told Carla and Owen to get off home too. It had been a long day and tomorrow would be no different. Uniform had been instructed to call if either of their two suspects were picked up, no matter the time of night. Fraser had taken on board everything that Carla had said but he couldn't shake his belief that the teenager was guilty.

'Aye, it's only me,' Fraser confirmed, as he always did. He supposed the routine greeting suited them. There was comfort in it for both of them.

He tossed his keys in the bowl and slid his size thirteen brown work shoes off, then tucked them on the shoe rack under the coat hooks in the hallway by the front door. He was careful to line them up neatly next to his other two pairs: one pair of walking shoes, and one pair of trainers. Both functional, not fussy or fancy. A bit like Fraser. The smell of lavender furniture polish and rosewater with an undertone of white vinegar hit him. Another comfort. Friday was polishing and window-cleaning day, and for a woman of her advanced years Jenny was still fit as a flea.

'Hey, Napoleon, how's your day been?'

Fraser fussed over his ten-year-old German shepherd-Irish wolfhound mix, whom he'd had since the dog was just six months

66

old. The strange-looking animal whined in reply as if Fraser knew what he meant, then walked back into the bedroom where he spent most of his time snoozing. Napoleon was a big softy. Much like his owner deep down. At six-foot-four Fraser didn't look out of place walking on the beach with such a large dog. Jenny, on the other hand, looked like she was leading a Shire horse around, but the gentle dog had never given her a moment of trouble in all the years she had been caring for him, and for Fraser.

'Shame you've had to come back early,' she said, as she peered around the kitchen door. 'Adam must have been disappointed. How was he?'

'It cannae be helped. He's all right. Would there be a pot of tea made?' Fraser lifted his post from the antique mahogany sideboard, flicking through the selection and filing most into the recycling bin. But a more official-looking envelope caught his attention.

Jenny Baird had known the two brothers since they were boys. Her heart had been shattered to learn what Adam had confessed to doing. But, much like Fraser, she still cared for him. She'd not forgotten the man he was before he committed his atrocious crimes and wasn't shy about defending herself on the subject.

'Aye, there's a fresh pot not long made. I've brought some leftover scones from the bake sale for you. Help yourself; I need to be going. Book club tonight and I cannot wait to tell the girls what I think about it.' The girls were her group of church friends, the youngest seventy-five.

Jenny slid her feet out of her slippers and into the size three ankle boots which looked like children's shoes next to Fraser's on the shoe rack.

'You'll be going in tomorrow, I expect,' she said. 'I'll pop in and let Napoleon out for you.'

'Thanks.' Fraser smiled, and watched the old woman close the door after herself.

He lifted a mug from the tree next to the kettle and yawned as he placed it on the immaculate worktop. He felt blessed that Jenny's standards were as high as his; he didn't know what he would do without her if he was honest. He laid the tea strainer over his mug and poured in the tea. Real tea. Not a luxury in his mind: a necessity. After adding a splash of milk, just enough to colour the tea, he sat to read his post, the top letter making him frown. Adam hadn't mentioned anything about a parole hearing, but then they hadn't had a long visit, he supposed. Then he recalled how his brother had seemed tense, and the phone call right before the futile chase of Ryan. Had he been going to tell Fraser then?

Adam's one surviving victim wouldn't be happy to hear this. Lisa Kendall would have been sent a copy of this letter too, perhaps inviting her to give evidence for the parole board.

Fraser opened his laptop and checked his emails. Sure enough there was a brief one from Lisa.

> *Hi Fraser*
>   *Hope you're well. Did you get the letter? I mean – wth?? Letting him out. Seriously?? I know you love your brother, I get that but . . . Seriously . . . You know more than anyone I really don't need this.*
>   *Lisa x*

Fraser stood to refill his cup, inhaling a long slow breath before blowing it out. He shook his head. Lisa was straight to the point as ever. Of course she would object, and he did not blame her one bit. Being attacked by Adam had often felt like a curse, but it was her witness testimony that had led to his arrest and conviction. Her bravery had stopped him. In a bizarre way that she would never understand, Lisa had helped Adam.

Fraser understood completely why people were baffled by their friendship. With no family of her own, he'd become the only person Lisa could talk to about it. And supporting her was the only thing he could do to atone for his brother's deeds.

> *Dear Lisa*
>   *Hope this email finds you well too. I only opened my letter five minutes ago, so I've not had a chance to talk to Adam. My visit was cut short. Work stuff. But I'll let you*

know as soon as I hear anything, I promise. Take care of yourself.
  Fraser

'Take care of yourself' always felt like such an empty platitude, but he meant it. Some of Lisa's injuries were permanent – physical and emotional. Her reply pinged back immediately.

Thanks, Fraser. I really appreciate that. You take care too. Keep in touch x

Perhaps it was the guilt, he wasn't sure, but he felt responsible for Lisa, whose experience with Adam had left her afraid to marry or have a proper relationship. He had helped her out in one way and another over the past thirty-five years. Mainly financially and emotionally, after her mental breakdown and PTSD following Adam's attack. Fraser didn't care what other people thought of their friendship.

An incoming video call on his laptop interrupted his train of thought. Lisa. He'd thought she might call him. He could do without it to be honest, but he clicked the 'answer call' button anyway.

'Hello, Lisa,' he greeted her, while failing to stifle a yawn.

'I haven't caught you at a bad time have I?' she asked, fiddling with the silver chain round her neck.

'Not at all. It's lovely to see you. How are you?'

'I was fine until I got this letter.'

Fraser saw her hold up the same letter that was in front of him. 'Aye, I can imagine it's got you worried but, listen, nothing will happen unless it is absolutely safe to do so.'

'Do you think he's safe to be released?'

What a question. How the hell could Fraser possibly answer her? He wished for nothing more in the world than to have his brother with him. The whole idea of Adam being freed was such a shock, and he'd barely had a minute to register that it was even a possibility. He didn't know what to say for the best. Lisa needed him to say something to make her feel better, so the truth about Fraser's own feelings was impossible to share. It would devastate her.

The tension in Lisa's voice was echoed in her tight body language. More than thirty years and thousands of pounds of counselling could only do so much. The fear of seeing Adam again had never left her. It often made Fraser wonder why she had felt so close to him for all these years, given that the men were twins. Not identical, but there was still some family resemblance. Psychologists would probably have an explanation of why they leaned on each other so much. Adam's victim and his twin brother. Fraser was fucked if he knew.

'What's been happening with you anyway? What are you working on at the moment?' He tried to change the subject, knowing that, as a writer, being asked about her books helped her relax.

But the moment she opened her mouth to answer, his ringtone sounded behind him. 'Sorry, Lisa, I better get this.'

'It's fine. Go ahead.' Her thin smile came and went quickly as she rubbed her thumb across the horizontal three-inch scar on her throat, a visible reminder of Adam's attack. It was a sign that her anxiety was hitting hard. But Fraser couldn't help that, and the call was from the prison. Adam must have saved up his telephone privilege time to use at this time of night so the call must be important.

'I'll talk to you soon,' he said to Lisa, as her face disappeared from his screen.

'How's it goin'? Long time no speak,' Adam chuckled.

'Aye, sure. All right, Adam. Sorry about rushing off earlier ... I was ...'

'I know, you said. Your case.'

'Aye. It's bloody horrific. I mean I only saw photos of the man, but . . .' He sucked air in through gritted teeth. 'It was bad.' Aware that the call might be recorded, he left the description there.

'You'll get it sorted though.'

Get it sorted. Adam's description of Fraser's work.

'I hope so. Never mind that. Why the hell didn't you tell me?'

The silence that followed meant Adam was trying to figure out what to say. Then, 'Tell you what?'

Fraser played along. 'The parole.'

'I didnae know how you'd react.'

Fair enough, Fraser thought. That was probably true. 'What do you think about it?'

Adam sighed heavily. 'Honestly, I really didnae ken what to think. I've been inside for thirty-five years, Fraser. What the hell will I do outside? I cannae work. How can I? I've never had a job since I was nineteen.'

His brother kept talking, barely taking a breath. A sure sign he was anxious.

'Coming on top of everything with Dad. I just cannae . . . Och, I don't know. What do you think?'

'They must think you'll cope all right.' Coping all right sounded better than *safe to be released*.

'Do you think I would? I mean where would I go? I cannae come and live with you, can I?'

The way he said it suggested that's what he'd want. But that just wasn't possible. Strands of the Lewis community couldn't cope, wouldn't tolerate, seeing him back amongst them. Ever. He'd probably be offered a fresh start on the mainland. Glasgow, maybe, or Edinburgh. Aberdeen would be nice. Far enough away to be anonymous.

'It's early days. That would all be sorted oot by folk whose job it is to assess everything like that.'

'The risk assessment,' Adam said plainly.

Fraser didn't want to talk about that. 'Partly, yes, but it's about more than that. Like you said, it's about how you'd cope on the outside as well. I'm sure that there would be a long period of rehabilitation before then.'

'I suppose you're right.'

'Do you want to be released?' Fraser asked.

He heard his brother take a breath down the line. 'I dinnae ken, Fraser. I really dinnae.' A brief silence was followed by, 'Would you like me to be oot?'

'Of course I would, ya daft bastard.' Fraser said it without having to give it any thought. His comment made Adam laugh. Fraser liked hearing him laugh. Selfish, he knew, but he couldn't help it.

'Listen, my call time's nearly finished. I'll speak to you tomorrow,' Adam told him then added, 'Thanks, Fraser. Love ya.'

'Love ya. Night, Adam.'

The call had cut off before Fraser had finished speaking. He hated when it did that. After talking to Adam, Ryan's face popped into his head again. Fraser couldn't shake the thought that he was like teenage Adam. When he closed his eyes, Fraser recalled Adam at sixteen.

After rummaging in the drawer of the sideboard in the hall, he pulled out a small photo album, a simple A5 red book that held memories that Fraser didn't often visit. The first image always quickened his heart rate. It was taken in the care home that first week when the boys were thirteen. They both looked so innocent. Fraser still struggled to recognise the boy standing next to him in this photo as the same man who had become a serial killer. On looking at that first photo, a pounding headache followed. That was enough.

It had been a long day, so he grabbed Napoleon's lead from the back of the kitchen door. A bit of fresh air would help. One short whistle brought the huge dog bounding from his bed.

'Come on then, you. Let's go for a walk.'

Standing on the white sands of a Western Isles beach, listening to the water – as Fraser was within minutes of leaving his house – helped him to breathe. Really breathe, as if the rest of the day had lacked oxygen. The air closer to the water hit the lungs differently somehow, the salty scent rushing through his nostrils. The soothing sound of the waves lapping the sand, some days hitting harder than others, was bliss. Napoleon loved getting his paws wet and, for such a large dog, he was an extremely agile swimmer. There was nothing quite like it anywhere else in the world, and Fraser should know. His army years had taken him to countless places, but nowhere compared to this. The smell of the ocean reminded him of his escape. He wished Adam could experience it. Maybe he soon would.

'Watch where you're fuckin' gawn.'

Adam's shoulder had smacked into a short, stocky man who was waiting to use the payphone after him.

'Aye, all right. Fuck's sake.'

'What did you say?'

'Fuck off,' Adam retorted and tried to pass until another inmate held out his foot to trip him up.

On the deck, with laughter ringing in his ears, Adam thought how easy it would be to get up and smack Andy Melrose in the face. The man was barely five-foot-eight, if that. Like Fraser, Adam towered above most people at six-foot-four. But was a moment's satisfaction worth the risk? Hell yes, it was. He got to his feet, but as he pulled his fist back Melrose just grinned. Then the memory of his chance of parole got to him.

'Come on then, big man.'

Adam looked at the small group that had gathered around him.

'Didnae think so,' Melrose sneered. 'Cos I'm no a wee defenceless lassie tied up in your fuckin' freaky murder dungeon, am I?' The men around them laughed. 'You wouldnae like it if I fought back. I'd gie you mair than a scar on yer cheek.'

Instinctively, Adam's hand touched his face where Lisa Kendall had sliced a shard of glass across his cheek during her escape. Every time he looked in the mirror he was reminded of the monster he had been.

He took a last look at Andy Melrose's triumphant face and turned to leave. He'd barely taken a few steps when he heard him say, 'Sounds like Sherlock Brodie's got a lot on his plate. What's the going rate these days for helping him catch killers? I mean, what do you charge, eh, Brodie?' Melrose laughed. 'Packet of Hula Hoops and a Mars bar. Maybe I should sign up. I wouldn't mind a wee packet of Monster Munch now and again.'

'Fuck off and die,' Adam mumbled to himself, clenching his hand into a fist.

13

1989

Fraser scanned the prison visitors' room for Adam. A life sentence with a minimum of thirty years to be served as a category A prisoner in HMP Perth. They were twenty years old so his brother wouldn't be free until he was a middle-aged man. The past three months had been surreal. Being summoned to his commanding officer at six o'clock in the morning was confusing enough – and then he'd been told the news. Fraser had immediately vomited, barely making it outside before chucking his guts onto the tarmac. He'd not been able to see Adam since his sentencing, and when he walked through the door Fraser wanted to cry, but he didn't dare. Someone had to be strong for Adam. Fraser was about to be deployed to Northern Ireland. He couldn't go without seeing his brother because he didn't think he'd be able to visit for a considerable time. And Adam had nobody else.

The man coming towards him was a stranger. Thin, pale, gaunt. Not the Adam that Fraser had left behind to join the army. God, was this his fault? If he hadn't left, maybe Adam wouldn't have done it. Fraser stood when Adam got to the table. He reached out his hand, noticing that it was shaking despite the warm room.

'No touching,' a voice called out.

Fraser snapped his hand back. His mouth was so dry. He could hear the sound of his pulse in his ears as he stared at his brother. They sat in silence for what felt like forever, until Adam said, quietly, 'It's so good to see you.'

Fraser spotted a deep blue, purple bruise, like finger marks, on Adam's bicep. There was also the remnant of an old bruise under his right eye, barely there but Fraser noticed it immediately. He frowned when his brother tugged the T-shirt's sleeve down but failed to cover the marks completely.

'What happened?'

'Nothing, it's fine.'

Words failed Fraser. What the hell could he say?

'Do you need me to get you anything?' he asked.

'No, Her Majesty provides everything,' Adam replied drily, a hint of a smile on his lips.

'Fer fuck's sake, Adam. This isnae fuckin' funny.'

'I ken it's no. Sorry. I just didnae ken what to say to you. This was a mistake. You should go. Try and forget aboot me, Fraser.'

The two brothers looked at each other. Fraser could feel tears forming so he coughed loudly, hoping they would get the message and piss off.

'You're no getting shot of me that easy,' Fraser cut in. 'Who the hell else is going to put up with your shite?'

Adam smiled, shook his head. 'What are you doin' here anyway?'

'Like I already said, who else will put up with you?'

Adam held Fraser's gaze and, for a split second, there was something glistening in them. He flicked his eyes to the side.

'Thanks,' Adam murmured.

Fraser nodded; he didn't need to say anything in return. He stared round the prison visitors' area. Adam looked nothing like these men. His brother wasn't like them. Was he?

'What's it like . . .' Fraser hesitated, searching for the rest of his question. '. . . here.'

'Well, I'll no be gien them a tip any time soon but it's adequate. Toilet arrangements could be better.'

His sense of humour was baffling, abhorrent under the circumstances. But Adam had always done that. Denied things, instead delivering ill-timed humour to cover his fear. Realising that his coping mechanism was murder had come too late to save the women he'd abducted.

14

'Hey, boss.' Carla greeted Fraser with a pair of gloves in her outstretched hand.

He'd barely managed to swallow a couple of gulps of tea before getting the call. Another victim. The second in two days.

'How bad is it?' Fraser asked, as the two detectives headed towards the derelict caravan parked near the beach at Uig Sands in the west of the island, thirty miles away from Carver's home in Stornoway. The stench hit him hard from the doorway.

'It's not pretty.'

'Is it like the Carver crime scene?'

Carla nodded. 'I'm afraid so.'

Fraser blew out a sharp breath through puffed cheeks. 'Who found him?'

'Reverend Martin. He's over there talking to Owen. Poor man, he's pretty shaken.'

'Have we got an ID yet?' Fraser asked while they walked.

'Yes, Mark Tait. Works on the fishing boats on and off. Off more than on recently. Rev Martin says he's got mental health issues. Diagnosed with schizophrenia a few years ago. They've already found a load of prescription anti-psychotics and hospital appointment cards inside the caravan.'

Fraser noticed Carla retch from the smell coming from inside.

'Do you need a minute?'

'No, it's fine. I'll be . . .' She turned to run as far as she could before vomiting.

It struck Fraser that the last time she'd done that was when she was pregnant with her first child, and he hoped this blip was not morning sickness again. He was as liberated as he was forced to be, but it really would be inconvenient for her to be pregnant right now.

He crouched closer to Mark's body, to see several stab wounds to the chest and neck. It was hard to make an accurate count because of all the blood. But it was the ghastly sight of his missing tongue that made even him retch.

'What do you reckon on a time of death?' Fraser noticed that Julia Carnegie looked quite pale herself. The noise her thermometer made when it was withdrawn from the body made him shiver.

'Twelve hours ago I'd say, given ambient temperature.' She screwed up her face. 'What a horrible place to live, and die.' Then composing herself she added, 'Same murder weapon too, I think.' She pointed at the body.

'I know it's a stupid question, but I have to ask,' Fraser began.

'Cause of death?' Julia replied.

'Aye.'

'Like our victim yesterday it could be any one of these stab wounds.' Julia shook her head. 'Have you ever seen anything like this before?'

'Not even in the army, and you know how bad Bosnia was.' He reminded her of her time in the armed forces too.

'It still shocks me what humans are capable of doing to each other.' Then she flicked her gaze sideways. It was something people did when the conversation reminded them of Adam. Fraser was grateful when Owen approached.

'Hey, boss.'

'You've been talking to the guy who found our victim. What did he say?'

'Aye. Reverend Denzil Martin. He says he was worried about our victim because he was distressed when he saw him yesterday. Wanted to check on him because he couldn't get hold of him on the phone.'

'Distressed. How?'

'He said he was rambling about the devil. Even had blood on him.'

77

Fraser stood tall. 'Blood, that's interesting.'

'Said it looked like he'd cut himself on something. The man's pretty shocked. I said someone would be over to take a statement in a bit.'

Carla rejoined the two men, looking queasy.

'Are you OK?' Fraser asked.

'Aye, I'm sorry about that. The mess just got to me there, but I'm fine.'

'Is there anything I need to know about?' His question was brusque.

Carla took a moment and licked her dry lips. 'I don't think so.' As if she understood his question perfectly.

'If or when there is, I need to know as soon as possible, all right?' He smiled at her, hoping that she took his comment as supportive, but moved away before she had a chance to answer.

'Ambulance is here,' she announced, and Fraser looked out to see the driver of the private ambulance park just outside the police line.

'Good, then maybe we can get this place ripped apart. See if this poor sod has received any suspicious post lately.'

The disgusting state of the place would make it harder to figure out what was important and what wasn't.

'You reckon it's the same guy? What with the tongue removal and all.'

'Excellent detective work, DS McIntosh,' Fraser teased. 'Cos if it's more than one then we really are in trouble here, aren't we.'

Fraser asked Carla to search one of the two bedrooms, the less filthy and chaotic of them, for anything that might help them figure out who wanted Tait dead. Owen got the short straw of searching the room Tait clearly used as a bedroom and occasional toilet, if the array of vile smells were anything to go by. The younger detective could be heard retching, mumbling expletives under his breath.

Fraser pulled open the drawer next to the sink in the cramped kitchen. It was crammed with notebooks filled with various lists, written and scrubbed out then written again. There were several beautiful drawings of boats and landscapes. Sketches of wildlife, and the sea eagles the tourists flocked here in droves to see. Otters and pine martens, too. There were umpteen drawings of vases filled with flowers, all varieties. Sunflowers, tulips, roses and some Fraser didn't recognise. The man clearly had a talent. *Shame*. He closed that drawer and peeled open the one next to the small, filthy fridge, where a coloured-pencil sketch of a pretty woman with long hair was held in place by a novelty fridge magnet. It was detailed down to a freckle on the model's neck, her bitten nails painted violet. The letter H with a kiss next to it was written at the bottom. A piece of crumpled paper caught his eye. Uncurling it carefully, he read a stomach-churningly familiar message. And the writing seemed to match that of the one found in Carver's home, too.

I know what you did. I'll be seeing you.

A vigilante killer.

Owen suddenly passed him, his face pale.

'Sorry, boss. I need air. He's got jars of his own shit in there.'

Fraser didn't blame him. He could smell the crap from out here. Inside the bedroom must be ten times worse.

Carla spotted a tatty envelope on the floor and picked it up. Inside was a bank statement. There were few entries on it, mainly benefit payments and a direct debit to O2. But one deposit immediately caught her attention. Propped up against a book on the table beside her there was a photo of two men. She lifted that to take a closer look too.

'DI Brodie,' she called out.

'What have you found?'

'Mark's bank statement proves the two men are connected.'

Fraser held out his hand. 'Give it here.'

He looked at Carla just as Owen poked his head back inside the caravan.

'Why was Simon Carver paying Mark Tait five hundred pounds every month?' Fraser asked. 'How do the two men know each other?'

'Boss, I think I've found something else.' She held up the photo and read the writing on the back. '*Me and Simon. Blackpool 2001.* They've known each other for more than twenty years.'

'They're old friends then,' Fraser mused. 'So what the hell did they do that got them killed?'

15

After giving the team a short break to get their heads straight after encountering such a horrific scene, Fraser was keen to get the investigation moving. He wasn't so hard-hearted that he didn't care about their mental welfare. Although, if he was honest, his motivation was more that he couldn't afford one of them succumbing to the stress of it all. His mind had taken a beating on seeing the crime scene too. He looked at his team and knew he could easily have felt overwhelmed by the task ahead. Two men, not just murdered but sliced, probably tortured then mutilated. Some uniforms had been sent to help with the legwork, otherwise they'd be stretched too thin. As he looked out at the expectant faces he flipped the lid from a marker pen and then approached the whiteboard. What was left of the men's bodies, unflinchingly displayed in photographs, was like something out of a horror film. He pinned the photo they'd found of the pair to the board. The men looked to be in their early twenties.

'Right. So, Simon Carver.' He tapped his pen on the man's smiling face. 'We know he's been depositing money into the bank account of Mark Tait' – he moved his pen to Mark's face – 'once a month, and both men received a threatening letter before being brutally murdered.'

Fraser spoke without looking at his detectives. 'What the hell is this letter about? *I know what you did. I'll be seeing you.*' He pressed the pen down hard on top of a photo of the note, tapping it gently a couple of times. He turned round. 'How old is the second victim, Mark Tait?'

Carla referred to her notebook. 'He's forty-four. Single, so not like Carver in that respect.'

'How old was Carver, remind me?'

'Forty-five,' Owen said. 'Do we think they're old school friends? Or was Mark Tait ever in care?' Owen asked. 'Like Simon Carver. Maybe they met there?'

'That's worth checking out, yes, but that would have been a long time ago.' The memory of his own time in the kids' home played briefly in Fraser's mind.

'So they led very different lives,' Carla continued. 'Simon worked full time. Happily married.'

'Their living arrangements too,' Owen pointed out. 'They couldn't be more different, could they? I mean, Carver's house was immaculate and Tait's was . . . Well, you saw it.'

'Who owns the land that the caravan sits on?' Fraser asked.

Carla flicked through a pile of paper on her desk, scanning the pages with her finger. 'It belongs to a Morag Thomson.'

Owen's phone rang on his desk. 'It's Forensics,' he said as he answered. 'Ah, right. OK, thanks for telling me. Yes, cheers. Catch you later, mate.'

Fraser stared at him. 'Well?'

'Erm, yes, so Carver's phone had nothing suspicious. All the messages were friendly. They're going to send me his contacts list soon. Laptop had nothing either. The only fingerprints are his as well.'

'That was quick,' Carla mentioned.

'Aye, good and efficient, just what I like,' Fraser commented. 'What about threatening messages from Sutherland?'

'No, none.'

'That's interesting,' Fraser said, looking at Carla. 'Did we find any devices at Tait's caravan?'

'No, not yet but there's still a forensics team at the scene,' Carla told him.

'Right, OK. Are there any messages to and from Mark Tait on Carver's phone?'

'Nothing obvious,' said Owen.

'That's weird,' Carla piped up. 'You give a man five hundred pounds every month but don't communicate with him?'

'I agree. That is strange. Carla, you go and speak to Morag Thomson. See how well she knew Mark. Ask her if she knew Carver.' Fraser pointed to the photo. 'Has she seen him at the caravan?'

'I'm going to see Molly Carver about this money,' Fraser informed them. He looked at the small group of uniformed officers. 'I'd like a door-to-door carried out, but try no to panic everyone. The last thing we want is nervous islanders ringing in with leads that take us nowhere. And remember, nothing to the press.'

All three of the detectives grabbed their keys and were headed for the door when Owen's phone rang again.

'It's the front desk,' he said, when he'd hung up. 'Reverend Martin is downstairs. I said I'd go and take a statement from him but looks like he's beat me to it.'

'Great, you go, lad.'

'Sure.'

'When you're done get onto CCTV from the area near the caravan, will you? Maybe his killer was captured somewhere along the road there. Farm security footage is good, too.'

As they went their separate ways, Fraser's phone buzzed with a text. Lisa Kendall. He didn't have time for this.

What has your brother decided about parole? Please text me back. This is driving me mad. I really don't think I could cope if they release him.

Fraser could not give her an answer of any kind, let alone the one she so desperately craved. He didn't know himself. He slid his phone into his pocket and got in his Range Rover, about to drive off when a knock on the driver's window made him jump. He didn't have time for this either.

'Sir.' It was Chief Superintendent Andrew Everett. The man's stale coffee breath was too close to Fraser's nostrils for comfort.

'A quick word, Fraser, before you head out. My office, ten minutes.'

Fraser wasn't given the opportunity to object as Everett walked back inside the station.

* * *

David Sutherland stared at the unopened bottle of vodka in his trembling hand. His head pounded, nausea clawing at his throat. His whole body itched from the withdrawal. Just one drink would stop all of that pain. Simon's face filled his mind. Handing himself in was the right thing to do but every time he thought of it, his heart raced at a million miles an hour. He couldn't do that to Eva. Or Wendy. But his memories were so jumbled, David didn't know what was true. So he did what he always did best, and with tears streaming down his face he opened the bottle and sank half of the contents without stopping.

16

Fraser waited outside Everett's office, wishing he could get on with his job. There was no need for the new chief superintendent to spend time in this office and Fraser was surprised he wanted to leave his comfortable Inverness base and slum it at the island station. There were certainly better golf courses on the mainland. Fraser realised that was a stereotype, but in this case it was true. The few times they'd met, Andrew Everett's tales of standing in the freezing rain on the Old Course at St Andrews had bored Fraser to tears. The recently retired CS Bailey had never ventured further than the Longman roundabout if he could help it – island-hopping had not been in his diary at all – but a double murder made Everett's presence important now.

'Come,' a voice said from the office, in sync with the sound of a phone being hung up.

Fraser walked in. Closing the door quietly behind him, he prayed this wouldn't take long. 'Sir.'

'Have a seat, Fraser. I'll try not to keep you.'

'Thank you, sir.'

Chief Superintendent Everett slid back into his padded black leather chair, his hefty frame causing the cushions to bend a little under his weight.

'Two murders in two days, DI Brodie.' Everett said it as if Fraser didn't already know. 'It's unheard of on Lewis, at least since . . .' Fraser's superior officer coughed before continuing. Both men knew his comment referred to Adam. 'You and your team are on top of things here, I hope?'

'Absolutely, sir, I was just on my way to talk to Simon Carver's wife again. DC Kelly is going through CCTV, and DS McIntosh is heading back up to Mark Tait's to talk to the woman who owns the farm his caravan was on. There are already several leads, sir. We should know more soon.'

'Good, good. We need to get a lid on this and fast. Tourist season and all that. The last thing we need is wildlife watchers traipsing over potential evidence.'

'I know, sir, and we are working as fast as we can.'

Everett was right. More than anything, they had to get on top of this case before anyone else got hurt. But if Fraser was right about Ryan, about his similarities to Adam, then Mark's death meant they had to find him fast or more lives would soon be lost.

'I'll sit in on tomorrow's briefing,' Everett told him. 'Keep myself up to speed so to speak.'

'Yes, sir.'

Great. More pressure. Just what Fraser needed.

'I want you to know I'm going to be more of a hands-on kind of leader. I realise my predecessor did things differently, but it wasn't all that long ago that I was out there pounding the pavements myself.'

'Thank you, sir, I'm very grateful for your help,' Fraser lied.

'Good, good. And I'll handle the press if and when that becomes something we have to contend with.'

Fraser was genuinely grateful to hear him say that. The last thing he wanted was to give press briefings. For him the press was an irritation he would prefer to avoid.

'Thank you, sir.'

'OK, I'll see you eight a.m. sharp tomorrow then, unless you and your team can have it wrapped up before then.'

The way he looked at him made Fraser feel like that was a challenge. He said his goodbyes and headed back to his car, trying not to be irritated by the hold-up.

When his phone rang in his pocket, Fraser was surprised to see it was from the prison. He had no time to deal with that now either. It was like his attention was being pulled in all directions at once. He forced himself to let the call to go to voicemail and accelerated quickly out of the station car park.

'Reverend Martin, thank you for coming in.'

Denzil Martin flattened down his unruly black hair as he stood up from the plastic chair in the reception area and shook Owen's outstretched hand.

'I had to, to be honest.' Denzil closed his eyes and exhaled sharply, shaking his head. 'I just can't get the image out of my mind. So much blood . . .' His words tailed off quickly.

Owen noticed that the man's hands were trembling. 'Come on through, we can chat in here. Can I get you a cup of tea or coffee?'

'No, no, thank you. Just maybe a glass of water.'

'Sure, you take a wee seat and I'll be back in a minute.'

Rev Martin nodded as he sat down at the table in the interview room. Owen felt sorry for him and wondered if he should have done more for him at the scene but, he supposed, there had been more pressing matters at hand.

'Here you go.'

'Thanks.' The glass shook as the man tried to raise it to his lips, spilling some drops onto the table. Denzil wiped them away with his fingers. 'Forgive me.'

'It's all right. Don't worry. It must have been a terrible shock to see Mark Tait like that.'

'Shock is an understatement, Detective.' He shook his head. 'I don't know how you detectives deal with that.'

'I know you told me earlier that you were checking on Mark this morning because you were worried about his mental health. Could you tell me more about that?'

'Of course. Yes. Mark suffers from schizophrenia and doesn't have a support system, so I do my best but, oh, he's such a lost soul. Was, I mean.' He stared at the floor, shaking his head again. 'Who would do something so awful to such a vulnerable man?'

'That's what we intend to find out, Reverend. You told me earlier that Mark was distressed when you last spoke to him?'

'That's right.' Denzil took a breath, fiddled with his collar. 'Mark's illness is . . . was predominantly filled with a delusion that the devil lived inside him.'

'You mentioned that he had blood on his hands?'

'Yes, he'd cut himself, I think. Yesterday is all such a blur now.'

'Did Mark ever talk about a man called Simon Carver?'

Denzil chewed his lip, seemingly thinking. 'He and a man called Simon were childhood friends, I believe. I don't know any more than that, I'm afraid.'

'Are you sure about that?'

'As sure as I can be. He occasionally mentioned a friend called Simon, although, to be honest, I can't remember if that was his surname. I'm sorry.'

Owen scrolled through the photos on his phone to find the one he'd snapped of the picture of Mark and Simon. He was keen to see what the Reverend knew about it, if anything.

'Can you tell me anything about the people in this photo?'

Denzil took the phone from him. Narrowing his eyes he stared. 'I'm sorry, can I just . . .' he asked, as he zoomed in on the image. 'I really should go and get some reading glasses.'

'It's fine, do whatever you need to.'

'I recognise Mark but I'm not so sure of the other man, I'm sorry.' He handed the phone back to Owen.

'That's all right,' Owen said, disappointed.

'He looks a little familiar but it's a small island, I suppose,' Rev Martin mentioned.

'How did Mark support himself, do you know? He didn't work, did he?'

'As far as I know he lived on invalidity, you know, sickness benefits. I'm not sure what the government are calling them these days. I didn't like to pry. You saw his caravan though. The man had nothing.' The Reverend dabbed the edge of his eye. 'Forgive me. The evil in this world is unrelenting.' Then he looked at Owen, recognition suddenly written on his face. 'Simon Carver. Molly's husband. Is that him in the photo?'

'That's right.'

'Does Simon have something to do with what happened to Mark?'

'In a way. I'm sorry to say that Simon Carver was also murdered.'

'What?! Oh, dear Lord. No. But . . .' Denzil couldn't speak. He opened his mouth but nothing came out. He ran his fingers over his collar, reaching for the glass of water again. 'But, so, was he . . . ?'

'Simon Carver was murdered in his home yesterday morning.'

Denzil clasped his hands to his face. 'Oh, how awful. Was he . . . was he? Has he also been stabbed?'

Owen nodded gently because he knew what the Reverend was asking.

'Oh,' he lifted his hand to his face, covering his mouth as he gasped. Closing his eyes, he shook his head. 'I don't know what to say, I . . . I . . .'

'Do you have any idea why someone would want to hurt these two men? In your dealings with people on the island have you noticed anyone acting strangely recently? Maybe out of character?'

Denzil sighed. Frowning, he shook his head. 'Not that I can think of. It was just Mark I was concerned about.'

Although not a church-goer himself, Owen knew that the church was the centre of the island community for many. He decided to press him further, hoping Brodie would be pleased with his initiative.

'Do you know a lad called Ryan Melrose?' Owen asked.

'Andy Melrose's boy. Yes. Why?'

'His fingerprints were found in Simon Carver's kitchen. Do you know of any connection between them?'

'Well, Ryan used to play football in the youth league, so I assume they would know each other through that.'

'Have you ever seen Ryan at Mark's caravan?'

'I haven't, but then I didn't visit often,' Denzil answered.

Owen made a note in his book. There were so many connections, but then that was to be expected on a small island. He looked up to see the man checking his watch.

'I'm so sorry but I forgot, what with all that's happened, I have an appointment. And I must get to Molly Carver after that. Will we be much longer?'

'No, all done. Thank you for coming in. You've been very helpful.'

'I hope so.' Denzil shook Owen's hand firmly this time. 'Such a terrible business. God rest their souls. I hope so.'

17

4th May, 1.30 p.m.

Owen finished the dregs of his coffee. After talking to Denzil Martin he'd started on his next job. Sandy had sent a text asking if Owen fancied watching a movie that night and he wished he could say yes. A cosy night in would be great, but this case was too pressing to make firm plans unfortunately. There were hours of CCTV to get through, even on fast forward. There wasn't much in the vicinity of Mark Tait's caravan, but there was a small private camera on a shed used by fishermen near the water – although there wasn't anything of use on that. The second camera that might help identify Mark's killer covered the farm track that led from Morag Thomson's tractor shed along a dirt track past the caravan, and ended at the entrance to the driveway that connected the farm to the main road.

What the hell? He paused the video. Rewound. Played it again. Owen leaned in, screwing his eyes up. The image on the screen was grainy, and the figure was dressed in black with their hood up. They must have known they would be caught on film because they were deliberately facing away from the camera. Owen took several screenshots of the figure, zooming in on them to try and get at least an approximate height. It was not immediately clear whether the person was male or female, but they were slim-built and not that tall, maybe five-foot-seven or five-foot-eight at most. It was hard to tell from the poor quality of the footage. The rucksack on their back looked to be black or dark in colour too. Navy even. But it had no branding on it. Did it contain the murder weapon or weapons? The figure had no distinguishing features in the way they walked, but they did not look like they were in any kind of hurry. Their gait was nondescript. He wondered if they had been so nonchalant on the return journey.

He played the video forward quickly and stopped it right on the two-hour mark. Two hours. If this was their killer they had been with Mark for two hours. What kind of torture the poor man had endured did not bear thinking about. What the hell did he do, Owen wondered, thinking of the note the killer had sent. On the retreat the figure moved faster, but not with any particular urgency. Owen tried to zoom in on the face, but this time it was hidden behind a scarf or bandana. Clever. Owen spotted a second figure at the edge of the screen and gasped. They were some distance from the hooded suspect but it was possible that they'd seen them. His DI needed to know this right away.

18

4th May, 2.45 p.m.

Fraser readied his ID for Molly to see, mulling over the information DC Owen Kelly had just given him. A potential suspect was a big development. Pity they were so difficult to identify. Someone in the technical department would be working on sharpening the image, and hopefully they'd have it before the next briefing.

Fraser rapped the letterbox loudly.

'Who is it?' A man's voice came from inside.

'Detective Inspector Fraser Brodie. I'm here to speak to Molly Carver.'

The sound of locks being opened followed, then a man appeared in the doorway. Fraser spotted Molly hovering behind.

'She's already spoken to your colleague. She's got nothing else to say.'

'And you are?' Fraser asked, irked by the man's attitude before he'd even set foot through the door.

'I'm Phil Harrison, a friend of the family and I'm also a lawyer. She won't be saying anything further without me being present.'

That was all Fraser needed. The wife of his victim being obstructive and insisting on a lawyer. Harrison's presence changed things. Fraser wondered if Molly thought she needed this guy, or if he had pushed himself into the situation without her consent. He looked the type. The poor woman appeared traumatised.

Fraser glared at Harrison, then allowed his eyes to drift and soften towards Molly.

'Is he right? You don't want to talk to me?'

Confusion crossed her face and, frowning, she shook her head slowly. She looked away as if avoiding his eye would help. Fraser's instinct was correct.

'Do you think you need a solicitor? Have you got something to hide, Mrs Carver?'

Molly looked back at him, surprised, but Harrison spoke first.

'I think we've made our position crystal clear, Detective, so if you don't mind.' He started to close the door but Fraser held his hand against it.

'Just answer me one question and then I'll leave.' He stared at Harrison then focused his attention on Molly. 'How long had Simon and Mark been friends?'

Phil stopped. 'I don't know what you're trying to pull, but I'll be speaking to your boss if you carry on. We've already told you our position.' He moved to close the door until Molly spoke.

'Why are you asking about Mark?' she said.

Instead of answering, Fraser paused, noting that Harrison's demeanour had changed; he seemed distracted now. Were those beads of sweat on his forehead?

Phil Harrison opened his mouth to speak but Molly laid a hand on his arm.

'Come in, Detective,' she said quietly.

Fraser stared at Harrison closely as he stepped past the man in the doorway. Harrison had to tilt his head to look up at him – Fraser was at least five inches taller, perhaps more. Molly showed Fraser into the living room and invited him to sit down.

'Catherine, my neighbour, has gone to her room. I don't think she knew what to say to me. I mean, what can you say to someone whose husband has been murdered? Although I don't think I'll ever be able to repay her kindness. We weren't even friends to be honest, just neighbours.' Molly opened the door at the end of the hall. 'Come through, we can talk in here.'

'Thank you, Mrs Carver, I won't keep you any longer than necessary.' Fraser spotted Harrison taking his phone out of his jeans pocket.

'I'll be recording this conversation, Detective Inspector.'

Fraser shrugged and turned his attention to Molly. He would be looking deeper into the solicitor.

'Did you know that your husband was giving Mark Tait five hundred pounds every month?'

'What's that got to do with anything?' Phil cut in.

'Mr Harrison, you of all people should know how important the first forty-eight hours are in a murder case. You should be reassured that my team and I are being diligent.'

The two men locked eyes across the coffee table, neither one wanting to look away first, but it was Harrison who flicked his gaze sideways before Fraser did.

'Phil, it's fine. I want to help.'

Harrison moved right back on the sofa and lifted his hands as if in defeat. 'OK, Molly, but as long as you understand my advice is to say nothing.' He pointed to his phone which was still recording the conversation.

Fraser could not help the feeling of satisfaction that ran through him, despite the darkness of the situation. He pressed on, turning to face Molly.

'So. Did you know?'

'No, I didn't.'

'So you weren't aware of what your husband was spending his money on?'

'For goodness' sake, she's just lost her husband. What kind of question is that? How is it even relevant?' Phil cut in, sitting back, arms crossed.

'It's relevant because Mark Tait was found dead this morning.'

Molly's eyes widened. 'No!'

It was Phil Harrison's response that drew Fraser's attention. The man's eyes flicked left and right, his collar suddenly seemingly too tight and troubling him. He coughed, immediately uncrossing his arms.

'He was found dead in his caravan earlier this morning,' Fraser informed them.

Molly turned to Phil. 'Oh, Phil, I'm so sorry.'

'I'm fine,' he sniffed, avoiding her eyes. 'Have you got any idea who, I mean, I'm sorry.' Phil held a hand up in front of him then, taking a deep breath, he continued. 'Simon and Mark were both friends of mine so if there's anything I can do to help . . . and I'm sorry about my brusqueness earlier.'

'Oh, Phil,' Molly repeated and enveloped his hand with hers.

He immediately pulled his hand away, the gesture seemingly unwelcome.

'Do you think it was the same person who killed both of them?' Molly asked, giving Phil a concerned glance.

'It looks that way,' Fraser admitted.

Phil's behaviour drew Fraser's attention. The man seemed nervous.

'So, Detective,' Phil asked. 'Erm, do you have any idea who has done this?'

'The police think that David killed Simon,' Molly told him. 'That's right, isn't it?'

'Why the hell would he? I mean, *how*? He can hardly stand up straight these days,' Phil said plainly, then sighed. 'Sad bastard.'

'Don't say that,' Molly scolded him.

'Why not? It's true isn't it,' Phil said.

'So you don't think Sutherland could be capable?' Fraser suggested.

'Absolutely not.'

'Have you got any idea why he would be searching specialist knife websites?' Fraser asked.

Phil frowned. 'David is a collector. He has a large collection that he keeps in a storage unit I believe.'

This piqued Fraser's interest immensely and his expression betrayed the fact.

'Oh, come on, Detective Brodie, a hobby doesn't make a killer,' Phil tutted. 'I collect them too.'

This development piqued Fraser's interest. 'Is that right?'

'Yes. Have you got any idea what antique weapons are worth?'

'No, I don't,' Fraser admitted, remembering Adam's quip about his retirement.

'Wendy always hated those damn swords,' Molly interrupted.

'Swords,' Fraser repeated.

'Yes,' Phil frowned. 'He's got a Jacobite Claymore worth thousands, amongst other extremely valuable pieces.'

'So why doesn't he sell the damn things?' Molly exclaimed. 'He and Wendy are desperate for money.' Tears came again.

'What about knives then? What kind of knives does he have in his collection?'

Phil's brow creased. 'I'm not sure. Knives are more my thing to be honest.' When he said it his eyes held Fraser's. 'Antique military, that kind of thing.'

'Each to their own,' Fraser admitted.

'Does this mean that David is your prime suspect?' Phil asked.

'He's a person of interest,' Fraser admitted. 'But there are other lines of inquiry that we're investigating.'

'Such as?' Phil pressed.

'Ryan Melrose is another person of interest.' Fraser watched them both carefully. 'Do either of you know him?'

Molly frowned, shaking her head. 'The name doesn't ring any bells.'

'He's that waste of space Andy Melrose's boy,' Phil said, scorn in his voice. 'Poor lad doesn't stand a chance with a scrote like that for a dad.'

'So you know Andy Melrose, then?' Fraser suggested.

'I do. He asked me to represent him but I said no. You must know him too,' Phil said plainly, seemingly without blinking. 'He's inside with your brother.'

Molly watched Fraser carefully, her eyes widening. 'It *is* you! The name Brodie, I should have twigged right away.' She chewed on her lip and fidgeted on her chair.

This conversation was too important for them to be distracted by Fraser's family history, as serious as it was, but Molly was clearly uncomfortable with him now.

'What makes Ryan a person of interest to you?' Phil probed.

'His prints are in the house.'

'That's it, is it? His prints. No DNA. No weapon.' Phil frowned. 'You need to do better than that, Detective.'

Fraser chose not to share that his gut was screaming it was the teenager, because hunches aren't enough to arrest someone.

'Wait, I do know that name,' Molly interjected. 'It was him and his dad who broke into the football clubhouse last year. The alarm went off and the police got there before they could take anything, and they explained it away as a misunderstanding.' She tapped Phil's arm. 'Remember? Simon decided not to press charges.' She tutted. 'Simon started helping the lad after that. Said he felt sorry for him. You must remember.'

'So Ryan's fingerprints would be in your home?' Fraser mooted.

'Maybe, but I can't think when he was last there. Must have been about six months. Probably before his dad got locked up.'

'That's right.' Phil lifted a finger up. 'He stopped helping him about the same time Andy went inside.'

'Have you got any idea why he stopped coming?' Fraser asked.

'I'm sorry, no, but— Actually, och, it's probably nothing,' Molly began. 'Simon's car was damaged a couple of months ago. I said I thought it was Ryan.'

'It was, that's right,' Phil agreed. 'Some wee shit keyed it outside the clubhouse.'

'Why would you suspect Ryan damaged the car?' Fraser asked, intrigued by her assumption.

'The way the boy acted around Simon, I can't explain it. We bumped into him one day, not long after and . . .' She shrugged. 'I'm sorry. I know what I mean, I just can't explain it.'

'Was it reported to the police?' Fraser asked, much to Phil's apparent amusement. 'Could it have been Ryan?'

'Come on. Cops don't give a shit about that sort of thing these days.' He scoffed. 'My Jag had its tyres slashed last week. You didn't see me making a report about it. It's pointless without a witness.'

'Slashed with a knife, perhaps,' Fraser suggested.

'I don't know, but I've set up a camera outside the driveway since. I'll catch the wee toe-rag if they try it again.'

Slashed tyres, scratched paintwork. Adam had started with vandalism. Fraser grabbed a card from his pocket and laid it onto the coffee table. The clock was ticking. Ryan Melrose was still missing.

'That's all for now but if either of you think of anything else please get in touch.'

'We will,' Molly told him.

Fraser glanced in Phil's direction before heading for the front door. 'I'll see myself out.'

As if waiting for him to leave, neither spoke until the front door closed after him.

'Why didn't you tell him—'

Molly's question was immediately shut down.

'Because he didn't need to know about that.'

'But . . .'

'I said he didn't need to know! Just leave it, will you. If the subject comes up then you say nothing.'

'But what if it helps them?'

Phil's mood darkened. 'Molly . . . I can handle it!'

'OK, OK.' She pushed past him and slammed the kitchen door behind her.

Phil watched from the living-room window until the detective's Range Rover disappeared from sight. He checked his phone to find a voicemail message. Irritated, he listened to it and called straight back. The fact his call went to her voicemail further aggravated him.

'Oh, for fuck's sakes, answer your phone,' he urged, as he paced up and down the room, nibbling on his thumbnail. 'We need to talk.'

19

'Mrs Thomson? I'm DS Carla McIntosh. We spoke on the phone.'
Carla smiled and held up her ID to show the elderly woman through
the glass pane in her front door.

The heavy rain had made the thirty-mile journey back up to
Uig Sands treacherous, and after being held up for over an hour
while an overturned tractor was recovered she was grateful to have
got there in one piece. The image Owen had sent on the way was
grainy, but Carla was hopeful Morag would recognise the figure. As
she waited for the old woman to open up, her eyes were drawn to
the immaculate rose and lavender bed out front. Morag Thomson
clearly loved her garden. From what she could see the rest of the
farm was rather chaotic and unkempt, but that was not surprising
given Morag's age.

'Oh, aye, hang on a minute.'

Carla heard the loud clicking of several locks before the huge oak
farmhouse door creaked open.

'Come in, come in, lass, come on through.' The old woman started
to walk back inside, shaking her head. 'Terrible business, this. Poor
Mark. God rest his soul.'

Carla wiped her feet and stepped inside, closing the heavy door
behind her. It was like stepping back to a time long gone. Outside
the property it was the twenty-first century, but inside it felt like
the nineteen-forties. Antique china plates were displayed along a
mahogany sideboard in the hallway. She followed Morag into the
farmhouse kitchen, where the huge range cooker gave off a blast of

warmth and the distinctive smell of baking wafted into her nostrils. It reminded Carla of her granny's old house.

Morag Thomson instructed an old collie to go to his bed, and invited Carla to sit down at the long, pine farmhouse kitchen table. Carla gratefully accepted, realising the smell was bread. She spotted a pot of tea and two cups with matching saucers on the table, next to a jug of milk and a bowl loaded with sugar cubes.

'I made a pot for us when you called to say you were coming, lass. Please have a seat.'

'That's very kind of you, thank you.' Carla sat down, sliding her hand over the thick wood of the table, wishing she could afford one like it. She probably never would, given her own family's precarious financial situation.

'Milk and sugar?'

'Just milk, thank you,' Carla replied, peeling off her cardigan in the heat of the kitchen.

'Here you go, can I get you something to eat? A sandwich maybe?'

'No, no, tea is fine, thank you.' Carla smiled and took a sip. *Real tea.* Brodie would be jealous.

Morag Thomson sat on the dining chair opposite. 'What can I do to help you, then, hen? I've already spoken to a lovely young constable earlier.'

'This is just a bit of follow-up, Mrs Thomson. We need to find out a bit more about Mark, and anyone in his life that we should know about. Friends, family, that kind of thing.' Carla laid her notepad onto the table and rummaged in her bag for a pen.

A sad look came over Morag's face. 'There weren't many people in poor Mark's life, I'm afraid. Apart from me and his community nurse, I don't think he spoke to anyone much. Not after he stopped working on the fishing boats.'

'When did he stop that?' Carla asked, sipping her tea.

'Oh, gosh, now you're asking. I don't think he'd been to sea for at least two years. Skipper had to let him go because of his behaviour. He said Mark was putting the rest of the crew in danger. I don't blame him I suppose. He had the whole crew's wellbeing to think about, not just Mark's.'

'I can imagine.'

'I was going to go and see Mark myself this morning but something came up. I should have made more effort.' Her eyes teared over. 'It was Reverend Martin who found Mark I believe. That must have been a terrible shock for him.'

'How long have you known Mark?'

A small smile crept onto Morag's lips. 'Since he was a boy. I grew up beside his mum too so . . .' She stopped suddenly and shuffled uncomfortably on her chair before picking fluff from her trousers.

'Mrs Thomson?' Carla pushed. 'Is there something you're not telling me? It sounds like you knew the family well.'

'Sadly, yes,' Morag informed her, as she poured her own cup of tea.

Carla's interest was piqued. 'Tell me about them.'

'Well, it's probably not relevant to what's happened, but Mark, you see, he didn't have a nice childhood. His mum was . . .' Morag sighed. 'She wasn't . . . She shouldn't have had children is all I'm saying. Letting every Tom, Dick and Harry into his life, some not exactly kind to the poor lad, so.'

'So?' Carla repeated, encouraging her to continue.

'Mark spent a bit of time in the Lodge when he was a teenager. He got taken off his mum and one of the step-dads. There were rumours of abuse at the time. A nasty business.'

A connection to Simon Carver.

'Do you know when he was in the Lodge? The year?' Carla asked.

'I couldn't be sure, lass. He was a teenager.'

'Does the name Simon Carver mean anything to you?' Carla asked. She put a photo of him on the table between them.

Morag shook her head. 'No, lass, I'm sorry. That name doesn't mean anything to me, I'm afraid.'

'You didn't ever see a man visiting Mark?'

'Like I said, Mark didn't really have anyone. His behaviour was rather off-putting.' Her brow creased as she studied the photograph. 'Did he have something to do with what happened to Mark? What did you say his name was again?'

'Simon Carver.'

'Do you think it was this Simon that killed him?'

'No, Mrs Thomson.' Carla said simply. She didn't want to alarm the old woman with the grisly details. 'Is there anything else you can tell me that might help me figure out who's done this to Mark? Did he have any enemies that you know of?'

'Mark didn't talk much to anyone, not even me really.'

'How often did you see him?'

'He'd come and give me a hand every couple of days, do odd jobs, that kind of thing. I'd always have him stay for a sandwich and a cup of tea, maybe take the dog for a walk, but he never used to say much to be honest. He was a sad soul, truth be told. I didn't mind the silence, though; I was just glad he was eating. I tried to make sure what I gave him was healthy – fruits, salads, that kind of thing – because I doubt very much whether he considered these things himself.'

'Is his mother still alive, do you know?'

Morag shook her head. 'No, no. She drank herself to death years ago. Not a huge loss if you ask me.'

'That must have been hard for him, do you think?'

'I don't know. Like I said, the man never said much about anything.' She tapped her temple. 'He seemed trapped in here if you know what I mean.'

Carla did know what she meant. Mark's life sounded desperately sad and lonely.

'How long had Mark been living in your caravan, Mrs Thomson?'

'Oh, ten years? Maybe more.'

Carla did not know why that surprised her. It was sad his illness had dominated so much of Mark's adult life, and she couldn't help fearing he had been let down by the sparse mental-health support on the island.

'When he left care, do you know what he did, where he lived?'

'He had a flat and a good job in Inverness. I forget what it was he did, but everything was great until he hit his thirties. That's when the illness started, and he's' – she paused to correct herself – 'he had been living with it ever since.'

'Did Mark ever marry?'

'I don't think so. If he did then I certainly never saw them.'

Morag went to refill Carla's cup.

'I won't take another, but thank you. One cup was enough for me.'

'All right then, hen. If you're sure. Are you positive you wouldn't like something to eat?'

'I'm sure. Just a couple more questions before I leave you in peace, Mrs Thomson. Do you remember . . .'

Before she could finish, Morag interrupted her, her expression changed. 'You work for him, don't you?'

Carla frowned, but quickly realised what she meant. 'Aye.'

'Well, I suppose if anyone knows how to catch a killer, it's Fraser Brodie. He's close to one after all.'

This was not a conversation Carla wanted, but Morag wasn't finished yet.

'What happened to those boys was a damn sin. It's no wonder one of them turned out the way he did.'

'Well, I can't really comment.'

Carla never knew what to say in these situations and was grateful that the old woman left it at that. Carla pressed on.

'Do you remember seeing anyone that you didn't recognise hanging around or even just passing through recently?'

Morag shook her head. 'Not that I recall I'm afraid, dear. I'm sure there will be plenty walking through soon when all the tourists return. I get hundreds traipsing across the edge of my fields to get to the hills. Walkers, photographers, you know . . . I used to do a bed and breakfast, but I'm too old to be bothering with all that now.'

She waved her hand as if waving away the notion like it was absurd. It made Carla smile. This woman might be in her late seventies, but she looked as fit as a flea. She wondered what the old woman would do though, now that Mark wasn't going to be around to help out.

Carla took out her phone and showed her the photo Owen had sent. 'We found this from a CCTV camera near Mark's trailer. Do you recognise this person?'

'Hang on till I put my glasses on.' She lifted a pair that had been dangling from a chain round her neck. 'OK, let me have a closer look. It's a bit fuzzy.'

Carla pointed at the other figure in the frame. 'Is that you?'

'Oh, yes. It looks like it. Gosh. I'm afraid I don't remember seeing anyone else though, I'm sorry.'

That was disappointing. 'It's all right, Mrs Thomson. You're right, it's not very clear, is it.'

The old woman handed back the phone. 'I suppose now I'll have to get my son up here more often to help me out.' Her expression looked like a grimace. 'As long as he doesn't bring that stuck-up wife of his. Thinks she's a cut above the rest of us, she does. Daughter of a London banker, you see.'

Carla was really starting to like Morag, and wished she could stay for more tea, but she had to press on.

'Thank you so much, Mrs Thomson, you've been really helpful.'

'You're very welcome. I'm not sure I've been much help, but I hope you catch the bastard that's done this to poor Mark. He didn't deserve that.'

The swear word came as a surprise, but Carla agreed with the sentiment. Mark had clearly had a rough start to his life, followed by chronic mental-health battles. She took one of her cards out of her pocket and handed it to Morag.

'My number is on here. If you think of anything else, no matter how small, please don't hesitate to call anytime.'

Morag looked at the card. 'I will, dear. Now you drive home safe, you hear.'

'I will. Thank you again.'

Carla walked back to her car, slightly spooked by the depth of the silence out here, even in the middle of the day. As irritating as it was that her neighbours might be in their hot tub at midnight, Carla wouldn't like to be so isolated – especially in an emergency. Who was she kidding? She and Dean would never be able to afford a place like this anyway. Not now.

Putting her own problems to the back of her mind, she thought about what Morag had said. So Mark had been in care. With Simon Carver, perhaps. Was that the reason for the money transfers? Did Carver feel sorry for the man who couldn't look after himself? Was it guilt money? Had something happened? Carla wondered if Carver blamed himself somehow for Mark's illness . . .

Just then, a text from her husband made her heart sink.

David Sutherland rummaged in his pocket for the keys to his storage unit. Swaying unsteadily on his feet after downing enough alcohol to stave off the pain of withdrawal, he smiled at the security guard, waiting until the man had passed before opening the door. He screwed up his eyes against the blinking, bright light and threw the black bag on the floor, pulling the door shut after him. It would be better for everyone if he stayed out of sight until he figured out what to do.

20

4th May, 4 p.m.

Phil Harrison peered in the window of the small art gallery, startling Hayley when he knocked on the glass. He'd made his excuses with Molly and headed straight there.

'Don't bloody do that!' she exclaimed, clasping a hand to her chest. She snatched open the door and ushered him inside. 'You nearly gave me a heart attack.'

'We need to talk about Simon and Mark.' He grabbed her arm and pulled her to the kitchen at the back of her studio, craning his neck to check they were alone.

'Ouch, let go, you're hurting me! What's going on?'

Phil closed the door to the back room. 'Have you heard what's happened to Simon and Mark?' he rasped.

Hayley frowned and tucked her long blonde hair behind her ears. 'What about them?'

'They're dead.'

Hayley gasped. 'What the hell? Oh my God. What happened?' she stammered.

Phil produced a piece of paper from his pocket and handed it to her. Hayley pushed her large, turquoise-framed glasses further up her nose and read the note.

'I got this yesterday,' Phil told her. 'Simon got one, too. The detective never mentioned Mark getting one but . . . you know what I'm saying.'

I know what you did. I'll be seeing you.

Hayley stared at him, then seemed to grasp what he was trying to suggest.

'Well, I haven't had one, if that's what you're getting at.' She stopped. 'If Mark didn't get one, then their deaths, as awful as they are, they can't be connected to . . .' She hesitated, looking past him. '. . . To what happened, can they?'

'Hayley, think about it.' He pressed his finger on her temple.

'Hey.' She shoved his hand away. 'Calm down, will you.'

'That detective thinks Melrose's boy did it,' Phil told her, nervously looking over his shoulder.

'Ryan? Why would he do something like that?' Hayley shook her head at him.

'I dunno, his prints are at Simon's house or something. That's not the point.'

'Why would Ryan kill them?' Hayley asked. Now he had her attention.

'I have no idea!' Phil exclaimed, pacing back and forth. 'Does he know?'

'How on earth could he possibly know what happened?' Hayley insisted.

Phil stared at her, heavy bags under his eyes. He had not managed a wink of sleep last night. Every noise in the darkness had made him jump. He moved quickly towards the small window and peered out from behind the blue velvet curtain, almost knocking his elbow against a huge bunch of tulips.

'Careful.'

'Never mind the damn flowers. Are you sure you've not had a letter?'

'Jeez, Phil, you really need to calm down.'

Phil slammed himself back down onto a chair and dropped his head into his hands. 'He cut out Simon's tongue, babe, nailed it to the wall.'

'Phil!' Hayley said firmly. 'Nobody knows what happened except us.'

'Molly knows,' Phil said quietly.

'What the hell,' Hayley hissed. 'Why on earth did Simon tell her?'

'It doesn't matter.' Phil took hold of Hayley's hands. 'Molly wouldn't tell anyone. Simon swore to me that she wouldn't.'

'Well, maybe Molly killed them, then.'

'Don't be stupid. She wouldn't kill Simon. She was besotted with him,' Phil reminded her. 'Anyway, why would she? It's Ryan we should watch out for.'

'I think your imagination is getting the better of you,' Hayley insisted. 'You're getting as paranoid as Mark.' Her phone rang in her pocket and she sighed when she read the caller ID. 'Look, I really have to take this. It's about my show. This exhibition could make or break me.'

'For goodness' sake, be careful, Hayley.' He squeezed her hands in his. 'I don't think you should be alone with Ryan, not if the police think he could be a killer.'

Hayley laughed. 'Ryan Melrose is a scrawny teenager. He doesn't scare me.'

The figure sloped back behind the wall of Hayley's art studio before Phil could see him. Phil looked worried. Good. Nice car he had. Jaguar, only a couple of years old. That house of his must have cost a pretty penny too. It was going to taste all the sweeter knowing none of that could save him now.

21

4th May, 5 p.m.

'Hey, boss,' Owen Kelly said, quickly slipping his feet off the desk.

Fraser nodded a greeting, as Carla handed him a cup of tea. 'Is there a pot made?' he asked plainly.

'Aye, there's a pot in the kitchen,' Carla replied.

'Perfect,' he said, without smiling. 'Just let me have this then we can get started.' He closed the door without waiting for her to respond.

'Has he always been like that?' Owen asked.

'Like what?'

'What do you mean, *like what*,' Owen repeated back at her. 'Fair enough, I already knew he was a bit aloof, but sometimes he's just plain rude.'

Carla looked in the window of Brodie's office door. 'He's got a lot going on at the moment. And he's the best detective you'll ever meet. There's nothing in the manual that says you have to be polite. You should know that.'

'Very funny. Do you think that's why he doesnae like me?'

'What, because you're a direct-entry detective and haven't spent years pounding the beat gaining priceless experience and knowledge?'

'Point taken.'

'Anyway, he doesn't dislike you.'

'But he doesn't like me either, does he,' Owen pointed out.

'He's just set in his ways. Stop worrying.'

'How long have you worked with him?' Owen asked.

'Six years, and I've learned more in that time than the first ten in the force.'

'Does he ever mention . . .' He leaned in closer and lowered his voice. 'Does he ever mention' – it was barely a whisper now – 'his brother?'

'Rarely, and I don't ask him. Neither should you,' she warned.

'I won't, but I'd love to know more. Wouldn't you?'

'It's none of our business.' Carla glared at him. 'I mean it.'

'Doesnae stop me being curious though, does it. They were in care as well, did you know that?' Owen asked.

'What are you talking about?'

'Brodie and his brother. In the seventies they were in a kids' home. The same one as our victims.'

'How the hell do you know that?' Carla asked.

'There's enough online about Adam Brodie. Psych reports, social work, everything—'

The conversation quickly ended as Fraser emerged from his office. He walked straight over to the whiteboard and stood with a red marker pen in his hand, shooting a brief scowl at Owen as if he had overheard their conversation. Owen blushed and flicked through sheets of paper, trying to look busy.

'Right, Carla: Morag Thomson. What's her story about Tait?'

'Lovely old woman.' Carla opened her notebook. 'Mark Tait worked on the fishing boats until a couple of years ago, she says. His mental illness made him too dangerous after that, she said he had to be let go.'

Carla scanned through her notes before continuing. 'Sounds like a pretty sad individual by all accounts. No friends to speak of, and she doesn't recall him having visitors. She did, however, confirm that Mark was in care.'

'At the Lodge?' Fraser asked. Carla nodded, knowing what he was thinking.

'OK, this could be the connection we need between the two victims. Owen, get straight onto social services, will you – get Carver's and Tait's files. It can't be a coincidence that they were in the Lodge together, so we need to know about their time there. And anyone else who might be connected. Who might even be next . . .'

'Sure,' Owen replied, gathering his things.

'In fact, go and see social services in person, dig around a bit. Ask if you can speak to someone who might have been around then: care workers, retired or otherwise, cleaners, maintenance workers . . . Anybody at all from that time.' Fraser's eyes barely blinked, and he pointed a finger at Owen. 'We need to know everything we can. Charm them,' he suggested unexpectedly. 'Would that be something they taught you at detective college?' The sarcasm oozed from his question, but his eyes twinkled.

'On it,' Owen said, ignoring the sarcastic comment.

'Before you go, any luck getting the CCTV cleaned up yet?'

Owen was about to answer when an email notification chirped on his laptop. He lifted a hand. 'Hang on, sir, this . . . could . . . be something,' he spoke slowly. 'Yes. It's still not clear, but a lot better. Maybe your lovely old woman will recognise him now, Carla.'

He turned the laptop round as Carla rolled her eyes. The sharper image showed the figure with something covering their face, and a woman who was clearly Morag Thomson a few metres away.

Carla yawned. 'I'll go back up there. I could have done with it being clearer earlier.'

'Thanks, Carla,' Fraser said. 'Let's regroup before you go. Owen, you're dismissed, and I want to know as soon as you find anything out from social services.'

'Yes, boss. See you guys later.' He grabbed his blazer from the back of his chair and headed straight out.

One thing Fraser did like about The Boy was how smartly he dressed. Not slouching around like some of the young detectives he'd seen over the years. The truth was, the newest member of his team wasn't half bad – as much as Fraser was planning to keep him on his toes. And it wasn't Owen Kelly's fault who his father was, or that the man had been in the squad that had arrested Adam. He was also not to blame for the fact that his father had kicked the shit out of Adam before backup arrived that night, leaving him with several broken ribs and a busted nose. Not that The Boy would ever find that out from him.

'Good job, Carla,' Fraser said, turning his attention back to her and smiling briefly. 'Let's get that all added to the victim profile, along with the details of his condition.'

'So what are you thinking?' Carla asked, staring at the newly sharpened image. 'Any ideas on this guy?'

Fraser squinted at the figure on the screen, and wished the answer were yes. The person he was looking at was short and slim but they had a male physique, and posture.

'I don't know.' He stared intently at the image. 'But I know who it isn't and so do you.'

Carla nodded. 'I know. That's not David Sutherland.'

'Do you think it could be Ryan Melrose?' Fraser asked.

'Hopefully Morag will be able to confirm if it is.' Carla grabbed her bag off the back of the chair and headed for the door. 'I'll let you know how I get on.'

'Aye, good lass, as soon as you can, please. I want to push forward on Melrose as soon as possible.'

22

Hayley was counting down the hours until tomorrow evening. Her big moment. It was the one she had dreamed about for so long that she had almost forgotten a time before she'd been working towards it. Her art was what had kept her sane these past few years, and this exhibition had been a long time in the planning, and years of hard work in the making. Art college, followed by years of shit jobs to earn a living, until she'd had the money to return to Lewis and open the studio. A helping hand from her childhood friend Phil had given her the leg up she'd needed. A knock on the door distracted her.

Hayley's phone rang as she popped back the snib of the lock and ushered in the vicar from the church down the road. His name escaped her, but she recognised him. Denzil, that was it. He had his hands full of pamphlets.

'This is Hayley Stevenson,' she said into the phone. She smiled at the vicar who was about to speak and raised a hand to ask him to wait. 'Mmm, yes, that's right,' she continued, before covering the mouthpiece and focusing on her visitor. 'I'll be with you in a minute,' she whispered.

'No problem,' he replied, moving away to admire the paintings.

'I'm sorry about that,' Hayley said, when she'd ended the call. 'Are you here to collect your tickets?'

Denzil looked confused. 'Tickets?'

'I'm so sorry, I thought you were here for tickets for my exhibition.'

Denzil glanced round the room. 'Your work is very impressive. So you're having an exhibition? That's wonderful.'

'Yes, first one. If you don't count my student ones, of course.' She laughed nervously.

'You're very talented.' He paused to read the name on the huge sign on the wall. 'Hayley.'

'Thanks, I try.' She smiled. 'So if you're not here for tickets, then what can I do for you?'

Denzil handed one of the pamphlets to her. 'I run a support group at the church for people with addiction problems. Have you heard of it?'

Hayley blushed, skimming through the pages without paying much attention. 'No, I haven't, sorry.'

'No bother. I've been visiting businesses and waiting rooms in hopes of being able to leave some leaflets. I'm trying to make the group more visible. We never know when we, or someone we love, might need it.'

Hayley held his gaze before flicking her eyes sideways. 'Yes, sure, you can leave a bunch here.'

'Thank you so much, Hayley, I really appreciate that.' Denzil narrowed his eyes at a painting of two alligators basking in some dense swamp land. 'These two look like something you wouldn't want to meet on a dark night.' He chuckled.

A grin spread across Hayley's face. 'I painted that from a photo I took in the Everglades last year.' She scrolled through the pictures on her phone. 'Here, look.'

Denzil took her phone to look more closely. 'Yikes,' he said and handed it back to her. 'But you really have captured the . . .' He paused as if searching for the right word. 'Menace,' he said.

'Menace!' Hayley exclaimed. 'What a brilliant word. That's exactly it. Do you know how many pet dogs get eaten by alligators every year?'

Denzil jokingly covered his ears. 'No, and I don't think I want to.' He laughed a little at her suggestion.

Hayley laughed and gently touched his arm. 'I'll keep that little gem to myself then.'

'Please do.'

Hayley dropped the leaflets onto the desk behind her and opened the drawer.

'And here,' she said. 'I'd love it if you would come along.' She handed Denzil two tickets for her exhibition. 'Bring a friend. I can't promise it will be the most exciting night out you'll ever have, but there will be champagne and pizza bites, might even be some sausage rolls. Real ones too, not vegan.' She screwed up her face.

'Oh, you're very kind. How much . . .' He slipped his hand into his pocket and took out his wallet until Hayley lifted her hand up.

'No, no, the tickets are on me.'

'Well, that's very kind of you, Hayley. I'll be sure to pop by.' He glanced down at his tickets. 'At eight o'clock on the dot.'

Hayley flashed a smile just as her phone rang again.

'No rest for the wicked, huh?' she joked, as she made off to take the call. 'I look forward to seeing you.'

'Yes, I'll see you then,' he said.

Denzil watched Hayley disappear into the back of the studio. The last thing he saw was her hand waving behind her before she clicked the door shut.

He looked at the tickets then stuffed them into his jeans pocket. The price tag on the bottom corner of the painting he was admiring made his eyes widen. Certainly out of his price range. Pity.

The bell on the top of the door chimed, shifting Denzil's attention to the heavily tattooed postman who was walking towards the desk with a parcel in his hands. He laid the package on the table.

'Hi there, Rev.' The postie smiled.

'All right, how's it going?' Denzil replied, heading for the door and holding it open for the postie, who had followed him back out of the gallery.

'Looks like we're in for a downpour,' the man said, nodding his head towards the black clouds that had begun to gather at the peaks of the nearby hills.

'Something's brewing for sure,' Denzil replied.

He pulled up the collar of his jacket and headed in the opposite direction of the postman's van, just as the first huge raindrops smashed into the pavement at his feet.

23

4th May, 6.15 p.m.

Fraser hated these video meetings, but they were a necessary evil if he wanted to be involved in decisions affecting Adam's future. Fraser was all his brother had, and the thought that decisions would be made for Adam appalled him. Lawyers didn't understand Adam like Fraser did. The good or the bad.

The bruise on his brother's cheek caught Fraser's attention immediately, even though it was obvious by the angle at which he sat that Adam was trying to hide it. The blue mark, barely the size of a ten-pence coin drew Fraser's gaze like a magnet. Adam must know he would have noticed immediately, but he said nothing. If Adam wanted to talk about it he would. Later. Maybe. It wasn't like it hadn't happened before. As a serial killer in Barlinnie he often had bruises that nobody talked about. Especially when his victims of choice had been young vulnerable women.

'Adam, how are you?' Fraser tried to adjust his seat so that his face was in the centre of the screen. It wasn't easy at six-foot-four. He frowned when he didn't recognise the face sitting next to his brother.

'Hello, Mr Brodie, I'm Sharon Pearson. I'll be representing Adam at his parole hearing.'

Fraser stared at the young woman, who looked barely in her twenties. She was smartly dressed and heavily made up, with not a single hair out of place. He watched Adam shake his head and roll his eyes as she looked down at some paperwork.

'Do you want to apply for parole?' Fraser asked Adam directly.

'I don't know,' Adam shrugged. Leaning back in the chair, he looked up and gave a long sigh.

Sharon Pearson shuffled the papers on the table in front of her. She looked flustered, and Adam yawned.

'Adam hasn't made any decisions yet, Ms Pearson,' Fraser told her. 'We need a bit more time to talk about it. I've been very busy with work.' He stopped there.

The woman put the papers down and looked right into the camera. 'I have another suggestion I wanted to talk over with both of you.'

It was clear to Fraser that she had got Adam's attention this time. She had certainly got his.

'I'm listening,' he said, as Adam sat forward again in his seat.

'There's a possibility that if we propose Adam be transferred to a category D prison, subject to meeting the criteria and passing the appropriate risk assessment, the parole board will give it consideration. Kind of a halfway option if you like.'

'An open prison,' Adam said, looking at Fraser. 'Where would that be?'

'There's only one in Scotland as far as I know. Castle Huntly.'

Adam frowned. 'Where's that?'

'Longforgan,' Fraser explained.

'Fucking Dundee!' Then Adam lifted a hand. 'I'm sorry for swearing, hen. Sorry.'

A brief silence fell and the two brothers stared at their screens. Neither of them had considered that to be an option. Lisa's face momentarily flashed into Fraser's mind. She would be fearful of exactly how open the prison would be.

'What do you think?' Adam spoke first.

'You don't have to decide right now,' said Pearson. 'I'll email all the information to you, DI Brodie.'

Adam grinned when she said that.

'I'm just Fraser in these meetings, Ms Pearson.'

'Of course, I'm sorry.'

The two men held each other's gaze on the screen until Fraser's phone rang. He snatched it up from his desk and frowned. Molly Carver. He needed to take this.

'It's fine, we'll talk soon,' Adam said. 'You get back to work.'

'Er, yes, of course. I'll be in touch,' Pearson added quickly, before their faces disappeared from the screen.

Cutting calls short always made Fraser feel bad . . . The heavy weight in the pit of his stomach told him he had let his brother down. It was a habit he wished he could break, but it was difficult in his line of work. Especially right now. His phone had stopped ringing, so he dialled Molly's number, which barely rang before she answered.

'Molly, hi. How are you?'

'Detective Inspector Brodie. Phil hasn't turned up when he promised he would.' Her voice sounded hoarse. 'His phone keeps going to voicemail. I'm worried about him. He and Simon were like brothers and now after what's happened to Mark . . .' She paused, seeming uncomfortable with the comment.

Given what had happened to both Simon and Mark, it was understandable that she was worried. Simon Carver and Mark Tait. Both former residents of the Lodge. Three friends, two dead, one unaccounted for. Fraser didn't want to use the word 'missing' just yet but a sick feeling was growing in his stomach. When he'd spoken with Molly and Phil all the man had admitted to was that they were school friends – but what if they were all in the kids' home together? He didn't want to reveal the potential connection to Molly yet, but he would make sure Owen asked social services about Phil too.

'Give me Phil's address and I'll go over there.'

'Detective Brodie, I'm scared that something terrible has happened.' Her voice broke, the tone urgent.

'Try to stay calm. I'm on my way now.'

What she said next chilled Fraser's bones.

'Please hurry. I found a letter on his desk. Like the one that was sent to Simon!'

Fraser's blood ran cold. Phil had received the same warning Simon and Mark had before they were brutally stabbed and mutilated. 'Unaccounted for' had become 'urgently missing'. Had something happened in that home?

'Where are you, Molly?'

'I'm here at Phil's house.'

'Go back to your neighbour's house and stay there. Lock the door. I'm sending officers round to sit with you. Do it now.'

Fraser didn't think Molly was a target, but it was better to be safe.

As he approached, Phil was appalled at the state of Mark's caravan, and guilt clutched at his gut. Watching through trees from a distance he saw people dressed in full forensic gear coming and going. He quickly wiped away a tear. They should have taken better care of Mark. It had been a long time since any of them had been to see him. Simon was giving him money, but they should have done more for him. He was supposed to be Mark's friend. They all were, but they had all abandoned him and gotten on with their own lives, leaving him behind. The thought of the horror that had unfolded in that shabby caravan made his blood run cold.

A noise behind him made Phil jump, his heart racing like a train. A twig had snapped and he spun around, steadying himself on the stump of a tree.

'Who's there?' His voice shook. 'Hello?'

He called out into the dense patch of woodland behind him, but saw nothing. It was probably just a squirrel. He remembered how Mark had always been feeding the damn things. It was no surprise his nerves were frayed, hanging on by a mere thread. He took a deep breath in an attempt to settle his anxiety, but it didn't stop his legs shaking.

Despite the state of the caravan, it looked like Mark had been busy. A large allotment had been dug in the space at the side of the filthy vehicle, and Phil could see shoots of potatoes peering out of the soil. What a simple life his friend had. Maybe he should envy Mark that.

Footsteps sounded behind him now. 'Terrible thing that, isn't it.'

'Argh.' Phil gasped, almost losing his footing with fright at the sudden arrival. 'I . . . erm . . .'

'It wasn't pretty, I hear. Nailed the poor sod's tongue to the wall.'

Phil's stomach lurched. It was the same as had happened to Simon, just as he'd feared. He struggled for air, a dizziness filling his head. His knees turned to jelly beneath him and gave way, dropping him into the dirt.

'Hey, man. Are you all right?'

Phil couldn't speak and tried to press Hayley's number on his phone, but it was as if his hands refused to work.

'Mark . . . Sim . . .' Phil's words became trapped in his throat. This had to be a bad dream. It couldn't be real, it just couldn't. Molly had described what had been done to Simon clearly enough for Phil to get a ghastly picture in his head. He had to warn Hayley.

'Here, let me help you.' The man bent down, took the phone out of his hand. 'Can I call someone for you?'

Phil was too weak to protest. 'Hayley . . .' he mumbled.

'Did you say Hayley? You want me to call Hayley?'

Phil managed to pull himself into a sitting position, the fog of shock starting to clear. He had to warn Hayley to lock her doors and call the police. He held out his hand to take his phone back. 'It's fine, mate, thank you. I can manage now.'

'Oh sure, that's good. I'm glad.'

Phil was confused. Why wasn't he handing back the phone? Then he watched him remove the SIM card and slip it into his pocket. Phil thought he was going to vomit from fear as he tossed the handset onto the ground, stamping on it until he had smashed it into hundreds of pieces. It was the killer and now he'd come for Phil.

'You won't be needing this now, Phil.' The man's sinister sneer made Phil's blood run cold. 'What say you and me go for a drive and have a little chat?'

It took Phil a minute, but when it hit him he recoiled in horror. Could it really be him?

24

4th May, 6.30 p.m.

Owen waited for the door to be unlocked. An on-call social worker had told him to come straight down and she would be happy to meet with him. He showed his ID to the young girl who let him in.

'Hi. I'm DC Owen Kelly. I'm here to speak to someone about the Lodge kids' home.'

'That place has been shut for years—' the young woman started to say.

'I'm aware of that, but I'm here to meet someone to talk to about it.'

'I'll just go and get Dianne for you.' She straightened the length of her skirt before pressing her badge onto a sensor and heading deeper into the 1960s building.

Owen took a seat in a row of uncomfortable black plastic chairs that were lined up under a wide rectangular noticeboard, covered with various leaflets about topics such as domestic abuse and living with dementia. A large, middle-aged woman bustled through the door.

'Hello, Detective.' The woman held out her hand. 'I'm the senior social worker on call tonight. Dianne Petrie.'

'DC Owen Kelly.' He pulled his ID back out and showed it to her.

The woman lifted her glasses from the chain around her neck to peer at it then let them fall, dangling above her chest.

'What can I do for you, Detective?'

Although the waiting area was empty, Owen looked around him for anyone who might overhear. The boss had made it plain that all details of this case needed to stay on a tight leash. 'I need to speak to someone about the Lodge, about two kids in particular, possibly three. It's very important.'

Petrie frowned. 'Come through, we can talk in my office. But I have to warn you now, I might not be able to help you much, data protection and confidentiality being as it is.'

'I understand.'

Owen followed her through the door into a warren of corridors, rooms peeling off left and right. This building was like the Tardis – so much bigger inside than the crumbling exterior suggested. He was also surprised by the modern decor.

'Please, take a seat.' Petrie pointed to a chair as they entered an office, then sat down behind a chaotic desk covered with files, with sticky notes all over the desktop computer.

'Thank you.'

Owen spotted a framed photo of what was clearly a much younger Petrie with a little smiling boy.

'It was two kids you said you would like to ask about. What were their names?'

'Yes, that's right. Simon Carver and Mark Tait. Also, if could you tell me if Phil Harrison ever spent time at the Lodge.'

Dianne Petrie's eyes widened. 'Awful news about Simon. Is that what this is about?'

Owen nodded. 'Did you know Mr Carver?'

'Everyone knew Simon.' Her thin smile came and went quickly. 'Poor Molly. She must be devastated.'

'What about Tait, did you know him?'

She pursed her lips with narrowed eyes, giving the impression she was trying to recall him. 'I can't say I know the name. Does he have something to do with what happened to Simon?'

'In a manner of speaking,' Owen answered carefully, unwilling to tell her everything yet. Mark's death had not yet been reported in the media. He found it surprising that she didn't know someone with his mental-health problems.

Dianne typed the names into her computer then sighed loudly. 'Bear with me a minute; my computer is so slow. Island Wi-Fi can be temperamental, can't it?'

'It has its moments,' Owen agreed, and glanced down at the text he'd just received from Brodie.

Meet me at Phil Harrison's place as soon as you've finished there. There's been a development.

He typed a quick reply while he waited, wondering what had happened. Petrie's frustration increased.

'I'm so sorry, the whole page has frozen,' she said. 'I'm going to have to see if I can do this the old-fashioned way. What years were they in the Lodge?'

'I was hoping you could clarify that, but as a starting point you could check '88 to '92?'

She got up from her desk and opened the top drawer of one of the huge, silver filing cabinets that lined the wall under the window looking out over views of the harbour. When she'd got through its contents she moved down to the next drawer and flicked from back to front.

'OK . . .' She frowned and looked at Owen before flicking through the files again. 'That's strange.'

Owen got up and joined her at the window. He did not like the sound of 'strange'. Nothing good ever came from it.

'What's wrong?'

'I can't find any of the paper files from '85 to '95.' She frowned. 'Unless they've been destroyed after digitalisation; hang on.'

Dianne kneeled down and opened the bottom drawer then shook her head as she pulled a thick pile of brown, dog-eared folders into her hand. She opened the top folder and ran her fingers through the pages.

'These go back to the seventies – look,' she said and handed it to him. 'This is strange.'

Owen flicked through the first couple of pages and instantly recognised a name before quickly slamming it shut. *Fraser Brodie.* Reading about his DI's childhood trauma would be wrong on so many levels. Not that it stopped his curiosity. Owen had never admitted it to Carla but his interest in Adam Brodie went back many years, long before he became a detective. But it wasn't just Adam that interested him, it was the twin brother who became a detective, too. Owen laid the thick brown folder onto the top of the cabinet closest to him.

With a serious expression on her face, the social worker went from one filing cabinet to the next, frowning as she rummaged through the drawers and folders. The loss of these files had to be a serious breach of security, and the woman was obviously harassed. But this was also inconvenient for their investigation and somewhat suspicious.

'Look, I can see there's been some sort of mix up here,' Owen said eventually. 'If I leave you my number could you give me a call as soon as possible when your computer unfreezes? My email is on there as well as my mobile.' He laid his card down next to the folder. 'I also wanted to ask if you know of anyone I could speak to who worked there during those years?'

'Sure, my mum. She worked there for twenty-five years. She retired in the late nineties.'

This was more promising. 'Do you have an address for her?' Owen knew Brodie would be impressed by his initiative with this, but he would be waiting forever for any praise.

'Of course,' Dianne stood back up. 'My mum lives with me. Twenty-six Croft Way. She'll be in the back garden if you don't get an answer. She might be in her eighties, but she spends every waking hour with her flowers.'

'That's great, thanks,' Owen said, glancing at his watch. 'I should be going.'

'I'll see you out,' Dianne Petrie insisted.

As they walked back through the hallway, the social worker turned to him and said, 'I'm sorry to ask. But do you have any idea who murdered Simon?'

'We're currently following several lines of inquiry,' he said, giving the standard reply. 'How well did you know him?'

'I didn't, not really. I mean, I knew him to speak to, but that was it.' When they reached the door, she held it open for him. 'I'll be in touch as soon as I've sorted that mess out. I am so sorry I couldn't help you.'

'I appreciate that, thanks. But I really need the information as soon as possible.'

As he stepped outside, Owen was grateful the rain had stopped. The heavy spring shower that fell earlier had battered the ground with some force. When his phone rang in his pocket, he knew it was Brodie before he looked at it.

'On my way, boss.'

Ryan answered the call as soon as he saw the caller ID. He'd been expecting it.

'How's it going son?' Andy Melrose asked.

'Fine.' Ryan kicked an empty Coke can along the road, much to the annoyance of an elderly man walking his little black terrier nearby. He shot the man a steely stare. 'How's it going with you?'

'All right, aye. I took that Brodie down a peg or two last night.' He chuckled. 'You should have seen his face. He wanted to smack my mouth so much it had to bloody hurt.'

'Excellent.' Ryan smiled. 'The one on the outside isnae having a great time either.'

'Have you seen her yet?' Andy asked.

'I went round there but she wasnae in. I'll try again tonight.'

'Good lad. But make sure nobody sees you,' Andy warned.

'I know what I'm doing, Dad,' Ryan insisted, irritated. 'I'm getting good at it now.'

25

4th May, 7.15 p.m.
'No, thank you, I'd better not.'

Carla declined the offer of more tea from Morag Thomson, knowing that Brodie wouldn't want her to be here a second longer than she needed to be. His message about Phil Harrison's disappearance was concerning, given his connection to their victims, but what she'd discovered on her second visit here had proven extremely useful. A lead.

'Are you sure?' Morag asked.

'I'm sure. I really need to be going.' She picked up her bag and rested it on her knee. 'You've been very helpful.'

'I just wish I'd remembered to mention about Ryan the last time I spoke to you.' She shook her head and tutted. 'My memory isn't what it was you see.'

Ryan Melrose had been positively identified as the figure in the CCTV image, and he had been walking towards Mark Tait's caravan. Plus his fingerprints were in Simon Carver's home. They had to find him.

'How well do you know Ryan?' Carla asked.

'I don't really,' Morag admitted. 'But I know his dad.' She tutted loudly. 'An awful man. I'd even go as far as to use the word evil. Drug dealing is the work of the devil.' She sneered. 'He was never a role model for that boy, that's for sure.'

'Have you any idea where he was going when you saw him?'

'Not really, but there were signs of a fire out in my top field and Ryan's been known to enjoy burning things.'

'Oh, yes?' Carla's mind turned over rapidly. That was one of the three key signs of a potential serial killer. Starting fires was a gateway crime according to her training. Cruelty to animals was another.

'Och, when he was thirteen he went in front of the children's panel for starting that fire in the auld primary-school building.' Morag stood to tidy their cups onto the tray before tapping her temple. 'I don't think he's quite right. Mind you, being raised by that family it's no surprise.' She tutted.

'Here, let me,' Carla insisted, lifting the cups and the teapot for her instead.

'Thank you, you are a lovely lass.' Morag smiled and sat back down.

'Not at all; it was very kind of you to go to all that trouble for me.' Carla carried the tray to the counter and dried her hands on the towel slung across the back of the chair. 'You've got my number if you think of anything else.'

Morag lifted the card out of her cardigan pocket and held it up with a sombre smile. 'Aye, I've got it, hen.' She dabbed a tear away from her cheek. 'I can't help thinking of that poor man. Mark never did a soul any harm.'

Carla lifted her bag and wanted to give the old woman a huge hug but resisted. She squeezed her shoulder gently instead.

'We're doing everything we can to catch the person who did this.'

Morag sniffed, and struggled to pull a tissue out from her sleeve. 'Och, I know you are,' she said, then blew her nose. 'Ignore me, I'm just being a silly old fool.'

'You're not silly, you care – that's all.'

Morag dabbed her face dry and exhaled sharply. 'Young Ryan can't have done this,' she insisted. 'He's sixteen. I mean, I know he used to tease Mark a bit and I'm not saying he's an angel, far from it, but . . .' She hesitated. 'Murder?'

'People do awful things to each other, I'm afraid,' Carla said, as she made her way to Morag's backdoor.

'Keep in touch, will you, let me know what happens?' Morag asked.

'I will.' Carla stepped outside. It looked like it was about to pour down again.

* * *

The figure stood still behind the large oak tree until the detective's car disappeared out of view. He hoped the old woman knew better than to open her big mouth, but he had thought it best to pay her a visit just to remind her.

'What do you want?' Morag asked, a hint of fear in her voice as she tried to close the door. A boot lodged in the gap.

'I think we need to talk, don't you?'

'I haven't said anything, I swear.' Morag tried to push him away, but before she knew it he had grabbed her arm, and she was swept away from the doorway.

26

4th May, 7.45 p.m.

'Boss,' Owen greeted Fraser, as he approached Phil Harrison's house.

'Did you get much from the social worker?' Fraser asked, without looking at him.

'Yes, she gave me a name and contact details. A care worker who was there in the late eighties, early nineties ...'

Before he could continue, Fraser's ringtone sounded.

'It's Carla,' he told Owen, then focused on what she had to say, hoping it was something useful. 'What did the old woman say?'

'She confirmed it was Ryan Melrose on the CCTV.'

'She's sure?'

'She's sure, boss.'

Positive news. 'Great work, Carla, get back as soon as you can. Phil Harrison is missing.'

'Was he in the Lodge too?' Carla asked.

'I think The Boy was about to tell me before you called,' Fraser raised his eyebrows at him.

Fraser hung up and focused his attention on his DC. 'Morag Thomson has identified the person as Ryan Melrose, so with his prints at the Carver crime scene we're looking at our suspect.'

'Detectives, what are you going to do to find Phil?' Molly asked, coming out of the house.

Fraser had been irritated to find her still at Phil's home, against his instructions, and now she was interrupting just as he was about to hear from Owen about his visit to the social worker.

'I asked you to go home, Molly,' Fraser reminded her.

'I know, but I want to wait. I want to be here when Phil comes back. I need to see him.'

'Owen, go and see if you can find his phone.'

'Sure, boss.'

As Owen headed inside, Fraser turned his attention to Molly.

'Has Phil had any recent contact with Ryan Melrose, do you know?' Fraser asked.

'I don't think so.'

He saw Molly check her phone for the umpteenth time.

'Where is he?' She paced back and forth. 'He knows how much I need him.' Tears fell quickly. 'It's not like him to ignore my calls, especially not . . . now.'

Fraser looked at her. She was genuinely worried about Phil. He and Simon were best friends. Simon and Mark were childhood friends. He had to ask.

'Do you know if Phil was in the Lodge with Simon and Mark?'

'Yes, he was.' Molly's face turned white as a sheet.

This was serious. His absence might still have an innocent explanation, but Fraser was growing increasingly concerned. They should have found out Phil had a link to the home much earlier. They might have had a chance to protect him but now they were a step behind the killer. They had to locate Phil fast.

'I need you to think really hard, Molly,' Fraser said. 'This is important. Has Phil mentioned Ryan Melrose to you recently? Has he said anything that he didn't tell me when we spoke before, did he express any concerns about the lad to you? It's really important, Molly,' he repeated.

'No, he hasn't.'

'Was David Sutherland in the home with them too?'

Molly shook her head, looked down at the floor.

'Molly, is there anything else I need to know?'

The woman shook her head again. 'No, please, you have to find Phil,' she urged him, before tears fell again.

How did the three men connect to Ryan Melrose? They weren't random victims at all. Fraser wondered whether what connected the victims, connected their killer to them.

'Molly, I need you to think carefully for me, all right. Did Simon ever mention whether he knew Andy Melrose from the Lodge?'

'I don't know . . .' she shook her head, nibbling her lip. 'I can't remember . . . I don't think so.' There was only one way to find out.

Next stop: a warrant for Ryan Melrose's arrest and a search of his home.

27

Phil peeled his eyes open. He had no idea where he was. There was a thick sour smell which made him retch. His wrists were bound, and his ankles were tied tight to the legs of an uncomfortable damp wooden chair, forcing him into a rigid sitting position. His head had obviously been flopped forward so long while he was unconscious that it pinched his neck painfully to lift it up. He shivered with cold. Water dripped nearby, each drop splashing into a puddle underneath. The fact he needed to pee urgently added to the humiliation of his current circumstances.

What time was it? How long had he been out of it? The last thing he remembered was being at that shambles of a caravan. A vague recollection of his phone being crushed made Phil sick to his stomach. Footsteps grew closer.

'I've brought you a bottle of water and a burger. Can't have you telling people I didn't treat you well!' The man's sinister laugh cut right through Phil.

'What do you want?' Phil asked. He had known the truth would come out one day, but not like this.

'You mean you don't know? A well-educated man like you must have figured it out by now, surely.'

The sensation of calm that washed over Phil seemed at odds with his situation. Had he been drugged? Was that why this felt so unreal? All attempts to wriggle his hands free were futile. They were trapped tight, and the thick dirty rope was cutting into his skin. His captor opened the bottle of water and held it to Phil's lips.

'Drink!'

Phil gulped until the bottle was swiped away again. It sickened him to feel grateful. Then he noticed bruising and small, sliced scratches on his captor's knuckles. They looked fresh. First Simon. Then Mark. Now him. It couldn't be a coincidence. Why do this now? Nothing could change what had happened. He thought of Hayley. Phil had tried to warn her, he really had, but she was too wrapped up in her damn exhibition.

The smell of the burger turned Phil's stomach.

'I'm not hungry,' he said, turning his head away as the greasy roll was placed in front of his face. The sound of angry breathing filled the silence that followed. Then Phil's head was tugged backwards, a handful of his hair snatched tightly in the man's fist.

'Eat it!'

The food was forced in and held there until chewing and swallowing it was the only option. Despite the grease, the roll tasted dry and stuck in his throat, making Phil gag as he got it all down.

Then, like a switch had been flicked, the atmosphere changed again.

'See, that wasn't so hard, was it?'

Phil jarred at the gentle slap on his cheek. The last piece of meat was stuck to his teeth, and he had to run his tongue over them several times to dislodge it.

'Can I have some more water?' he asked, grateful to see the bottle offered immediately. It was the perfect opportunity to mount what little defence he had, and he spat the mouthful directly into the man's face.

The man pulled his hand back to slap Phil's face but stopped short before the palm made contact. Phil recoiled in anticipation and raucous laughter followed. Phil slowly peeled open his eyes to see his attacker wiping his face with a filthy towel before tossing it back down in a heap.

'That was clever. I have to admit, I didn't see that coming.' A finger pressed Phil's head with just enough force to hurt. 'Well done, and by the way, it won't make any difference to what's about to happen, so . . .' A sinister shrug followed.

When it looked like he was leaving, Phil called out. 'Where are you going?'

All he got in return was a wave.

'You can't just leave me here!'

The door behind Phil slammed shut and a bolt flipped across before the unmistakeable sound of two keys being turned in locks echoed into the large, cold room.

'*Bastard!*'

Desperate, all Phil could think to do was to try and wriggle his hands free. He flinched from the agony of the cuts on his wrists that oozed blood onto his hands. It stung to move them even an inch, but he couldn't just sit here doing nothing. Trying to keep the panic at bay, he wondered how long this monster planned to keep him tied up, before torturing him the way he had terrorised Simon and Mark.

His legs were stuck fast, pinned to the chair with even thicker rope than his hands. Pins and needles tingled his feet, stabbing and pinching them painfully. Rocking his body from side to side he managed to upend the chair, sending himself crashing to the concrete floor with a thud.

'Argh,' he whimpered, panting to catch his breath.

If he could shuffle this chair to the window he could call for help. The floor was wet, soaked from the rain lashing in through holes in the roof. Holes that meant Phil could catch a glimpse of the sky poking through the clouds. Why hadn't he taken the time to notice that more? This island was beautiful and filled with so many happy memories – not just bad ones.

The effort to move even a few centimetres was taking its toll, and Phil had to stop to save his strength. Getting the six or so feet to the cracked window was going to be a marathon, not a sprint. Slowly, steadily. Nearly there.

Footsteps outside.

'Hello, is there somebody there?' he called out urgently. A surge of adrenaline poured into him. 'I'm in here! Please, you have to help me!'

The footsteps moved away without a response.

'Hello?' Phil yelled. 'Don't leave me here!'

He dropped his face to the concrete in defeat. But then the sound of a key turning in a lock echoed and the bolt was slammed across.

Phil didn't look up. He squeezed his eyes tight to stop the trickle of tears that had started to flow. The footsteps splashed through the puddles in the sunken patches of floor.

'Leaving so soon?'

Phil's body was unceremoniously hoisted up as the chair was dragged back to the centre of the filthy room. He was forced to make eye contact with the man they had underestimated; the sinister grin gave Phil chills. A dribble of piss leaked out, the warm liquid bizarrely comforting.

Smirking as he walked away, the man added, 'Don't go yet, Phil. The fun's just getting started.'

28

5th May, 8.30 a.m.

Something's come up Molly. I'm sorry but I've had to take a trip to the mainland. I'll call you soon x

Molly was so relieved to get a text from Phil's number as she was making her breakfast that she immediately cried – heaving, snotty tears. The kind that would have embarrassed her if she'd been in public.

As well as being grateful to be able to go home to her own house, this news was a huge relief. A text meant Phil was OK. She knew she should contact the detectives first, but she couldn't wait to talk to Phil. She dialled his number, eager to speak to him, but when she couldn't get through she hung up. No need to leave him a message. He was probably busy, although she was curious to know what could have taken him away so suddenly, so soon after Simon's death. The two men had been like brothers after meeting the way they did, in the kids' home when they were both teenagers. It was strange Phil would leave like that, especially when he had seen how devastated she was – but at least he had let her know he was OK.

A moment later the doorbell rang, interrupting her train of thought. She would call Phil back in a while – perhaps she would catch him then – and let the detectives know he had made contact.

'Hello.' Molly smiled at the vicar as he stood on her doorstep. Although she and Simon were not regular churchgoers, they had been to a few Christmas and Easter services over the years. Reverend Martin was new, though.

'Hello, Mrs Carver, I'm sorry to turn up unannounced like this, but I wanted to see how you were doing.'

'Thank you, Reverend Martin. That's very kind of you.'

'When I heard about what happened to your husband I knew I had to come and offer my condolences, and to let you know that I'm here for you.' He reached for her arm. 'I can't begin to imagine how awful it's been for you.'

The touch made Molly's lip tremble. Perhaps it was because he was a man of God, but Molly couldn't help herself. It was no use, the tears couldn't be stopped.

'I told him I would kill him if he ever lied to me again.' She sobbed. 'How terrible is that? I wished him dead and now . . .' Her words faded. She had to control herself.

'Hey, hey, we've all said things when we're upset. Shh, come on. I'm so sorry, I didn't mean to upset you.' Denzil moved up a step to be on the same level as her and laid an arm around her shoulder. 'How about I come in and make you a cup of tea? Hmm?'

Molly nodded and turned, moving in the direction he was guiding her, helpless to do anything to stop it. Not that she wanted to stop him. The tears were tumbling out unchecked, whether she wanted them to or not. It was as if he had uncorked a bottle of grief that she'd been trying hard to control.

Denzil helped her to a seat at the kitchen table.

'You sit there. I'll sort the tea.' He filled the kettle, then opened each of the cupboards in search of mugs. 'Ah, here we are.'

Molly struggled to speak as the vicar made them both a cup of hot, sweet tea and sat down next to her. She picked up a green checked tea-towel draped over the back of her chair and dabbed her wet face.

'I'm sorry,' she mumbled.

'You don't have anything to apologise for.'

Molly smiled awkwardly. 'I do really appreciate you checking on me.'

Denzil reached across the table to take her hand. 'That's what the church is for. You're going through the worst thing imaginable, Mrs Carver. I don't blame you for feeling overwhelmed. You're grieving.'

He squeezed then released his grip, bringing his hand back to his mug. 'Crying is good, it's the right thing to do.'

'You're very kind,' Molly said.

'Not at all, I'm glad to help.'

Molly shook her head and stared down at the table. 'I was worried that perhaps another of Simon's friends might be in trouble because . . .' She stopped short of mentioning Mark. 'I was worried about his friend Phil but I've just had a text from him.'

'Oh, that must be a relief, then.'

Molly nodded, a thin smile replacing the tears as she wiped her face. 'Yes, thank God. Pardon me, Vicar.'

'He's a friend of your husband though, you said? He must be devastated by his loss too.'

'He is.' She sighed. 'They go back a long way, Phil and Simon. They're more like brothers to be honest.'

'He must be taking your husband's death very hard.'

'Phil is absolutely devastated.'

'I'm sure you'll be a great support to each other during this awful time.'

Molly smiled. 'Phil is a wonderful man. Like Simon, his childhood wasn't great, but he's overcome so many obstacles to get where he is today.'

'Sounds like he's very special to you.'

'He is, and he had me worried there for a while. I'm just so glad he's fine.' She let out a small sob and wiped her face again.

'I am glad,' Reverend Martin said gently. 'The last thing you need is more worry.'

'Nobody tells you what grief is like,' she said. 'My stomach is in knots, and it feels like I've been run over by a train.'

'It's not something you can understand until you've been through it yourself,' he mused.

'Have you lost someone?' Molly asked.

'I have,' he said softly.

'So you know how it feels,' Molly said, in more of a question than a statement as she reached for her mug. She didn't know if it was the warm sweet liquid that comforted her or the man who had prepared it.

'Yes. I lost my dad when I was very young, but I remember the grief, the overwhelming physical and emotional pain, like it was yesterday. It's why I turned to God. He pulled me through my darkest times.'

'Knowing how it feels . . .' Molly said. 'Perhaps it's what makes you so good at your job.' Moisture glistened in her eyes.

'Perhaps.'

The ringtone from her phone interrupted their conversation.

'I'm sorry, I need to take this. It's Carla, I mean DS McIntosh,' she corrected herself. 'Excuse me a minute, please, Reverend, will you?'

Denzil gathered up his phone and keys from the table and stood to leave, swallowing down the remainder of his tea.

'I'll leave you to it.' Before he walked away he laid a piece of paper on the table. 'My number's on there; please, do call, if you need anything.' He rested a hand gently on her arm. 'I'll see myself out.'

'Thank you,' Molly called out to him as she watched him disappear into the hall. She heard the front door close just as she answered the call.

'Hello, Detective. Yes, I'm fine, thank you. I was just about to call you, actually. I've had a text from him. Phil has had to go away suddenly on business. Something on the mainland. I don't know what, but he's OK.' She listened to the detective's reply then added, 'Yes, it's such a relief.'

Phil's swollen eyes peeled open just enough to see out of. Warm liquid from the cut above his right eye dribbled into the eyeball, causing him to blink painfully. He had wet himself and the damp denim stuck to him. The warm piss had cooled and stung the irritated skin. He couldn't be sure how long he had been out of it and wondered how and why he was still alive.

Every movement stung and the bloody, metallic taste in his mouth made his guts churn. He had one missing tooth, and another was hanging badly. The nerves were exposed sending pulses of agony through every part of his face. Death would be a blessed relief. Seeing that bastard slip his SIM card into another phone and send a text with an evil smirk on his face had made Phil angry that this evil murderer was pretending to be him, sending texts to people who could be concerned about him. He thought of Molly. Hayley. He had to be going after them next.

If it didn't hurt like a bitch to move his face, Phil would have cried knowing this was the punishment for what they did.

29

5th May, 9 a.m.

Fraser hammered the front door with his fist. Waiting for that damn warrant had been frustrating. A minute later Suzanne Melrose opened the door, yawning.

'What do you want?'

'We're looking for Ryan,' Fraser said and stepped closer to the red door. There were chips of paint flaking off all over it, more gathered in piles on the step.

When he moved forward, Suzanne did too. She pulled the door behind her but left it wide enough for him to see the mess inside. She moved faster than Fraser anticipated, given that her eyes struggled to focus on him. She'd taken something already. A toddler wandered from the living room wearing only a nappy and vest, snot and chocolate stains on their face. The state of the child meant Fraser couldn't tell which of her twins it was.

'Ryan's no in,' Suzanne Melrose told him, but avoided his gaze when she spoke.

'I have a warrant that says I can come in and check for myself.'

Fraser's path was blocked.

'I told you, he's no here.'

He held up the warrant without saying anything else and stepped forward again.

'You can't just barge in here,' Suzanne protested. 'Wait, you can't—' But before she could say more, a door slammed loudly from inside.

'Owen, go and join the uniforms round the back!' Fraser shouted and pushed past Suzanne without a word, sending her reeling backwards. 'We don't want him slipping out there again.'

'That wasn't a good idea,' Carla warned Suzanne. 'It's an offence to harbour a suspect.'

'Suspect! What suspect?' She followed the detectives inside. 'Wait a minute, you can't just barge into my home like this.' She tried to keep up but struggled, now carrying a toddler on her hip. 'Andy doesn't live here now. You know that, Fraser Brodie. He's in Bar-L.' She pursued Fraser relentlessly. 'Beside your murdering, freak, scumbag brother!'

Fraser ignored her jibe. It wasn't as if he hadn't heard it all countless times before. He moved through the hall and into the filthy kitchen, shuddering that children were being brought up in a place like this.

The sound of raised voices echoed towards him, and he was relieved to look out the window and see Ryan being marched, his hands in cuffs, round to the front of the house. The state of Owen's hair made a wry smile grow on Fraser's face. His immaculately styled barnet was in disarray. Owen must have had to work hard to subdue him.

Fraser called for a car to come and take the teenager to the station. He wanted to get a head start on searching the place. He had a forensics team on call, ready to dive in at a moment's notice. Fraser and his team would go over the place first, then head back to formally interview the teenager. It would take time for an appropriate adult and a solicitor to get there, and it wouldn't hurt to let Ryan sweat a little.

'Stay with him until backup arrives, DC Kelly, then come and join us,' Fraser called out, then returned his focus to the kitchen. He forced his hands into a pair of gloves, squeezing his fingers together to make them fit.

'You can't do this!' Suzanne screamed at him. 'My Ryan is a good boy. He hasn't done anything. He's no like his dad . . .' She sobbed.

Fraser produced the warrant from his pocket and tried to hand it to her. When she refused to take it from him, glaring with venom instead, he laid it onto the only available space on the kitchen table which wasn't covered in a mixture of dirty dishes and laundry. He flattened the paper out.

'All the information you need is on there. I suggest you read it, Suzanne.'

Suzanne pulled out a chair and dropped down in defeat without saying anything else. Fraser looked at Carla.

'You take the lad's room,' Fraser instructed. 'Bag anything you think is relevant; you know the drill.'

'Sure thing,' Carla replied and shot a sympathetic glance at Suzanne before leaving.

Fraser began opening drawers, starting with the one next to the fridge, which was wedged tight shut by something blocking the runner. As he slipped his fingers in to dislodge the obstruction his eyes drifted over the various papers stuck onto the fridge with a selection of novelty fridge magnets. He was surprised to see artwork that had clearly been done by the toddlers on it. A piece of paper with a mobile phone number written on it and the takeaway menu filled the rest of what should have been a white surface but was more a grey, beige, dirty colour, particularly around the door handle.

A few tweaks freed the pen that was jammed inside the drawer and Fraser slid it open easily. He flicked through the chaotic pile of receipts and letters, including a selection from social workers addressed to Suzanne. There were lots of white envelopes with REMINDER printed in large red lettering.

None of the drawers gave Fraser anything at all, apart from an insight into the sad situation Ryan was growing up in. Even more memories of his and Adam's childhood hit him.

He noted that the knife block on the counter had two knives missing; one space looked like a large knife should be there, the other, something smaller.

'Where are these two knives?' He pointed at the empty spaces.

'What?' Suzanne snapped. 'How should I know? I'm a wee bit behind with my housekeeping, or haven't you noticed that?' She dropped her head, heaving a huge sigh.

Fraser bagged the knife block. Matching the murder weapons to these spaces would be crucial. He and Suzanne stared at each other in silence. She looked broken. All the fire had gone, and her head flopped into her hands.

'You don't have to go to the station. I'll get a social worker to sit in on his interview,' he said.

Suzanne sighed, then looked up. 'Thank you.'

Fraser nodded. 'No problem.'

'DI Brodie!' Carla's voice echoed loudly through the house.

'Excuse me a minute,' Fraser said and followed the sound of Carla's voice. When he got to Ryan's bedroom he was appalled to see his bed was no more than a mattress on the floor, and again he had to force down the awful memories from his own childhood that slammed into him. 'What have you got?'

Carla held something up in a gloved hand.

'Where did you find that?' Fraser's heart thudded.

'Stuffed under the mattress.' She pointed down. 'Poor lad doesn't even have a proper bed.'

Fraser's eyes took in every inch of the knife in her hand, noticing the remnants of blood dried on the edges. It was obvious even from where he was standing.

'Aye, but not having a proper bed doesn't mean you become a murderer, DS McIntosh.' He left a short pause and stared around the room. 'Not always.'

'Boss,' she replied sheepishly.

They took the knife Carla had just discovered and tentatively placed it into one of the vacant slots in the knife block. The two detectives looked at each other without saying anything. The knife fit.

'Bag it, and let's get the forensics guys to go over the whole place. I want nothing left to chance.'

Carla pulled a clear plastic bag from her pocket and carefully placed the knife inside, slipping the tape across to seal it.

'What do you want me to do with Suzanne and the kids?' she asked.

'See if there's a relative that can put them up for a couple of days, or a neighbour. We'll need to take possession of this place pronto, but I'll leave that to you.' He began to walk away then stopped and turned back round. 'I'm going to let The Boy sit in on this one.' Then he stalked out without waiting for her response.

Fraser walked past the police car that had arrived and already had Ryan Melrose handcuffed in the back next to Owen Kelly. He indicated for Owen to get out, after sending a uniformed officer to take his place.

'Boss,' Owen said and wiped his palm over his messy hair.

'Come on, let's get back and get you a strong cup of tea. You're doing the interview with me.'

Fraser didn't see Owen's astonished face because he was focused on the death glare he was getting from Ryan Melrose. If looks could kill, Fraser would have fallen dead on the spot. Maybe he imagined it, but Fraser was sure the lad's eyes were black. Black as night. A chilling recollection sprang to mind of the way Adam's eyes had once been described.

'Detective.' Suzanne's voice came from behind him as the police car drove away.

Fraser turned to see her standing in the doorway, a look of resignation on her face.

'Look after him,' she said. 'He's not a bad boy.'

'We will,' Fraser said and headed back to his car, wondering how well she knew her son.

Denzil parked his car outside the church hall. He tightened the handbrake and, yawning, laid his head back on the headrest. Lack of sleep was catching up with him.

Instead of a day of committee meetings and more visits to parishioners, what he really wanted to do was go home, have a shower and get ready to go to Hayley's exhibition tonight. Not something he would have chosen before today, but she had charmed him. The least he could do was go and support her.

A police car roared past, startling him. It was moving at speed round to what Denzil assumed was the custody suite at the back of the station, not far from the church hall. Denzil had managed to catch a brief glimpse of the occupant before the tall gates shut the car and its passengers inside. He frowned and pursed his lips.

What on earth had Ryan been up to now?

30

5th May, 10 a.m.

Fraser tucked his phone away after another text from Lisa. He understood why she was anxious; they'd never been in this position before, facing Adam's potential release. She wouldn't cope with learning of his possible move to an open prison either, so Fraser kept that to himself for now. Her mental health was fragile as it was. Castle Huntly . . . It was a long way from Barlinnie, but at least Loganair flew into Dundee airport; it was a tiny place compared to Glasgow. He'd not had time to read through the information Sharon Pearson had emailed him yet. Something like that needed his full and undivided attention, but so did this case. No matter how hard it was, the brutal murder of two men had to come first – especially when there were others at risk.

'Boss.'

Fraser was pleasantly surprised to see his DC hold a cup of tea out to him, but feared it would in no way match up to Carla's standard given he'd had six years to train her in the method of the perfect brew. Cautiously he took a sip. It was surprisingly good. Easily a seven out of ten.

'Mmm, nice,' he said, conscious that Owen was desperate for his approval in everything he did. Fraser wouldn't admit it to him but he saw a lot of his own early enthusiasm in The Boy.

'You're welcome.'

Fraser acknowledged a harassed-looking young woman who rushed past them into the interview room. The social worker on call, he assumed.

'Come on then, are you ready?' Fraser handed his mug to the uniformed officer next to him, and gestured to Owen.

Owen exhaled slowly, looking half guilty, half excited. People had died to give him the opportunity to sit in on this interview. They owed it to Simon Carver and Mark Tait not to mess this up.

As they entered the interview room it smelled like the social worker had grabbed a quick coffee before starting work. The smell on her breath churned Fraser's stomach. Memories of being forced to make his father's black coffees still lingered after all these years.

Then he saw those eyes. Black as soot on first glance. Ryan's resemblance to Andy Melrose was astonishing, but if the charges were valid he had surpassed his father's depths of depravity by miles. Ryan's gaze never shifted from Fraser, which he knew was intended to intimidate. It was a tactic that had never worked on Fraser. Living with Johnny Brodie had been good training for dealing with violent offenders. Nobody had ever scared Fraser the way his dad had; he'd vowed a long time ago that he wouldn't let anyone do that to him again.

Fraser was keen to get started, but things would happen his way. Once the formalities were over, and introductions made for the recording, he sat in silence, lips pursed, staring back at Ryan Melrose's scowl.

The atmosphere in the small interview room was electric. Fraser could sense Owen's discomfort, but he would cope a minute longer. He would learn a valuable lesson in the process: something the books couldn't teach him.

It was Melrose that Fraser wanted to feel uncomfortable, but the teenager didn't flinch. Fraser was sure he had not even blinked the whole time they had been staring at each other. Ryan had seen his father's attitude to the police. That was his own training for today.

Fraser cleared his throat and let his shoulders droop, just a little. He opened the brown folder on the table to reveal a plastic bag that had been concealed inside the front cover. His gaze flicked to the side to see the social worker's eyes widen briefly before she refocused her attention on the notepad she had been writing in.

Melrose's duty solicitor, however, didn't seem fazed. A well-dressed man, nearing retirement, he looked like he had seen it all before. Either that or he genuinely didn't give a toss any longer.

Fraser held up the bag, but Ryan's eyes did not move from staring him directly in the eye. Not even for a second.

'Ryan, could you explain why this was found under the mattress in your bedroom?' Fraser asked. 'Or why it matches the empty slot in your mum's knife block.'

Ryan didn't move an inch until his solicitor leaned in and mumbled something into his client's ear. It was then that the teenager's lips finally moved.

'No comment.'

This response was exactly what Fraser had anticipated. Even at the tender age of sixteen, Ryan Melrose knew the score. His father, Andy, had been the same. Ryan knew the burden of proof was on Fraser and the prosecution.

'Could you tell me whose blood that is on the knife?'

Silence filled the space between them, but the hint of a smirk grew on Ryan's lips before he took a breath and answered. He leaned back in the chair and stretched out his legs under the table.

'No comment.'

Melrose's solicitor scribbled something on his pad. Fraser watched the way the older man's brow dipped and widened as he wrote. He noticed the solicitor's receding hairline too.

'Hasn't your mum been looking for it?' Fraser persisted.

'No comment.' This time there was no dramatic pause before answering. Ryan crossed one ankle over the other under the table, then yawned.

'Where were you at nine o'clock in the morning on the third of May?'

'No comment.' Ryan just seemed bored now, and Fraser was irritated to see the solicitor lean in to whisper again.

'Ryan, I would like to remind you that this is a very serious murder investigation,' Fraser said slowly. 'Now, do you know either of these two men?' He slid two photos towards him. 'Or perhaps this is how you remember them?' He pushed one of the gruesome crime-scene images towards Ryan.

'Detective Inspector Brodie, my client is a minor. This is inappropriate,' the social worker intervened.

Without responding, Fraser tucked them back into the folder. Carla had told him that Molly had received a text from Phil, but that wasn't the same as actually seeing or talking to the man.

'Where's Phil Harrison?' Fraser asked.

Ryan smirked. 'Who?'

This lad really was boiling Fraser's piss. 'Phil Harrison. He's a friend of these two men.' He pointed to the photos.

Ryan sniffed and glanced down at the pictures, took a breath and looked at his solicitor. 'No comment.'

Fraser sat back, deciding to try something else. 'Does your dad know what you've done?'

Ryan's eyes blinked several times. Finally something they could work with. Fraser was cutting through the bullshit at last. The rattled teenager flashed a quick glance to his right at the social worker, who seemed to be reassuring him. Then he looked at his solicitor, who didn't return the glance until he must have felt Ryan's eyes burning into him.

'You're not obliged to say anything,' his solicitor said, then wrote something on his pad.

Ryan sat up straight and stared down at his hands, seemingly examining them in detail, picking at the chapped skin on his palms then peeling dirt from his fingernails. All the while Fraser waited.

'Are you all right, Ryan? Do you need a glass of water or a break?'

Bloody social workers. Fraser tried not to show his irritation. Ryan coughed, then rubbed his throat.

'Actually, can I have a can of Coke or something?'

'This isn't a café,' Fraser informed him. 'We don't take orders. DC Kelly, please get Mr Melrose a cup of water.'

'Sure.' Owen stood up from the table, and the sound of his chair scraping across the hard floor grated.

'Detective Constable Kelly has left the interview room,' Fraser said for the tape.

He sighed at the social worker's intervention, because Fraser knew he'd been getting somewhere. Why did that bloody woman have to mollycoddle the little toe-rag? He doubted that Adam had been treated like this back then. But Fraser knew he couldn't justify asking Ryan anything while they waited for his water. And he knew Ryan knew that too.

Fraser glanced down at his watch. They didn't have long to charge him or let him go. The knife was compelling evidence, but the recent discovery that Ryan's prints weren't on it made things difficult. But his prints were in Carver's home. It didn't rule out the possibility he had worn gloves when he'd used the knife, but a clear print would have been more helpful. They had their eyewitness, of sorts, in Morag Thomson, but she didn't see him actually go into Mark Tait's caravan. She had only confirmed that he passed by her property on the day Tait was murdered.

The interview-room door opened.

'Here you go.' Owen laid a paper cup on the table and sat back down.

Fraser was intrigued to see a small tremor in the lad's hand as he lifted the cup. Interesting.

'Are you OK to continue?' Fraser asked. When Ryan nodded he added, 'For the tape, lad.'

'Sorry, er, yes,' Ryan replied quietly, between sips.

Finally the solicitor seemed to wake up. 'Ryan, I'd like to remind you that you have the right to remain silent.'

Fraser wanted to say 'Give it a bloody rest' but chose not to. He didn't want Owen picking up bad habits.

'I know.' Ryan's voice was barely a whisper as he put the cup back down.

Maybe that social worker had done the right thing after all . . . Ryan looked ready to answer questions now. Fraser was surprised, he had to admit. He lifted up the plastic bag with the knife again, then slid it across the table towards Ryan.

'Why was this under your mattress?'

Ryan swallowed hard and avoided looking at the bloodstained weapon this time. Fraser felt like he was looking at a teenage boy for the first time.

'I don't know.'

'Did you put it there?' Fraser persisted.

'No.' Ryan shook his head and avoided eye contact.

Fraser narrowed his eyes at the lad, then shot a quick glance at Owen. 'Who put it there then?'

'I don't know,' Ryan insisted.

'Was it your mum?'

'No!' Ryan replied hotly.

'If you don't know who put it there, how can you say it wasn't your mum?'

'Just . . . It just wasn't, all right?' Ryan blasted.

'So it wasn't you, and it wasn't your mum. Who was it?' Fraser was turning the screw, but gently, to keep the social worker and solicitor sweet.

'I don't know.' Ryan's eyes caught Fraser's this time. 'I don't know.'

'He's answered that question, Detective Inspector,' the solicitor interrupted, making another note in his pad.

Fraser pursed his lips, considering his next words until someone knocked on the interview-room door. Irritated by the interruption he bawled, 'Yes!'

'Sir, this has just come in.' A flustered young, uniformed officer handed him a sheet of paper and left without saying another word. She didn't stay long enough to hear him mumble thanks.

Fraser showed it to Owen, then laid it down in front of him. Forensics had confirmed whose blood was on the knife.

'Ryan, the blood on the knife is Simon Carver's, who was murdered on the morning of Friday, the third of May. So I'm going to ask you again, and I want you to think very carefully before answering.' Fraser stared at the solicitor then looked at Ryan. 'Can you explain why a knife with Simon Carver's blood on it was found under your mattress?'

The atmosphere in the room darkened, and the sullen teenager who had become timid suddenly morphed again into a frightened animal. His breathing changed, becoming more like a growl. A snarl.

'Boss, watch your—' Owen called out, but Ryan was too quick. He overturned the table – sending it flying straight at Fraser's shoulder, which made a horrible cracking sound when the steel connected with it.

'Argh!' Fraser shouted, as the two uniformed officers who had been posted outside the room ran in and wrestled the lad to the ground. Fraser clutched his arm. 'Take him back to the cells.'

'Are you all right, boss?' Owen asked, as he righted the table onto its legs in front of the speechless social worker. Ryan was dragged, struggling, from the room, followed by his solicitor and social worker.

'Yes, yes, don't fuss.' Fraser rubbed his arm, which stung from the impact of the heavy table. Why the hell wasn't it bolted to the floor? Well, the lad clearly had strength. Strength enough to overpower and stab two middle-aged men to death? He was also prone to volatile mood swings. What had Carla told Fraser? The teenager had a history of starting fires. Speak of the devil: Carla entered the interview room.

'I heard the commotion.' Her eyes narrowed in concern. 'Jeez, I think you need to get that shoulder looked at.'

'Will the two of you stop with the fussing,' Fraser insisted, moving his arm cautiously. The initial pain was easing slightly. 'I'm fine.'

Carla shot Owen a look and he shrugged. 'Can I at least get you a cup of tea?' she suggested to Fraser. 'And what's happening to Melrose? Will he need a psych evaluation now?'

'Naw, that would take ages to organise, and we've not got time for that. Just give him a bit of time to calm down. I think that was all for show anyway: a distraction.'

'Are you sure?' Carla countered. 'Anything we get while he's . . .'

The look Fraser gave silenced her. Carla bit her lip.

'Sorry,' Fraser barked. 'Just trust me. I know what I'm doing.' Neither Carla nor Owen would dare argue with that.

Fraser tentatively moved his arm again. It wasn't broken, luckily for Ryan. It stung like a bitch though. Maybe police work was a young man's game, he thought momentarily. Twenty years ago he could have dodged that incoming table no problem. Maybe Adam was right about retirement.

Fraser refocused on Carla. 'I want you to go back to Morag's place again. You seem to have built a relationship with our star witness. Have her take you up to Ryan's fire spot. See if you can see anything useful there.' He pointed to Owen. 'You go with her. I'm going to head over and have a word with Molly Carver. See what else she can tell me about young Ryan.'

'Sure boss,' Carla said, as Owen walked out ahead of her. 'You sure you're OK?'

'Aye, I'm all right.' The veteran detective did appreciate her concern.

'OK then, I'll see you later.'

Andy Melrose dialled Ryan's number for the third time, anxious at not getting a reply.

'Shit,' he muttered under his breath as he hung up. He tried Suzanne's mobile number and waited. 'Answer the phone you damn— Hello, Suz, how's it going?'

'What the hell have you got Ryan mixed up in?' she said sternly.

'Hello to you, too, darlin'.'

'Well!'

'Dinnae you worry aboot it. Is he there? I've been trying to reach him?'

'As if you don't know.'

Andy could picture her face when he heard that jibe. He'd seen it often enough. 'I don't know so tell me.' He was growing impatient.

'That bloody Brodie took him in. What the hell have you done?'

Andy took a breath. Closing his eyes he exhaled slowly, loudly. He curled his hand into a fist, but he knew he had to keep calm. There was too much to lose if he lost it now. What the hell was he thinking trusting Ryan to do it? He was just a kid. There had been plenty of other options on offer to carry out the job, and Andy cursed his own greed. He'd thought why pay someone when Ryan could take care of everything? Keeping the circle small was the plan given the seriousness of the task. For obvious reasons, the fewer people involved the better. He'd never had to take this kind of action before but there was no other option.

'Andy, are you still there?' Suzanne's tinny voice broke into his thoughts.

'When did he take him?'

'Not that long ago.' Her voice trembled. 'Maybe about a couple of hours. I've had cops all over the place, snooping, trashing everything. They even searched the bairns' beds.' She was crying now. 'Oh, Andy, what's going on?'

'Look, I'm sorry, Suz, I have to go. I'll call you later,' he replied, and hung up without acknowledging her tears. He didn't have time for that; he had a shitshow to fix. There was too much at stake to fail now.

Adam Brodie passed him as he walked away, the two men glaring at each other without speaking until Andy couldn't resist.

'Ryan won't talk to him,' he whispered close to Adam's ear. 'Family comes first.'

Before he had a chance to reply, Andy was swallowed up by the crowd of prisoners in the middle of C Hall.

31

5th May, 11.30 a.m.

Owen's phone buzzed as Carla indicated left out of the station car park. He opened the incoming text. Good news.

> *Sorry about the computer glitch. Everything up and running. Sending bits to you now. Mum says she's happy to talk to you. Don't hesitate to get back to me if I can help with anything else.*

'Something useful?' Carla asked, as her car joined the winding road towards Morag's farm.

'Just the case notes from the home. There was some kind of computer problem earlier and she couldn't find the paper files either.' Owen frowned.

'Mmm,' Carla replied. 'Sounds like your gut is telling you something there.'

'Thought us book detectives didn't have gut feelings?' he teased. 'I thought we learned it all from the page not the pavement.'

'You got me there. But, seriously, you do think something's up, don't you?'

'Nah, I'm probably just seeing stuff that's not there.'

'What does the text say?' she asked.

Owen read out the message, then tucked his phone back into his blue blazer pocket. 'The address is on the way to Morag's,' he said, in a statement that came out more like a suggestion.

'Well, then, DC Kelly, what say you and me pay the old woman a visit on the way?'

Owen fell quiet. 'The boss won't like it,' he said eventually.

'Why not, we're using our initiative aren't we?' Carla said. 'He's not the control freak you think he is.'

'I never said he was!' Owen insisted. 'I hope you've never told him I said that.'

'Of course not,' Carla teased.

Owen shook his head, a small smile growing on his lips. 'Do you think that . . .' He hesitated, pondering how to put the next bit. 'Never mind.'

'No, come on, spit it out.'

Owen allowed himself a breath before adding, 'Well, his brother must affect Brodie's work, don't you think? Not in a bad way. Maybe it's what makes him such a good detective.' He ended with a shrug.

'I don't know,' Carla replied honestly.

'Would you visit your brother if he did what Adam Brodie did?' Owen asked.

'I'd rather not think about it, Owen.'

'You're right. That was a stupid thing to say. Sorry.'

Carla listed their options as they approached a fork in the road. The left turn took them out to Morag's farm, and the right led to Dianne Petrie and her mum. She indicated right.

'A quick chat with her mum can't hurt,' she said. 'Open up the files she's sent you and have a quick look before we get there.'

'Sure,' Owen replied, and began reading as he tried to ignore the travel sickness that hit him on the winding road. When the sign for Croft Road came into view Carla indicated onto it.

'What number do we want?' she asked.

'Twenty-six Croft Way,' she said.'

'Shit, this is Croft Road, hang on.' Carla pulled into the car park of a small shop and turned the car round. 'I noticed Croft Way a little further back.'

Owen felt a surge of nausea claw his stomach with the momentum. 'Calm down, Jenson Button.'

'Very funny.' Carla laughed.

Five minutes later they were parked outside an old cottage which had a huge, well-maintained garden both front and back. A variety of fruit trees, with pink-and-white blossom buds on display, lined the drive leading to a front door that had picture-postcard roses round it, and a bed of lavender nearby. The far-reaching views to the white sands and sea were stunning.

'Let's go in and see what Mrs Petrie has to say,' Carla added.

'Nice place,' Owen muttered as they waited at the front door. 'She might be round the back,' he suggested, when they got no answer. 'The old woman loves her garden apparently.'

Carla turned and took in the view. 'So would I if I lived here. This is beautiful.'

The two detectives followed a path bordered by immaculate flower-beds interspersed with herbs. The fragrance caught on the small breeze. Every available space was packed with plants in all shades and sizes. Carla was admiring the display when a voice came from behind them.

'Can I help you?'

Mrs Petrie removed her gardening gloves and tossed them onto a basket of foliage on the ground. Holding up her ID, Carla asked, 'Mrs Petrie? I wondered if we could have a few moments of your time to talk about the Lodge kids' home. About two residents in particular.'

Mrs Petrie walked towards them, and that was when Carla noticed the small scar on her left arm. Then she noticed a long white line that ran the length of her right arm. As if she had been spotted, she pulled down the sleeves of her cardigan.

'You two had better come inside then.'

'This is a beautiful spot, Mrs Petrie,' Owen said, as the two detectives followed her inside.

'Please, call me Celia. Aye, it's a bit special isn't it?' Celia Petrie lifted the kettle and filled it. 'Tea?'

Carla and Owen looked at each other until Carla spoke for both of them. 'No, thanks, Mrs Petrie, we'll not keep you long.'

The old woman dried her hands and pointed to the kitchen table. 'Then, please, sit. How can I help you?'

'Your daughter Dianne said you worked in the kids' home in the eighties and nineties,' Carla said.

'That's right.'

'Do you remember a couple of residents: Simon Carver and Mark Tait? Or Phil Harrison? Does that name mean anything?' Owen asked.

They watched the old woman look as if she was searching some kind of database in her mind. She was staring out of the kitchen window, her eyes narrowed.

'Simon Carver and Mark Tait,' she repeated. 'Carver ... Carver ... That name rings a bell.' She let out a long slow breath and frowned. 'What was the other name you said again?'

'Mark Tait,' Carla reminded her, but she suspected the old woman's memory problem was a symptom of something more serious. It was then she noticed that Celia's T-shirt was inside out before she added, 'Or Phil Harrison.'

'I'm sorry, can you tell me those names again?' Celia said. 'My mind doesn't hold things like it used to.'

'Simon Carver and Mark Tait,' Carla repeated slowly, sensing the woman's embarrassment at her poor memory, and omitting Phil's details this time to reduce the confusion. 'They were in the Lodge in the late eighties, early nineties. I believe you were a senior care worker at that time.'

A warm smile crossed Celia's lips.

'It's a crying shame that the council have shut that place down.' She looked Carla in the eye and lifted a finger. 'Some of those kids thrived in there, once they were taken away from the parents. It was the best thing that ever happened to them. Dianne tells me stories that just make me cry. Some folk shouldn't be allowed to have kids.'

Ryan Melrose's face shot into Carla's mind when she heard that. 'You're probably right,' she said, then noticed Owen was surprised by her comment.

'Aye, well, there's nothing I can do for them now, is there.' She sighed. 'Did you say you wanted tea?'

'No, thank you, Celia,' Carla said gently. 'We were just wondering about Simon and Mark.' Using the boy's first names might help her remember them.

'Oh, yes,' Celia smiled. 'Simon and Mark.'

Owen and Carla exchanged glances as Celia sat down at the table.

'Do you remember them?' Owen asked.

Celia frowned and seemed flustered, then fidgeted with a tea-towel on the table.

'I'm sorry, young man, how did you say you take your tea?'

Carla could see the old woman was growing more confused and feared Celia would not be able to help them. Her memory problems seemed serious. She stood up from the table but decided to try one last thing. A potential connection.

'How is Andy getting on?'

Owen's frown conveyed that he had no idea what Carla was doing.

'I'm sorry, dear.' Celia shook her head. 'I don't know anyone called Andy.'

'My mistake.' Carla stood and pushed her chair under the table. 'We'll leave you to get back to your beautiful garden.'

'Aye, it is. Dianne wants me to get some help, but I said not while I'm still standing, we won't.'

'Thank you for your time,' Owen said.

'You two make a very handsome couple.'

Carla suppressed a laugh, uncertain which one of them was more shocked. 'Er, thanks,' she replied to Celia's suggestion. 'We'll see ourselves out.'

They looked back at the house before getting into Carla's car to see Celia waving from the kitchen window with a mobile phone in her hand.

'She's a funny old bird, isn't she,' Owen commented, as he put on his seatbelt. 'Good call asking about Ryan's dad.'

'Thanks, it just seemed like a good idea. I thought she might be able to tell us about a social-work connection. Doesn't matter now because she couldn't.'

'Good hunch, though,' Owen told her.

'It's a damn shame that, isn't it. She's obviously got some kind of dementia. Didn't her daughter mention it?'

Owen shook his head. 'Nah. Strange. She must have known her mum wouldn't be much help.'

Carla indicated towards the fork in the road again. This time she joined the winding single-track road that snaked the two miles to Morag's farmhouse.

'I can see why you came back here after uni,' Owen said, without taking his eyes off the stunning scenery. He frowned when Carla didn't respond. 'Are you OK?'

Carla sighed. 'Aye, aye, I'm all right,' she said, just as her phone rang. Owen picked Carla's bag up from the floor of the passenger footwell.

'No!'

He dropped the bag, startled on hearing her raise her voice.

'Erm, OK. Are you going to tell me why you've just made me almost shit myself?'

'It's nothing. I'm sorry,' Carla said. 'Can you see who it was? It might be Brodie.'

'That's what I was about to do before I needed a bloody change of boxers.' Owen took Carla's phone out and held it up so she could take a look.

'Withheld number. It's probably some scam,' Owen suggested.

'Yes, probably,' Carla replied, as she pulled up outside Morag Thomson's front door. Both detectives spotted the open door. They got out and slowly approached the farmhouse.

'That doesn't look right,' Owen remarked.

'No, it does not,' Carla agreed. 'Wait.' She grabbed Owen's arm before he walked much further.

'Let me go in first,' Owen suggested.

Carla nodded. 'OK,' she whispered.

As Owen stepped through the open door, Morag's dog started barking. He pressed a finger against the door that led into the kitchen and it squealed as it moved.

'Try the living room,' he whispered.

As Carla moved quietly into the room, he looked past her and was alarmed to see the coffee table overturned and the contents scattered over the floor, a puddle of tea next to the fireplace.

'Owen,' she called out. 'In here.'

'A fight?' Owen suggested as he came in.

Carla didn't answer. Instead she moved through to the backdoor, petting the dog's head as it came bounding to meet her. There were red spots on the dog's coat and around its muzzle.

'Shit.' She kneeled to take a closer look. The blood was dry to the touch.

'Out the back?' Owen added.

Carla nodded.

They looked at each other before quickly snatching open the backdoor to find Morag Thomson lying sprawled face down on the grass, a pool of blood around her head.

Molly Carver stared at the pages of the notebook, the photo she loved glued inside the cover. She should have stopped writing a diary years ago. She wasn't a teenager, for goodness' sake. Allowing herself a small smile at her memories she let the diary drop into the flames of the garden incinerator. The faces on the photo grimaced and curled as they melted in the red-hot heat. In seconds there was no trace of them. Then she took the envelope from her pocket. Opening it, her hands trembled as she took the paper out: a newspaper article. Something caught her attention out of the corner of her eye; it was her neighbour Catherine, watching from the window. Molly turned, smiled and waved until the curtain moved back in place.

Molly took a deep breath, the smoke causing her to cough, then threw the paper into the fire. There was no going back.

32

5th May, 1.30 p.m.
'Morag!'

Carla ran down the two steps outside the backdoor and frantically searched for a pulse. She looked at Owen and shook her head.

'I'll call it in,' Owen said and moved away.

'Thanks.' Carla didn't look up from Morag's body which was cool to the touch but not yet ice cold. She hated that sensation. Her revulsion was immediately followed by guilt. This might not have happened if they had come straight here instead of making that futile visit to Celia Petrie.

'The boss is on his way. He wants us to preserve the scene and not touch anything.'

'We should have come here first,' Carla said, as she got back to her feet and pointed to the gaping head wound that was leaking all over the back patio. 'Who does that to an old woman?'

Before Owen could answer, the sound of the backdoor squeaking open caught their attention.

'Morag!' Dianne Petrie's anguished cries hit them, and she surged forward until Owen intercepted her.

'Whoa, I can't let you do that, this is a crime scene.' He had to hold the woman tight as she struggled to get to Morag.

'Come on, let's go back inside,' he said and guided her gently towards the kitchen.

'I don't understand, what's . . . how . . .'

Owen helped Dianne to a chair in the kitchen. She was crying now, shock etched on her face.

'Carla, this is Dianne Petrie, Celia's daughter.'

'I'm so sorry you've had to see that,' Carla sympathised. 'How did you know Morag?'

Dianne sniffed and wiped her face, unable to answer as she struggled to catch her breath. Her hands trembled. Carla poured her a glass of water and helped it into her shaking hand.

'Thank you.'

Carla nodded. The thin smile she gave Dianne was all she could offer. She watched her sip and then spill the water down her lilac polo shirt.

'Oh, God,' Dianne exclaimed, putting the glass on the long wooden table, her hands trembling. She looked dead into Carla's face, her eyes wide and staring. 'Mum. How am I going to tell Mum?'

'Is your mother a close friend of Morag's?' Owen asked.

'No,' Dianne sobbed. 'She's her sister.'

Carla crouched down next to her. 'I'm so sorry for your loss. When did you last speak to your aunt?'

'I . . . I don't know.' Dianne swallowed a sip of water, this time her hand steadier, her eyes more focused. 'Er, no, it was last night. But she spoke to Mum this morning, she asked if I would bring her some bread.' Dianne's tears started again. 'I'm sorry, this is just so . . .'

'It's OK, you've had a huge shock, Dianne,' Carla reassured her. 'Do you have any idea what time your mum spoke to her?'

'Well, no . . . I left for the office at eight and it wasn't before then. I'm sorry,' she repeated.

Carla gently tapped Dianne's shoulder, then stood when she spotted Fraser arrive. 'Excuse me a wee minute,' she said, as she and Owen went to meet him at the doorway.

'Boss,' Carla said, as the three detectives stepped into the garden.

'This is your witness, Morag Thomson,' Fraser confirmed. 'I saw the upturned coffee table, is that the only disturbance?'

'Aye, and that's Dianne Petrie. She's her niece.' Carla told him. 'Thank God we were here before her.'

'Dianne is the senior social worker I spoke to,' Owen added. 'As well as the daughter of a former care worker at the home, boss.'

The sound of a van on the gravel driveway caught their attention.

'Good, that's Forensics.' Fraser peered through the open door at Morag's distraught niece then turned back to his team. 'Do we know where Melrose was this morning before we brought him in?'

'Do you think Ryan Melrose did this?' Carla asked.

'It's possible. He had motive and opportunity.'

'Aye but it would be tight for time. Him getting up here, doing this, then back home.'

'But not impossible,' Fraser mused.

'Not impossible, but . . .'

'She identified him from the CCTV,' Fraser said plainly. 'That's as good a motive to whack her over the head as any.' Fraser started to walk away, leaving that suggestion hanging in the air between Carla and Owen, but called back to them before he was out of sight. 'Take her niece home, will you Carla, and talk to the mum, see how well she knows the Melrose lad. Kelly, you're with me, son. Oh, and arrange for someone to take care of the dog, will you?'

Owen was barely able to contain his excitement that Fraser had chosen him, again. He followed Fraser to where Morag's body lay.

'Right, what do you see?' Fraser asked, while he slipped his hands into a pair of latex gloves and pointed to Morag's body lying face down on the patio.

Owen's eyes surveyed the scene carefully. 'There's no blood trail so she was attacked out here and fell where she's landed.'

'And the upturned table?'

'A fight. She tried to fend off her attacker and ran out here where he caught up with her and hit her over the head.'

'Look around you. Is there anything else out of place in the garden?' Fraser raised one of his hands and indicated the land around them.

'We've not had a chance to check yet,' Owen had to admit. 'Dianne turned up not long after we got here.'

Fraser indicated for him to follow him. He pointed to a broken piece of fence.

'The attacker's escape route?' Owen suggested.

Then Fraser turned and pointed up at the roof of the farmhouse. 'What do you see up there?'

It took Owen a minute to spot it: a security camera, facing towards the field over the other side of the fence. A buzzard circling above them caught his eye and he considered how useful it would be to interview the bird. If only life was so simple. Fraser's words pulled Owen out of his thoughts.

'The camera might not give us the attack, but it should show us the bastard that left through that fence.'

33

5th May, 2.30 p.m.

'You really didn't have to go to all this trouble,' Dianne Petrie said, as Carla pulled her car up outside her house for the second time that day.

Carla got out and locked the vehicle. 'It was no trouble. I couldn't let you drive yourself home after a shock like that. I'll make sure your car is brought back here for you.'

'Thank you. You've been so kind.' Pooling tears made Dianne's eyes glisten.

'That's OK.' Carla touched Dianne's arm gently.

'You still need to talk to Mum don't you?'

'I'm afraid so,' Carla replied. 'She was possibly the last person to talk to your aunt before the attack.'

'I understand, but it's unlikely that she'll remember.'

Dianne reached for the door handle but stopped before going inside. She looked down and heaved a huge breath, then turned to face Carla.

'Look, there's something you need to know about Mum. She's been having some memory problems lately and gets confused easily.'

'It's OK, I know.'

Dianne frowned. 'You do?'

'Yes. DC Kelly and I popped by this afternoon on our way to . . .'

'Of course. He asked me earlier if he could talk to her when he came to see me about those residents. I should've mentioned her memory issues to him beforehand.'

'That's right. Simon Carver and Mark Tait.' Carla mentioned their names again to see if she got a reaction and was disappointed when Dianne didn't flinch.

'That's them, yes.' Dianne nodded and tightened her grip on the door handle. 'Can you let me tell Mum about Auntie Morag? It will sound worse coming from a stranger. I know you said you met her earlier, but she won't remember who you are.'

Carla felt sorry for her. She didn't envy her that task one bit. 'Sure.'

'Thank you,' Dianne said, in almost a whisper.

As soon as they stepped inside, the stench of burning wafted from the kitchen. Carla ran ahead of Dianne and pushed the kitchen door open where she found a pot that had boiled dry on the hob. Inside it were two eggs, smoking. She grabbed the handle and tossed the pot into the sink. Dianne switched off the ring on the cooker and opened a window as she coughed against the acrid smell.

'Mum!' Dianne snatched open the French doors leading to the garden. It clearly wasn't the first time Celia had forgotten about a pot on the cooker and gone out into the garden. When Dianne didn't get an answer she ran outside. 'Mum!'

Carla joined her and headed for the shed at the bottom of the garden. She pulled open the door, but Celia wasn't there either.

'I'll check upstairs,' Dianne said.

Carla followed her back inside but waited in the kitchen. A mobile phone was plugged into the charger next to the kettle. She heard Dianne's footsteps getting further away so Carla picked up the phone. She wasn't sure exactly what she was looking for but assumed this was Celia's phone.

'Shit,' she mumbled when it flicked to a password screen.

She laid the phone back down, and a selection of books caught her attention. All of them were about finding ways to improve your memory. How sad, she thought, as she heard Dianne's footsteps approaching. Poor old woman still has hope that she can help herself.

'No sign?'

'No,' Dianne replied. The fear on her face showed her age, with the wrinkles on her brow line more obvious now.

'She can't have gone far.' Carla grabbed her keys from her pocket. 'Let's head back out and see if we can find her. We'll give it ten minutes, then if there's still no sign I'll get some uniforms out looking for your mum.'

Dianne looked past Carla. 'She's left her phone as well,' she gasped. 'I've told her a million times to always keep it with her so if she gets lost she can ring me.' Tears came again. 'First Morag, now this.'

'What on earth!' Denzil slammed on his brakes, skidding to a stop just feet from the old woman who was walking by the side of the road in her slippers. 'My goodness, Celia!' he exclaimed, and pulled on his handbrake. He grabbed his jacket from the back seat before leaping out.

'Hey, you, what are you doing out here?' he said gently, as he wrapped his jacket round her shoulders. 'You're freezing. Come on I'll take you home.'

'No,' the old woman protested. 'I need to get to work. I'm already late. Peter won't like it if I'm late again.'

'It's fine, he says it's all right.' Denzil humoured her, realising that she was confused. 'He gave you today off.'

Celia looked at him in confusion. 'Did he?'

Denzil nodded gently, smiling as he did. 'Yes. Now, come on, let's you and me get in my nice warm car out of this cold, shall we?'

Celia finally seemed to recognise him. 'Och, Denzil, it's you. I didn't recognise you.'

'Yes, it's me,' he replied as he fastened the seatbelt for her. He clutched her hands in his. They were ice cold. The smell of urine hit him, and he had to turn away.

'You've always been a good lad.' Celia smiled and touched his cheek. 'You better get home before your dad finds out you've snuck out with his car.' She laughed. 'I bet you've not finished your homework either, have you?'

Denzil held his hands up in playful surrender. 'Ah, you caught me.' Then he pressed a finger to his lips. 'Shhh, this can be our secret.'

'Och, you silly boy.' Celia waved her hand at him. 'Your dad will tan both our arses for this.' She chuckled.

'I doubt that,' Denzil whispered, as he shut the passenger door and wiped away the stray tear that had trickled out of his eye before getting back into the driver's seat. 'Brrr. Let's get out of this cold.' He smiled across at the old woman who was staring over at him.

'Aye, you're a good boy.'

'Och, stop it, you'll have me blushing in a minute.' Denzil laughed.

Ryan Melrose slammed his shoulder into the cell door then fell back.

'Hello!' he yelled, then hammered on the thick steel barrier between him and the outside. 'I want to speak to my lawyer!' He banged again, over and over. 'Did you hear what I said?' This time he kicked out with his foot before pressing his face against the opening in the door. 'You can tell that bastard Brodie he's wasting his time. I'm no talking to him . . .'

Keys jangled in the lock before the cell door creaked open. 'About fucking time.'

34

'Any joy with the footage from the farmhouse camera?' Fraser asked.

Owen shook his head, grimacing at the look of disappointment on his boss's face. 'It wasn't connected, boss.'

'You're bloody joking!'

'I'm afraid not. I looked into it and the company came out to look for a fault a couple of months ago, according to their records, but for some reason the job never got done.'

Fraser turned to his whiteboard to see Morag's smiling face looking out at him next to Simon Carver and Mark Tait. Why attack her? Was it really as simple as the fact that she could identify Melrose in a court of law as having been close to Tait's caravan? It took a cruel heart to attack an old woman. Did Ryan have that cruel streak? Evidence suggested yes.

And where the hell was Phil Harrison? Getting a text from him wasn't enough; Fraser wanted to speak to the man himself. He had assigned a couple of uniformed officers to examine CCTV near Harrison's home and office as well as the ferry port and airport, although there was no record of him on any manifest heading to the mainland or surrounding islands. His disappearance was extremely troubling. Fraser glanced at the clock above the office door when Carla came rushing in, her face red from running.

'I'm sorry. I got held up. Dianne Petrie's mum wandered off, so I gave her a quick hand to find her.'

'Shit, is she OK?' Owen asked.

171

'Aye, thanks to that vicar.'

Fraser frowned. 'Who?'

'Denzil Martin. The witness who found Mark's body. He said he found Celia wandering out on the old Croft Road – nearly hit her with his car, actually – so he gave her a run home.'

'This is the old woman who used to work at the Lodge when our victims were there?' Fraser flicked through notes on the table in front of him.

'That's her,' Owen cut in. 'Her daughter said we could talk to her but failed to mention the old woman's memory issues.'

'I see. Thanks, Owen. Strange that she didn't mention the memory problems.'

Fraser turned to Carla. 'Did you manage to talk to her after the vicar brought her home?'

Carla shook her head.

'What, nothing at all?'

'She was in a horrible mess, and in no fit state to make a statement about her dead sister. I've asked Dianne to have a chat, see if she can get anything out of her, but honestly I don't fancy her chances. She was pretty confused.'

'That's no help to us,' Fraser exclaimed, before the sound of Carla's phone irritated him further.

Carla grabbed it from her pocket. 'It's Dianne, hang on,' she said and stepped away from them to take the call.

Fraser threw his focus in Owen's direction. Owen waited, looking uncomfortable. He at least knew now it was best not to try and fill Fraser's silences.

'Go and talk to Ryan Melrose again.' He finally broke the silence. 'See what shakes out now he's had time to reflect on our earlier conversation. Mention Morag's name as well. See how he reacts.'

'Er, hasn't that social worker left, and his solicitor too?' Owen hesitated.

'And?'

Owen clearly wasn't comfortable with where this was going. 'But, boss, I'm not sure . . .'

'I'm not saying interview the lad. It's just a wee welfare check. Ask him if he's needing anything.' Fraser turned back to the board. The conversation was finished as far as he was concerned.

'Sure boss, I'll go and have a word,' Owen said and slipped his arms into his blazer.

Fraser turned to see him shoot a worried, wide eyed glance at Carla as he past her. She frowned back at him.

Carla hung up and slid the phone away. 'Where's he going?'

'Never mind that. What did Petrie say?' Fraser said abruptly.

'No joy from her mum. She can't even remember speaking to Morag this morning.'

Carla jumped when Fraser slammed the red marker pen onto his desk with force. She watched as he flopped down hard on his chair, the cushioned leather giving way under his weight.

'Cup of tea, boss?'

'I don't have time for tea,' he insisted. Luckily his DS seemed to realise how much he needed it.

'I'll go and put the kettle on.'

The sound of his phone ringing made Fraser swear. Something he didn't do often, or at least not in front of Carla. He was old-fashioned that way. The screen identified the caller as Johnny Brodie's care home. Fraser couldn't face that yet. Switching it to silent for a while wouldn't do any harm.

'Here, you look like you need this.' Carla laid his cup and saucer in front of him and took a KitKat from her pocket. 'And some chocolate as well.'

That made Fraser smile, the lass knew him well. 'Aye, thanks. You're right enough.' The first sip was bliss. Perfectly brewed with just a splash of milk. She wasn't wrong about the biscuit either.

'So, what evidence have we got on Melrose?' Carla asked.

'This for a start, and a good one at that.' Fraser held up the bag with the bloody knife in it. 'Fingerprints at the Carver crime scene. CCTV footage close to Tait's caravan, with the old woman's statement identifying him. If that camera facing the back of the farmhouse had been connected, we could have the wee toe-rag for sure. The fact that his father spent time in the home with our victims is also significant.'

'But we've only got Morag's word that it's him near Tait's place. The image isn't exactly perfect.'

'Tell me something I don't know.' He snapped the biscuit in half and took a bite.

Carla sank half of her cup of tea before challenging the evidence. She grabbed the pen and stood next to the whiteboard.

'Right, so Morag's.' She jabbed Ryan's photo with the tip of the pen. 'Has he been there? DNA on her body? Murder weapon must have been a damn heavy thing he whacked her with if it was him. Hammer maybe? Where is it now?'

'Mmm,' Fraser acknowledged.

'The knife under the mattress is a bit obvious, don't you think?' she suggested.

'He's just a kid, Carla. He probably didn't think things through properly.'

'I agree with you there. But even a teenager would know to wash the weapon, and why aren't his prints on it? Why is there so much blood but no prints?'

'What are you saying?'

'I'm not saying anything. I'm challenging the evidence the way his defence will. Andy's connection to the home could be ruled a coincidence if we don't find out what happened there.'

Fraser had to stifle a yawn. The sleepless nights were catching up with him, and that was the last thing he needed. Cases like this always disrupted his sleep. Adam's potential freedom was weighing on his mind too. Surprisingly his father's imminent death took third place in his thoughts. It had only been two days but it felt like a lifetime since he was sitting opposite his brother at Barlinnie with nothing on his mind but a burger and chips. The vibration of another incoming call rubbed against his leg. He didn't need this either.

'Get off home to your family,' Fraser said. 'We'll pick it up again first thing. Can you get here for half seven?'

'Aye, of course.' Carla's smile was genuine.

Fraser's thin smile stifled another yawn, and he didn't like the way she was narrowing her eyes at him. 'Spit it out, what is it?'

'Is everything all right?' she asked.

'With?'

'I don't know.' She shrugged cautiously. 'Everything, I guess.'

'Adam's fine, if that's what you're getting at.'

His candour made Carla blush because she knew he didn't like to talk about his brother.

'Good, good, but if . . .'

'I'm fine, DS McIntosh,' he insisted.

'Yes, of course. I'm sorry.'

Carla grabbed her bag and took out her keys.

'And tell The Boy to get home, too. He's down in the cells talking to Melrose.'

'What?!'

'Just tell him, will you?' Fraser snapped, as the vibration from his phone hit again.

'OK. Night then,' she answered, clearly keen not to irritate him further.

He watched the back of her disappear out the double doors and snatched his phone out.

'Hello?' he said.

Fraser's heart raced and seemed to skip a beat or two while he listened. It was the nursing home. Here it was at last. The call. A cold chill ran through him. Fraser hadn't known how he was going to feel when this call inevitably came, but he didn't think it would be like this.

'Right,' he said, swallowing hard. 'Thanks for letting me know.' He closed his eyes and listened. 'No, I can't come right now. I'll have to call you back with the arrangements.'

Fraser put down his phone and sat back in his chair. That was that then. Johnny Brodie, the man who had brutalised Fraser and Adam as boys, was dead.

35

5th May, 8 p.m.

Denzil hated being late and, by the looks of the turnout for her exhibition, Hayley could have done with him getting there earlier. But Celia had been in a horrible state. His dad would never have forgiven him if he had left her out there; he and Celia went way back. The relief on Dianne's face when she had clocked her mum sitting in his passenger seat was lovely. He'd recognised that other woman with her as one of those detectives – the friendlier of them if his memory served him correctly.

He straightened his dog collar and looked around at the half-dozen people milling around the room, which wasn't huge but still seemed empty. Their faces weren't filled with enthusiasm. There appeared to be more waiting staff than visitors. Denzil couldn't help feeling sorry for Hayley and smiled when she made a beeline for him as soon she spotted him.

'Dennis, you came.' She handed him a tall glass of bubbles.

'Yes, and it's Denzil,' he corrected her.

'Oh, of course, I'm sorry. I'm so glad you could make it.' She sipped from her glass, then gulped.

'So how is it all going?' he asked.

Hayley leaned forward and drew in close to his ear, close enough that Denzil could smell that she had been drinking for a while. A faint whiff of weed wafted towards him too.

'Most of these people don't know the first thing about art.' She gulped from her glass again. 'Every one of them has had a free ticket off me.'

'Oh,' Denzil replied. 'A bit like me then,' he added in a whisper.

For some reason Hayley found this utterly hilarious and roared with laughter. Maybe she'd had even more bubbly than he realised.

'You are a funny man,' she boomed. 'I think I like you.'

Denzil was shocked that her words sounded like an attempt to flirt with him. Surely not. He was a vicar. Besides, she could have any man in this room. Not that there were many, but the tall guy standing next to the painting of huge waves crashing below a lighthouse was much better-looking than him. That man looked like he was far more her type. Given her age he wondered if Hayley had ever been married. She had to be mid-forties.

If she *was* flirting with him then Denzil had to admit he quite liked it. It was nice to know he still had some appeal, even if his commitments were elsewhere. He sipped his drink: champagne. He was impressed.

When three of the guests handed their empty glasses to a waiter and gave Hayley an embarrassed nod before exiting her studio, she looked like she was about to burst into tears. Denzil felt he should say something. He leaned in closer.

'They didn't look like they could afford your work anyway,' he said quietly, assuming that would placate her. He could not have been more wrong.

Hayley thrust her empty glass into his hand and rushed through to the back of the studio, out of sight, banging the door shut after her. Denzil jumped with fright on hearing the loud crash. Murmurs trickled around the room before the rest of the guests drifted out the door. Denzil sank the rest of his champagne and handed the glass to the waiter.

'Looks like you guys can get off early,' he said.

'What about our money?'

'Er, can you come back in the . . .'

'It's fine.' Hayley's voice appeared behind him. 'Here.'

She opened her purse and handed a wad of notes to the lad who distributed it amongst the other waiting staff. They thanked her and took their jackets from the coat-rack then left, chatting and laughing as if they hadn't a care in the world.

Denzil lifted the tray of glasses. 'Where do you want these?'

'You don't have to do that; you get off home.' Hayley poured more champagne into her own glass. 'I'll tidy this lot up in the morning. Thanks for coming.'

'It's no trouble, honestly,' he insisted and carried on clearing up.

'Why can't everyone be as nice as you?' she said, tears trickling down her cheeks.

'Hey, it can't be that bad.' Denzil hugged her, noticing how beautiful her hair smelled. Like strawberry and something else he couldn't place. He ran his hand gently up and down her back. 'So tonight didn't go as well as you thought it might, there's always tomorrow.'

He felt Hayley cling on tight and sob into his shirt. She was saying something he couldn't make out. She pulled away and looked up at him, her barely five-two height dwarfed even by his five-foot-nine.

'My best friend didn't even turn up,' she mumbled.

'I'm sorry.' Denzil tidied stray strands of her long blonde hair behind her ear. It was hard not to feel sorry for her with the tip of her nose pink and her red eyes staring up at him.

Before he realised what was happening they were kissing. He stepped back.

'Er, I'm sorry if I gave you the wrong impression,' he said urgently. 'I'm not. I mean . . .' He stuttered.

Hayley looked like she wanted the world to open up and swallow her. Denzil knew how that felt. That kind of rejection was horrible. Painfully humiliating.

'It's OK, you didn't, it was me. I misread . . .'

'I think I'd better go.' Denzil turned to leave. 'Will you be all right?'

'Please don't go. I'm sorry. I shouldn't have done that, but I don't want to be on my own.'

This was awkward. He did have somewhere else he needed to be, but he didn't have the heart to say no. He had a feeling that Hayley usually got what she wanted. Denzil thought of a compromise.

'Sure, but how about I make us some coffee?'

'Thank you.' She moved forward with her arms open. 'Can I hug you? I promise I won't try and kiss you again.'

Denzil had to smile. 'Sure, another hug can't hurt.'

* * *

David Sutherland awoke with a start, hungover and trembling after blacking out again. He watched the movement inside Hayley's studio, waiting for the last of her guests to leave so that he could ask her for help. Hayley had always been good in a crisis. She would know what to do. He was about to cross the road when a man opened the door.

What the hell was he doing there?

36

5th May, 8.30 p.m.

A headache had begun brewing moments after he'd got the news. Johnny Brodie was dead. The senior nurse in his care home had said that his father had passed away peacefully this afternoon. Just, it seemed, as Fraser was looking at Morag Thomson's body. He wondered how Adam had reacted when he was told. Talk to Adam, have a cup of tea, go to bed. That's all Fraser craved right now.

The front door opened before he could give it much more thought. He smiled and gave Jenny Baird a small wave, before getting out and locking up his Range Rover. Napoleon came bounding off the front step to greet him, wagging his tail furiously against Fraser's leg.

'Hello, lad.' He looked at Jenny when he got to the front step. 'I'm sorry I'm a bit later. Work was . . .'

'I know. It's fine. You should know by now, young man, I understand.'

Young man. Such a strange way to address a man in his mid-fifties but it felt right coming from her. She was the only proper mother figure Fraser remembered.

'I'll be getting off then. Napoleon has had his dinner so don't let him tell you otherwise.'

The dog whined as if understanding what she'd said. Fraser smiled. 'Thanks, Jenny.'

'I'll be over first thing. I want to hoover and I've an appointment in Ullapool in the afternoon.'

Jenny said goodnight as Fraser grabbed Napoleon's lead and headed for the beach. The water was calm as he sat on the sand, the evening breeze wafting the smell of salt into the air. Eyes closed, Fraser inhaled a huge breath and held it, savouring every molecule of fresh oxygen, before letting it out again. Sitting there, focusing on the simple act of breathing in and out, helped him think. He watched a seagull land a few feet away. Fraser smiled, knowing Napoleon would have his sights on it. Right on cue the huge, clumsy old dog lumbered in the bird's direction, reaching the spot long after the grey-and-white bird had flown off.

'Oh, Nap, lad, you'll never learn, will you?' The dog panted, as if he'd run a marathon. Barking once, he turned away to continue snuffling in the sand.

A WhatsApp video call request arrived. Wishing it would be Adam was futile. Fraser know who it was before looking. Lisa Kendall. He took the phone out of his pocket and painted on a smile.

'Hello Lisa. How're you doing?'

'Have you heard from Adam today?' she asked without a greeting, clearly anxious.

'Not today, but to be honest I've been pretty busy with work.'

He watched her look away from the screen and pick up a half-filled wine glass and sink a huge gulp.

'They can't let him out, Fraser. They just can't.'

As much as he cared for the woman, in that moment, an awareness of her selfishness came over him. He pushed that to the back of his mind. Was it actually his selfishness, not hers? Did he want Adam's freedom more than he cared about her?

Fraser could only support her up to a point, because they could never feel the same. Fraser wasn't the one who had been beaten, strangled and left for dead by Adam.

'Adam hasn't even decided if it's what he wants, so we should wait and cross that bridge when we come to it.'

'How can he not know?' Lisa gulped more wine and topped up the glass. 'He's had thirty-five years to think about it.'

Fraser realised he didn't have an answer to that. Then he noticed that she was frowning at him.

'Are you all right?' she asked.

Her question threw him.

He swallowed back a well of unwelcome emotion that had not so much crept up but crashed into him. Coughing had always done the trick before. Why wasn't it wiping away his feelings this time?

'Fraser?' She looked worried.

'Dad's gone,' he blurted out, surprising himself as much as Lisa. 'He died this afternoon.'

She snatched a hand to her mouth. 'Oh Fraser, I'm so sorry,' she said, like a reflex.

'Thanks,' he choked out.

'I know you didn't get on and hadn't spoken to him for a long time.'

Lisa seemed to have a selective memory about the extracts of the psychiatric social-work reports from Adam's court case which had left little detail to the imagination about the childhood they had endured with Johnny Brodie. The neglect. The abuse. The violence. The cruelty.

'That's right,' he agreed quietly. It was easier than trying to explain.

'Does Adam know?'

'I assume so by now,' Fraser said, fearing his complicated twin brother's reaction could have gone in any direction. Was this what grief felt like?

'It's just you and Adam, isn't it? I suppose you'll have to make all the arrangements.'

That thought hadn't escaped Fraser's mind. 'Yes, I suppose so,' he shrugged. 'But it'll just be a simple cremation.'

'I can help. I mean if you need help that is.'

'That's very kind of you to offer, but I think I'll manage.'

'What will you do with the ashes? I'm sorry, that was wrong of me to ask that.' She held up her hand.

Fraser was grateful that the image on the screen started to buffer. Divine intervention. The conversation was dragging Fraser way out of his comfort zone. He didn't do feelings, and certainly not his own. Some people thought he had none anyway. Seconds later the screen went black, the words CALL FAILED flashing across it. That suited Fraser perfectly. He didn't want to talk about Johnny Brodie's ashes. Didn't even want to think about them.

'Come on then, lad.' Fraser stood. Wiping sand from his trousers he headed back on the short walk to his house, Napoleon always several steps behind him, sniffing and pissing.

As he got closer to the front door his phone rang and he quickly went inside, tossing his keys in the wooden bowl on the hall table before he answered. Thank God. Adam.

'Adam. I'm so glad you called.'

There was a fleeting silence before – 'That's it then. He's dead at last.'

'Aye.' Fraser didn't know what else to say.

'They allowed me a late call so I thought I better gie you a phone. See if you're all right.'

'Are you all right?' Fraser asked.

'Am I all right?' Adam repeated, a hint of a laugh in his voice. 'I've been counting doon the hours to this day since I was born.'

This statement was actually true, and his brother had had plenty of time to think about it.

'Well, that's it now, then. He's gone,' Fraser said. 'No more thinking about it.'

'If only it was that simple, eh,' Adam said quietly.

'What do you mean?'

'Well, you know what I mean. Everything that happened,' Adam paused. 'Back then.'

That caught Fraser off guard. 'It was a long time ago.'

'It doesnae feel like that to me sometimes. Do you remember when we got taken to the home?'

Remember. Fraser would never forget. It was the first night in his life that he had ever felt safe.

'What do you remember?' Fraser asked.

'My first memory is how warm it was. Do you mind that?'

'God, yes. The kitchen was always so hot, wasn't it?' Fraser said.

'Mind the steam when they were doing the washing on a Saturday?' Adam laughed. 'The care worker's specs used to fog up.'

'Oh, aye. That's right, and mind the trouble that new worker got into for hanging washing oot on the Sunday.'

Adam laughed down the line. 'Oh, I'd forgotten aboot that. She never lasted long in the job, did she.'

Fraser was so glad that Adam had called. Neither of the brothers knew exactly what to say to each other but it was important that they tried. For both their sakes. After they'd said goodnight, Fraser had settled on the couch with Napoleon napping on his lap and a pot of tea, and had dozed off. So when his phone rang it woke him with a start. He coughed to clear his throat.

'Brodie,' he said sharply and listened with incredulity to what he was being told. 'Get McIntosh and Kelly back to the station. I'll be there as soon as I can.'

There would be no more reminiscing.

Fraser grabbed his coat and car keys. This was unbelievable. It took a lot to get Fraser flustered, but this – he didn't have words for this.

Ryan Melrose was missing.

Andy Melrose yawned, turned over in his bed and pulled the covers up to his chin, but before he could get comfortable the door opened. He looked across at the figure blocking the light from the hall. He yawned again as he sat up, tilting his head from left to right, a cracking noise resulting.

Rubbing warmth into his cold arms he asked, 'Is it done?'

'Aye, it's done,' a man's voice replied, before the cell door closed again.

37

'All right, boys, put your bags in here then I'll show you round.'

The man who had brought them from the hospital seemed nice, but Adam warned Fraser that they should watch their backs. He'd heard men who worked with kids were weirdos who liked touching them. Fraser didn't know what that meant and he didn't care. As long as he wasn't a punchbag anymore. He'd never forget the expression on Jenny Baird's face when she'd looked in the living-room window and seen what their father was doing. Blood had been pouring from Adam's nose and Fraser's legs were black and blue.

'This is the bathroom. You can have a bath whenever you want, but just check the rota first because someone else might already need it. There's a sheet in the office.'

Fraser couldn't believe how nice the room smelled. Soaps and shampoos he'd never seen before sat on the shelf next to a green bath. He didn't know baths came in other colours. It was so clean. No marks on the walls or ripped wallpaper. No stains, blood or otherwise.

'Probably so he kens when his favourite resident is having one,' Adam muttered in Fraser's ear. 'So he can watch.'

Fraser glared at him. Adam could be so horrible.

'And this is the kitchen.'

The smell of roast chicken hit Fraser first. It was so good. He saw bowls filled with all the trimmings on the dining table. Roast potatoes. Sprouts. Some other stuff he didn't even recognise. He was starving.

'Sit yourself down, lads. I'll get yous each a plate.'

Fraser fought back the urge as much as he could but it was no use.

185

Feeling safe at last he burst into tears. There had been times Fraser had feared he'd never reach his teens, but now at thirteen he could stop worrying. Adam looked on in surprise.

'What's wrong with you?' he asked.

'Nothing. Nothing.' Fraser wiped his face. 'It's perfect.'

38

Denzil had been so sweet when Hayley had humiliated herself so spectacularly but, fair play to him, he had not taken advantage of her the way some men in her life had. He wasn't that bad to look at either, though not exactly Brad Pitt with his thin, wiry frame and short stature. Short for a man anyway. He was certainly shorter than anyone she had been out with before and his haircut looked like something his mum would give him. But for a vicar he was nice.

There was something about him. His smile. His kind words. She couldn't decide which it was. He had helped her wash and dry all the glasses and plates before leaving, saying he had an early start in the morning. It was disappointing because she had enjoyed his company. David arriving soon after Denzil left had been irritating, him ranting about doing something to Simon when he was shit-faced. It had taken over an hour for Hayley to convince him to go home to Wendy. She would be worried about him.

Hayley was disappointed Phil had not bothered to show up tonight. He hadn't returned the three texts she had sent him that day either, which was unusual. The only time he had ever done that in the past had been when he was involved in a serious case at the High Court in Edinburgh and even then he had been so apologetic. Hayley knew he preferred to stick to working on the island these days though. Phil was upset about Simon and Mark. Hayley was too.

The pair had been through so much together. With the exception of the sex, which was always good, they would say they were like brother and sister. Phil's ex-wife was less keen on Hayley. But then, in Hayley's experience, sadly being someone's brother didn't stop you from having sex with them. Or their father. Or their uncle. Or their disgusting, fat friends. Having an alcoholic mother had only exacerbated an already traumatic experience. Being taken off her parents had been the best thing that had ever happened to Hayley. Meeting Phil in the Lodge kids' home had probably saved Hayley's life. He, Mark and Simon had become her new family.

She stared at her reflection in the bathroom mirror and patted the puffiness around her eyes, which stung a little to the touch. She looked awful, but sobbing like a baby will do that to a person.

A text startled her, chirping into the silence. Her heart leaped to see it said it was from Phil. At last.

So sorry I missed your show. I couldn't get out of a work thing babe. Bet it went brilliantly. Speak soon. Love you x

She typed a quick reply.

No problem just glad you're ok. Show was shit but will fill you in later. Nite hun x

She waited for his final text that always contained just a single x and was confused when it didn't appear. He must be tired, she thought, and stuffed her phone in her bag, grabbed her keys and switched off the light. The flickering streetlight outside the studio caught her attention, and she wished the council would hurry up and replace the bulb.

There was a loud crash behind her. Breaking glass. Great. Something else had gone wrong tonight. Hayley frowned. Wait a minute. Were they footsteps? She turned but couldn't make out who the figure was in the blackness at the other end of the room.

'Who's there?' she called out helplessly and rummaged fruitlessly in the bottom of her bag for her phone. 'I'm calling the police so you might as well go. If you leave now then I'll hang up and we'll say no more about it.' She edged backwards towards to the front door but tripped over something in the dark.

'Ow,' she cried out, twisting her wrist as she landed.

Footsteps grew closer. The sound they made on the wood floor was menacing. A brief view of a face was dimly lit up by the flickering streetlights. She couldn't make it out clearly. They had something in their hand. Hayley didn't know what it was before it came smashing down on the top of her head.

39

'Did you miss me? I got held up, sorry.'

The sinister tone made Phil shudder. He tried to peel open his swollen eyes but failed miserably although he didn't want to see the psycho anyway.

The ropes on Phil's arms were loosened and his body was dragged into a sitting position. The outline of a water bottle came closer and the gag in his mouth was ripped out, making him whimper. The cuts on the edges of his mouth stung.

'Drink,' the voice instructed.

Phil didn't have to be told twice. He was gasping. His tongue was so dry and cracked it felt like it was bleeding.

The cold water was so good, he didn't want it to end. A greasy burger was forced into his broken hand and the man grew frustrated when he couldn't grip it. He held it next to Phil's lips so he could bite a chunk off. Phil didn't care that the pickles hadn't been removed. That had been such a minor complaint before. He was starving and had been forced to consider the possibility that starving him to death was the plan. As he drifted in and out of consciousness, he'd thought that death would have been a blessed relief.

With his mouth and throat lubricated, Phil attempted to speak.

'You don't have to do this. Just let me go; I won't say a word to anyone.' His voice was scratchy, and his throat stung with the effort, but he had got the words out.

A sharp slap came at him fast.

'Shut it! I didn't say you could speak.'

Phil gave in to the tears that he had tried hard to stop this psycho from seeing. What was the point in hiding it now? This guy was going to kill him anyway. It was the when, not if, that bothered Phil. Keeping him waiting for the killer blow was torture. It made Phil wonder how many days Mark had had to endure this. Mercifully Simon had been killed faster given the presence of Molly in his life. A different tactic had had to be applied there.

The effort of holding his head up had grown harder, and Phil allowed it to flop forward, but it seemed his captor had other plans. A fistful of his short hair was snatched up, sending a shooting pain through his skull as his head was quickly forced back up.

'Take a good look at me,' the voice snarled. 'Because this is the last face you'll ever see.'

Even if Phil could have seen out of his swollen eyes he didn't think he would want to. That last beating had broken his nose, causing the skin round his eyes to swell. All he could make out was the dark shadowy outline of a figure moving around him. He felt the anger well enough though. Tremors of venom vibrated through the floor at him. The realisation that something they'd done as kids was motivation for this was horrendous, but it was the only explanation.

The intense pain coming from his broken hands was making Phil feel sick, waves of nausea clawing at his stomach. He feared what little food and water he had been given was about to make an undignified return. If he vomited it would anger this guy even more. Or it might amuse him. Either option was possible.

The broken nose and cheekbone he could handle. It wasn't like he had never had the shit kicked out of him before. His childhood had been blighted by his stepfather's outbursts. But his shattered hands stung with every breath and the slightest movement sent pulses of agony up his arms and shooting into his head. That was probably why this monster did what he did next. Every snapped finger was twisted back and forth, accompanied by sickening laughter.

Phil screamed. The noise that exited his own body was like nothing he had ever heard before and it left him panting and gasping for air. This level of cruelty could only be dished out by a psychopath. The sounds of his evil amusement drifted into the cloudy sensation swimming round Phil's head. Footsteps retreated. Seconds later he passed out again.

40

6th May, 12.30 a.m.

'Roadblocks are in place, boss,' Carla said.

'Good, then he won't get far. Every officer on the island is looking for him.'

'They're trying to go through CCTV outside the station now, boss, but there's been a glitch,' Owen mentioned.

'What do you mean a glitch?' Fraser asked, alarmed.

'That's all I've been told,' Owen replied.

Just what they needed, another computer issue, just like the social-work files. Either they were very unlucky or there was something fishy going on with the technology round there.

'You two get over to his mother's place. Check if he's turned up there.'

Suzanne Melrose and her young sons had gone to stay with her parents while Forensics took over her house, and straightaway Carla was shocked by the contrast in the two homes. The attractive semi-detached bungalow in a newbuild development with an immaculately kept garden was a surprise. She was sad to think how far Suzanne must have fallen because of her drug and alcohol habit. The detectives had gone to the family home but Ryan wasn't there. Carla hadn't been expecting to find anything there. Ryan wasn't stupid.

'What's going on? Have you got any idea what time it is?' A tall, middle-aged woman opened the front door dressed in a long, green, fluffy dressing gown and slippers.

Choosing to ignore her question about the hour Carla said, 'Hello,

I'm Detective Sergeant McIntosh and this is Detective Constable Kelly. Could we come in and have a word with Suzanne?'

The woman narrowed her eyes at their ID, then sighed as she held the door wide open for them.

'You had better come in, but I highly doubt my daughter will be much help to you.' She scowled and opened a door to the right of them.

Carla and Owen stepped inside an exquisitely decorated hallway and peered inside the adjacent – and equally beautifully decorated – room to see Suzanne snoring loudly on the bed. Carla shot a concerned glance at Owen whose gentle shrug didn't fill her with confidence.

'Has she taken something?' Carla asked.

'Has she taken something,' Suzanne's mother scoffed. 'Of course she has, look at her! I came home from my church committee meeting earlier and found the twins in the front garden wearing only their nappies.' She closed the door again.

'This must be an incredibly difficult time for you,' Carla said, hoping for some warmth from the woman. She would be disappointed.

'Suzanne has made her own choices. I told her a long time ago that her father and I wanted nothing to do with her unless she got a grip of herself and stopped the drugs.'

'Do you have five minutes to talk to us instead?' Carla asked.

The woman didn't even try to hide her disdain for the inconvenience, as she adjusted the collar of her dressing gown. 'Yes, I suppose so, come through.'

The two detectives stared at each other then followed her along the hall and into a stunning living room. Two red leather sofas sat across from each other with an antique pine coffee table between them. The television hanging on the opposite wall wasn't a huge monstrosity. A large bookcase lined the entire back wall and was filled from top to bottom with an eclectic mix from political biographies to crime novels by the likes of Agatha Christie and Frederick Forsyth. A copy of the *Telegraph* lay over the arm of one of the sofas, folded open to the crossword page, with a pair of silver spectacles on top.

'Please, take a seat. I'm not sure how much help I can be, but I'll try.'

Carla and Owen sat at opposite sides of the room. An unconscious plan to scope the entire place? Or to force this woman into feeling trapped into giving them information?

'This is a little bit delicate Mrs . . . I'm sorry, I don't think I got your name.'

'Mrs Duncan-Bell, and please, spit it out, whatever it is. It's late.' She fiddled with her cuffs as she sat down in an armchair positioned under a long bay window. A biography of Margaret Thatcher sat on the arm of the chair with a thick leather bookmark peeking out.

Carla began to wonder if the hard exterior was a coping mechanism that helped her deal with the nightmare her daughter's life had become.

'Your grandson Ryan has—' Carla was interrupted immediately.

'That boy is turning out just like his father.' Mrs Duncan-Bell shook her head. 'No, worse in fact. At least Andy didn't hurt anyone.'

Carla decided not to point out the damage caused by Class A drugs, something she should already be aware of.

'That may be,' Carla said. 'But I need to know if Ryan has been in touch with his mother, or you, in the past few hours.'

Suzanne's mother frowned. 'I didn't know he was allowed to make calls in custody.'

Carla and Owen looked at each other, but before either could speak Suzanne's mother continued.

'He's not in custody any longer, is he?'

Carla opened her mouth to explain what had happened when the sound of running footsteps on gravel came from outside. Owen leaped from his seat and ran to find the front door wide open. He and Carla raced to check the driveway. When neither of them could see anyone they turned back and saw Suzanne standing bleary-eyed, her hair stuck to her face as if she had been wakened suddenly, next to her mother. The two women stared at the two detectives. Carla shook her head at them but was angry with herself as well, for allowing the older woman to dupe her.

'Was he here?' Carla spat.

Neither woman said a word, instead staring at each other and then at the floor.

'I'll call it in,' Owen said and walked away.

Carla scowled at the two women. She was more disappointed in Suzanne's mum than her drug-addled daughter.

'I think you've both got some explaining to do, don't you?'

41

6th May, 3.30 a.m.
Fraser sat helpless watching Adam take the beating. Neither boy spoke. Instead they had to bite their tongues until the ordeal was over, which would be whenever Johnny Brodie ran out of steam. If only Adam would listen to him. Why didn't he ever try and do what Fraser did? Don't answer back. Don't challenge him, especially when he's drunk. But Adam never listened. Fraser couldn't understand it.

Wait, he was coming over. Fraser cowered behind the stinking floral armchair, the stench of Johnny Brodie's stale sweat and booze wafting from the fabric, catching in his throat.

'You're next,' Johnny Brodie slurred, his belt tightly gripped in his hand. 'Think you can make a fool of me, do you?'

Fraser searched his mind for what they had done to make a fool of him. That was a futile exercise, but Fraser seemed unable to stop himself.

Johnny Brodie snatched a fistful of Fraser's hair into his hand and dragged him out of his hiding place. Fraser knew better than to cry out, but his scalp stung when he was thrown over the couch.

'Get off him,' Adam roared and punched his twelve-year-old fists against his father's back, until with one slap he was on the floor.

'Get to your fucking room. I'll be in to deal with you again after I've given this little bastard what he deserves.'

The two boys looked at each other. Fraser pleaded with his eyes for Adam to leave. It was better just to get this over with.

Adam got up. Small dribbles of piss stained his pyjama bottoms.

'Get out of my sight,' Johnny growled, his expression deadly serious.

The real monster was about to be unleashed and Adam knew it. He mouthed 'I'm sorry'. Then he ran out of the room.

Fraser looked up at his father's towering frame. He was a hugely muscular man of six-foot-two. His eyes were black as soot. Johnny Brodie picked up a mug from the fireplace and took a long leisurely sip. Fraser's heart raced and he could smell the coffee wafting towards him. In his other hand he had Fraser's chin squeezed between his fingers. The speed of his heart terrified him. Fraser wanted to be sick. That pungent, bitter smell, it always signalled the pain that was to come.

Here it came. Fraser felt his body tugged down the couch, his pyjama bottoms ripped off to reveal the already scarred skin, before he heard the whip of leather through the air . . .

Fraser woke in a cold sweat, panting to catch his breath. That dream. It was the same every time. Right before that first strike, he would wake up in a pool of sweat, his mouth dry and his heart racing. He was shocked to learn that Adam never dreamed about it.

Fraser lay for a moment to allow his breathing to return to normal. He laid a hand on his heart and felt the rhythm slow. He closed his eyes and inhaled a long, soothing breath, then exhaled. Then again – in and out. In and out. Fraser reminded himself that he was safe. He was a middle-aged man in his own bed in his comfortable home. Not a frightened little boy living in a chaotic, filthy house with a monster.

The fear that man had instilled in Adam and Fraser was indescribable. He wondered if it was that last beating that plagued his dreams because it was the one that got social services involved. The medical examination which revealed the scars and burns on both boys' bodies meant they couldn't live with Johnny Brodie anymore. Charges were never brought, though. He was told to stop drinking and get his life together, then maybe they could come home, but luckily for the boys he never did.

The evil man's death had brought it all back but, in reality, no matter how hard Fraser had tried, it had never really gone away.

The time on his alarm clock read three twenty-eight. He had not got to bed until well after one o'clock after having to deal with the nightmare that had been caused by Ryan's escape. The teenager's whereabouts, and how he had managed to slip away, remained a mystery. Fraser had ordered an immediate inquiry and didn't look forward to his meeting with Superintendent Everett in the morning.

He had also torn strips off Suzanne Melrose and her mother, and told them there would be consequences for not telling police he had turned up there. He advised them to arrange for solicitors to help them because they were going to need it.

He'd ordered two canine officers and their handlers to join the search; they would still be out looking for the teenager now. Fraser would be there himself were he not completely exhausted. He'd known only too well that he'd be no good to anyone without at least a few hours' sleep. The fact that they were on an island worked in the police's favour. He was quietly hopeful Ryan would soon be back in custody.

His phone rang on the bedside table. 'Brodie,' he answered, and shuffled his body to the edge of his bed, suddenly aware of his naked chest in the cold chill of his bedroom. The words he heard the officer say next made him want to get up and punch the air. 'Thank God,' he said. 'Get an officer to stay with him for the rest of the night. I'll be there first thing.'

He hung up and tossed his phone back down then let out a huge sigh of relief. After downing the glass of water by his bed he walked across to his bedroom window. Pulling back the curtain he stared out into the darkness. The isolation of his home hit him suddenly. He'd just been told that Melrose had been picked up a mile away, with blood all over his hands.

42

6th May, 9 a.m.

Denzil smiled at the young lad delivering papers to the houses on either side of Hayley's studio. She had been so disappointed last night that the turnout for her exhibition was poor. He felt really sorry for her. Her paintings were decent, but obviously not to everyone's taste.

Through the frosted glass he saw the outline of something large on the floor just inside the door that had not been there last night. He tried the door, but it wouldn't budge. He glanced anxiously behind him and shoved his weight against the door, but the obstruction was heavy. It took a couple of good shoves until the heavy mass eventually slid over and he could push open the door. Denzil was horrified by the sight that greeted him.

He leaned down to see if Hayley was breathing then searched for a pulse. She was alive, thank goodness.

'Hayley, can you hear me?' Denzil tapped her cheek. 'Hayley, it's Denzil.' He raised his voice and shook her shoulders as he grabbed his phone to dial for help.

The moaning sound meant she could hear him. 'Hayley, wake up. Help's coming, love.'

He stroked her cheek and looked around at the chaos. Shelves had been tossed on the floor. Drawers left wide open. Paintings smashed on the floor. Paintbrushes scattered all over the room. An easel had been smashed, the pieces thrown everywhere.

There was a small pool of partially dried blood on the floor by Hayley's head. Sirens echoed in the distance when Hayley's eyes finally opened.

'Denzil,' she mumbled.

'Hey, you.' He smiled. 'You gave me quite the scare there.'

'My head hurts.' She tried to lift her hand to touch it. 'What's happened . . .'

'No, no, you just take it easy until you've been checked over. There's an ambulance coming.'

Denzil was sure he saw her try and smile.

'I must look a right state.' She closed her eyes again. 'My head really hurts,' she whispered, just as a paramedic arrived in the studio.

From the side window Denzil saw two police officers get out of a patrol car. He slid the window open and called to them.

'In here. I'll let you in the backdoor!'

The two officers were at the backdoor before Denzil, and he unlocked it for them.

'The paramedics are already here.' Denzil shut the door after them. 'Just through that door there,' he pointed. 'The main room is through there.'

'Thanks,' the younger of the two officers replied over his shoulder, while the older man stayed with Denzil and took out a notebook.

'And you are?'

'I'm Denzil Martin. I'm a . . .' He thought for a minute, then decided on, 'I'm a friend of Hayley's.'

The officer nodded and made a note of that. 'It was you that found the victim, is that right?'

Denzil tried to peer past to see how she was. 'I'm sorry, can I just go and . . .'

'When we're finished,' the officer insisted.

Denzil scratched at his head anxiously. 'OK, of course. Yes, it was me that found her. I wanted to see if she was OK after last night.'

'What happened last night?' the officer asked quickly, noting something down in his book. 'Why wouldn't she be OK?'

'She put on an art exhibition and it was a bit of a disaster. She was upset so I thought I'd better come and check on her.'

'I see. And were you at this exhibition yourself?'

'Yes.'

'What time did it end?'

'About nine, I think . . . Then I stayed behind to help her tidy up.' Denzil didn't like the way the officer was looking at him. 'We had a coffee and I left around ten.'

'So you were the last person to see her before the attack?'

Denzil was not enjoying the direction this was taking. 'Hayley was fine when I left her.'

'Mmm.' The officer wrote something down again.

'Look, are you trying to accuse me of something? Hayley's a friend, and—'

Before he could finish, one of the paramedics called out to him. 'We're taking her now, do you want to come with us in the ambulance?'

Denzil looked at the officer.

'If you could give me your contact details first. Someone might need to talk to you again later.'

'Yes, of course, of course,' he replied quickly and gave him the address and phone number of the manse.

Denzil rushed past him and caught up with the two paramedics loading the trolley into the back of the ambulance. A small crowd had gathered. A young woman with a sleeping toddler in a buggy was chatting to an elderly couple about what might be going on. Eva Sutherland was watching from the crowd, running late for school, stopping to gawp at the commotion. The postman had stopped and was probably trying to decide what to do with Hayley's post.

'Denzil,' Hayley's voice was weak.

'I'm here,' he reassured her and sat down on the empty seat in the back.

'Put your belt on,' the paramedic instructed. Denzil did as he was told. Without opening her eyes, Hayley reached for him. Denzil took her hand and squeezed a little: just enough to comfort her, he hoped.

'Don't leave me,' she urged. 'I don't have anyone . . .'

'It's OK, I'm right here. I'm not going anywhere,' Denzil said, briefly catching the eye of the paramedic who was also travelling in the back of the ambulance. The unexpected flush of heat on his cheeks took Denzil by surprise. He smiled awkwardly then focused on Hayley.

'I won't leave,' he repeated. 'I promise.'

43

6th May, 9.30 a.m.

Fraser yawned, then smiled awkwardly at the young nurse who he realised had caught him. Waiting to talk to Ryan Melrose felt like it was taking forever, so when the doctor stepped out of the room Fraser sat up sharply, jarring his back slightly on the uncomfortable plastic chair.

'Doctor, do you have a minute?'

'Yes, but only a minute.' The doctor checked his watch. 'You've probably noticed how busy we are.'

The island's only hospital had a small accident-and-emergency department, run by one doctor and a handful of other staff. Melrose coming in with deep cuts to his wrists had caused extra logistical problems, because he had to be supervised at all times.

'Can I talk to him?'

'You can, but I've asked for a psychiatric evaluation so I can't let you have long.' The harassed-looking man took a final glance at the uniformed officer standing guard outside the room. 'We don't have any secure beds on the island, as I'm sure you're aware, so he'll have to be transferred if that's what the psychiatrist feels is for the best.'

Their conversation was cut short by a trolley being wheeled at speed along the corridor and into resus. Fraser stepped aside to let the group move past. The face of the man who had been told to wait outside was familiar, but Fraser couldn't place him until he spotted the dog collar. Reverend Martin. The man looked concerned about whomever had been rushed through those double doors. Fraser nodded back at him then looked away.

A psych evaluation on Ryan Melrose was the last thing Fraser wanted. It was a complication this case did not need.

'Thank you,' Fraser replied to the back of the retreating doctor. What else could he say?

He opened the door and acknowledged the nurse – who looked barely into his twenties, a student most likely – who had been assigned to Ryan. Suicide watch. The thick bandages on both wrists looked worse than Fraser was expecting. The wounds hadn't damaged nerves but had required a lot of stitching. An elderly man having a late-night walk with his dog had spotted Melrose and called police. A mile further down the road and he'd have reached Fraser's; he couldn't help wondering if the lad had been deliberately heading towards his place.

Ryan's eyes opened at the sound of the door closing and he gave a long sigh. Turning his back to Fraser appeared painful, but it was what a petulant teenager does to authority, Fraser thought. It wasn't going to stop him.

'How are you, Ryan?' Fraser asked, after walking to the other side of the bed so they could talk face-to-face. He pulled an uncomfortable-looking plastic chair over and sat close to the bed, running his fingers across the stubble he had not had time to shave off this morning.

'Don't pretend you care about me.'

'You've got your mum and granny in a lot of trouble,' Fraser said. He couldn't help but look again at the thick bandages.

A little smirk. 'That stuck-up cow will not like you saying that.'

'Sounds like you don't like your granny very much.'

'Wouldn't matter if I did.' He lifted a hand and winced. 'She's never liked me or Dad. Don't think she even likes her own daughter.'

'Then why go there?'

'I needed money, didn't I, and she's got plenty of it,' Ryan told him. 'But then you lot arrived, and I had to go before I got the chance to get any.'

Something in the teenager's face looked different, but Fraser couldn't put his finger on it. His features seemed softer, and his eyes were red and tired.

'What were you going to do when you had the money?'

'Get as far away from here as possible.'

'And how did you plan to do that? You must have known you'd never have been able to board the ferry without being seen. You'd have been waiting hours for one anyway. Which one would you have got. Ullapool? Uig? Or did you plan to catch a plane from Stornoway? You knew we'd be looking for you.'

'I had to try something, didn't I?' The fight had returned to his voice. 'I had to see Dad, he'd know what to do.'

Fraser wondered if he envied the lad's blind faith in his father. What must that be like?

'You're in pretty serious trouble, Ryan. Is that why you did that?' He pointed to Ryan's wrists. 'Do you feel guilty?'

'I'm not talking to you anymore. Tell him,' Ryan urged the nurse. 'Tell him I need to rest.'

Fraser lifted a hand to silence the young nurse before his lips had even moved. 'I'm going in a minute.'

'Then fucking go!' Ryan shouted.

Fraser had to stop the agitated young nurse from going for help. 'Stay there,' he pointed a finger in his direction.

'But . . .' He tried to insist but the look on Fraser's face made him retreat.

'Ryan, look at me,' Fraser instructed him. 'Look at me,' he repeated.

Ryan did look up, but with a face full of teenage defiance. 'You can't do this, I have rights.'

The ringtone from his jacket pocket irritated Fraser and he snatched his phone out. 'What?' he said, then he listened with interest. 'Great, thanks.' Fraser stared at Ryan and tried to picture the horrifying scenario that the evidence now revealed. Forensics had come back with a match for prints found at Morag's.

'What?' Ryan stared him down.

'Can you explain why your prints were on the backdoor of Morag Thomson's farmhouse?'

'I don't know,' Ryan said, without meeting Fraser's eye. 'You're the detective, you tell me.'

'Why Morag, what's she ever done to you? Was it because she could identify you being up near Tait's caravan?'

'What are you talking about, why would I want to go to that nut job's disgusting caravan?' He stared past Fraser as he spoke.

'So you do know Mark Tait.'

'Everybody knows that nutter. Going about talking to himself. Nutcase.'

'But why kill him, Ryan? What had he done to you to make you do that to him?' Fraser's heart was pounding; this interview wasn't exactly legit. He'd not read Ryan his rights, but he didn't want to stop when he was sure a confession was coming. That young nurse was a witness.

'I'm not saying anything else, so you might as well go.'

The tension in that small, stuffy room was electric, and Ryan stared at him, shaking his head.

'The knife was under your bed,' Fraser continued, until the room's door swung open. It was Carla. 'What?' Fraser snapped.

'You'd better come, boss. There's been another attack; it happened last night.'

Fraser stared at Ryan, who was smirking at him now. Then he looked at the young nurse.

'That boy does not move! Is that clear?'

44

6th May, 10 a.m.

Fraser followed Carla into the ward to see the Reverend Martin sitting next to Hayley Stevenson: the victim of another attack, which had taken place during the hours Ryan Melrose was at large. Fraser felt sick at the thought they were responsible for letting this happen, but the fact she was still alive was a miracle, and he hoped she could help identify her attacker. The killer. The writing daubed on the wall was evidence of a connection:

I know what you did. I'll be seeing you.

It was exactly what Tait and Carver had been told. But why was she still alive? Was it because she was a woman? Their killer's actions didn't suggest compassion for the fairer sex – or for anyone. Given that he had also received the threatening message, finding Phil Harrison was growing increasingly urgent. The search of his house had given them nothing to go on. Had anybody actually had a conversation with him?

'Hayley, I'm Detective Inspector Fraser Brodie.' He held his ID out and acknowledged Denzil sat next to the bed. 'Do you feel up to talking about what happened last night?'

'I'll leave you to it.' Denzil squeezed Hayley's hand in his. 'I'll go and grab a coffee or something.'

Fraser recalled the report he had just read. The vicar had been the one who had called the ambulance.

Hayley's eyes welled with tears. 'I dread to think what would have happened if he hadn't found me.'

'Sounds like they really trashed your place too.'

'I don't care about that right now. Like Denzil said it's just stuff. I can paint more pictures and buy more paints.'

'Sounds like a good friend you've got there.'

'He is.' She smiled. 'I've only known him a couple of days. I'm not much of a churchgoer but he's been really kind to me. My exhibition was a bit of a disaster, you see, and I suppose my pride was hurt a bit.'

'What can you remember? Could you identify the person who hit you?' Fraser asked, steering the conversation back to her assault.

'I'm afraid not, it was dark,' she said, and Fraser's spirits sank. 'I remember David coming to see me. I think. It's all so fuzzy now.'

'Do you mean David Sutherland?'

'Yes. I think he came but maybe I'm mixing up my days. I'm sorry.'

Fraser noted her comment. Sutherland's whereabouts still hadn't been confirmed. Was Fraser focusing too much on Ryan? But it wasn't Sutherland on the CCTV near Mark's caravan. They knew that for sure. What they needed was a concrete alibi for Sutherland's whereabouts before he could be officially ruled out.

'What about the writing daubed on the wall? Does that mean anything to you?'

Hayley's frown was as disappointing as her answer. 'What writing?' she asked, glancing over Fraser's shoulder and smiling to see Denzil with two cups of coffee in his hands.

The smell wafting from the paper cups made Fraser back away instinctively, his stomach turning at the bitter stench.

'Here you go. I put a little sugar in; I wasn't sure what you'd want,' he said, as he laid a cup on the table, shifting his gaze briefly to Fraser then back to Hayley.

'Detective . . . I'm sorry, I can't remember your name,' Hayley began.

'Brodie.'

She turned to Denzil. 'He's asking about writing on the wall; did you see anything?'

Denzil shook his head. 'No, I'm sorry. I don't remember. It's all such a blur, to be honest. As soon as I saw Hayley, my body went into autopilot.'

'OK, then, does this mean anything to you? *I know what you did. I'll be seeing you.*'

'No, I'm sorry. Like I said, I didn't notice anything like that. I was too busy concentrating on Hayley, but that's a strange thing to write,' Denzil suggested, looking at Hayley.

Her eyes had narrowed. She was searching her mind. There was something, Fraser knew it. Then her eyes snapped wide open.

'Phil!' she urged. 'Phil said something about it. You have to talk to Phil.'

'Do you mean Phil Harrison?'

'Yes, Phil's one of my oldest and best friends. He came to me the other day and told me something about a letter.' Her fragile mind was obviously hurting. 'God, I told him not to be so paranoid. That Simon had probably pissed off someone's husband . . .' Hayley broke down in tears.

'How do you know Simon Carver?' Fraser said. 'What about Mark Tait?'

'Can't this wait?' Denzil interjected, soothing Hayley as she sobbed.

'Phil, you have to talk to Phil. You have to warn him.'

'Have you spoken to him recently?' Fraser pressed.

'No, but he's texted me.' Hayley started to rummage around for her phone until she found it on the locker. She scrolled through her messages and showed the screen to Fraser. 'Here.'

Fraser took the phone and hit Phil's number. When it went straight to voicemail he hung up in frustration. For some reason tracing Phil's number was proving difficult. He shot off a text to Owen.

Keep on trying to trace Harrison's phone. There have been texts from his number. I don't like this. Keep me posted.

'Hayley, did you spend time in the Lodge kids' home?' Fraser asked, fearing that she was part of the group, and wondering how many others there were out there.

She nodded. 'Yes, that's where I met Phil and the others.'

'The others,' Fraser repeated expectantly.

'I moved into the Lodge in 1991, and me and Phil hit it off

straightaway.' A small smile crossed her lips then she took a breath, rubbing her forehead. 'Oh, it feels like I've been hit by a truck.'

'The others,' Fraser urged. 'Who are the others?'

'It was me and Phil and Mark and Simon. We kind of became a bit of a . . .' Then she stopped abruptly, fidgeting on the bed. 'I'm sorry, I really don't feel well.'

'Can't this wait?' Denzil said quietly. 'I know you've got a job to do, but I can bring Hayley to the station when she's up to it.' He looked at Hayley. 'Is that all right?'

Fraser did want to ask Hayley one more thing, then he'd have another officer stationed close for her protection. Just to be on the safe side.

'Do you know a teenager called Ryan Melrose, Andy's son?'

'Did you say Melrose?' She flashed a worried look in Fraser's direction.

'Yes, Ryan Melrose, sixteen years old, do you know him?'

'Erm, yes, I do, but . . .' She was staring at Reverend Martin now.

'Hayley, do you know this boy?' Denzil Martin repeated Fraser's question.

Hayley took a huge deep breath, exhaling slowly. The anticipation was killing Fraser.

'I knew his dad Andy briefly from my time in . . .' She stopped. 'I, erm . . . I gave evidence against Andy Melrose. He's in Barlinnie now based on the evidence I gave them about his drug dealing.'

'From your time where?' Fraser urged. 'Did you meet him in the kids' home?'

Hayley nodded. 'Yes, I did.'

45

6th May, 11 a.m.

Fraser had hoped that Superintendent Everett hadn't seen him, but the sound of his name being called said otherwise.

'Go and get the kettle on,' Fraser told Carla. 'I'll catch you up. Is The Boy here yet?'

Carla told him Owen had been waiting for them to return from the hospital after finally being able to view the CCTV, the cause of the glitch still unknown.

'Sir,' Carla said, as she passed Everett.

'Fraser, I think we need to talk, don't you?'

Fraser knew his balls were about to be handed to him after Melrose's escape, and he didn't have time for it. Building the case against Melrose had to take priority as did finding Phil Harrison before it was too late.

'Yes, sir,' he replied, following him into his office.

'Close the door, Fraser,' Everett insisted, flopping down behind his desk.

Fraser did as he was told. Andrew Everett was nice enough, but it was obvious he'd had his head bitten off by his own superiors already.

'Look, sir . . .'

'Sit down, Fraser,' Everett interrupted.

'Sir.'

'I don't have to emphasise the seriousness of this, do I?' Everett's composure was rattled. 'I need to know. Is Melrose your man?'

'I believe so, sir.'

'Jesus, and we let him walk right out of here to attack someone else. Is the woman all right?'

'Hayley's fine, and I have every confidence the inquiry will get to the bottom of what happened,' Fraser countered. 'Melrose is back in custody now.'

Beads of sweat had gathered on Everett's brow in the time they'd been together. He reached in his drawer for what he claimed were mints, but Fraser knew they were antacids. The guy was stressed. If he wasn't careful he'd give himself an ulcer. Shouldn't it be Fraser developing the ulcer? He was the one out there trying to catch killers.

'He's to be assessed by a psychiatrist before things proceed any further,' Everett suggested. 'Suicide risk, apparently. Is that right?'

'He attempted to take his life, yes.'

'Well, at least he didn't do *that* in our care.' The remark seemed a little in bad taste to Fraser.

Everett looked over at a knock on his door. 'Come in.'

A sheepish-looking Owen was at the door, a laptop in his hand. 'Sorry to interrupt, sir. I think you both need to see this.'

'Come in, come in,' Everett cleared a space on his desk and Owen clicked to play the footage.

Fraser watched in disbelief as a large-framed uniformed police officer, who kept his back to the camera, was seen ushering Ryan through a side entrance. Owen scrolled forward to footage of Suzanne's mother waiting in a BMW. Ryan got into the car, and the camera followed them until out of range.

'Bloody hell,' Everett hissed. 'Fraser, you concentrate on Melrose. I'll deal with . . .' He pointed at the screen. 'This.'

'Sir.' Fraser stood and indicated for Owen to gather up his laptop and go.

Once Owen was out of earshot, he said, 'Sir, I wouldn't be surprised if Andy Melrose was involved in springing his son from custody. You and I both know he's got a long reach, even in Bar-L.'

'What are you suggesting?'

'I thought I could go over and talk to him.' Fraser paused to find the right words and turned to ensure the door was closed. 'I'd like to see Adam as well. You'll probably find out soon enough, but our father died yesterday.'

'Fraser, I'm so sorry. If there's anything you need, just ask.'

'Thank you, sir. I appreciate that.'

'Take the time you need to make arrangements and what not. I'm very sorry for your loss.'

'Thanks. I'll go and see if I can get on the next flight. It'll be tight for time but hopefully I'll make it.' He glanced at his watch. 'I'll check in as soon as I've spoken to Melrose.'

'I can get someone to cover for you, if you'd like a few days?'

Fraser shook his head. 'I'm fine, honestly. You know me, I'd rather be working.'

'With the shitshow unfolding here at the moment, I won't fight you, Fraser. But are you sure you're OK?'

'I am, sir. And there's not much we can do with the lad until the psych evaluation now, so a couple of days won't hurt.' Fraser reached for the door handle. 'Thank you, sir. Listen, could we keep this between the two of us for now?'

'Of course,' Everett assured him. 'Tell Adam . . .' Then he stopped, his discomfort apparent.

'I will, sir.' Fraser's rare smile revealed how much he appreciated the gesture.

Andy Melrose paced back and forth, a headache developing fast. Things were not going as he had planned. At least getting a psych evaluation meant the police had to wait to talk to Ryan again. Out of the corner of his eye he spotted Adam Brodie walking towards him. Just like his damn brother, he was always there, watching. The damn man was staring.

'What the hell are you looking at?' Andy glared at him before Adam turned away, seemingly trying to avoid a confrontation. 'Aye, you better walk away, Brodie, and if your brother knows what's good for him he'll do the same.'

46

6th May, 11.45 a.m.

Phil's eyes remained shut, no matter how hard he tried to prise them open. He could feel thick, stinking pus oozing from the sides. The wounds must be infected. *Septic shock*. Was that what would be written on his death certificate? The racing he had felt in his heart earlier had changed. It beat slower now, less urgent, more thready. The pain in his hands was not gone, but was certainly less. Blessed relief. The nerves were dying he supposed. If he could open his eyes to look he didn't think he'd want to. It wouldn't be a pretty sight.

Phil mused that perhaps the calm that was washing over him was what death felt like, and he was grateful. Thankful that the fear was gone. The terrifying anticipation had been worse than the beatings. The tight chest. The dry throat. The hammering heartbeat. Bracing himself for impact. That was all gone now, and he supposed everything was shutting down, except his sense of smell was strangely still strong. Against the stench of his own blood, sweat and piss he picked out another fragrance, something much nicer. Dare he say heavenly. Was that where he was heading? Phil didn't think he deserved to end up there. Wherever he was headed Simon and Mark would be there waiting for him, he was sure. Friends forever, just like they'd promised all those years ago. He feared for Hayley's safety but all he could do was hope that DI Brodie caught this guy before he got to her.

The smell was floral yet fruity. The fact that when one sense dies the others were heightened wasn't lost on him. His eyes were fucked. All he heard now was a whooshing noise; presumably his eardrums had burst. The disgusting copper taste of blood and the agonising rubbing pain from piss-stained clothes and ropes were gone. Sight, hearing, taste and touch. All he had left was smell.

Phil was resigned to his fate, relished it even; it smelled so good. Warm and comforting like a hug, but not a quick squeeze from a friend. No, this was an emotional, even sensual embrace from someone who loves you, really loves you, unconditionally. They were holding him, and he was breathing it in. In and out. In and out. Squeezing tighter now. In and out. In . . .

47

6th May, 11.50 a.m.

Dianne Petrie had called in sick because she couldn't face the office. The rest of them could cope without her for a day, maybe even two. She was exhausted. Celia hadn't slept well last night, and therefore neither had Dianne. It wasn't her mum's fault, of course; since those detectives had come and spoken to her the agitation had increased. She had a good mind to make a complaint, but that McIntosh woman had been kind when Celia went missing. Dianne didn't have the heart. If Denzil hadn't found Celia she dreaded to think where she'd have ended up. The bottom of the quarry, perhaps, which was on the other side of the site of the derelict former kids' home. It was almost guaranteed the old woman would have got lost and taken a fall.

Dianne lived for Celia's lucid moments these days, which, while infrequent, were important. But her mother was living more and more in the past. Her assertion that she still worked at the kids' home was hard to shift. Dianne had lost count of the number of times Celia had said she was late for work – that Peter would be cross if she didn't hurry. Denzil had explained that was what Celia had said to him when he'd found her. It had been a long time since Peter Crichton was cross with anyone, sadly. The pain of that still stung.

'Mum? It's just me,' Dianne called out and tossed her keys onto the hall table.

The bits of shopping would keep them going for a few days. Although she usually took her mum with her, Dianne hadn't wanted to risk her confusion upsetting her when they were in the middle of Tesco.

'Mum!' She listened for movement upstairs. 'Where are you?' she muttered under her breath. She opened her mouth to call again when Celia's face appeared round the kitchen door.

'There's no need to shout,' Celia said, taking one of the bags out of Dianne's hand. 'You'll wake the dead with that noise.' She laid the bag onto the counter and started to empty it.

'Why didn't you answer me the first time then?'

'Am I not allowed to go to the bathroom now?' Celia's brittle mood had deteriorated in the time Dianne had been gone.

Dianne thought it best to leave it at that. There was no point poking the bear more. She noticed the answering machine was flashing but the message was empty so she deleted it. The caller must have changed their mind.

'Where have you been?' Celia asked, as she placed the butter into the freezer.

'What does it look like? I was at Tesco. Look, I wrote it down for you.' Dianne pointed to the note she'd made on the whiteboard she'd got for her mother.

'Yes, of course. Sorry, I forgot.' Celia's mood softened.

'I know, it's OK.' Dianne took the butter back out of the freezer. 'Why don't you go and have a seat in the living room. Read the paper or something. I'll finish this and make us a pot of tea.'

Dianne watched until the old woman turned into the living room. The past few days had shown a marked deterioration. She definitely needed to see someone about it. Perhaps her medication needed tweaking a bit.

The kettle had barely boiled when Dianne heard a racket coming from the living room. She raced through and was alarmed to see every drawer pulled out. The contents of the sideboard and television unit were all tossed onto the floor.

'Mum, what are you doing? Stop that, let me help you find whatever you're looking for.'

'Where is it? What have you done with it? The meeting is today; I need their notes.' Celia spat.

Dianne stepped back, tears flooding her eyes. She brushed them roughly away; her mum didn't need her to collapse into a heap.

Kneeling down next to Celia she gently said, 'Tell me what you've lost,' the way she had been trained to do as a social worker, never imagining all those years ago she would be practicing it on her own mother. 'Maybe I can help you.'

Celia narrowed her eyes suspiciously at her with a look of confusion. 'Who are you and what are you doing in my house?'

Dianne had to keep her cool. She repeated the mantra – *they're not giving you a hard time, they're having a hard time.*

'Mum, it's Dianne.' She smiled and reached for her mum's hand.

Celia frowned; there was a flash of recognition then it was gone again. 'Have you got their files? I can't find the filing cabinet.' She picked up the piece of paper closest to her and threw it away. 'Why do people keep moving things around in here?'

There was only one thing for it. 'Which files are you looking for?' Dianne smiled. 'Maybe I know where they've been put.'

'Do you?'

'Perhaps,' Dianne repeated. 'Whose files do you need?'

'Let me think,' Celia said, her mood calmer. 'I need Hayley's, Simon's, Mark's and I can't remember the fourth one . . . Och, it'll come to me.'

'Take your time.' Dianne got down onto the floor and leaned her back against the wall.

'The meeting is today, you know, and Peter will be so cross.' Celia started rummaging in the drawers again. 'Phillip, that's it, have you got Phillip's file there? What a to-do he's been causing. Dragging those others in with him.' Her face fell deadly serious. 'Peter just doesn't know what to do with him.'

48

6th May, 12.30 p.m.

'Not a fan of flying?' The red-headed woman smiled at Fraser. Her accent wasn't a local one. Edinburgh, perhaps, maybe even Perth.

'Is it that obvious?' Grateful to have been allowed on the flight at such short notice, Fraser had hoped he had hidden his fear of taking off better this time.

'Don't worry, my husband is a terrible flyer. He avoids it as much as he can. Silly fool still gets the ferry.'

Fraser considered that flying was the best of the two options. 'Must be bad if he would rather get rolled about for nearly three hours in the Minch.'

The plane vibrated and Fraser's hands squeezed the arm rest, in an involuntary response. Damn take-offs. Mixed feelings about leaving the island hit him every time. He looked down on the ivory white sands; they were a sight to behold.

'Don't worry, fifty-five minutes and we'll be down again.' Her attempt to reassure him was nice. 'Are you heading to the mainland for business?'

Fraser would definitely not be telling this stranger the real nature of his trip. 'Aye, something like that.'

'What is it you do?'

Her small talk had now passed the socially acceptable limit. 'I'm a detective.' That should be enough to quell the need to continue this conversation.

'Oh, right,' she answered, a gentle pink hue on her cheeks. Her nervous laugh filled the space between them.

Fraser smiled, which was enough for her to turn her attention to the sunlit view from the window.

'Hello again.' The taxi driver waiting at the rank had driven Fraser to Barlinnie many times before. He extinguished his cigarette, pressing his foot down on it before opening the backdoor for him.

'Usual,' Fraser informed him.

'Of course.' The man got into the driver's seat and indicated out of the airport.

Fraser braced himself for more small talk for the next twenty minutes, maybe thirty depending on traffic. At least he would be able to claim the cost back for this one because of the business aspect of the trip. Including the cost of the plane tickets a couple of hundred quid wasn't to be sniffed at.

'Have you been busy?' the driver asked.

'Steady, I suppose,' he answered. Wasn't that what he was supposed to ask the driver? 'What about yourself?'

'Same. Steady, but enough to keep the wolf from the door.'

Fraser scrolled through the messages on his phone, hoping that would cut the chat short. For once, it did, and nineteen minutes later he was handing over forty quid for a thirty quid fare.

'Keep the change,' Fraser said.

'Thanks, mate. Give me a call when you're wanting picking up.' He handed Fraser his card.

'Thanks.' He was getting a late flight back, so having a reliable lift was good. 'I will.'

Fraser waited in the room the governor had allocated for his interview with Andy Melrose. Finding out that he'd spent a short time in the home was significant. It gave Ryan a connection to their victims. Fraser couldn't decide what the rancid smell was. Sweat, perhaps, with a stale sweet tinge that he couldn't explain. He turned when the door opened and a squat, wiry man walked in, a tattoo of a spider web on his neck. Fraser remained seated while Melrose sat opposite.

'You better be looking after my boy,' Melrose sneered. 'I got told he'd slit his wrists.'

'Ryan is fine. He's being taken care of.'

The two men stared at each other until Melrose broke the silence.

'Good. So what are you wanting with me?'

'I'll tell you something that intrigues me, shall I?' Fraser answered his question with a question.

Melrose folded his arms across his chest. 'Go on.'

'How did you do it?

'Do what?'

'Get Ryan out of custody?'

Melrose shrugged, his arms tightening. 'Don't know what you're talking about.'

'Come on, Andy,' Fraser pressed. 'Neither of us is stupid enough to believe that.'

His lips pursed, Melrose said, 'No comment.'

'I'm impressed. It must have been hard keeping it quiet.'

'No comment,' Melrose repeated.

'Do you realise what your son is accused of? I mean, really?'

Melrose opened his mouth to speak. 'No—'

'Yes, yes, I know. No comment. Change the record.'

He stood up and walked round to Melrose's side of the table and bent his face close to his, fighting against the stench of stale coffee that was churning his stomach.

'If I order a search of your cell, have you hidden that burner phone well enough? You'll not be wanting that found will you?' Fraser bluffed, before straightening up and returning to his own seat. 'So I'll ask you again—'

'All right, all right,' Melrose said, 'there's no need for that. What do you want from me?'

'Do you know what Ryan's done?'

'I'm sure you're about to tell me,' Melrose sneered.

'Your son has been arrested for the murders of two people. He may also be implicated in the disappearance of another individual. People you spent time in care with.'

Melrose balked, his face turning white, and sat bolt upright. 'Whoa, whoa, no way. Wait a minute. Ryan wouldn't do something like that. He's sixteen, for fuck's sake.'

'So why did you think he was in custody?'

'I didn't . . . I mean . . .' He stopped himself. 'No comment.'

'You're no helping your boy by keeping schtum you know. Or yourself.'

'No comment.'

Fraser noted that he was rattled. 'Aiding and abetting is a serious crime. How long is it you've still got to go in here again? Remind me.'

'All right, all right! I wanted him out to do some deliveries for me and maybe just . . .'

'I cannae imagine you mean Avon.'

'Ha fucking ha!' Melrose dropped his head into his hands. 'I cannae believe this,' he mumbled. 'Oh my God. That's not what I wanted him to do.'

Fraser looked at the man. Colour had drained from his already pasty face.

'What's not?'

'Hang on a minute, hang on a minute,' Melrose blasted. 'Gie me a chance to think.'

'What are you not telling me?' Fraser insisted.

'Please, DI Brodie, don't. I just wanted him . . . My boy.' Melrose looked broken. 'He didnae do that, he couldnae kill someone.'

'We have evidence to the contrary.'

Melrose fell back in the chair. 'I cannae believe this. Is he all right?'

'Like I already said. We're taking care of him.'

Melrose exhaled a shaky breath. 'Is Suzanne all right?'

Choosing his words carefully Fraser told him, 'She's coping.'

'Good, good. That's good at least.' Another long, shaky sigh, then, 'I thought he'd been picked up for the weed. Naebody telt me it was . . . that. If I knew that I'd . . . I'd—'

'You'd what?' Fraser asked.

'I only asked him to scare them a bit. Get them to pay their debts quicker.'

'Do you mean you asked him to threaten people?' Fraser suggested. 'Which people?'

'Hayley and Phil. They owed me more than money; they put me in here.'

'Who else?'

'Simon and Mark owed me money.'

'The same people you were in the home with. You're telling me that was a coincidence. And where's Phil Harrison?' Fraser urged.

'What? I don't know, I swear, I don't know.'

'Where has Ryan taken him?'

'I don't know. I didn't know he'd taken anybody anywhere!' Melrose shouted.

'Defeating the ends of justice will add a considerable amount of time to your sentence,' Fraser threatened him.

'I don't know anything!'

'I don't like it when folk lie to me, Andy. You should already know that.'

Melrose quickly leaned forward. 'Please, you have to understand. Ryan was always a bit different.'

'In what way?'

'He just was. He struggled to read like the other kids, and you know how cruel kids are to each other.'

'Aye, I do.' Memories of being bullied for being in care came back to Fraser.

'Ryan struggled to concentrate and was always skipping school,' Melrose continued. 'Having explosive outbursts. Rages even.'

On hearing that, Adam's face filled Fraser's mind. Ryan was like his brother in so many ways. The thought was horrifying.

'What did the school do about that?' Fraser was curious. School had done nothing to help Adam back then. The fact that he hadn't done anything for Adam either was a cross he bore every single day. Melrose's answer saddened Fraser.

Melrose scoffed. 'School did fuck all, that's what they did.'

Nothing had changed it seemed. Vulnerable kids were still being let down and people were still getting hurt as a result, and worse.

'So you and Suzanne, what did you do to help your son?'

Fraser's question seemed to knock him off guard.

'What could we do, we're not teachers.'

'I hear Ryan likes to start fires,' Fraser said. 'Up at Morag Thomson's place.'

'Interfering old cow told you he was there, did she?'

'Your son was caught on CCTV in that area.'

'Yes, well, don't go listening to that old witch, she doesn't know what she's talking about. Was she the only eyewitness?'

'It was Morag that identified him from the CCTV.'

'Well, I'd take that with a pinch of salt, Detective.'

'Why's that then?'

'She's got it in for me, so saying it was Ryan would have been the perfect opportunity to stick the boot in.'

Fraser stopped for a moment and watched Melrose's body language. Defensive, yes, but there was something else. Concern? Maybe anxiety.

'Why would she have it in for you?'

'I'm sure you've read my record; figure it out for yourself.'

'Tell me anyway.'

'I broke into the farmhouse a couple of times.'

'Why?'

'I was teaching Ryan,' Melrose said.

'Let me get this right. You were teaching your son how to burgle.' Fraser was appalled.

'Aye, he needed to know how to provide for Suzanne and the bairns if I got put away. Which turned out to be the case, didn't it? Thanks to you.'

'Seems a bit of a stretch to suggest that she would allow your boy to be charged with something as horrific as murder because of that.'

'I'm just telling you how it is from my side,' Melrose insisted. 'Have you spoken to Suzanne?' His voice grew softer when he said her name.

'Your wife has helped us with our inquiries, yes. Both she and her mother are assisting with our investigation into Ryan's escape too.'

Melrose's gaze fell to the floor. 'I'm not proud of the shit I've done to them.'

Fraser was surprised by his statement. 'I suppose being in here gives you plenty of time to reflect.'

Melrose coughed and turned his head away. Fraser hadn't seen that coming. He waited a moment before his next question.

'So. How well did you know Simon Carver and Mark Tait? Did something happen in the home?'

Melrose's gaze lifted from the table, and he focused dead straight on him. 'Carver. Was he one of them that got killed?'

Fraser nodded. 'Simon Carver and Mark Tait, along with Morag.'

'Morag! You never said she was . . . that she was . . . No. Please, no, she's just an old woman.'

'I'm afraid so.'

'My God. No, I didn't . . . not an old woman, no . . .' The news seemed to throw him. 'I've done some bad shit, but killing old women, that's a whole other level.' His disgust was obvious. 'You're not suggesting my Ryan has done that . . . Really?' His eyes seemed to be searching for something.

'All the evidence suggests his guilt, I'm afraid, but he will get a fair hearing. Just like everyone else.'

Melrose stiffened on hearing that. 'Yes, right. He's Andy Melrose's son. That fact alone works in the prosecution's favour, doesn't it.'

'I don't blame your suspicion, Andy, but your son, whether guilty or not, is being looked after and will be given as robust a defence as . . .'

'Defence! What kind of defence can me and Suzanne afford?'

'I believe your mother-in-law is funding your son's defence.'

Melrose looked shocked.

'That surprises you,' Fraser suggested.

'Have you met her?'

'Not yet, but I'm sure I'll have that pleasure soon.'

Melrose fell silent, then he sighed and asked quietly, 'What will happen to Ryan if he's found guilty? Will he go to young offenders at Polmont? He's just a bairn.'

Fraser thought about the answer carefully, because this question was asked out of genuine concern for his son. He felt that coming across the table at him.

'He's being assessed today by a psychiatrist and . . .'

'Good, good. So it'll depend what he finds, will it?'

His eyes pleaded with Fraser for an answer to comfort him. Fraser nodded.

'Good, good.' Melrose's body started to loosen, and his shoulders dropped. Then he sat forward again. 'I suppose this must feel like history repeating to you then.'

It took Fraser only a second to realise that he meant Adam. His own discomfort shocked him. But Melrose wasn't finished.

'I know your brother well,' he said. 'But then, everybody does, don't they.'

The case was too important for Fraser to allow his feelings to cloud the conversation. They had to find Phil before it was too late.

'This has absolutely nothing to do with Adam.'

'Of course it does,' Melrose pointed out. 'Everything you do is tainted by your brother.'

Fraser saw what was happening. Andy was trying to redirect the conversation away from Ryan, but time could be running out.

'Where's Phil Harrison?' Fraser urged again.

'I don't know!'

'If you're lying to me . . .'

'If I knew where he was I would tell you, I swear . . .'

Fraser was shocked to see tears on Andy Melrose's cheeks and couldn't help wondering if Johnny Brodie had ever shed a tear for the monster he had created.

49

6th May, 2 p.m.

Hayley's head still hurt, but her scan was clear. She was discharged with a hefty dose of painkillers, and was delighted to get out of there. For one thing, she couldn't wait to get out of the clothes she had been wearing and get clean. A boil wash was the next best thing to throwing her jeans out. They were 501s that she had found on a vintage site, and she hoped they would survive the wash. She'd been told that a patrol car would be parked outside her house just in case, and sure enough there was a skinny lad watching the building when she got home. That was reassuring, although she hoped he wouldn't be on his phone the whole time. Hayley wished she could remember what happened but the last image in her head was Denzil's concerned face looking down at her.

It was probably because he was a vicar, but Denzil had been so kind again, bringing her home from the hospital and offering to get her a few bits of shopping so she'd be able to stay at home and rest for the next two or three days like the doctor had suggested.

'Just me,' Denzil's voice called through the hall of her one-bedroomed flat above the studio.

'I'm in the kitchen. Kettle's on.'

'Great, I'm parched.' Denzil laid the three carrier bags onto the floor beside her then handed her a bunch of carnations.

'Aw, that's really kind of you.' She blushed.

'Don't get too excited. They were in the reduced bucket.' He smiled. 'But I thought you'd like them.'

'I love them.' She tried to stand but winced from the pain in her head.

'Let me.' Denzil laid them in the sink. 'You sit down.'

Hayley gave a playful salute. 'Yes, boss. But you really shouldn't have gone to so much trouble.' She grabbed her purse from the counter behind her. 'What do I owe you for that little lot?'

Denzil helped himself to a mug from the steel tree next to her kettle and poured water over the teabag.

'It doesn't matter. You just get yourself rested up.' He poured some milk into his mug and stirred before joining her at the table. He reached into one of the bags and lifted out a plastic box of chocolate doughnuts. 'I thought these might perk you up, too.'

'Oh, they look tasty.' Hayley helped herself, taking a large bite and savouring the sweet taste. 'Delicious,' she said, her mouth full of doughnut.

'Pig,' Denzil teased then reached into his pocket at the sound of his phone buzzing. 'Must be yours,' he said, after checking the screen of his.

'It might be Phil. I texted to let him know I was OK.' Hayley lifted her phone from the counter behind her but felt disappointment wash over her.

'Bad news?'

Hayley frowned. 'It wasn't Phil.'

'Who was it?'

Hayley was sure her face made it clear that the sender wasn't one of her favourite people. 'My mum.'

'She must have been worried about you.'

'Trust me. The only person my mum cares about is my mum.'

'Oh, sorry. So you two don't get on then.'

'You could say that.' Hayley slid her phone back onto the counter. 'I'm surprised not to hear back from Phil though.' She glanced at her watch. 'I guess he must be pretty busy.' She picked up her phone again and dialled Phil's number. 'Why does it keep going to voicemail?'

Denzil shrugged. 'Maybe he's lost his phone?'

'Then how can he text me?'

'Oh, I didn't realise he'd text you.'

'I'm really worried about him.' Hayley gripped Denzil's arm.

Denzil dropped his hand on top of hers. 'I'm sure he'll get in touch soon.'

'I hope so.' Hayley rubbed her fingers across her brow distractedly.

'Is your head still sore?'

'Aye, but it's more of a dull ache, I suppose. They said it would hurt for a while. I'll get a couple of painkillers.'

'I'll get them.'

'Thanks. I'm not sure what I would've done without you these past two days.'

'Just think of me as your good Samaritan.'

Denzil patted her shoulder then pressed two tablets from the blister pack and handed her a glass of cold water. 'Here you go. Look, would you like me to pop in on your pal? Tell him you'd like to see him.'

'Och, no, I can't ask you to do that,' Hayley insisted.

'It's no trouble, really. Maybe then you can relax properly,' he suggested. 'What's his address?'

'Thank you.' Hayley quickly scribbled it on a piece of paper.

Denzil's phone rang as she swallowed the tablets. 'It might be work,' he said, as he stepped into the hall. 'This is Reverend Martin, yes,' she heard him say, as he closed the kitchen door after himself.

Hayley drained the dregs of her own cup of tea and carefully stood up to make a second one. She stared out at the far-reaching view across the harbour.

'I'm sorry I have to go. As I suspected, it's work.' Denzil grabbed his jacket from the back of the chair and kissed her cheek. Hayley was unsure which of them was more shocked by his gesture. 'Er, I'll call you later?'

'Yes. Talk to you later,' Hayley smiled. 'And, listen, thanks again for everything you've done for me.'

'You're welcome. I'm just glad that you're all right.'

Denzil pulled the front door shut after himself. He nodded to the officer stationed in the patrol car across the street, then jumped when David Sutherland appeared from around the corner. He looked paler than he'd ever seen him. His addiction had hold of him again for sure.

'Rev,' David murmured, before walking in the opposite direction.

Denzil could only have been gone for ten or fifteen minutes when the knock sounded on her door. Hayley was confused not to find anyone standing there, but a box on her doormat caught her attention. It was addressed to her, handwritten, but had no postage, so she glanced around to see if she could spot who had left it. The box was about the size of a paperback, and the handwriting was neat. It was like something Amazon would send a book in, except it wasn't their packaging. She took the parcel inside and closed the door. It was light, lighter than a book. Her curiosity made her rip the heavy tape, flicking pieces onto the hall table as she struggled to get the thing opened. With the last piece of tape ripped off she tore into the top of the box. An odour hit her as soon as the end was exposed. It wasn't pleasant, but not bad enough to make her turn away.

Hayley peered inside the open end, then screamed and dropped the box. Some of the contents spilled out onto the laminate floor, a tinge of red staining the wood. Her heart raced, and the shooting pain in her head made every nerve in her body tingle. She barely made it to the toilet before she vomited.

Who would do something so awful to another human being, then send it as a macabre gift? A tongue. Maybe it wasn't real. Maybe it was someone's idea of a sick joke, but she wasn't hanging about to find out. It had to be the same person who had attacked her and ransacked her studio.

She snatched her gym bag from the top of her wardrobe and tossed it onto her bed. Whoever sent that abomination knew her address, and they weren't afraid to let her know they could find her. She wouldn't need to pack much. Just enough for a couple of days.

With her bag packed, Hayley tried Phil's number again, this time with a sickening feeling in the pit of her stomach. Her eyes welled with tears as she paced up and down her hallway.

'Come on, Phil, where are you?'

Hayley hung up then hit the call button again and again. 'Phil,' she begged. 'Please call me. I just need to know you're OK.'

50

6th May, 3 p.m.

Fraser stood to greet his brother when he was brought into the private room.

'Adam.'

'Fraser,' Adam replied. 'This is a surprise. First I get a compassion phone call, now this. Shame Dad couldn't die more often.' He chuckled.

'How are you doing?' Fraser asked, choosing not to tell him he was also there on a case.

'I'm fine, Fraser. How do you feel about it?'

Good question.

'I'm not sure his death has sunk in yet.'

'We knew it was coming.' Adam shrugged.

'Aye, we did, but . . .' Fraser took a breath. 'It's still weird.'

'When are you burning the old bastard?' Adam didn't mince his words at the best of times, but this was cold.

'I've not even begun to think about his funeral yet.'

'What about taking him out on a boat and chucking his body in the sea?' Adam's steely stare made the suggestion sound serious. 'Mind you I wouldnae wish his foul, stinking corpse on the sea-life. They dinnae deserve that.'

'That's not a realistic option, is it, Adam.'

'True, why waste money hiring a boat. You and Jenny should have a wee bonfire in the back garden.' He grinned. 'You'd probably need to take a Black and Decker to him first, though. God, I wish I could be there for that. We could toast some marshmallows on the bastard's flames.'

Fraser chose not to respond. 'Will you be applying to attend the funeral?' he asked. 'I'll need to factor that into the arrangements. I reckon the governor will allow it if I vouch for you.'

Adam grinned again. 'With you being such an upstanding member of society.'

'Maybe.' He smiled back.

'Nah, I'll pass. Send me a photo of his body, though. If I'm feeling low, I can take it out to cheer myself up.'

'I'll see what I can do,' Fraser replied sarcastically. 'Seriously though, Adam, how do you feel? Now that Dad's gone.'

Adam shrugged. 'Good. Actually, I feel great. What about you?'

'Aye, the same I suppose.'

'You only suppose,' Adam pointed out. 'I'd have thought you'd be just as delighted as me. I mean, you were there, too.'

'I know.' Fraser shuddered at the remark. 'How could I forget? I am happy. I am, I just feel a bit numb. Do you ken what I mean?'

'I'm afraid on this we are poles apart,' Adam said. 'There's no numbness here.' He patted his chest. 'Pure joy has replaced pure hate at last.'

Fraser knew he meant that. Maybe he was jealous of the simplicity in Adam's emotion. His brother's next comment was a surprise.

'How's Lisa?' Adam said quietly. 'I know how close you two are.' It was clear he wasn't sure how Fraser would respond, given the fact he had only uttered her name twice, perhaps three times, in the past thirty-plus years.

'She's fine.' Fraser stretched the truth rather than lied.

'She's still scared of me, isn't she?'

Why was he asking him this? Why now, of all times? Fraser took a moment and tried to look at his brother through Lisa's eyes. Wide staring eyes, frenzied like that of a madman, weren't what Fraser saw. But it was Adam's hands . . . What those hands had done appalled him. But he still loved the man, if not the monster. Adam was opening up. Was this Fraser's chance to ask about Ryan, about the similarities he saw in them?

'What was going through your head, Adam?'

His brother looked at him in confusion. 'What do you mean?'

'Back then . . .' Why was Fraser's heart racing like that?

Adam's eyes widened. 'Oh, you mean, *back then*.'

Fraser nodded, chewing on his lip. 'Aye.'

'There wasn't any room for anything in my head.' Adam tapped his temple. 'Except rage. Pure black, evil rage. It was suffocating me.'

Rage. That's what Melrose had said about Ryan.

Fraser swallowed hard. 'I didn't realise.'

'How could you? You had your own pain, mate.' He avoided catching his eye, coughing to clear his throat. 'Shit, Fraser, where's this come from?'

'I dunno,' Fraser lied. 'Maybe Dad, I dunno.' He should know better than to try and lie to Adam.

'That's no it.' Adam stared, narrowing his eyes. 'It's this case. I'm right, aren't I?'

Fraser heaved a sigh. 'Aye.'

'I knew there was something.' Adam pointed at him. 'Why did you ask me that?'

Fraser considered his next comment carefully, watching Adam's every gesture, every blink.

'My suspect is a teenage boy.' There it was. He'd said it. But he stopped short of saying it was Andy Melrose's boy.

Shit, Adam was shuffling uncomfortably in his chair.

'You think he's like me,' Adam said quietly.

'Not exactly, it's just . . .'

'Tell me about him,' Adam cut in, seeming more relaxed with the topic of conversation.

'He's sixteen.' Adam was the first person who hadn't been immediately appalled by this fact. He didn't even flinch. Fraser couldn't decide if he was relieved or scared by that.

'And you definitely think he's your man . . . boy.'

'Aye. I do.' Fraser chose not to share that he feared history was repeating itself.

'What's he done?'

'He's murdered three people, one of whom was an elderly woman, attacked another, and we suspect he's responsible for a disappearance.'

'And you think *I* can help you with that.'

'Yes and no.' Fraser shrugged.

'Is that because you think he's like me?' Adam stared, unblinking.

'No, not like you, Adam. Like you were back then. You're not that man now.'

'What do you want me to say?' Adam asked.

'Och, I don't know.' Fraser sat back in the chair. 'Forget I asked. It was stupid of me. I'm sorry.'

There was a brief awkward silence as Adam stared around the small room, and Fraser examined his fingernails. Anything to distract from his discomfort.

'So,' Adam began tentatively. 'You need my help. Is that what you're saying?'

'Don't worry about it; it's fine. I shouldn't have asked you to talk about the past. It was stupid and cruel.'

A brief smile came and went quickly from Adam's lips. 'I'd like to help. What else do you need to know?'

'How do I talk to him, Adam? I need to find Phil, I mean, our missing person. Urgently. Ryan is in custody but . . .' Fraser was flustered, realising he shouldn't have said names. 'The other victims were killed in their homes but there's no trace of our missing person anywhere.'

'Mmm.' Adam pursed his lips. 'I'm assuming all the victims are connected.'

'Yes, and they all received a suspicious letter.'

Adam's eyes widened. 'What did it say exactly?'

Fraser weighed up whether it was right to tell him. This was evidence, and Adam wasn't a police officer. He had to make a choice.

'I know what you did. I'll be seeing you.' There, he'd said it; there was no going back now.

Adam leaned forward, narrowed his eyes. 'Do you know what they did?'

Fraser shook his head. 'Not yet.'

'How are they connected?' Adam asked, just as a prison officer came into the room.

'Just five more minutes, mate,' Fraser urged.

The balding officer glanced at his watch, then threw a serious stare at Adam. 'You've got five minutes, no more,' he said and began to walk away again. 'Only out of courtesy to you DI Brodie.'

'Thank you,' Fraser replied.

'So you were about to tell me how they're connected.' Adam threw a look at the door behind him. 'Before we were so rudely interrupted.'

Fraser noticed that Adam's eyes had changed: his pupils were dilated; his body language suggested he was enjoying this.

'They all lived in the Lodge around the same time in the early nineties. My suspect is the son of a man who spent time there too.'

'Wow. The Lodge.'

'Aye.' Then Fraser frowned. 'It was after our time, obviously.'

'The early nineties?'

'Aye, do you know something?'

Adam screwed up his face, seemingly reaching for something. 'D'you ken what. I think there was something, but I'm damned if I can remember.' As he opened his mouth to continue, the door opened behind him again.

Fraser muttered an expletive under his breath as he held up his hand. 'All right, mate, I'm going.'

'If it comes back to me I'll call you,' Adam said as he rose.

'Sure, thanks, Adam. Take care.'

When Adam reached the doorway he stopped and turned to face his brother, seemingly with an idea.

'Your missing man. He's the key. He's getting extra attention.'

Fraser swiped through his phone as he got into the taxi for the airport, scrolling his contacts for Owen's number. Adam's words whirred round his head.

'He's getting extra attention.'

Phil hadn't been attacked at home or at his office. He'd been taken somewhere else.

'Owen, get over to Molly Carver again. I've got an idea,' he said, choosing not to elaborate on the source of the information. 'Ask her if Simon ever told her anything about Phil. Ask why he would be more important than the rest.' Shaking his head he listened, irritated, to Owen's questions. 'Just do it. I'm on my way back.'

As the taxi drew up to join a line of traffic Fraser called Carla, who was on her way to talk to Ryan.

'Ask him why Phil in particular. See how he responds to the focus being on Phil. I think he's the key to all this. It has to be something he did.'

51

The outcome of Ryan's psychiatric evaluation had come faster than any of them had anticipated. The forensic psychiatrist had deemed him not to be a suicide risk now, but concluded that keeping him in custody would be detrimental to his mental health. A secure foster home was the alternative she wanted for him, with strict conditions and a curfew. A footnote added that Ryan was the product of a chaotic and unbalanced home life. That wasn't a surprise.

It was a fair and honest review, Carla thought, as she drove to the house he had been placed in. She knew the family well: an older couple who had been fostering for two decades already. The conditions of his bail had been explained, and they had signed the necessary paperwork without fuss. Ryan had been fitted with an electronic tag; if he tried to leave he would be picked up immediately. The farmhouse was in the middle of nowhere and surrounded on all sides by acres of open farmland.

Carla pulled up outside the property and was struck by the silence, apart from the occasional call of the oystercatchers she knew to be in the area. Before she got out of the car, her phone rang. Dreading another call about her dire financial state, she was glad to see the station number on the caller ID. It was the uniformed officer who had been tasked with watching CCTV in an attempt to trace David Sutherland's movements: not a job she envied.

'Really?' she exclaimed, as the update filled in gaps that helped to clear David Sutherland. It saddened her to learn how difficult his life was, especially knowing about the family's financial problems.

'So the security footage from Ravi's has Sutherland there at the time. That's great. Thanks for letting me know,' she replied, then hung up and got out of the car.

Despite the daylight, the security light outside the backdoor blinked on. She had to shield her eyes when it temporarily blinded her. Nodding her head to acknowledge the uniformed officer stationed outside the property, she turned on hearing the door being unlocked.

'Are you DS McIntosh?'

'Yes, that's right.' Carla reached for her ID. 'Thanks for letting me come over.'

'That's no problem.' Penny Simpson held the door wide open for her and pointed inside. 'Please, come in.'

As she stepped in, Carla was met by the sight of a sheepish-looking Ryan Melrose sitting at a long pine dining table. The teenager flicked his eyes up briefly to acknowledge her before staring at the floor again.

'Hello, Ryan.' Carla smiled and took a seat opposite him.

Penny pulled out a chair from the dining table and sat. 'I'll sit in.'

'That's fine,' Carla agreed.

The sound of dogs barking echoed from another room.

'There are dogs here. That's nice. Do you like dogs, Ryan?' Whether they liked it or not, and as abhorrent as his alleged crimes were, Ryan was still a kid. 'What kind of dogs are they?'

When her question was met with a wall of silence while Ryan sipped from the mug he had been cradling, she added, 'Lovely place they've got here isn't it? Nice and cosy.' She removed her coat and slung it across the chair next to her.

This boy was proving a tough nut to crack, but Carla could be just as stubborn as Ryan. She stopped talking and sat right back in the chair, sinking into the thick cushions. She allowed her gaze to drift around the room, but without removing her attention completely from him. She required all of her senses to be on high alert. She envied the huge range cooker, and the large fireplace at the other end of the vast room, with what looked like a bread oven in the space above it. Carla knew the farmhouse dated to the sixteenth century with associated beams and low doorways.

'I don't know what you're wanting me to say. I'm not talking to you. Any of you,' Ryan finally said. 'And if he thinks sending a lassie will make a difference,' he scoffed, 'then he's even dumber than he looks.'

'All I'm asking is that you answer the few questions we've been trying to ask you, which, I'm sure you'll admit yourself, you've been rather stubborn about.' Carla looked directly into his eyes as she spoke, holding eye contact until he flicked his gaze briefly to the side. Then she was pleasantly surprised to see he returned his focus to her completely.

He leaned down and scratched the skin above his ankle bracelet.

'Is that bothering you?' Carla nodded down at his leg.

'No.' Ryan sat back up straight.

'It's better than the alternative, huh.'

'I suppose.'

'The Simpsons are nice,' Carla suggested.

'I suppose,' he repeated and slouched in the chair.

Carla found herself instinctively mirroring his slouched posture. This boy didn't look capable of committing the horrors she'd seen. He was a thin lad, not tall but not short either. Just kind of average. So average that it was unnerving to think how easily he could blend in. But Fraser was right, they had to follow the evidence.

'Do you understand why it looks like you've committed these terrible crimes?' she asked.

Ryan looked her dead in the eye, his demeanour changing. 'No comment.'

Carla sighed. She wasn't getting through to him at all.

'Tell me about Phil Harrison,' she asked, as Fraser had instructed. Ryan didn't flinch. 'And the kids' home your dad stayed in. Did he and Phil know each other?'

'No comment.'

'Where did you take him?' Fraser had been positive that Phil was at the centre of this.

'No comment,' Ryan repeated.

'Why did you—'

Before she could finish, Ryan cut in, 'You can't ask me these things. There isn't a solicitor here and you haven't read me my rights.'

He wasn't wrong. She would have to tackle this differently.

'Murder is a very serious crime to be accused of,' she reminded him.

'No comment,' Ryan replied again.

'Why was the murder weapon under your bed?' she persevered.

'I don't know.'

An answer at last. Carla spotted a bead of sweat glistening on his forehead. 'Ryan, look at me,' she murmured. The teenager squeezed his eyes shut then sniffed back what looked like real emotion. Carla frowned.

'I don't know how it got there, all right.'

'Who else had access to your room?' Carla asked.

Ryan sighed. 'Nobody else, but I didn't put any knife anywhere and I didn't kill those people. I wouldn't be surprised if you lot put it there.'

Finally a comment they could work with. It was baffling. Ryan's fingerprints weren't on the knife but Carver's blood was. His prints were in both Carver's and Tait's homes, though. They were waiting for confirmation whether they were at Phil Harrison's or Hayley's studio.

What Ryan said next shocked her.

'I didn't kill Morag either.' Ryan's eyes filled with tears.

At last he was talking. He looked like a teenager now, a child even, visibly upset when he said Morag's name.

'Did you know Morag well?'

Ryan nodded. 'She could sometimes be a nosy bitch but she was all right,' he sniffed, wiping his nose with the back of his hand. 'Me and Dad weren't very nice to her though and that makes me feel like shit sometimes.'

It seemed like he was about to add something. Carla waited patiently, as hurrying him might stop his flow. Her instinct proved right.

'That weirdo, Mark something, I ken she helped him as well.' He stared down at his hands, picking the skin from round his thumbnail.

'Do you mean Mark Tait?'

'I cannae mind his surname but the guy that lived in the caravan.'

'Have you been to the caravan, Ryan?' Carla asked. This was promising.

Just as she thought she was making progress Ryan stared right at her and frowned, seemingly considering this answer more carefully.

'Did Morag say I had?' he said, eventually.

'You were caught on CCTV near the caravan.'

Ryan shrugged. 'So?'

'Your prints are in the caravan.'

'So?' He shrugged again, looking away from her.

This was ridiculous. He was playing her. Was he stalling because he knew where Phil was and that time would eventually run out? Perhaps that was his plan for Phil.

'Did Phil deserve it?' she asked, unsure who was more surprised, her or Ryan.

'You've got no idea.'

'Then tell me, Ryan. Maybe Phil did; he sounds a bit dodgy to me, to be honest.' This was risky, what would the boss say about this technique? 'You can't have done this alone. It's too big. The letters, what are they all about?' She might as well jump in with both feet. Phil's life was at stake. 'Ryan, please, just tell me what happened. Who are you protecting?'

A look of confusion crossed his face. 'I'm not protecting anyone.'

'Ryan.' Carla was pleading now. 'Let us help you. This doesn't have to go any further. Just tell me where Phil is.'

What he said next was confusing, but in keeping with how this interview had gone.

'I found her, all right?' he shouted, staring dead straight in Carla's eyes before dissolving into a flood of tears. 'I went to see Morag, and she was just lying there. I tried to help her, but it was too late.' He struggled to keep his emotions under control. 'So I panicked and left her. I just left her.' He was sobbing now, and his words sounded like a weight had been lifted off him. 'I don't know anything about Phil or Mark or that Carver guy, all right.'

'I think you've asked him enough,' Penny Simpson said bluntly.

'Did you touch Morag's body?' Carla asked urgently.

Ryan's eyes were red from crying. 'Yes, of course. I had to check if she was breathing, but . . .' His words dissolved into tears again.

'I think that's enough, don't you?' Penny Simpson had moved closer to the backdoor and was unlocking it as Carla grabbed her bag and coat.

Carla reached out her hand and laid it on top of Ryan's.

'Thank you, Ryan. I'm sorry I've upset you, but you've been really helpful.'

Carla was almost at the door when he called after her.

'I did see someone up at the farm. Don't know him but I think he was helping Mum a while back. A vicar from the community centre started coming round after Dad got sent down.'

'Do you know this man's name?'

Ryan shook his head. 'You'll have to ask Mum.'

Carla shot him a brief smile then nodded at Penny Simpson, who shut the backdoor barely seconds after Carla had stepped outside. She scrolled quickly to Fraser's number.

'Boss, it's me. Ryan has just told me he saw someone up at Morag's. I'm going to check it out.'

Then a text hit her phone. It was the bank: a payment reminder. Carla wiped away an involuntary tear and got in her car. She had no idea where she and Dean would find the one thousand pounds they needed to clear the outstanding mortgage payments by the end of the month. The stress of their problems was taking its toll. She felt terrible about the way she had snapped at Owen in the car when he'd nearly answered her phone. If she wasn't so humiliated by it all, she would explain. Fraser had always said she should come to him if she needed help. Maybe it was time to take him up on his offer.

Molly flopped down onto the sofa, dropping her rucksack on the floor at her feet. A tear formed in her right eye when she saw their wedding album on the coffee table. She picked it up and, her heart pounding heavily, she flicked through the pretty silver pages. Simon had been so handsome and she had felt like a princess. A cliché but true.

They had been married for ten years before Simon had told her. Ten years, two weeks and three days to be precise. She'd never seen her husband cry like that, either before or since. The enormity of it meant the day was etched irreversibly in her mind.

Molly had promised him that day that she would keep his secret, no matter what.

52

6th May, 6 p.m.

Owen indicated onto the road towards Molly Carver's place. Fraser wanted him to press her about Phil Harrison, believing that he was the key to all this. The thought struck Owen, and not for the first time since starting work for Fraser Brodie, that a little bird had given him a clue. A little jail bird. His *unpaid consultant*. Unless crisps and chocolate bars were written up as petty cash. But who better to have an insight into this kind of brutality than Adam Brodie?

The scenery on Lewis, which some might call bleak and empty, was stunning to Owen and made navigating the single-track roads a pleasure – if you didn't mind the loose suicidal sheep. When he had first moved to the island he thought every sheep in the world must graze that landscape. A few near misses had helped teach him to adapt his driving style.

Molly opened her front door as he turned into her driveway. Her expression suggested she was expecting to see DI Brodie instead of his underling.

'Hello again, Mrs Carver,' Owen said, as he locked his car.

'Come in,' she said and walked away, leaving the front door wide open for him to follow her back inside.

Owen closed the door after himself and headed into the kitchen after her.

'Have you found Phil yet?' she asked, tension in her voice. She looked like she'd been crying.

'Not yet, but we're working on it as a matter of urgency.' He tried to reassure her, but Molly didn't look convinced.

'Something's wrong, I know it is. Haven't you been able to locate his phone or something . . . First Simon, then Mark, now . . .' She didn't finish the sentence.

'We're working on it, Mrs Carver, don't worry.'

'Oh, I know, I know, it's just . . .'

'Is it unusual for Mr Harrison to not respond?'

'Highly unusual. He should be back by now, and I can't understand why he hasn't phoned me. He missed Hayley's art exhibition as well. That was weird. The two of them are joined at the hip.'

Owen took his notebook out of his blazer pocket and noticed that Molly's hands were trembling.

'I'm sorry, please sit.' Molly pulled a chair out.

'Thank you.'

Molly rummaged in the drawer next to the fridge then shut it before moving to the sideboard. 'Where is it . . .' She closed one drawer and opened the next. 'Ah, here.'

Molly pulled a heavy-looking photo album out, as well as a handful of loose photographs, and dropped them onto the table in front of Owen. She flicked through the photos then slid one across to him. 'This is the most recent one of Phil I've got.'

Owen picked it up. Phil's smiling face stared back at him. He was holding up a huge fish. Not being really knowledgeable about fish, Owen assumed it to be either salmon or brown trout.

'Would you mind if I keep hold of this one?' he asked.

'Of course, of course.' Molly flipped open the album and thumbed the pages until she found what she was looking for. She turned the album to face Owen.

She pressed her thumb onto one in particular. This photo showed four children, probably mid-teens, smiling and standing outside a large building Owen knew to be the kids' home. The Lodge. As he looked closer he recognised a very young-looking Mark Tait and Simon Carver. He glanced between the page and the recent photo of Phil Harrison. Another one of the group looked a bit like him but the boy in the picture wore his hair very long. If this was Phil he was looking very chummy with a pretty blonde girl who was beaming at the camera. His arm was draped across her shoulder, their heads leaning against each other. The four friends. Two dead. One seriously assaulted. One missing.

'Is this Phil?'

Molly leaned over and pressed a finger on the picture.

'Simon, Mark, Phil and Hayley,' she said, dragging her finger over each of them as she said their names. 'David, my brother-in-law, was friends with them too, but he was more on the periphery if you know what I mean. He didn't live in the kids' home like the others did. He wanted to be as close as they were, but they never really let him in.'

As Owen opened his mouth to ask something else, a car screeched to a shuddering halt on the driveway, almost hitting Molly's front doorstep. He got up and peered out through the kitchen curtain to see a terrified-looking woman come running their way. The sound of the door bursting open was accompanied by shouting.

'Molly!' she screamed. 'Molly! Lock the door, he's after me. He knows where I live.'

Owen intercepted her in the hallway. 'Hey, hey, what's happened?'

The woman was shaking so much her legs were twitching.

'Hayley!' Molly pushed past him. 'Come on, come through.' She helped Hayley to a seat at the kitchen table. 'I'll get you a glass of water.'

Hayley's teeth were chattering loudly. Molly had to help her hold the glass.

'What's happened?' Owen pressed her.

'My bag, it's in my bag,' she stuttered, dropping her face into her hands.

Owen slipped on a pair of gloves from his pocket then carefully unzipped the bag. He removed the box and peered down, unsure at first what he was looking at.

'What's in it?' Molly exclaimed, wrapping her arm around Hayley's shoulder.

'I can't look at it again, I just can't. Get it away from me.'

Owen reached his gloved hand a little way into the box. The contents felt cold and firm. A pungent odour wafted into his nostrils.

'God, I can't. I just can't.' Hayley ran from the room, with Molly following close behind her.

Owen heard Molly trying to calm her down as he peered in the open end.

'Bloody hell,' he shuddered, almost dropping the box.

He fished a plastic evidence bag out of his blazer and sealed the package away. He ripped off the gloves and stepped outside. Glad to be out in the fresh air, he scrolled through his contacts for DI Brodie's number.

'Owen. What's up?' Fraser yawned at the other end of the phone. Owen could hear the sound of an airport tannoy in the background as he updated him. 'Where the hell was the officer that was supposed to be watching the place?' Fraser said, horrified. 'You and Carla get over to Harrison's place. This isn't looking good at all. I'll meet you there when I can.'

Mark, Simon, Hayley and Phil. Childhood friends with a secret. Something that had made someone very angry indeed. It was time someone told them exactly what it was.

53

6th May, 7 p.m.

It was Suzanne Melrose who opened the front door. Carla needed her to confirm her suspicions about a certain vicar.

'What do you want?' she asked abruptly.

'I need to talk to you again,' Carla told her. 'Can I come in?'

'Can I say no?'

Carla considered this. 'I suppose you can, yes, but it's about your son.'

Suzanne walked away without replying, leaving the door wide open. Carla closed it after herself.

'Is he all right?' Suzanne asked.

'Ryan is fine, yes.'

'That couple are looking after him all right, are they?'

'They're a nice family. Don't worry. He's safe.'

Suzanne's gaze fell to the floor. 'Listen, I'm sorry about what we did. It was wrong to help him.'

'It wasn't very clever. You've got yourselves into a heap of trouble.'

'I know.' Suzanne sighed.

Carla chose to move the conversation forward. 'Ryan told us about a man who has been helping you recently. He couldn't remember his name.'

Suzanne frowned as she lit a cigarette, took a huge draw and blew smoke towards Carla. 'What man?'

'He said it was the vicar from the community centre. Has someone been coming round?'

Suzanne flicked her gaze sideways. 'Maybe. What's that got to do with anything?'

'Who?' Carla asked.

'Look, it's no secret that I've been struggling since Andy went to Barlinnie.' Suzanne sucked another huge draw and tapped the cigarette into a round, glass ashtray on the coffee table. The living room door opened.

'I've told you before I don't want you smoking inside.' It was Suzanne's mother. 'Oh, hello, Detective. I didn't see you.'

'Hello again.'

Carla watched Suzanne stub the cigarette straight out.

'I'll leave you to it,' her mother added and left as quickly as she had arrived.

'My mum doesn't like me smoking in the house.'

'I heard her,' Carla said. 'So who's been helping you?'

'Like you said, the vicar. He brings me shopping and he's collected my prescription a couple of times.'

'Which vicar? Which church?'

'Oh, I cannae mind which church. I dinnae bother with all that. It was my social worker that put me in touch with a group at the community centre. You know, a parent-and-toddler group.'

'Was it Reverend Martin?'

'Reverend Martin. That's right.'

Carla's mind ticked over fast. 'Denzil Martin.'

'Yes, that's right. That's what I said.'

Carla's phone rang as she headed back to her car. Owen.

'I'm on my way,' she said and headed straight to Phil Harrison's place, thinking that they should have another talk to Reverend Martin.

54

6th May, 8.15 p.m.

Carla looked surprised to see the Range Rover pull up outside Harrison's house. Fraser had come straight there from the airport.

Fraser quickly joined her and Owen outside the bungalow. He popped his head in the front door to see Forensics sweeping the place. He shuddered to think of the shock it must have been for the two women seeing the contents of the parcel Hayley had received.

'Do we think that the tongue is Phil Harrison's?' Owen asked.

'Well, if it's not then there's another poor sod out there that we don't know about yet,' Fraser said bluntly. 'What did Hayley say about it? Did she see who left it? Where the hell was the officer who was supposed to be watching?'

'The officer is adamant he saw nobody. We're still trying to figure it out, because he insists he never left the patrol car. Hayley said her friend had just left and minutes later her doorbell went and the box was there.'

'Friend. What friend?'

'Reverend Martin,' Owen said.

Carla frowned. 'Did you say Martin?'

'Aye, he brought her home from the hospital.'

'Mmm,' Carla replied. 'That man seems to get everywhere, doesn't he.'

Fraser caught her eye. 'What are you thinking?'

'This Reverend Martin seems to be a one-man support network for this town,' she suggested.

'It's his job though, isn't it,' Owen said. 'Stornoway isn't exactly a big place.'

'Owen, organise a background check on him,' Fraser insisted. 'Find out everything you can and see where he was before coming to Stornoway.'

'Will do.'

Then Fraser looked at Carla. 'Go and speak to the two women again. I want to know everything there is to know about Phil Harrison. He is the key. He has to be.'

'Aye, will do,' she replied.

As Owen retreated Fraser called out, 'When you're done, grab a mask and a pair of overshoes. You're coming into the house with me.'

'Sure, boss.'

As he walked from room to room Fraser noted that Phil Harrison kept a clean home. The bed was made. Floors were clear. Kitchen was tidy apart from a single glass, bowl and spoon on the draining board. It was the home of a man who lived alone. There was a vase of tulips on the kitchen window ledge which he hadn't expected to see. Fraser pointed to the dishes.

'Dust these for prints then bag them.'

In Harrison's bedroom there was a walnut desk with two drawers on either side. Fraser pulled open the top one, finding nothing but work stuff. Notebooks, files. He flicked through every one, but there was nothing to indicate where Harrison was. He sat back in the chair, staring round the neat, well-kept room. There wasn't a single item of clothing out of place, no dirty washing on the floor. The smell of fresh sheets wafted towards him.

Owen's face peered round the bedroom door. 'This place is clean, boss. No sign of a struggle. Nothing.'

'What does this say to you, Owen?' Fraser pressed him.

Owen took a breath before answering. 'Whatever happened to him didn't happen here. The dog hasn't picked up anything either.'

'Come on, let's go,' Fraser said as he stood, Adam's words still whirring round his brain. '*He's getting extra attention.*'

Based on Hayley's sinister parcel, Fraser feared they were already too late to save the man.

* * *

As he pulled into his drive, the figure standing in the doorway with Napoleon at her side wasn't a surprise. It wasn't convenient, but she was there now.

'I hope you don't mind but I let myself in with your spare key.'

'Hello, Lisa,' Fraser replied. 'Of course I don't mind.'

'I should've asked if it was all right but . . .' She shrugged. 'I was on the ferry before I'd thought much about it to be honest.'

Fraser stared through the doorway at the small suitcase behind her. Living so close to the ferry port in Skye that sailed to the isle of Harris and Lewis made these kinds of last-minute trips easy for Lisa.

'It's fine. I've told you before, you're welcome here any time.' He dropped a single, gentle kiss on Lisa's cheek. 'How was the ferry?'

'It was all right,' she replied, flicking her black fringe out of her blue eyes. 'How's work?'

'Busy,' was all he could say.

'You look tired.'

As soon as she'd said that Fraser yawned. 'Och, I'm all right.'

'Go and sit down. I'll make us some tea,' Lisa smiled at him. 'Have you eaten?'

As inconvenient as her visit was, the sound of a pot of tea right then was bliss. Realising he couldn't remember when he'd last had a proper meal, his stomach rumbled.

'I wouldn't mind a sandwich, actually,' he admitted, following Lisa into the kitchen. He flopped down onto one of his oak dining chairs. Yawning again, he said, 'I'm sorry. You're right. I'm knackered.'

'Maybe the job is too much for you these days. You're not getting any younger,' Lisa suggested.

Fraser laughed. 'Aye that's what Ad—' Then he stopped.

They both knew what he had been about to say.

Carla smiled gently as she sat down on Molly's sofa, haunting memories of three days ago still very fresh in her mind.

Hayley closed her eyes. 'I can still see it now. God, it was horrible.' She shivered.

'I know this is a daft question,' Molly asked. 'But it was definitely, you know Phil's . . .'

'Stop it!' Hayley shouted. 'Stop, please. Don't say it.'

'I'm sorry,' Molly took her hand. 'I'm sorry.' She looked at Carla. 'I just can't believe this is happening. I keep hoping someone is going to shake me and wake me up from a horrible, horrible nightmare.'

'Do you still have the texts that you've received from Phil's number?' Carla asked.

Molly nodded and handed her phone to her. 'Haven't you been able to trace his phone?'

'I'm afraid not,' Carla told her, disappointed not to have better news.

'That's strange,' Molly added. 'Don't you think? It's like one minute it's on, then it's not.'

'Oh, shut up, Molly!' Hayley shouted. 'Just shut up.'

'Hayley, come on. Calm down; that's not helping,' Carla insisted.

'Well, someone has to do something! He can't have just disappeared off the face of the earth!'

'Do you still have the messages you got?' Carla asked.

'Of course I do.' Hayley scrolled. 'Here.' She handed her iPhone over.

'Thank you.' Carla took it and read through the messages. At first glance it appeared Phil was genuinely away on business. He'd said the same thing to both women.

'He's dead, isn't he?' Hayley said it without looking up from fiddling with her cuffs. 'I mean, he has to be, doesn't he?'

What the hell could Carla say? Except the truth. But then Molly took over.

'Come on. We can't fall apart now. Phil needs us to be strong. He needs you. He loves you, Hayley.'

'I know,' Hayley sobbed. 'I love him too. I always have.'

'Oh, sweetheart.' Molly hugged her tight.

'Phil was always there for me.' Hayley was sobbing, clinging on to Molly's shirt. 'Even when . . .' Suddenly she stopped, wiped her face and sat up. Looking straight at Carla she added, 'I'm sorry. It's just that he was . . . is . . . was . . . oh, I don't know,' she cried. 'My best friend.'

'What's going to happen now?' Molly asked.

'Well, we're going to arrange for somewhere for Hayley to stay.'

'You mean like a safe house!' Hayley exclaimed. 'Oh my God. He's forcing me into hiding.' She stood and walked to the window. 'I'm here, come and get me! I'm not hiding from you! Come and get me!'

Molly shot a concerned look at Carla. 'Why don't you let her stay here? I'll take care of Hayley. It's what Simon would want.'

'No, I don't think that would be a good idea,' Carla told her, as she approached Hayley at the window. 'Come on away from there. Let's go and sit down.' She took her arm. 'Come on.'

'Why can't she stay here?' Molly said. 'If he wanted to get me he would have done it by now. He knows I'm alone now.'

Hayley allowed her body to soften to Carla's touch, then she pulled away.

'He doesn't want to hurt you, Molly.' Hayley heaved a weary sigh. 'I would only be putting you at risk by staying here. It's me he wants.'

55

7th May, 9 a.m.

CS Andrew Everett had joined the morning's briefing, his serious expression a reminder of how bad things were. He had suggested to Fraser that another couple of detectives from Inverness should join them, but Fraser had declined for now. A couple of the island's uniforms had been seconded instead. The experience would do the pair good, he assured Everett. The truth was Fraser didn't want anyone else trampling over his case.

'Morning, boss,' Carla said quietly.

Fraser noticed she looked tired, and wondered if her sleep was as disturbed as his was as a result of this case.

'Carla. Did Hayley get settled all right?' he asked.

'Aye, after she calmed down she did,' she replied. 'Poor woman was a nervous wreck. She wanted Molly to come but obviously I explained why that wasn't possible. Molly actually suggested that Hayley stay with her. The two women seem close.'

'Good, good, I'll head up there and talk to her myself after this bloody—' He looked at Everett and stopped to correct himself. 'After this press conference.'

Fraser hated the damn things, even if it was just a small handful of journos who would send the copy over to the major networks for him. He had been disappointed not to find Everett offering to do it. Knowing his face would be seen on Facebook and Twitter – or X, or whatever it was called these days – was a new burden he had to shoulder. But if it helped them find Phil Harrison he'd do a hundred conferences.

'OK, so the tongue has been sent off for DNA but I think it's safe to assume at this stage that it belongs to our missing person, Phil Harrison,' Fraser said. 'We've taken a toothbrush from the house for comparison, haven't we?' he asked for clarification.

'Aye,' Owen answered him.

The phone on Carla's desk in front of him rang, the interruption irritating Fraser. But before she had a chance to pick it up he did it. He listened intently to the caller before hanging up. 'Reverend Martin is in reception. Carla, when we're done here, could you go and talk to him? Apparently he's quite insistent on talking to one of us. Has the background check been carried out?'

'We're waiting for the details, boss,' Owen informed him.

'He's here?' Carla said. 'Interesting.'

CS Everett's phone chirped with a text, and he blushed slightly when he read the message before making his excuses and scurrying out of the room. Weird, Fraser thought. The man had been adamant he wanted to be there.

'So these four were in the home together. Andy Melrose too but Hayley insists he wasn't part of their group.' Fraser pointed at the old photo of Simon, Mark, Hayley and Phil that he'd pinned to the board. 'Have you got the file the social worker sent over?'

'I have, yes, but there's something weird,' Owen said.

'Weird how?'

'There seems to be some information missing.' He opened a file on his laptop to show him the anomaly he had spotted. 'See how this jumps from there' – he tapped his finger on the screen then dragged it down – 'to there.'

Fraser and Carla both stared, noticing how the dates jumped by two months.

'And here, look, it's the same on Phil's and Mark's.'

'That can't be a coincidence,' Carla pointed out. 'What's that all about?'

Fraser scanned the entries on all four teenagers' social-work files, his eyes coming to a halt on Hayley's.

'Good work, well spotted.' Fraser stepped back. 'Owen, you go to Dianne Petrie's, see if she can explain that. Ask her what happened during that period and why it would be left out.'

Owen made a note on his pad as a ping sounded from his laptop. 'Hang on, boss. Here's the background on Reverend Martin.' He scrolled as Fraser stared over his shoulder.

'Ah, that's interesting,' Owen said and turned to Carla. 'He's only been a minister for a couple of years. Stornoway is his first parish.'

'What did he do before that?' Fraser asked.

'He was a banker in Edinburgh.'

'Unusual career move,' Carla suggested.

'His accent sounds like he's from here though. How old is he?' Fraser pressed Owen.

'Erm, forty-one.'

'A mid-life thing, maybe,' Carla said, as she grabbed her bag from the back of her chair.

'I'm sure you'll ask him that when you speak to him.'

'Will do.'

Ryan Melrose looked up from eating his cornflakes when Penny Simpson brought the landline phone to him.

'There's a call for you.'

'Who is it?' Ryan asked sullenly, wiping milk from his chin.

'It's your dad.'

Ryan's eyes stretched wide as he quickly took the phone from her.

'Five minutes,' Penny insisted before leaving him alone in the kitchen.

'Whatever,' he muttered, placing the handset to his ear. 'Dad, I didn't know you were allowed to phone me.'

'Aye, son, but I'm no allowed long. I just wanted to see that you're all right.'

'I'm fine, Dad.'

'Are they looking after you all right?'

'They've put a tag thing on me and there's a cop outside, but . . .' Ryan sighed. 'But it's fine.'

'Good, good. I've been worried.'

'Don't worry. I'm OK.' Ryan paused, took a breath then said quietly, 'I miss you, Dad.'

'I miss you too, son,' Andy replied. 'So *everything* is all right then.'

'Aye, Dad, there's no need for you to worry. Absolutely *everything* is better than all right.'

56

7th May, 10 a.m.

'Reverend Martin, please follow me,' Carla said and led him through into one of the interview rooms. She ran a finger over the radiator and realised it must be on full blast given the heat in the small room.

'Thank you.'

'Take a seat.' She pointed to the chair opposite her, as she removed her cardigan and slung it across the back of the chair. 'What can I do for you?'

'It's Hayley. I can't find her and she's not answering my calls.'

'Reverend, I can see that you're worried about your friend, but I can assure you she's perfectly fine.'

Denzil frowned. 'Then where is she? She's had a head injury recently and I'm worried about her.'

'I understand that but I can assure you that she's fine.'

'So you keep saying,' Denzil said sternly. 'But where is she?'

'Like I said, Hayley is fine. She's safe.'

Denzil frowned. 'What does that mean, *safe*?'

'Like I said, please don't worry about your friend, she's all right.'

'I'm just concerned, that's all.'

Carla noted that his jaw had tensed.

'She's a very vulnerable woman and her recent head injury makes her even more so.'

'We're aware of her head injury, Reverend Martin,' Carla mentioned.

'Look, there's something else that I can't really, I mean, I shouldn't really say but . . .'

'Oh, yes?'

261

'It's something very personal. She wouldn't want people knowing. So, please, just tell me where she is so that I can check on her.'

'And like *I* said, she's fine. Your concern is noted and will be passed on to Hayley.'

Denzil leaned forward sharply in the chair, gesticulating with his hands. 'Look, I don't think you understand the seriousness of . . .'

'And you don't seem to be getting the message, Reverend Martin.'

Denzil leaned back again. 'Forgive me. I'm just worried, what with everything that's been happening.'

'I know. We're taking care of her, I promise.'

A look of confusion filled his face again. 'You're taking care of her. What does that mean exactly?' Then his eyes stretched wide. 'Has Hayley been arrested for something? Oh my God, what is she supposed to have done? Because I can assure you she's pretty much been with me since the attack.'

'Hayley hasn't been arrested.'

'Then what's going on?'

'I'm not in a position to tell you any more than that at this time,' Carla said.

Denzil reached for her arm. 'You're scaring me now. Is she hurt?'

Carla's brief hesitation in answering made him gasp. 'Oh God, she is, isn't she? I need to see her. Where is she?'

'I'm sorry, but that's all I can tell you for now. Why don't you leave a number I can contact you on, and I'll let you have more information when I can.'

'Never mind.' Denzil stood up quickly and knocked his chair backwards, before picking it back up and apologising.

'I can see you're worried but, please, trust me, she's fine.'

A thin smile crossed Denzil's lips. 'I don't have any choice but to believe you, do I?'

'Before you go,' said Carla, 'how well do you know Hayley?'

Denzil sniffed. 'Not that well.'

'Do you know any of her other friends?'

'I know of one, some bloke called Phil that she's been trying to get hold of. I offered to go and check on him for her actually.'

'Oh,' Carla's eyes widened. 'And did you talk to Phil?'

Denzil shook his head. 'No, I couldn't get an answer. She does seem pretty worried about the guy. He didn't even turn up to her exhibition which was odd. Apparently they're best friends.'

'Thank you, Reverend, I'll take that on board.' The more she talked to him, the more Carla found she didn't like the man. She should probably feel bad about that, because he was a man of God. Carla decided to press him on the information they had just discovered. 'I gather you've not been a minister on the island for long,' she said.

Denzil frowned at her. 'Why on earth are you asking me that?'

'Where were you on the morning of the third of May between eight and ten?' Carla looked him dead in the eye. 'And that night.'

'What day was the . . . third? Friday, erm . . . Just let me get my diary.' Denzil rummaged inside his jacket pocket while Carla waited, quietly watching. 'Why are you asking me this?' he added, flicking through the pages.

'Where were you?' Carla repeated plainly.

'Well, on the third I was doing my weekly visit to the nursing home at Carloway and then I took the evening service. Which was the reason I couldn't check on poor Mark until the following morning.'

The pair stared at each other until Carla looked away first. She would be checking those alibis as soon as possible.

'Now if there's nothing else, I really need to be going,' Denzil said, as he stood.

Carla had no choice but to watch the man walk out.

57

7th May, 11 a.m.

Hayley poured boiling water over the teabag of a brand she didn't recognise, in a mug she didn't own, from a kettle she didn't like, in a tiny flat that wasn't hers. All because some sick freak was trying to scare her – very successfully. Tears weren't far away every time she breathed out.

Images of the disgusting contents of that parcel kept flashing into her mind no matter how hard she tried to shut them out. A horrible pink tongue. Hayley hadn't slept last night; she didn't think she would sleep ever again.

She was grateful to find a bottle of white wine in the fridge, which she thought a little strange but wasn't going to question. She opened the cupboard above the kettle, then closed it. No wine glasses. It seemed the horrid little flat didn't have any, so she filled a mug with wine. It was a brand she knew to be cheap but didn't care. It was a bit early for a drink, but under the circumstances who would blame her?

She flopped down on the sofa, the cushions flattened through years of use. A pile of magazines on the coffee table caught her attention. She picked one up, flicked through it then tossed it down. Then another. Then another. It was no use. Hayley couldn't concentrate. Focusing on anything other than the image of the tongue was impossible. That sight would forever be etched in her mind. It was a struggle to remember Phil's face properly. He was always such a good-looking guy, even as a teenager – tall, dark and handsome – and he had liked her, really liked her, from the moment they met in the home. He'd paid her attention, listened to her, always supported her. No matter what. But perhaps if he hadn't, then . . . Hayley had to push those thoughts down. It was too horrible to contemplate.

But now he was gone, and so were Simon and Mark. She felt alone in the world. Molly was lovely, but she wasn't a friend like the others. Hayley felt closer to Denzil than Molly for some reason despite only knowing him for a couple of days. There was a warmth to him, probably because of his job and there was a familiarity about him. Whatever it was, she was grateful he cared.

The horrifying conclusion that she was next on this sick, twisted killer's list sent shivers that she couldn't control over her whole body. But that detective kept asking her about Ryan Melrose. Why would he hurt them? It made no sense to Hayley. It didn't even make sense for Andy Melrose to do this. They may have all spent time in the home but Melrose didn't know anything, did he? Who the hell had found out their secret?

She sank half of the mugful of wine. The warmth it sent through her finally distracted her from her fear. The next gulp was bliss too. She swallowed back the remainder and went back to the fridge to refill it. She thought of Reverend Martin. Such a sweet man. He'd been so kind to her, even making her see that her disastrous exhibition hadn't been so bad. There was always next time.

She took the refilled mug of wine through to the bedroom and flopped down onto the edge of the bed. The lumpy mattress made her come to a sudden stop, spilling some of the wine onto the hideous pink carpet.

'Oh, bugger,' she whispered and rubbed the spill in with her bare foot. She sighed and gulped half of the mug's contents down in one, struggling briefly to swallow it. Then she guzzled down some more.

The relaxing sensation that was washing over her felt good. Even her shoulders felt less tight. She sank the remainder of the cup then fell back onto the bed. The ceiling had stains on it. One big one with a trail of thinner ones shooting away from it. Water marks. Hayley shuddered to think of the state of the bathroom in the flat upstairs. Her eyes wandered through the intricate pattern of lines and swirls, sending her into an almost hypnotic trance. She was aware of the fuzzy head the wine had given her – she had drunk half a bottle in ten minutes, fifteen at a push. That wasn't a sensible idea given there was a madman out to kill her. There was no way she could fight off a killer in her state.

She noticed there was a phone plugged into the wall on a dated glass cabinet in the corner of the room. Hayley needed to talk to someone. One call couldn't hurt.

'Come on, come on,' she urged as she listened to it ring. Twice, three times, four times, five times then, 'Hi, it's me,' she cried.

58

In the end Andrew Everett did make a loose offer to do the press briefing, but said it in such a way that he left Fraser feeling he had to refuse. The superintendent looked distracted as he left the briefing.

Fraser prepared himself to face the half-dozen journalists in front of him. A couple of freelancers he recognised were there too. It seemed news of this case had already spread. He coughed to clear his throat and took a long sip from the glass of water on the table behind him.

'Hello everyone, and thanks for coming at such short notice.' Fraser held up the photo of Phil. The picture had been blown up to A3 size in hopes the camera could pick out the details better.

'Our concerns are growing for the whereabouts of this man. Phil Harrison has not been seen for two days and his friends are becoming increasingly worried about him, because it's out of character for him to stay out of contact for this length of time. He has a close network of friends on the island who are anxious to talk to him, as are we.'

Fraser's heart was racing the whole time, but he knew he had to continue. He took a deep breath and ploughed on, regardless of his anxiety.

'If anyone has seen or spoken to Mr Harrison in the past two days, or knows where he is, then please contact your local police. I'm not in a position to take any questions at this time, however details will be made available through Police Scotland's social media. Thank you.'

He started to walk away, the sound of mumbling voices behind him, before a woman's voice broke above the noise.

'DI Brodie, is Mr Harrison a suspect in your murder inquiry?'

Fraser turned back to face her. He recognised her as one of the freelancers who was well known for the more salacious stories.

'I won't be taking questions at this time,' he repeated, attempting to walk away again.

'Perhaps the public will be more willing to help if they have the full story,' she added.

Fraser could happily have throttled the woman, and all the eyes on him made him feel uncomfortable.

'As I've already explained, I'm not in a position to answer any questions at this time.'

If her first attempts had irritated him, then what she said next floored him.

'What about the tongue? Do you believe it's Phil Harrison's tongue?' She didn't take her eyes off him once when she spoke. 'If it is then surely you must assume he's already dead.'

Fraser stared at her in disbelief. How the hell could she know about that? How could she say that?

He wasn't hanging around to hear what else she had to say and shoved open the door to the back of the station, muttering expletives under his breath. Paying her a visit to find out where she got that information had just been added to his list of tasks. But first he wanted to talk to Hayley Stevenson himself.

'Looks like your brother's got a lot on his plate, doesn't it?'

Adam Brodie turned away from the television to see Andy Melrose standing behind him.

'Looks that way, yes.'

'I'm surprised he had time to come and visit me, then,' Andy added.

The comment briefly unsettled Adam. 'Why did he need to talk to you?'

Andy grinned. 'I'm afraid I won't be taking questions at this time.'

He walked away, leaving Adam wondering if it really had been him Fraser had come to see at all. Or was that visit just something he'd felt he had to do while he was there? A swirl of anger built in him and he tried to push it down. Fraser wouldn't do that. But it niggled him. The suggestion that Andy was the real reason for his visit spun in Adam's mind. Life in Barlinnie was damn hard and the knowledge that his brother cared kept him going. Fraser was the only person he had in the entire world. The women who'd written to him over the years begging to marry him didn't really care for him. There was a name for believing you're in love with a serial killer, but he couldn't recall what it was. He got up and followed Melrose, catching up to him quickly. He tugged his shirt to get his attention.

'What did Fraser want with you?'

'What's the matter? Are you jealous?'

Andy laughed and tried to turn away, but Adam punched him once, hard on the jaw, dropping him like a stone to the floor.

Roars rang out round them.

'Whoa, come on, Andy, man, you just gonna lie there and take that?' A voice came from the crowd.

Adam heard his heart thump loudly in his ears. Images of his father flooded his mind until it was Johnny Brodie he saw on the floor. He dropped to his knees and pounded his fists into Andy Melrose over and over and over until the man stopped moving.

'He's bloody killed him,' a man's voice rang in Adam's ears.

59

7th May, 12.30 p.m.

'Yes, can I help you?'

'Hello Celia, I was wondering if I could come in and have a word with Dianne.' Owen smiled at her, although the look she was giving him said she had no memory of ever meeting him before. Seeing her again confirmed that it was odd that Dianne didn't mention her mum's memory problems.

He reached into his blazer pocket and showed her his ID, which made her frown, peering from behind her glasses to examine it closely. The old woman looked worse than before. The clothes she had on were dirty and the stench of stale urine made him want to turn into the fresher air behind him.

'Mum, who is it? Oh, hello Detective.' Dianne Petrie joined them at the door with a towel and a pair of pyjamas in her hand. It was then Owen noticed the faint sound of a bath running in the background. 'Go and wait inside, Mum, I'll be in in a minute.'

Celia turned to walk away, but not before saying, 'I'm sorry I forgot your name, dear.'

'It's fine, Mrs Petrie. I'm Owen.'

'Owen, that's right.' The old woman pointed her finger knowingly at him. 'Owen.'

He watched the back of the frail old woman until she disappeared through the kitchen door at the end of the hall.

'I'm sorry, but you've caught us at quite a bad time. I was just running Mum a bath.' Dianne indicated upstairs. 'But come in, come in. I'll go and switch off the taps. I'll not be a minute.' The sound of a mobile phone came from the kitchen. Dianne sighed. 'Please go through,' she said, as Celia walked towards her with the mobile in her hand.

'This is ringing again,' Celia said, as she handed the phone to Dianne.

Owen shot Dianne a sympathetic glance.

'It's OK, Mum, I'll call them back.' Dianne took the phone. Her jaw tightened momentarily before she declined the call and stuffed the phone into her pocket. 'Excuse me, I'll not be a tick,' she said and headed upstairs.

Owen smiled at Celia who was staring at him, her eyebrows narrowed.

'I'm Owen,' he reminded her.

The old woman's eyes widened. 'Yes, that's right, Owen. Can I get you a cup of tea?'

'No, thank you. I'm fine.'

It wasn't long before Dianne had rejoined them.

'Right.' She blew out a sharp breath, a pink flush to her cheeks like she had been running. 'What can I do for you?' she asked and flopped down on the red sofa under the living-room window, opening it a crack to allow the breeze to cool her face. She looked at Celia. 'Sit down, Mum. Owen is here to talk to me.'

'Ah, right, yes, yes, of course.' Celia sat down on a large armchair just inside the living-room door.

'Please, have a seat,' Dianne pointed to the other end of the sofa.

Owen sank into the cool leather cushion. Being able to give his tired legs a rest was bliss. He tried to stifle a yawn; he didn't want to appear rude, but this case was taking a toll. He took out his phone and pulled up the link to the case notes with the missing entries, then handed it to Dianne who grabbed a pair of reading glasses from a drawer in the glass-topped coffee table.

'What's this?' she asked.

'I was wondering if you would know why these have been removed?' He shuffled closer until he was so close he could smell her floral perfume.

'I'm not sure what I'm looking at here.' Dianne frowned and scrolled through the entries.

Owen took the phone back, pointing to show her exactly what he meant. 'Why do all four of these kids' files have the same gaps in their notes?'

Dianne removed her glasses and tossed them onto the table. She sank back into the sofa.

'There couldn't have been anything noteworthy to say,' she suggested, avoiding his eyes.

Owen closed the document and then put his phone back in his blazer pocket, disappointed and a little perturbed at the same time. Either there really was nothing to see – although it would be a hell of a coincidence to see it in all four files – or she was being evasive. But why?

'Could it have something to do with the technical breakdown the other day, do you think?' He watched her frown momentarily before seemingly remembering.

'No, but you weren't the only person to fall foul of that IT crisis that day. Our entire elderly social-care team had a blackout, leaving twenty old people in distress that day.'

'What about the paper notes?' he pressed her.

'That I can explain,' she smiled. 'I found them in the wrong filing cabinet.'

'And they match what I just showed you?'

'I imagine so. I can't see why it would be any different.'

'I'd like to take a look at the paper copies, just to reassure myself. I'm sure you understand.'

'Of course,' Dianne agreed, just as her phone rang again.

Again Owen watched her clock who the caller was and decline the call. Her body language stiffened, and she stuffed the phone in her pocket.

'Dianne, I need the bathroom.' Celia stood up slowly. 'Oh,' she added, as urine leaked down her leg.

'I'll leave you to it. I can see you've got a lot going on.' Owen shot a small smile at Celia as he passed. 'But if you could arrange to have those notes delivered as soon as possible today that would be great. I'll see myself out.'

* * *

Dianne watched him go, sighing as her phone rang again.

'Dianne!' Celia insisted. 'I need the toilet.'

'Hang on, Mum.' Dianne lifted a finger and headed into the kitchen to answer the call privately. 'Hello. I'm sorry I couldn't pick up earlier. Things have been a bit hectic here.'

Dianne listened to what the caller said.

'Hang on a minute.' She covered the mouthpiece. 'I'm just coming, Mum.'

Dianne returned her focus to the call and peered out through the kitchen curtain, watching the detective's car reverse out of her drive.

'Text me the details,' she replied to the caller, unsure how she felt about what she'd heard. She walked to the bottom of the stairs and heard Celia humming a tune to herself. 'Just give me half an hour to get Mum sorted.'

60

Fraser took the flight of stairs two at a time to the flat Hayley had been tucked away in, which was three miles away from the centre of Stornoway. It was a simple block of four flats, built in the early nineteen-eighties. It was basic, blending quietly into its surroundings with neighbours unaware of this particular property's purpose. Hayley's phone had been taken from her so there wouldn't be any way for the killer to find her. Fraser certainly hoped so anyway. Her life was in their hands right now. Finding that tongue must have been terrifying, especially when it looked increasingly likely that it belonged to her best friend Phil Harrison. Fraser's brief press conference had so far given them zero useful information from the public, but it was early days and official news spread very slowly on the island. Unofficial whisperings were gathering momentum, he imagined. Everett had asked him why Fraser felt she needed protection when Ryan Melrose was already in custody. His answer was simple. Ryan couldn't have delivered that gruesome package to her home so there must be someone else willing to do his dirty work for him.

Fraser pressed the doorbell, listening to it ring loudly inside the flat, and waited for Hayley to answer. When he heard no movement he rang again. Perhaps she'd fallen asleep. This time he held his finger on the bell for longer. Still nothing. He leaned closer to the door and hammered his knuckles on the wood, trying the door handle too.

'Hayley,' he called out.

While he waited for a response he received a text from Owen. It was disappointing to read that Dianne had not been helpful, although hopefully once she sent over the paper files they would get to the bottom of the suspicious gap in the timeline.

Someone had asked Fraser something many years ago – he'd forgotten who it was now, but remembered their question as if it had been asked yesterday. Did he ever want to read his own social-work file? He recalled his answer clearly too. It was an absolute no. That time in his life was over, and that's how it would remain. There was never any point in raking up the past.

When his knock got no answer he slammed his palm on the door and listened for movement inside. He opened the letterbox and called out.

'Hayley, it's DI Brodie, could you open the door please?' He kept his ear pressed up against the chipped paint of the door frame.

'Shit,' he rasped when there was no response.

He snatched his phone out while he banged again.

'Aye, this is Fraser Brodie. I need urgent assistance at the Cromwell Street flats. Possible danger to life so I need to gain entry for a welfare check.'

Fraser scrolled through his iPhone contacts for the phone number of the property.

'Come on, come on.' At last he found it, immediately hitting the call button. If she was asleep the sound of the phone would surely wake her.

Fraser heard it ring and ring and ring.

'Shit.' He hung up and hammered the door with his fist. 'Hayley. It's DI Brodie. Come and open the door!' He banged on the door again, rattling the letterbox at the same time.

The din had obviously disturbed the neighbour – Fraser turned to see the door of the flat opposite opening. A elderly woman's curious face appeared.

'What's all the racket about?' she began to say, until Fraser held his ID out to her.

'Have you seen the woman who's been staying in this property?' he asked.

'I didn't know there was anybody living there these days.' The old woman gave him a blank stare and closed her door again.

Fraser crouched to peer through the letterbox and hit redial for the flat's number. This didn't look good.

'How much longer for backup?' he snapped down the phone to the station, not pleased with their answer. He pressed the end call option and stuffed his phone away before surging towards the heavy door, instantly regretting it. Pain immediately spread over his shoulder, making him wince. His arm still hurt from Ryan Melrose upturning the table at him. 'Fuck . . .' he started to say, when Owen's face appeared at the top of the stairs.

'I heard the call,' Owen said.

'I cannae get any answer and she's not answering the landline in there either.'

'Stand back.'

Owen gave the door one perfectly timed kick in exactly the right spot which sent the door flying open for them to run inside. Fraser entered the property first and surged from room to room calling Hayley's name. Everything about the emptiness in the place felt wrong. She knew not to leave the flat and was instructed not to let anyone in either. Where the hell would she want to go? Hayley had been scared stiff. Scared enough to do exactly as she was told – or so they had thought.

'Anything?' Owen asked.

Fraser shook his head. 'Shit. We've got her phone.'

'I'll check who the last caller to this landline was,' Owen said. He dialled a number then shook this head. 'Nothing.'

'Did she make any calls?' Fraser asked.

'Hang on.' Owen hit redial, then looked at Fraser. 'It's a mobile but it's switched off.'

The sound of sirens meant the backup was finally close. 'Bloody typical. Late as usual,' Fraser muttered while he rubbed his painful shoulder.

He watched the two female officers running from their patrol car into the block. 'Stand down,' he instructed them as they ran towards the front door.

'Sorry, DI Brodie, we got here as fast as we could.'

Fraser sneaked a glance at his watch to see that it had only taken them eight minutes and, under normal circumstances, given the single-track roads they'd had to race through, that might not have been too bad. But what if Hayley had been lying unconscious inside the property? Now wasn't the time for recriminations. Finding Hayley was the priority.

Fraser turned to Owen, 'Get that number traced as soon as possible!'

Hayley exhaled slowly and sank back into the passenger seat. She leaned her head gently against the window and yawned.

'Close your eyes and get forty winks,' Denzil suggested.

Hayley lifted her head up and faced him with a gentle smile. 'Nah, I'm fine. I feel better already now that I'm out of that disgusting hovel. Did you see the stains on the ceiling?' She shivered and yawned again. 'I'm sorry.'

'Don't be.' He reached his hand over and ran his fingers over her cheek gently.

Hayley squeezed her eyes tight shut, but failed to halt the single tear that ran onto his hand.

'Hey, you're OK. You're safe now.'

'I know.' Hayley snuffled and pulled away to clean her face. 'I don't know what I would have done without you,' she said, while gazing out of the window.

'I'm happy to help.'

Denzil turned onto the single-track road that led out of town, the sparse landscape opening up in front of them as far as the eye could see. The road was overshadowed by hills on either side. He narrowly avoided a sheep once they were on the other side of the cattle grid.

'Where are we heading?' Hayley asked as she yawned again.

'You said you wanted to get away from it all.'

'Yes.'

'Well, that's exactly what we're doing,' Denzil said, scanning the empty road behind him in his rear-view mirror. 'Help yourself to a bottle of water if you like. There's some in the bag at your feet.'

He turned to smile at her then refocused on the huge open expanse of road in front of them, the flash of white from a white-tailed eagle catching his eye above them. Such a majestic creature, he thought.

'Thanks, Denzil,' Hayley said, as she took a bottle out and sank almost half in one gulp.

'You're welcome.'

61

7th May, 2 p.m.

Carla was on her way out of the station to visit the Carloway nursing home to check out the Reverend's alibi. The senior nurse had said she would be happy to talk to Carla and would check the visitor's book once she found it, stating that things were a little chaotic in the home at present due to staff shortages. Typical, Carla thought before she heard, 'Can I get some help here?' A harassed-looking taxi driver, his balding head glowing with drops of sweat, helped Celia into one of the black plastic chairs lined up in a row inside the police-station foyer.

'It's fine, I'll handle this,' Carla told him, alarmed to see the dishevelled sight of the old woman, who had a large pile of brown folders in her hand. Her hair was still wet and all she had on was a pair of pyjamas.

'She was just wandering and so I stopped. She's a bit confused the poor auld soul.'

'Thanks for bringing her here.' Carla patted his arm. 'You've done the right thing.'

She approached Celia who was eyeing her suspiciously, her glare a sign she was trying to recall her name.

'Hello Celia, what brings you here?' Carla asked with a smile, crouching down to her level.

'I had to tell someone,' Celia insisted and thrust the folders towards Carla's face, sending her almost flying backwards.

'OK,' Carla replied, as she stood back up. 'Why don't we go and have a chat, then?'

'With all due respect, lass, you're not a policeman, are you?' Celia said. 'I'll wait for one of the policemen, so if you could tell him I'm here that would be great.'

Carla didn't argue with her. In Celia's mind Carla didn't seem like a police officer. To Celia's generation, especially in her mental state, police officers were all men.

'Why don't I take you through to find one, then.'

Celia frowned and stood to follow her, clutching the folders tightly. 'That would be great. Thank you, dear.'

Carla led the old woman away from the front desk and unlocked a side room. This time Carla was glad the little room was as warm as it was. Celia looked freezing, not to mention fragile. It appeared that her confusion had increased rapidly in recent days.

'Take a seat, Celia, I'll go and see if I can find a policeman for you.'

Carla walked out, looking back at the old woman's smiling but concerned face. She was still unwilling to loosen her grip on the folders. Carla took out her phone to send a quick text to Fraser about Celia, and saw that the message she'd written earlier about Denzil Martin hadn't sent. Damn the station Wi-Fi, it was as hit and miss as the phone signal on the island. She'd wanted him to know how frantic the Reverend had been when she wouldn't tell him where Hayley was. How she was beginning to think they needed to talk to him further . . . Something was off with that man.

A text came in as she resent the message. It was DI Brodie. Carla was appalled to read that Hayley wasn't in the safe house and that they were tracing the number she'd called. She rang Fraser immediately.

'Hi boss, check out if that number is Reverend Martin's. They seem close. He's been chummy with Suzanne Melrose recently too. He must know Ryan.'

Sure, being sent a tongue was horrific, but Hayley should not have left the safe house, with him or anybody. Carla didn't trust him.

'Hello again, Celia,' Carla said, as she sat down opposite the old woman, who was still holding the folder in her hands.

Celia's expression was serious as she stared at Carla.

'I'm DS McIntosh.' Carla tapped her own chest.

'Oh, yes, that's right,' Celia replied, slowly uncurling her grip on the folders.

'What's this you've got here then?'

'Peter will be so cross with me when he finds out but . . .' She stopped and slid the folders closer to Carla. 'I've not been able to sleep a wink since . . .'

'Peter who?' Carla asked and took the folders from her.

'Crichton, Peter Crichton, he's the senior care worker at the Lodge,' Celia informed her, looking at her as if she should know him. 'I'm a care worker there too, you see, and . . .' The old woman became distressed. 'Oh, I shouldn't have come.' She tried to snatch the folders back.

'Whoa there.' Carla laid her palm over them. 'It's all right, this conversation is strictly between you and me.'

It seemed to take Celia a moment to process what Carla had said. 'I'm not sure . . .'

'I promise Peter doesn't have to know.' Carla lowered her voice and laid her hand on Celia's. The subtle human touch had an immediate effect, and as she watched Celia relax, Carla wondered what year the woman thought it was. She had described working at the Lodge in the present tense.

'I know it's a silly question, but what date is it today, Celia?'

'What?'

'What's today's date?' Carla repeated gently, as she clicked the pen on. 'Just for my notes.'

'It's the third of, erm, no, it's the fourth.' Celia fiddled with the fabric on her pyjama sleeve.

'That's right, thank you,' Carla reassured her. 'And what year is it again?' she added, hoping the question didn't sound too ridiculous.

'It's 1992, of course.' Her expression changed again. Her concern was growing. 'You're sure Peter won't have to know?'

'I promise.'

Just as Carla had suspected. Whatever Celia was here to report was something she thought had happened recently.

'If you're sure.' Celia's searching eyes met Carla's and a thin smile grew on the old woman's face, her wet hair hanging limp across her shoulders.

Carla gave her hand a squeeze, then opened the first page of the folder on top of the pile. Her eyes scanned the sheet of A4 in disbelief until Celia frowned at her.

'You didn't tell me your name, dear.'

'I'm Carla.'

'Carla. What a lovely name.'

Carla needed to focus her whole attention on these seemingly innocent sheets of paper in her hand, though there was nothing innocent about the alleged behaviour reported here. But that wasn't the most horrifying part. The handwriting on the pages was almost a complete match for that on the threatening letters each of the victims had received. Carla was sure they'd seen it somewhere else before, too . . .

'Excuse me a wee minute, Celia.' Carla quickly left the room and dialled Fraser's number.

'Boss,' she urged down the line. 'You need to see this.'

62

Molly Carver sipped the tea that had gone cold while she had been going through another photo album. She wiped her face that was wet from crying and got up to switch the kettle on again. Looking out of the kitchen window while she waited for it to boil, she stared at Simon's BMW. She had always hated that car, and the irony that she was now free to get rid of it wasn't lost on her. There had been so many times she would have dearly loved to see the back of it, but there was no way she could part with it now.

She snatched up the keys and headed outside. She tightened her grey cardigan closer against the cool breeze. She felt her hair hanging lankly, realising that she had not showered that day. Molly waved to her next-door neighbour, Catherine. She had been so kind since Simon's death, letting her stay when the police needed to take over her house because it was an active crime scene. She didn't have to do that, but Molly was grateful for the support. The neighbours had never been particularly close but a tragedy like that was exactly the kind of thing to pull a community together.

That first step back into the house, the home she had always shared with Simon, had been horrific.

Sitting in the car made her feel closer to him. She sat in the passenger seat and looked across at the driver's seat. Molly could see him there, his wide grin staring back at her. That goofy grin had frustrated her so many times over the years. It had also softened her when the couple had argued. She could smell him as if he was sitting right next to her. Closing her eyes gently, she inhaled, savouring his scent as if he'd never left her.

Simon was so kind. The whole town must wonder why someone would do something like this to a man who did nothing but help the community. He'd run the local amateur football league as well as the kids' team. Surely they didn't believe that young Melrose boy to be capable of doing something so vile. Molly couldn't. She knew his father to be a bad man, but the carnage and horror she had found that morning . . . No teenager could do that, could they?

Molly knew she should be angry with Simon. If he'd come clean all those years ago then he would still be alive. Maybe *she* should've spoken up once she learned the truth. Was that the source of her gut-burning guilt: her lack of action? But she had made him a promise that she couldn't break.

Thoughts of his funeral forced their way into her head. How the hell was she going to get through that? Where did she even start in organising it? Reverend Martin would have to explain everything to her. Simon didn't even believe in God; after his childhood he'd said there couldn't be one. Would it be right to have the funeral in a church? Her mind whirled in a confused fog.

The sound of her ringtone in her cardigan pocket woke her from her trance, and she reached across the seat as the image of Simon smiling at her fizzled away. Her eyes stretched wide when she saw the call was from Phil's number. This didn't make sense.

'Phil, is that you?' she said anxiously. When her words were met with silence she repeated, 'Phil!'

The sound of breathing echoed down the line.

'Phil,' she said again, softly. 'Is that you?'

It couldn't be him, could it? How she prayed it was. Molly wished his whole disappearance was a misunderstanding and that this was Phil reaching out to her. Perhaps he feared she was angry with him for leaving her alone to grieve. Or was he in hiding? Something that he wouldn't be blamed for under the circumstances. Molly wasn't angry. She just wanted him home, safe. But the tongue, that horrible tongue . . .

'Phil?' she called out one more time, before the line went dead.

Molly called him back immediately and listened to the call go straight to voicemail.

'Phil, it's me. I just want to know you're all right. We've been so worried. Me and Hayley. Something horrible has happened.' She knew she was rambling. 'The police have taken her to a safe house. Please, Phil, just call back.'

There were so many things she wanted to say. She hung up and exhaled a long slow breath before trying his number again. This time she heard a digital voice tell her that the number had been disconnected. Thoughts spun in circles in her mind. What the hell was going on? She typed a short text.

Call me back. I need to hear from you. Something's happened to Hayley.

Molly thought mentioning Hayley would get his attention. She knew how he felt about her and had done since they were teenagers. The four of them had been thick as thieves back then. Simon, Mark, Phil and Hayley, but it was Phil and Hayley that were the closest. They had always been closer than the others. Now it seemed that what had bonded the group was tearing them apart.

The reply wasn't what Molly wanted to see. She frowned.

Message not delivered.

She frantically called the number again and hung up before the digital voice could finish its message. She tried to send the same text again, then again and again until the tears came.

Message not delivered.

'Oh, Phil, what's happened to you?'

Molly tried one last time before dropping her phone onto her lap and breaking down completely. This didn't make any sense. Tears fell again, as Molly wondered how she could possibly have any left.

Message not delivered.

Ryan Melrose paced up and down, struggling to catch his breath. It felt like all the oxygen in the room had been sucked out. He had to get out of there. As he headed for the door, his foster carer entered the room.

'Ryan, what's wrong?' As she reached out to help him, he pushed her away.

'Get off me.' He was hyperventilating now, fearing he was having a heart attack.

The enormity of it all was getting to him, overwhelming him. He snatched open the backdoor and ran outside to catch his breath. Fresh air had never tasted so pure, even the cow shit smelled good.

'What are you doing?' the officer on guard duty asked, startled by Ryan's sudden appearance.

For a moment Ryan didn't know what to say but this had gone far enough. Too many people had already been hurt.

'Erm.' The teenager took a huge breath. His dad was going to be angry, but Ryan just couldn't do this anymore. 'I need to speak to a detective,' he said. 'That woman though, not the big old guy. It's urgent.'

63

7th May, 3 p.m.

As soon as the detectives had returned to the station to regroup and figure out their next move, Carla was about to share the full details of what she'd discovered from Celia when her phone rang.

'Hang on, it's the foster carer's number,' she said.

'Is it?' Owen asked, frowning. 'What's happened?'

Carla screwed up her face and waved her hand at him, instructing him to leave her be. 'Hello Penny, this is DS McIntosh.' She listened to her say that Ryan wanted to talk to her, emphasising that it had to be her. 'I'm not able to come right now.'

The sound of the phone being snatched from Penny came next. 'Carla, is that you?'

'Yes, Ryan, it's DS McIntosh. Are you all right?'

'Aye, I'm fine.' He stopped, seemingly wondering what to say next.

'Penny says you want to speak to me.' Carla filled the silence for him.

'Erm, yes, I . . .' He was stuttering now.

'It's OK to tell me, Ryan,' Carla reassured him, hearing the tension in his voice.

'This is a bad idea. I'm sorry I bothered you,' he blurted, but before he hung up Carla managed to intervene.

'Ryan, it's OK to tell me. I'm here, I'm listening.' This felt huge.

'Dad told me to!' The teenager's words came at her in a rush.

Carla flashed a wide-eyed glance at Fraser. This conversation should be under caution. On speaker-phone at least. Her heart was pounding but if she put Ryan off, he might never speak again.

'All right, Ryan,' she said softly, sweat gathering under the collar of her white shirt.

Fraser was frowning at her, his full attention on this call. 'Keep calm,' he whispered. 'You got this.' He threw a glance at Owen and indicated for him to step back.

Carla didn't feel the confidence that he was suggesting.

'He'll be so angry with me.' The teenager was crying now.

'He's your dad, he loves you. He will want what's best for you.' Carla feared that fact wasn't exactly true but it was what Ryan needed to hear.

Heavy, choked breathing came down the line before:

'He told me to hurt them, to scare them, said he needed to send them a message that he shouldn't be messed with.' Ryan sobbed. 'But . . . but . . . I didn't . . . I swear I didn't.'

'Who did your dad want you to hurt?' Carla asked, keeping her voice low, steady, teasing the facts from him. 'It's OK, Ryan, you can tell me.'

The short silence was followed by, 'Simon, Mark, Hayley and . . .'

'And who, Ryan, tell me,' Carla urged.

'Phil Harrison, but I didn't hurt him.'

'Do you know where he is? If you do you have to tell me . . .'

Carla looked at Fraser, a flush of heat spreading on her face.

'I don't know, I swear. I don't know where he is. I didn't take him. I didn't hurt any of them.'

'All right, Ryan, that's really good. You've done the right thing.'

'Have I? Then why doesn't it feel like that?' Ryan asked, sniffing back tears.

'Because sometimes doing the right thing is the hardest thing. Did your dad tell you why?' Carla pressed him further, feeling the pressure of the two sets of eyes on her.

'He thought they were the ones that got him put away, said they needed to pay, but I didn't, I promise I never hurt anyone.'

'Who else knew about all this? Did your mum know?'

The answer came quick and sharp. 'No! My mum doesn't know anything about any of this. I . . . we . . . didn't kill those people. You have to find who did before that guy gets hurt!'

Before she could respond the call ended abruptly. 'Ryan . . .'

'Well, what did he say?' Fraser urged as his own phone buzzed. He looked surprised when he saw the number calling. 'I need to take this,' he told the two detectives and walked away, closing his office door softly behind him.

'What did Ryan say?' Owen asked Carla.

'That his dad asked him to scare them, nothing more. The lad is bricking it. He's terrified he's going to be jailed for murder. This is so messed up. We've been looking at a teenager when, all along, there's been someone else out there, probably laughing at us.'

'The killer is in those notes, Carla, we'll get him, don't worry.' Owen pointed to the case files that Celia had brought in. 'Come on.' He sat, grabbing the folder on the top of the pile. Mark Taits's social-work file.

'Look at the writing,' Carla urged. 'The circle over the I instead of a dot.'

'Is that . . .' Owen gasped.

Carla opened her mouth to speak but the sharp tone of her phone ringing cut her off. 'DS McIntosh,' she answered. It was the senior nurse telling her exactly what she had suspected. 'Thanks, you've been really helpful.' Carla's hunch about the man was right.

'What is it?' Owen urged.

'The rev wasn't in Carloway when he said he was.'

'Hi, what's going on?' Fraser asked abruptly. He had been surprised to see the governor on his caller ID; he had only called Fraser twice in all the years Adam had been inside, and neither time had been for a good reason.

'It's me.'

Fraser was confused to hear Adam's voice. 'Aye, I can hear that, what are you doing phoning me on this line? What's happened? This number coming up on caller ID scared the shit oot of me.'

'I've lost my phone privileges so . . .'

'What, then how are you able to call me now?' Fraser's confusion only deepened.

'Never mind that. Governor realised this was too important to wait,' Adam urged. 'I found out what happened in the home. It was bugging me since we spoke so I asked around. We had left by then, but there's a guy in here that lived there at the time. Says that one of the care workers was accused of sexually abusing a kid there. Lost his job but that's not all. He went and topped himself. Left behind a wife and son.'

'When was this?'

'Early nineties. A lassie said he touched her. She had a couple of pals that corroborated her story as well.'

'*I know what you did, I'll be seeing you,*' Fraser muttered.

'Fraser, are you still there?'

'Aye, aye, I'm here.'

'The wife topped herself soon after, couldn't cope with it all. Son became a banker apparently, moved off the island. He says he thinks he might be a vicar now. Goes by his mum's maiden name, the guy said.'

'A vicar!' Fraser blurted. 'What's his mum's maiden name?'

'Erm, oh God, Maxwell, I think, or Marshall. Something with an M. Aye, I don't know how much help that is but . . .'

'Could it be Martin?' Fraser's mind whirred. How did they not see this?

'That's it, yes, Martin.'

'Adam, you have no idea how helpful you've been.'

'Does this mean I get an extra packet of Hula Hoops next time then?' Adam's attempt at a joke made Fraser feel uncomfortable.

'Listen, I have to go, Adam.'

'Sure, see you . . .'

Fraser had hung up before Adam had finished. This was too important to wait. The missing entries in the files. Someone didn't want them to find out about the accusations. He would have to find out why Adam had lost his phone privileges later.

64

7th May, 3.45 p.m.

Hayley struggled to open her eyes and was disturbed by the ringing sound in her ears. She was cold. It was so cold that her teeth chattered. Confusion was quickly followed by fear when she realised her hands were tied to the chair and her bare legs were bound at the ankles by thick rope. Her head felt fuzzy like she'd been drugged.

What had happened to her clothes? All she was wearing was a thin T-shirt and a pair of knickers. Voices carried through the fog in her mind, but they sounded far away and distorted, like a radio struggling to find signal. Why did her head hurt so much . . . and that smell, what was that foul smell?

'She's awake,' a woman's voice said tentatively.

Hayley wriggled her hands, but they were tied tight. Footsteps grew closer.

'Welcome back. Your nap was a little longer than I had planned.' The man's laugh was sinister. 'You had me worried there for a minute. I thought I'd messed up the dose in all the excitement.'

'Denzil? Is that you?' she slurred, drops of saliva dripping from her lips.

'Hello Hayley.' He smiled. 'How does it feel to be betrayed?' He stared at her, a manic look in his eye, before looking away. 'I'd like to be able to say I'm sorry that it's come to this . . .' He tutted, shaking his head. 'But I'm a man of the cloth, Hayley. I'm afraid I can't *lie*.'

'Denzil, why are you doing this?' Hayley cried.

'Are you really going to pretend you don't know? But then you do like *make-believe*, don't you, Hayley?' He stroked her cheek, his thumbnail scratching the skin, causing her to pull back.

'Oh, I'm sorry, am I hurting you?' His sarcastic tone was undeniable.

'Please, Denzil, I thought we were friends.'

Her comment was met with booming laughter. 'Oh, you crack me up, Hayley. Friends! That is funny.' Denzil ran his fingers through her hair, before snatching a handful in his fist and pulling.

'Argh,' Hayley jerked back, tears trickling down her face.

A woman's terrified voice called out, 'No, Denzil, you've done enough. Look at her, she's terrified. Isn't that punishment enough?'

He tugged on Hayley's hair again, but this time he'd turned away. 'If you can't handle this, Dianne, then go and wait outside, but I thought you would want to be part of this one. She is the reason for all of this after all.'

'I know she is but, please . . .' Dianne begged, taking a step forward until Denzil flashed a blade towards her. 'He wouldn't want this.'

'How do you know what he would want?' Denzil shouted.

'Because we loved each other,' Dianne called back, angrily now. 'We were going to leave the island together. Start again somewhere else.'

Denzil's derisory laugh filled the air. 'Oh, I'm sure you were.' He ran the blade across Hayley's cheek, slowly, taunting her. 'You know, I should cut your tongue out right now.' Tapping the tip on her nose he added, 'Maybe I'll make you eat it afterwards.'

Hayley couldn't breathe, fearing the tiniest movement would cause the blade to cut her. She tried to piece together a coherent sentence. Jumbled thoughts struggled to arrange themselves in her head.

'She deserves to be punished, but not like this,' Dianne pleaded. 'Why not make her live with what she did to those friends of hers. The men she had wrapped around her fingers.'

'Mmm,' Denzil replied. 'I could, but . . .'

Hayley felt the blade slice through the skin on her cheek, blood trickling towards her jaw.

'Argh, no, Denzil, please,' she begged.

Denzil laughed. 'Where would be the fun in letting her live?'

'I can't do this, I can't.' Dianne ran to the door.

'Get back here!'

Denzil's command caused her to freeze. Dianne turned back.

'Good girl,' he said, then pointed to the floor. 'Move that away, the stink is making me feel sick.'

Hayley stared in the direction he'd pointed and broke down, overwhelmed by the horror. The source of the foul smell was Phil's decomposing body, blood-soaked with mottled flesh. His eyes, although swollen, were closed as if he was asleep.

'Don't worry,' Denzil sneered. 'You two will be together again soon.'

Hayley's eyes met Dianne's, the other woman seemingly acknowledging that they were both trapped. Dianne struggled to drag the heavy corpse to the other side of the room, sobbing as she moved.

'Oh, Phil, I'm so sorry,' Hayley sobbed. 'I'm so, so sorry.'

'Ah, poor Phil. What about Simon and Mark, are you sorry for them, too?'

Despite knowing it was futile, Hayley tried one last time. 'I won't tell anyone about this, just let me go, please,' she begged.

'You won't tell anyone,' Denzil muttered, sneering. 'Forgive me if I don't believe you. We know you have history in that department. You love telling people things, don't you?'

'We've finally got a hit on Reverend Martin's phone, boss!' Carla exclaimed. 'Hang on, they're sending me the location now. Wait a minute. Phil Harrison's number is coming up too. They're together.'

'Really?' Fraser asked urgently. 'Do we have DNA from the tongue?'

'Not yet,' Carla replied. 'Could he still be alive?'

'Come on, hurry up,' Fraser urged, grabbing his car keys. 'We need to get there and fast.'

Of course, Fraser thought. Where else would he take her?

65

7th May, 4.30 p.m.

If Denzil was going to take Hayley anywhere, it was there: the place it all began. Traffic cams had caught his car not far away an hour ago, and Fraser desperately hoped he wasn't too late. A killer hiding in plain sight. He was the knight in shining armour who had found her. He had saved her from the attack on her studio. He had gone to the hospital with her and dutifully sat by her bedside. Could Phil really be there, alive, or was that just wishful thinking? It was more probable that they'd only find the man's phone.

Fraser feared the loss of his father had affected his judgement. Had distracted him. He had been so positive of Ryan's guilt. He had even disregarded David Sutherland too easily when the evidence initially pointed towards him, although the man had since been ruled out thanks to the wonders of CCTV. But there had been Ryan's troubled family background, the fingerprints, the witness . . . most of all, the weapon. Whether consciously or not Fraser had been so wrapped up in his own guilt at not stopping Adam that he'd thrown everything into pursuing Ryan Melrose. But if it wasn't him, then how did the murder weapon get into that house? Had the investigation been deliberately steered in that direction?

All that would have to wait. For now, it was the writing on the threatening letters that had sealed it.

I know what you did. I'll be seeing you.

It was Denzil Martin's and it had been there for them to see when they'd visited Suzanne Melrose, if only they had noticed it at the time. His handwriting was almost exactly the same as his father's,

Peter Crichton, the author of the entries in the case files. The same sloping features with a circle above the I instead of a simple dot, a familial quirk. Denzil's name and number had been stuck to the fridge at Suzanne's by some innocent magnet, hiding in plain sight all along. In her confusion Celia had brought the motive straight to them in the case files. Adam's digging had provided the final piece.

'Poor Celia, she thinks it's only just happened. I know they were just kids but . . . to let a lie go so far,' Carla said.

Fraser thought of his father and the dementia that had ravaged his mind.

'Her mental condition is none of our concern, but without it we might not have found out until it was too late for Hayley. As it is, we still might not get to her on time.' He accelerated, his Range Rover already exceeding the speed limit. 'Owen should be just about there already, and I've got a few uniforms heading out to meet us,' Fraser said as the Range Rover cornered an open bend at fifty miles an hour, acres of moorland on either side. 'Sorry,' he apologised to Carla when he saw the colour drain from her face. 'But if you puke you're cleaning it up.'

'I'm fine,' she said. She looked like her guts felt like they'd been put through a blender.

'There's Owen's car. Good lad, he's stayed back like I told him.' Fraser pulled in close behind Owen's car, and the two of them ran to join him.

The three detectives gathered around Owen's car. The derelict kids' home was visible through the trees. The place had been empty for twenty years; the crumbling walls had been strangled by years of untamed growth by nature. Ivy and other shrubs that Fraser didn't recognise had reclaimed the space. Every window had been smashed and piles of fly-tipped rubbish were piled up nearby.

'Boss, I've seen Reverend Martin's car but Dianne Petrie's is there as well. Look.' Owen pointed across to their left.

'That explains why we can't get hold of her. What the hell has she got to do with all this?'

'She worked at the home early in her career, didn't she? Before she trained as a social worker,' Fraser suggested, wiping a line of sweat from his top lip. Adrenaline rushed through him. Hayley's life was in their hands. If she were still alive that was.

'Are we waiting for backup on this?' Owen asked.

Fraser considered his options. If they waited it might be too late.

'Let's go,' he said and headed off in the direction of the trees. 'We've seen what he's capable of, we don't have time to wait.'

Fraser checked his watch and tried to calculate how long Hayley had been in there having God knows what done to her. 'Stay as low as you can, and don't make a sound.'

66

'Denzil,' Hayley whimpered, tears streaming down her face. She searched his face for a shred of humanity, but there was none.

She knew what she had done all those years ago, but she couldn't possibly have anticipated the consequences. They were just stupid, mixed-up kids who had been abused and neglected before being thrown together in the Lodge. Phil had listened to her, believed her without question or interrogation. It had felt good. She had felt loved for the first time in her life. Hayley didn't want to lose that, but she couldn't possibly have known the chain of events that would lead to here. By the time she had broken down and confessed to Phil that she had lied it had been too late: a man was dead. The four of them knew the truth and swore they would never tell. They had stuck to the story for thirty years. But now their lies had caught up with them.

'I'm sorry for what happened,' she murmured and froze, resigning herself to the inevitable as he lifted her T-shirt, running the blade of the knife slowly up and down. There was a coldness in his eyes. This wasn't the man she had thought she knew. He was a stranger.

Her body became loose, every ounce of fight gone. Was this what the others had done? Is this what happens when you know you're about to die?

'You think saying sorry now makes up for what you did to my dad,' he rasped in her ear.

All hope that he had any empathy was gone.

Hayley said nothing. He was right. She should have spoken up at the time, admitted she had made the whole thing up. What was the worst that could have happened? The police would have given her a warning. Instead a man was dead, a woman a widow and a son left without his father. And then made an orphan.

'Liars always get found out,' Denzil whispered in her ear. 'Some take longer than others, but justice always gets done.'

She heard footsteps pacing behind her head.

'Oh my God, Denzil, the police are here,' Dianne called out anxiously.

Hayley's heart sped up. Was there a chance she might get away? She craned her neck to see until Denzil tugged a clump of her hair to keep her head still, but Hayley's heart leaped at the thought of rescue. They had come to save her. From nowhere strength surged through her body.

'Help!' she screamed. There was nothing to lose by trying. 'Help me, please!'

Denzil slammed a hand over her mouth and pressed down hard.

'Shut up,' he spat as his palm moved up to cover her nose too. 'If you know what's good for you you'll keep your trap shut.'

Hayley couldn't breathe. Was this it? Was he going to suffocate her? That was better than the fate her three childhood friends had suffered at least. Once she passed out she would feel nothing, but panic surged through her, nonetheless. An involuntary reflex to survive.

'No,' she struggled to say, thrashing her body around, causing him to momentarily lose his grip. He slapped her cheek with the back of his hand. Hayley's face stung.

Dianne's panicked voice came again. 'What should we do? They'll be in here any minute. They're probably surrounding the building.'

Denzil ran to one of the broken windows and looked out. Then he untied Hayley and forced her to her feet, dragging her through a gap in the wall where several bricks had fallen down.

'You're coming with me.'

Fraser pointed at Owen. 'Look for a way in there lad, but only go in if you're absolutely sure it's safe for you to do so. Don't be a bloody hero.'

'On it,' Owen replied, running through thick, overgrown shrubs round the side of the building.

The sight of this place left Fraser with mixed feelings. If he and Adam hadn't been sent there, their father might have eventually killed one or both of them. But he feared it was also the place where Adam had evolved from a troubled, abused teenage boy into a killer. The juxtaposition haunted him.

Fraser grabbed hold of Carla's arm.

'There isn't time to wait for anyone else. You take Dianne,' he instructed her. 'I'll arrest Martin. But like I said to The Boy, be careful; we don't know what they have in there. And I need you alive.'

67

7th May, 6 p.m.

Owen kept his distance, but followed Denzil as he dragged a terrified Hayley behind him. They had fled out the back entrance of the derelict building. Owen could see that he had a knife in one hand and his other was tightly gripping Hayley's arm. They were headed for the quarry. Hayley turned and spotted Owen.

'Shit,' Owen murmured.

'Help me!' she screamed. 'Help—'

Denzil wrapped his arm around her throat and dragged her close to him, holding the knife close to her skin.

'Don't come any closer. Or I'll cut the lying bitch's throat.'

Owen stopped and held his hands up in front of him. 'I'm not moving. Just put the knife down and we can talk.'

Hayley looked terrified as Denzil crept backwards, holding the knife pressed against her throat.

'I'm sorry, Detective, there's nothing I want to say, and I certainly don't have time to listen to any of your bullshit.'

Owen had to think on his feet. He was on his own. Negotiation training was something he had enjoyed, but this was different. This wasn't him and his mates going through a script where nobody's life was actually in danger.

'Denzil,' he said. Always use the first name, develop a rapport, that was essential. 'I understand you're angry.' Empathy, equally important.

Owen knew what to do, so why was his heart pounding so violently in his chest and his forehead pouring with sweat? His skin was clammy. Now knowing the whole sickening story, Owen did understand Denzil's anger – that wasn't a lie – but he couldn't let him channel his fury and grief into murder.

'So you know what she did back then!' Denzil shouted back.

Opening a dialogue. This was good.

'Yes, I do.' Keep the answer simple. Let him digest your answer. Don't over-complicate things. Then – 'And I can help you. Please, Denzil, put down the knife so we can talk.'

A roar of laughter. Owen could see Hayley was crying.

'I heard you're one of those book detectives. Get full marks in hostage-negotiation class, did you?' Denzil squeezed Hayley closer to him. 'Well, this bitch is going nowhere except hell, where she belongs.' He pressed the knife harder into her neck.

Hayley cried out in terror. 'Stop! I'm sorry, I never meant for it go that far!' She was screaming now.

'What the hell did you think would happen when you said my dad abused you?'

'I don't know. I don't know. I wasn't thinking.' Hayley sobbed. 'I'm sorry.'

Denzil snatched a handful of her hair and started to move away, dragging her behind him. He waved the knife at Owen. 'Stay back or I'll cut out her tongue right here, right now.'

Hayley screamed in terror.

'All right, all right.' Owen held up his hands. 'I won't move. Just let her come to me and we can talk about this.'

Denzil kept walking away as Hayley struggled to get free. 'It's a bit late for talking now, Detective.'

'This isn't what your father would want.'

It was the last-resort phrase, but it worked. Denzil stopped, turning round to face Owen.

'And how would you know what my father would want?'

Owen had to think fast.

'I never met your dad, but I know he was a good man, and good men don't want this.' God, please let this work. 'He would be proud to know you've been working to help people.' Owen was sweating profusely now. 'Please, put down the knife, Denzil, and let Hayley go. It's what your dad would—'

'That detective is right, your dad was a good man,' Hayley cut in. 'He didn't deserve it. You're right. I'll confess. I'll go to prison for lying if that's what you want but, please, don't kill me.'

For a split second it looked like Denzil was thinking about her suggestion, but to Owen's horror, as if time stood still, the knife plunged towards Hayley's stomach. She gave a single, gut-wrenching moan as Denzil stabbed her before he let her drop to the ground.

'There you go, Detective, she gets to keep her lying tongue,' Denzil shouted and ran away through the trees.

68

Carla tightened the handcuffs onto Dianne Petrie's wrists, but the woman didn't struggle.

'That detective won't be able to stop him,' Dianne warned her, tears streaming down her face. 'He's lost his mind.'

Carla didn't respond. She wasn't playing games with this woman. It was Dianne's job to help people, not hurt them. She balked to think how much the social worker was involved. Whether she had taken part in any of the torture, the stabbings.

'When I agreed to help him, I didn't know how far he was going to go,' Dianne swore. 'I didn't know he was going to kill them, and once I did it was too late, I was already involved. I was so close to telling you but . . . I just couldn't. I was scared of what he would do to me.'

'You'll have plenty of time to talk later,' Carla said.

'He said he wanted to make them pay for what they did to his family and I didn't blame him so I did whatever I could to help. It was sick, and ended up killing a man who didn't deserve any of it.' Her sobs grew louder, harder. 'I loved Peter. We were going to be a family.'

'Did that help include tampering with social-work records?'

'Yes, it did but I had no idea . . .'

'There will be plenty of time to explain everything when you're being interviewed,' Carla said.

'No. I need you to understand. Hayley's lie destroyed so many lives. She killed my baby, mine and Peter's. I was pregnant when he died. The doctor said it was the shock and grief that caused my miscarriage.' Her words were barely audible through tears now. 'She was beautiful. We should have been a family but she stole all of that away.'

Dianne wasn't finished talking, this time directing her anger at Carla. 'If you lot had done your job none of this would've happened. Peter was a good man. He didn't deserve what those four did to him. He didn't touch her, not once, ever!'

Carla turned to see Fraser join them.

'Boss.'

Screams of terror came from the other side of the building.

'Put her in the car,' Fraser urged and ran in the direction of the cries. 'Then follow me. It sounds like they're close to the quarry.'

Fraser set off running, dodging boulders strewn on the path between the derelict kids' home and quarry mouth, both places long since emptied of life. A heavy, thick black cloud overhead echoed the dark, sombre atmosphere. Reverend Denzil Martin. Son of senior care worker Peter Crichton, a man who had worked in the Lodge after Fraser's time there. Using his mother's maiden name, Denzil had become a Church of Scotland minister. Peter and Celia both worked in the home in the eighties and early nineties. Dianne had started her social-work career in the home too, and she and Peter had an affair which resulted in a pregnancy. It sickened Fraser to know what had happened. His blood ran cold when he reached Owen and Hayley.

'I couldn't stop him,' Owen cried out.

His hands were caked in Hayley's blood, as he pressed down on his shirt that he'd removed to pack into the wound in her stomach. 'He just stabbed her and ran, I couldn't stop him!'

'Which way did he go?' Fraser urged.

'He went that way, through those trees.'

Fraser took off again.

'There's an ambulance on its way.' Owen tried to reassure Hayley.

'Please don't let me die,' Hayley whispered.

'Hang in there, help's coming.'

Her voice strained, Hayley continued, determined to speak. 'I

know it was a terrible thing to do, but . . .' She groaned from the pain.
'He hugged me, that's all, but my mind, it was such a mess back then.
It was years later that I found out I had PTSD from the abuse. His
touch triggered a flashback.'

'Don't try and speak,' Owen reassured her.

'But I should have said something, I should've . . .'

As Carla joined them, the sound of sirens was a relief to everyone.

'Where's Brodie?' Carla asked.

'He's gone after him,' Owen said, flashing her a look of concern.

Hayley moaned through the pain. 'Someone needs to help him.
Denzil will kill him.'

69

7th May, 7 p.m.

'Denzil, stop!' Fraser called out. 'There's nowhere left to go.'

Denzil turned round and looked back at him for a moment, then behind him towards the gaping quarry. He waved the knife in Fraser's direction.

'You know what she did!' Denzil yelled.

Fraser became aware of Owen's approach behind him. He lifted a hand to stop him getting any closer, pleased to sense Owen falling back, hopefully out of sight. 'There's nothing any of us can do about that now but I need you to step back from the edge.'

'Why?'

'Come on, Denzil. You need help, and I can get you that help.'

Denzil burst into fits of laughter, catching Fraser off guard. He risked a glance at Owen, then back at Denzil.

'What's so funny?'

'You are, Detective. Offering me help. Do you think I'm stupid?'

'No, of course I don't. I want to help you.'

'I don't need help anymore.' Denzil edged closer to the quarry face, the knife still clutched tightly in his hand.

Fraser heard loose pieces of gravel tumble down the rock face.

'Come back from the edge, Denzil.'

Fraser knew he was running out of time. He knew where this was heading, and it wasn't to the station for an interview. Fraser had no option. He shot Owen a last glance and started walking towards Denzil.

'Stop right there!' Denzil screamed, startling a murder of crows nearby whose eerie caws rang out loudly as they took flight.

Fraser held his hands up in front of him as he edged closer. 'I can't do that, Denzil. Too many people have been hurt already.'

Denzil waved the knife towards him. 'I said stay back!'

Fraser stopped. 'You come closer to me then.'

Denzil peered over the quarry's edge and gripped the knife.

'All I wanted was justice for my dad.'

'I know,' Fraser acknowledged. 'I'm sorry for what happened to your dad.'

'Sorry?' Denzil scoffed. 'He was treated like a criminal, like some kind of child molester!' The anger dripped from every word. 'They came and took him and locked him up because of her lies.'

'I know, and I'm sorry.'

'My dad was a good man and your lot chose to believe that lying bitch over him. A man who'd spent his life caring for unwanted and neglected kids!' Tears streamed down Denzil's face. 'It didn't only kill my dad. It killed my mum too! She couldn't take the grief and ended it with a bottle of pills.'

'The police had to do their job, Denzil.'

'Innocent until proven guilty! My father's life was ruined by her lies. He lost his job. We had bricks thrown through our windows. Dog shit pushed through our letterbox.'

'I'm sorry that happened to you.'

'Yes, well, it was a bit late for sorry once my dad ended up down there.' He pointed to the foot of the quarry.

'Your father's suicide was a terrible thing, and I'm sorry.'

'You keep saying sorry as if it matters,' Denzil called back. 'They've been punished. Sorry isn't necessary when they've been sent to hell. Where they belong.'

Suddenly Denzil looked even thinner than before. He looked pale and fragile as if the light had been extinguished from him.

'Why don't you come back from there. Let me help you. Nobody else needs to die, do they?'

'After my mum took her life there was nobody left to look after me.'

'I'm sorry,' Fraser said.

'So you keep saying!' Denzil screamed. 'But it wasn't your fault, was it? It was theirs! If they hadn't lied . . . If she hadn't made up a lie about Dad touching her, he wouldn't have died, and my mum would have been able to take care of me!'

'What about Dianne?' Fraser asked.

Denzil's expression changed on hearing her name. 'I had no idea about Dianne until I went to the social-work office that day,' he smiled thinly. 'I had no idea how I was going to find out where they lived until I met her. We got talking and it turned out she knew my dad – very well as it happened.'

'They were having an affair.'

'Yes, but that didn't matter. Mum would've forgiven him.'

A thought occurred to Fraser.

'How did you know Hayley had lied?' He realised he had made a hash of the question when the look on Denzil's face oozed fury. 'No, I mean, I know you don't want to think something like that about your dad, but what I mean is how can you prove his innocence?' He paused. 'Hayley's guilt.'

'I wondered when you were going to ask that.' Denzil tightened his grip on the knife. 'I found out quite by accident, Detective.'

70

Three months ago

Mark Tait pushed open the door to his caravan and stared at the slim, brown-haired man standing outside.

'Yes,' he said. 'Can I help you?'

'Mark Tait?' his visitor asked.

'Who wants to know?'

'My name is Reverend Denzil Martin. I'm here to see if you're OK after your recent burglary.'

'How do you know about that?'

'The officer who helped you thought that you might need someone to talk to.'

'Oh. I'm fine, thanks.' Mark started to close the door, then stopped as if listening to someone and muttered to himself. 'I know, I know.'

Denzil frowned. 'Are you all right?'

'Yes, why?' Mark snapped, then continued mumbling to himself.

'Are you sure I can't help you?' Denzil asked again. 'You look like you could do with someone to talk to.'

'They won't leave me alone!' Mark shouted, starting to hit his own head. 'The voices are getting so loud.'

'Hey, come on, why don't I come inside and have a cup of tea? See if I can help you maybe,' Denzil suggested.

Mark tried to close the caravan door. 'I don't need anyone's help. They won't like it if I let you in.' He turned as if looking at someone.

Denzil was concerned for Mark's welfare. 'I'm sure they won't mind me coming in for five minutes,' he said softly.

Mark frowned and glanced behind himself again, then sighed. 'Five minutes, then you'll have to go.'

'There you go.' Denzil laid a cup of tea in front of Mark, who looked like he hadn't slept in days. The caravan looked terrible. It was thick with filth, and the smell made Denzil want to be sick. This man was obviously very unwell. As soon as he'd finished there he'd head over to let the mental-health team at the surgery know what he'd found.

'Thanks.' Mark sniffed the mug before taking a small sip.

'Can I make you a sandwich or something?' Denzil offered.

'No, I'm not hungry.'

Denzil figured paranoia about being poisoned probably meant he didn't want a stranger messing about with his food. He was surprised to have been allowed to make him a cup of tea. Mind you he hadn't drunk it yet, and by the way he'd sniffed it Denzil realised Mark didn't trust him one hundred percent.

'So you're OK, then.' Denzil watched Mark look around the room anxiously and bite his filthy nails. 'Are you sure?'

'Why do you ask? Did they send you?'

Denzil knew he had to remain calm. To not say anything to make Mark even more suspicious.

'Nobody sent me. I'm just here to help you.' Denzil glanced around the small space and clocked a drawing of a girl with long hair stuck to the fridge, held in place by a magnet that had Blackpool tower on it. 'Did you draw that?' He pointed in the direction of the fridge.

Mark turned. 'Yes.'

'Is she a friend of yours?'

'That's Hayley.'

'She's very pretty.' Denzil was glad they'd started a neutral conversation.

'Yes, she is. Hayley is an artist too. She has a studio. She gives me pencils and paper and any bits I need. I help her out if she's got any jobs needing doing around the place.'

'That's nice. What did you say her name was? I must check out her work.'

Mark's mood darkened, his eyes narrowing suspiciously, and he stood up and pushed the caravan door open, spilling his tea as he did. 'I think you should go.'

Denzil frowned and grabbed a tea-towel to mop up the mess. 'I'm sorry, I didn't mean to upset you.'

Mark stared at him, then started to pace back and forth. 'They're going to know you're here,' he said, slapping his head.

'I'm sorry,' Denzil repeated.

'They'll be so mad with me if they know you were here. I mustn't tell, they warned me I mustn't tell.'

Denzil was growing increasingly worried about him.

'It has to stay a secret. It has to stay a secret. Nobody can know she lied.' Mark paced back and forth, a look of panic growing on his face. He stared at Denzil. 'How did you find out?'

Denzil was confused and unsure what to say.

'I don't know what you're talking about,' he told him. 'Who lied? About what?'

'You're lying!' Mark's tone was becoming more aggressive. 'They said you would come if I told anyone.' Then his face changed. 'Oh God, what have I done? I shouldn't have let you in.'

Denzil dropped the cloth. This was more than he could handle. He checked his watch. He hoped that he would catch the nurse on duty if he hurried.

As he walked away, amongst the chaos of items strewn outside, a large, framed painting leaning up against the caravan caught his eye. It must be one of Hayley's, he thought. On closer inspection he spotted the signature.

Denzil's blood ran cold. It couldn't be her. Could it? If it was, then he knew exactly what she'd lied about. He knocked on the door again, his heart hammering loudly.

'I said I don't need help,' Mark told him. 'Now, please, you have to go.'

'I promise I'll go if you just confirm one thing for me.'

'What is it?'

'Were you and Hayley in the Lodge kids' home together?'

Footsteps behind him made Denzil turn round.

'Are you OK, Mark?' Phil Harrison asked, looking right at Denzil. 'Can I help you, mate?'

Denzil stared at Phil, and in that moment he knew. He looked at Mark then back at Phil. It was like everything had happened just yesterday. Their friend Hayley was the centre of it all, but he would recognise Phil Harrison's face anywhere. He had corroborated Hayley's statement. His dad had always protested his innocence, said the girl had been lying, and now Denzil knew he'd been telling the truth. He knew it would haunt him forever if he didn't do something about it. Denzil had to stay calm, but feared the two men could hear his heart banging against his ribcage. But where was the other one? He had to find him first. All four of them had to pay for it. A light-headed sensation swept fast over him. Denzil had to get out of there.

'I'm sorry to have troubled you, Mark,' Denzil managed to say quietly, before walking away.

Instead of leaving, he hid round the side of the caravan and listened to the conversation inside. For the first time he had absolute proof that Hayley had lied. He knew now that this was the real reason he had been drawn back to Stornoway, had left his old life behind . . . Not making a sound, he quickly ran away. He had to hold it together until he was far enough away to gather his thoughts. Looking back in the direction he'd come, his legs weak beneath him, Denzil vomited where he stood.

71

'So you see, Detective,' Denzil said. 'That's how I knew for sure.' He inhaled a long slow breath, and exhaled as he tapped the bloodstained knife in his palm. 'They'd carried on with their lives, not giving a shit that they had destroyed mine with their lies. They'd grown up, made good lives for themselves.'

'I think Mark Tait had suffered, don't you?' Fraser countered.

'Are you suggesting I should feel sorry for him?' Denzil said angrily. 'He got what he deserved. They all did, eventually.'

'But why the Melrose laddie?' Fraser asked. 'Why did you drag him into it?'

'I wasn't going to let you think it was Ryan for long. I'm not so bad that I would let him take the fall. I know all about Adam so I knew you would see similarities in him and I was right.'

It was as if Denzil could see inside Fraser's mind. Like he could read how he thought of Adam when he looked at Ryan, manipulating Fraser's weakness.

'You figured it out for yourself, didn't you,' Denzil continued. 'I just needed enough time to sort everything out.'

'How did you manage to get the bloody knife under his bed?'

Denzil scoffed. 'His mother wasn't a problem. I took one of her knives for Carver then stashed it when I visited her as part of my church work.' He looked down. 'I'm not proud of bringing Ryan in but I gather you lot are helping him. Silver linings.' Denzil shrugged.

'What about Morag?' Fraser probed. 'Why her?'

'Yes, poor, sweet, innocent Morag,' Denzil sneered. 'Now that really was an accident.' He gave a short, derisory laugh. 'She was starting to figure out something was wrong. I only wanted to talk to her but the silly old woman insisted on running, didn't she, and fell and banged her head.' He shrugged. 'Shame, really, because I actually quite liked her.'

The sound of his phone ringing in his coat pocket bothered Fraser and he took it out. Denzil seemed to get more agitated by the noise and stepped closer to the edge. Fraser saw the caller ID was the prison but it would have to wait.

'Denzil, it's all right, I've switched my phone off. Please come away from the edge so we can talk some more.'

Another group of rocks broke away, tumbling rapidly to the bottom and smashing loudly when they landed. Denzil peered over.

'That's what happened to my dad. His body was smashed, just like those rocks.' He snapped his head round to face Fraser. 'So you see I had to punish them. They left me with no choice. You lot didn't do anything about it, did you?'

'I know it looks that way, but—'

'Are you suggesting *I'm* a liar now?'

Fraser felt like he'd been hit by the force of the venom in Denzil's question.

'No, of course not.'

'Then what are you saying?'

'I'm saying it wasn't up to you to punish them. That's not your job. There are avenues we could have pursued in order to convict them on charges of making false accusations and wasting police time.'

'Wasting police time!' Denzil scoffed. 'Is that what my dad's life is worth to you?'

Fraser feared he was making things worse with his clumsy suggestion. Suddenly Carla's voice piped up from behind him.

'Your dad was a wonderful man, Denzil.'

Fraser was alarmed to see Carla continue on past him. He shot a concerned glance at Owen, who had also emerged from his hiding place.

'Carla, what are you doing?' he bristled, but she kept on walking closer to Denzil.

'What the hell is she doing?' Owen asked anxiously.

'Getting herself killed if she's not careful.'

'Do you want me to go?' Owen suggested.

'No, I can't be losing both of you.'

'Do you mind if I sit?' Carla pointed to a large boulder not far from the edge.

Denzil frowned, then shrugged. 'I can't stop you, can I?'

'True,' Carla replied and lowered herself onto the lumpy slab of rock.

'My dad used to take me walking round here when I was a kid you know,' she said. 'Just me and him.'

'I'm sure that was lovely for you.'

'It was, and I still miss those days, even now.'

A thin smile spread across Denzil's lips. 'I'm not stupid. I can see what you're trying to do. You're *establishing a rapport*. Showing me that we have something in common.'

Carla sighed and held her hands up. 'Busted.'

'Nice try, though. You've done better in the two minutes you've been here than your boss did.'

Carla looked back at the anxious expression on Fraser and Owen's faces then refocused her attention on Denzil.

'Fraser Brodie isn't so bad.'

'I'll take your word for it.'

'He cares what happens to people. Just like you do,' she said cautiously. 'Your dad would be proud to see that you're helping people in your work as a minister.'

Denzil fell silent momentarily, then looked right at her. 'I know about Brodie's brother.'

Carla nodded and stole a quick glance behind her. Most of the island's population were aware of Adam Brodie's crimes.

'It's admirable the way he's stuck by him.'

Fraser could see that his grip on the knife was loosening.

'I certainly admire him,' Carla said.

'He's brave,' Denzil admitted. 'Lots of people would have abandoned him.'

'He certainly is.' She stole another quick glance at Fraser, probably fearing she was incurring the full force of his wrath for this. 'Come on, why don't you give me the knife and we can get away from this place? Get a cup of tea and continue our talk. What do you say?'

Tears filled Denzil's eyes and Carla offered him a gentle smile. She stood up slowly and held out her hand.

Denzil rubbed away the tears with the sleeve of his blood-caked shirt. Fraser's heart pounded. This was it. He was going to give her the knife. She was going to take him in unharmed.

He was wrong.

Denzil lifted the blade of the knife to his neck. He sliced a single, deep line across the front of his throat, causing a thread of crimson to quickly become a river of red that soaked into his collar.

'No!'

Carla surged forward but she wasn't quick enough. It happened in slow motion like in a dream. It was too late to stop Denzil falling backwards to the quarry floor below, his bloodied body audible on the rocks seconds later.

'Carla! Get back from there!' Fraser pulled her by the arm, before pushing her towards Owen who was standing behind them. 'Take her back to my car.'

'Boss,' Owen replied and wrapped his arm around Carla's shoulder. 'Come on. Let's go.'

'Fuck!' Fraser yelled into the quarry, kicking loose stones angrily and sending them hurtling over the edge.

He leaned over to see Denzil Martin's body smashed and broken on the quarry floor below, the blood oozing from his neck wound visible even from up there.

What a waste. So many people had died for the sake of one single lie told by a mixed-up, abused, traumatised teenage girl.

72

Fraser stared at Dianne, sitting in the back of the patrol car, waiting to be taken to the station. He wondered how someone who had been in the care profession for all of her adult life could have been involved in something so evil. The woman looked shell-shocked, but he struggled to believe her protestations that she hadn't known what Denzil had planned. Just how deeply her involvement went was something he intended to find out very soon. The affair with Peter Crichton – it couldn't be just that. Could it? Carla had told him what she'd said about the grief and the miscarriage but that didn't excuse any of this. Whatever the case, Dianne Petrie would be jailed for a long time for her part in this.

'Take her back to the station,' Fraser instructed the young officer in the driver's seat. 'I'll meet you there.' Then he turned his full attention to Carla, who was standing with Owen nearby.

Her lips had barely moved before he lifted a hand to stop her, his expression solemn.

'Do you have any idea how reckless that was?'

'Yes, I do, and I'm sorry.'

'Owen, could you give us a minute?' Fraser asked.

Owen flashed a look of support at Carla, before heading back to his car.

'I'm sorry, Fraser,' Carla repeated. 'I was sure I could talk him down.'

'Oh, you made that quite clear!'

'I didn't think he would—'

'That's just it: you didn't think,' Fraser said sharply. 'He could have hurt you. Or worse, taken you over the edge with him.'

'I know,' Carla murmured.

'Do you?'

Carla nodded. 'I know what I did was stupid, and I'm sorry.'

The look of contrition on her face was piercing Fraser's hard exterior – which wasn't just made from anger, but also fear. Fear that he would lose not just a colleague but a good friend. Something Fraser Brodie had never made easily in his life.

'Come here.' He held open his arms and Carla fell into him. 'I don't know what I would've done if anything had happened to you, you daft woman,' he added as she clung on to him.

'I know . . . I promise I won't be so stupid in the future.'

Fraser pulled back. 'Don't make promises you know you can't keep, DS McIntosh,' he smiled. 'And another thing. Who the hell is going to make my tea if something happens to you? Because I sure as hell won't be letting The Boy do it!'

Epilogue

One month later

Fraser was glad that Carla had finally admitted the extent of her and Dean's financial troubles. She had promised to pay him back every penny, but Fraser didn't want her to. It was better to say it was a gift right from the start. He didn't want anything hanging over them. A fresh start was all he wanted for her. He'd added a little extra so the couple could take a break too. Carla deserved it. Fraser had always been good with his money and living a simple life with no ties meant he'd saved a fair bit. If he could help those in need, he would. Carla had apologised for allowing herself to become distracted, but Fraser had to be honest: she had hidden it well.

Maybe he had been distracted too. Fraser may have hated his father, but his death had still affected him. How could it not? Johnny Brodie had made Fraser the man he was. But he'd created Adam too.

He smiled when he saw Adam walk through the door of the visiting room. He stood up as his brother approached, then spotted Andy Melrose walking a few paces behind. They nodded solemnly at each other. Adam turned and shot a serious look at Melrose, then joined Fraser at the table. He reached out a hand to shake his brother's.

'It's good to see you,' Fraser said as he sat. He lifted a carrier bag up and slid the contents across the table.

Adam lifted a bar of chocolate and ripped it open, devouring almost half in one bite before rummaging through the contents of the bag.

'No cheese and onion,' Adam pointed out.

'I'm afraid not. You should have sent me your shopping list.'

'Oh, very funny. Looks like I'll have to send my concierge out for them, then.'

'Looks like it, yes.' Fraser shook his head and smiled, glad to see that Adam's sense of humour was still going strong after the tumultuous weeks behind them.

'How's things with Melrose?' he added.

'You don't need to worry about that. Me and your man there have come to an arrangement.'

'Should I be worried about this arrangement?'

Fraser took another quick look at Melrose, who had turned his attention back to the woman who sat opposite him. Fraser assumed it was the man's mother, given the resemblance. He had heard that Ryan was getting ready to start a new college course and was receiving counselling, which Carla had arranged. She had also encouraged David Sutherland to take a place on an alcohol rehab course on the outskirts of Inverness, one with a good track record at helping people stay sober. After finding blood on his clothes the man had spent several tortured days fearing that he had killed his best friend and been unable to remember. Fraser admired what he called her *aftercare*. Some of it might rub off on The Boy, who knew? The sole survivor of Denzil's reign of terror had plans to make major life changes too. After spending weeks in hospital recovering from the injuries she'd sustained as a result of the stab wound which had damaged both her bowel and stomach, Hayley had discovered that Phil had left his entire estate to her. The house, the car and all of his savings.

'Nah.' Adam ripped open a second bar of chocolate. 'You've nothing to worry about with me and him. He's not tried chucking his weight around since I gave him a couple of slaps.'

'Good.'

'How's things with you?'

'Not so bad.'

'I meant to ask you something,' Adam said.

'Oh yes, what was that?'

'What happened to the guy that let Ryan get out of custody?'

Fraser's eyes widened. 'How do you know about that?'

'A little bird might have told me.' Adam looked across the room, catching Andy Melrose's eye.

'That's being dealt with,' Fraser explained. 'Never mind about that. I picked up the ashes yesterday,' Fraser said. He was unable to avoid the issue. Skirting round it wouldn't do either of them any good. 'I didn't want to do anything with them without talking to you first.'

Adam said nothing.

'Did you hear what I said?' Fraser pressed.

'I heard you,' Adam replied, without looking up from staring at the scratches on the grey table between them. 'I'm just surprised you haven't already chucked the bastard's ashes in with the rubbish yet.'

Fraser was expecting this response, but he had to ask. Just because Adam was locked up, it didn't mean he had no say. He'd already had so much of his freedom taken from him.

'How many turned out for the funeral?' Adam asked, finally meeting Fraser's eyes.

'There was just me and a couple of others.'

Adam's eyes narrowed. 'Oh, yes, and who were those couple of others?'

'Jenny was there. She says to give you her love.'

A wide smile grew on Adam's face for a second, then disappeared. 'How is the old witch?'

'She's good.'

'Still cleaning up after you is she?'

'Aye, and she takes Napoleon out for me.'

'How old is she now? That dog of yours looks like a horse, how does she cope with him?'

Fraser felt bad that Adam had only ever seen his unusual-looking dog in photos.

'He's a good boy; he never gives her any problem.'

'I don't think I'd argue with Jenny Baird, right enough.' Adam smiled before his expression tensed. It was obvious the light-hearted teasing was a cover. 'And the others?'

Fraser took a deep breath. 'Lisa came to the crematorium.'

'Oh,' Adam said, almost in a whisper, then quickly cleared his throat. 'How, er, how is she?'

'She's good.'

'Did she know about the open prison being on the table?'

Fraser shook his head. 'No. I didn't mention it to her.'

'Well, you won't have to now at least.' Adam shot a quick glance at Andy Melrose.

Fraser had already wondered whether Adam's outburst was more about the possibility of freedom than anything else, but it was something he would never ask him. Despite everything he did, Adam had the right to keep some things to himself.

As the visit came to an end the two men shook hands one more time before Fraser watched Adam disappear out of the room. It was a moment that still brought a lump to his throat, even after all this time.

Once he'd got back outside, Fraser tugged up the collar of his raincoat against the lashing summer rain. Next on the agenda was a roast dinner in his favourite restaurant followed by apple pie and ice cream, washed down with a couple of pints. Maybe even a whisky chaser or two. Fraser was definitely off-duty and would be for the next two weeks, because he was taking a long overdue holiday.

He took a last look behind him at the tall prison walls, like he always did as his taxi pulled out of the gates. Fraser Brodie hated leaving his brother in there, but there was nothing he could do about it. All he could do was support him because, despite everything, Adam was his brother and he loved him. He always would.

Acknowledgements

It goes without saying that this book wouldn't be possible without a considerable amount of other people. An author has an idea, writes a book, then tries to bring the story to the world and that isn't possible without a huge team of supporters. So to Saskia for her unwavering enthusiasm for Fraser and Adam. For all of her cheerleading for me and my books to succeed. And for the delicious curry in Harrogate! Thank you! I'm grateful also to Mel, Jane and everyone at Embla for taking a chance on me and Fraser and for helping the story come to life. Thank you for seeing that special something about him too.

Thank you to my family who encourage and allow me every day to follow my dreams and listen to me talking endlessly about the book as if the characters are real people. But the thing is, characters do become real people to writers. They live and breathe, laugh and cry, live and die. So to be a friend to a writer in the midst of a first draft, where the characters are at their most fragile, cantankerous, dangerous, unpredictable and downright awkward is a brave thing indeed. You deserve a medal.

A huge thanks must go to Smokey Quartz, Pyrite, Labradorite and Amazonite for doing the heavy lifting when it was needed. For The Honest Guys, who took me running with wolves whenever I asked them to.

To my racehorses who amaze and bring me to tears of joy every time whether they win or not.

Finally to the enthusiastic communities of readers on social media who talk, review and recommend – thank you!

Oh, one last thing – like Fraser, I couldn't do any of this without copious amounts of tea, although, unlike Fraser, a humble tea bag does me.

A Note from the Author

Hello,

Thank you for reading *Bury Your Secrets* and choosing to get to know Fraser Brodie and his brother Adam. Two men, unique in their own ways, who grew up together but who took opposite paths. Both men have their own strengths and weaknesses. The setting for this book is a place that I love. The Isle of Lewis and Harris is a place of stunning contrast which I would encourage everyone to visit at least once. But I would advise that you pack a sturdy waterproof jacket!

If you have enjoyed this book then I would love it if you would consider leaving a review, just a couple of words, to let people know you liked it. Tell your friends, family, doctor, dentist, everyone.

I always enjoy hearing from readers and can be found on social media, mainly sharing memes and chatting nonsense.

Much love

Kerry x

About the Author

Kerry Watts was born and grew up in Perth where she still lives today. The daughter of a Rangers-mad window cleaner and Daniel O'Donnell-loving dinner lady. She began writing over twenty-five years ago after reading Isla Dewar's book *Giving up on Ordinary* and decided she wanted to do that. Becoming a bestselling author is a dream come true.

Authors who inspire her are anyone capable of creating a character who lives inside her head long after she has closed the book. Her favourite fictional characters are Dexter Morgan, created by Jeff Lindsay, as well as Hannibal Lecter created by Thomas Harris. She doesn't have a favourite genre as a reader. Kerry will read anything. Written by anyone. If the blurb has a good feel about it she's hooked.

When she's not writing she loves to spend time following her other passions – dogs, particularly rescue mutts, and horse racing. The sight of a thoroughbred racehorse at full stretch has been known to move her to tears, not just lump-in-the-throat stuff but full-on blubbing. And for that she is unashamed.

She also had a small role in a film called *The Rocket Post* but decided acting wasn't for her. She would rather create a character than play one. All of her books are brought to you through the super powers of Tetley tea.

About Embla Books

Embla Books is a digital-first publisher of standout commercial adult fiction. Passionate about storytelling, the team at Embla publish books that will make you 'laugh, love, look over your shoulder and lose sleep'. Launched by Bonnier Books UK in 2021, the imprint is named after the first woman from the creation myth in Norse mythology, who was carved by the gods from a tree trunk found on the seashore – an image of the kind of creative work and crafting that writers do, and a symbol of how stories shape our lives.

Find out about some of our other books and stay in touch:

X, Facebook, Instagram: @emblabooks
Newsletter: https://bit.ly/emblanewsletter